A Suitable Necklace

By Kim Akhtar

Central Park South Publishing

Kim Akhtar/ Central Park South Publishing
Publisher: Central Park South Publishing

website: www.langtonsinternational.com

Publisher's Note: *This is a work of fiction. Names, characters, places, and incidents are a product of the author's imagination. Locales and public names are sometimes used for atmospheric purposes. Any resemblance to actual people, living or dead, or to businesses, companies, events, institutions, or locales is completely coincidental.*

Book Layout & Cover Image – **alien artifacts**

A Suitable Necklace/ Kim Akhtar. -- 1st ed.
ISBN 978-1-0878-9159-0

For my faithful Baxter Wheaten, my muse whose love knows no bounds

Chapter 1

"We will be landing in Delhi in about an hour," said a soft female voice. "May I offer you a glass of wine, madam?" she offered. "Or champagne?"

"Champagne," the woman nodded in a pleasant husky voice.

The stewardess disappeared, returning almost immediately with a glass on a silver tray.

"Thank you," the woman took the glass and sat back in her large comfortable seat, looking out of the small window at the lights of the city below.

Five years...

It was impossible to tell her age, her smooth olive complexion free of any obvious wrinkles. Her face was oval with prominent chiseled cheekbones, her eyes, olive-green and cat-like, slanted upwards, her nose long and her lips full and luscious. Her light brown hair with natural glints of gold was short, prone to unruly curls, but mostly just wavy. It was only her manner that belied her age, the way she spoke with quiet authority, her gaze direct and confident that put her in her very late 40's...or perhaps even 50.

When the plane came to a stop, she got up, slipped quickly into the perfectly-tailored white linen blazer the stewardess held out for her, casually threw a black chiffon scarf with tassels around her neck, placed big dark sunglasses on her eyes, picked up her Hermes bag and walked towards the entrance.

As she did, a man who'd been sitting in the seat in front of her, turned around to watch her exit the plane. Only then did he get up.   .

"Your jacket, sir," the stewardess held out a navy-blue blazer.

"Thank you," he said as she helped him put it on.

"Have a pleasant stay in Delhi."

*

"Madam," a young man wearing the airline uniform smiled as he greeted the woman just outside the plane's door. "If you would come with me please," his hands behind his back as he walked a couple of feet ahead of her. "We have arranged for you to go through passport control and customs privately."

"Thank you," she said. She followed the young man who showed her into the airline's lounge where a passport officer was waiting for her in the entrance.

"Where are you coming from today?" he took her passport.

"Rome."

"Would you mind taking off your glasses, madam...Kumar?" he looked at the photo in the document. "Miss Sabine Kumar..." he frowned as though the name rang a bell.

She complied.

"The purpose of your visit to India?"

"Catching up with some old friends...."

The man nodded. "When was the last time you were in India?"

"About 5 years."

"A long time," the officer reached for a rubber stamp, flicking through the pages of her passport, occasionally stopping at a visa.

"Yes," she said. "It certainly has."

"What were you doing in Azerbaijan?"

"I was there for some work."

"Beirut, Damascus, Abu Dhabi, Doha, Amsterdam, Paris, London...interesting.

"What sort of work do you do?"

"I'm in the art world."

"I see," the officer stamped her passport. "We have a lot of beautiful art here in India."

"Yes, I know," the woman smiled and put her passport in her bag.

"Welcome to India."

Just after she left, the man who'd been sitting in front of her on the plane came into the lounge, also accompanied by an airline representative who took him to the same immigration officer. He walked with a black walking stick with a silver swan on the tip.

"Mr. Singh," the officer looked from the passport photo to the man.

"Yes."

"Your current residence is London?"

"Yes."

"What is the purpose of your trip to India?"

"I want to see some friends I have lost touch with."

"Yes..." the immigration officer smiled knowingly. "Friends always seem to provide the best reasons for a visit."

"Sometimes."

The officer stamped his passport.

"Miss Kumar, I am Mr. Vivek, the General Manager," a small man wearing a dark suit, white shirt and a red and black striped tie, bowed low as Sabine, her jacket casually over her shoulders, walked into the main lobby of the Oberoi hotel. "Welcome to the Oberoi."

"Hello Mr. Vivek," she smiled as he remained bent over in reverence.

"May I extend my condolences on the passing of your father?" he said. "Such a tragic accident...lost control of the car...those small sports cars, just not sturdy enough..."

"Thank you," Sabine said.

"And he was still so young..."

"Just 70."

"He looked so much younger," Mr. Vivek said. "It's because his spirit was so youthful...

"Where did it happen?"

"South of France..."

"Oh!" Mr. Vivek exclaimed. "How he loved that part of the world...Cannes, Nice, Cap d'Antibes..." he trailed off, "...used to say there was nothing like it...but he always came back to Delhi.

"Yes," Mr. Vivek nodded. "He could always be found in the private Club Room with a glass of whiskey at 6 o'clock, sharp.

"I can still see him walking through those glass doors," he reminisced. "Perfect grey suit, white shirt, striped tie, a crisp white handkerchief in his breast pocket, his hair slicked back, a twinkle in his eye and a smile and a kind word for everyone, no matter who you were...from the doorman to the general manager."

"He loved this hotel," Sabine nodded, quickly covering her eyes with the dark sunglasses that were on top of her head holding back her unruly hair.

"Such a perfect gentleman," he sighed. "An elegant, sophisticated man...a dying breed, I'm sad to say."

"Well..." Sabine began.

"And a Maharajah if ever I've seen one," Vivek interrupted. "Such a pity the government revoked their titles in 1971.

"But of course, they'd already lost so much by then," he continued. "Bit by bit, they broke the power of the aristocracy

"Such a pity..." he repeated, shaking his head.

"Mr. Vivek..." Sabine tried again.

"Thousands of years of Maharajahs and then in one fell swoop...poof! They're gone...

"What about your lovely mother?" Mr. Vivek put his hands together reverently. "We only saw her once, but so beautiful...like a movie star...she was French, was she not?"

Sabine nodded.

"I wonder we only saw her that one time...?"

"Mr. Vivek," Sabine smiled tightly. "I don't mean to be rude, but I've just come off an airplane from Rome..."

"Of course! I'm so sorry, Miss Kumar," Mr. Vivek apologized. "You must be exhausted and here I am going on and on like a broken record.

"You will be staying in the Eastern Star suite, where your father liked to stay," he clicked his fingers and a bellman appeared immediately with her suitcase. "He said he enjoyed seeing the sun rise over his beloved city.

"It is perfect for you, princess," he bowed.

"Thank you, but I do not have the title."

"If I were in charge, you would."

"Thank you."

"Shall I send the butler up in a few minutes to help you un-pack?"

"You are very kind."

"Will you be with us long?"

"I'm not sure...there are a few things I have to take care of."

"Consider this your home," he pressed the button to the el-evator.

"The hotel is looking as beautiful as ever," she gazed around the bright, shiny marble lobby and it's black and white check-ered floor.

"Thank you, Miss Kumar," he bowed again.

"When were you last in our fair city?"

"About five years."

"Please call me directly if you need anything at all, any time, day or night," he bowed and handed her his card. "May I accom-pany you to the suite?"

"I think I can find my way," she smiled and pressed the but-ton of the penthouse floor.

*

Downstairs in the lobby, the man with the black walking stick with the silver swan tip, walked to the reception desk.

"I am Mr. Singh," he said, his voice deep and sultry. "I believe I have a reservation."

"Yes," the young woman smiled. "We have been expecting you, sir. I hope you had a good journey."

The man nodded.

"The bellman will accompany you to the Western Star suite as you requested."

*

As he walked away, Mr. Vivek stared at him until he reached the lift. When he disappeared inside, he went to the reception desk.

"Who was that man who just checked in?" he asked the young woman.

"Sir?"

"The man with the cane."

"That is..." she looked down at her computer screen, "Mr. Raminder Singh."

"Where did he come from?"

"He arrived on a British Airways flight...from London, via Rome."

"Raminder Singh..." Mr. Vivek nodded.

"Is there something wrong, sir?"

"He looks familiar," Mr. Vivek reached for his cellphone in his inner breast pocket and put the name into Google. Before he could investigate further,

"Mr. Vivek, please sir...a problem with the air conditioning in the restaurant," someone called to him and he put away his phone and walked back into the lobby.

*

Sabine walked off the elevator and headed down the hall where the bellman was waiting for her with her luggage.

As she did, she heard the second set of elevator doors open. She glanced behind her to see a man walking to the other end of the hallway.

"Welcome to the Eastern Star Suite, Miss Kumar," the bellman said as she walked past him into the large living room with its bay window that overlooked the Delhi Golf Course and the lights of the old city twinkling in the distance. Candles had been lit, lamps turned on to their dimmest settings, vases were filled with white flowers of all kinds and the sultry notes of a saxophone reached her ears. She touched the velvet petals of a tuberose and put her nose to it, inhaling the heavy scent.

"Shall I unpack for you, madam?" said a voice behind her.

"Actually, can you come back later?"

"Of course," the voice melted away into the shadows.

She walked over to the drinks cabinet near the window and picked out a bottle of champagne from the fridge and opened it, pouring herself a glass. She threw off her linen jacket and flopped down on the sofa, putting her feet up on the large, low square coffee table as she reached for the remote to the large screen television and turned it on.

"*And next,*" said the presenter, "*it is being touted as the party of the decade...Celebrity Art collector, JJ Singh is said to be mounting a reception worthy of a Maharajah's darbar for Bollywood couple Priya Chopra and Randy Singh who recently eloped and got married in Italy.*

"*The party will be held at an as yet undisclosed location about a month from now, but 'Entertain India's' informants have been told that it will probably be at Mr. Singh's home in Chattarpur and will be the hottest invitation in India.*

"*Let me turn to my colleague in the fashion world for a moment...*" the camera focused on a young man, dressed flamboyantly in a red paisley brocade jacket that looked like a Victorian dressing gown. "*Who do you think will be designing Priya's outfit?*"

The man smiled. "*She usually goes with Tarun Tahliani or Sabyasachi, so I would bet that it will be one of them. But frankly, it's anyone's game at this point..."*

"Whoever it is, she will look spectacular," the female presenter said.

"As she always does."

"Thank you very much and keep us posted."

Sabine smiled, staring at the television before looking at her cell phone. 6am. Much too early to call. But perhaps a text. *'Call me when you see this,'* she typed. She put her phone down but reached for it again.

'Thanks for the painless arrival. It was nice not to have to wait in the immigration line.'

'My pleasure,' came the response. *'Good to know I still have some pull in this country.'*

'I suppose a drink is out of the question.'

'A drink would be unwise...especially at this hour. We are, after all, in India.'

She nodded and put the phone down next to her. Seconds later, it buzzed.

'You sure you want to do this?' said the message.

'Why? Have you changed your mind?'

'No, I never go back on my word.'

'That's what my father used to say about you,' she replied.

'But sometimes, my dear, just knowing a job will work is enough.'

'You don't want me to do this, do you?'

'You are your father's daughter and will do what you want to do.'

'The necklace was on Dad's list. It was the jewel in the crown.'

'I know it was, but you don't have to do it.'

'It meant something to him and it means something to me.'

'*To him, it was a job, Sabine, like so many others...to you, it's something else.*'

'*I'll be in touch,*' she replied, staring at the text message thread for a few moments.

*

She took her glass of champagne and walked around the suite, opening cupboards and drawers. Besides the living room, there was a study and a bedroom with a small sitting area and a bathroom that was almost as big as the bedroom with a bathtub in the middle of it, next to a floor-to-ceiling window with views of the tops of the trees on the golf course and the Emperor Humayun's Tomb.

She ran herself a bath, lit some candles and got in, sinking into the soapy, bubbly, rose-scented water, and lay her head on the carved headrest to watch the sun as it rose. She drained her glass of champagne, placed it on the ledge and slipped into the water.

*

"*Namaste,* Indi *bibi,*" a slight woman wearing a pink and white sari drew the curtains drenching the bedroom in bright morning light.

"*Namaste* Laxmi," a woman emerged from under a quilt.

Laxmi came over to the bed and plumped up the pillows. "Thank you, Laxmi,' the woman sat up and reached for the cellphone that was at the edge of the night table.

"Well, well," she said as she read a message.

"Here's your breakfast, *bibi,*" Laxmi brought over a tray, and placed it on the bed in front of her. "Toast, marmalade and a pot of tea."

"Thank you, Laxmi."

"Good news this morning?" Laxmi asked.

"I don't know, but it seems as if Sabine is back in town."

"She texted me at 6 am."

"Sabine *bibi*? She has been away for a long time."

"She certainly has," the woman nodded as she dialed a number. "Voicemail," she shook her head. "I'll try her later."

"It'll be good to have her back in town," Laxmi went around picking up clothes and tidying up.

"Hmmm," the woman said and bit into a piece of toast. "I don't know Laxmi...I'm too old to get into trouble anymore."

*

The elevator doors opened and Sabine, wearing a slim black dress, high-heeled sandals, a white silk trench-style coat, her hair waving around her and her big dark glasses shielding her eyes, struck quite a figure, striding quickly through the lobby towards the entrance.

"Ah...Miss Kumar," Mr. Vivek appeared seemingly out of nowhere by her side, walking quickly to keep up with her. "How is the suite?"

"Lovely, thank you."

"How is your stay so far?" he asked.

"I've only been here 12 hours."

"Yes, yes," he laughed

"What may I get you this evening?"

"I need a car and driver."

"Of course," he bowed slightly. "Let me tell the doorman..." They walked together to the front door.

"Call Shiv," he instructed the uniformed man at the door. "And tell him to bring the white Mercedes for Miss Kumar.

"Nothing but the best for you," he turned to Sabine.

"Thank you," she said.

"You are very welcome, Miss. Kumar," he opened the door of the car that pulled up. "I wish you a very pleasant evening."

"Where shall I take you, Madam?" Shiv the driver doffed his cap.

"The Singh Gallery in Vasant Vihar," she said, settling into the back seat.

As they sped through Delhi, Sabine looked out the window. In a way, it *was* good to be back, *I wonder if I could live here again*, she thought.

Her phone beeped with an incoming message. *'Tried calling. Your phone was off. See you tonight?'*

'Yes,' she replied. *'Have something to do first. Your Address?'*

'Same. West End A-7.'

"Here we are, Madam," the driver said as they pulled up to a very modern building on a side street in one of Delhi's poshest neighbourhoods. A red carpet stretched from the edge of the pavement to the large glass doors, with black ropes on either side holding back the paparazzi and fans holding out pieces of paper and pens for autographs from arriving celebrities.

A large man wearing a black suit and an earpiece opened the car door.

"Who is that?" Sabine heard several of the photographers ask one another.

"Don't know...but take her photo...you never know."

"She looks famous."

"This way please, miss," several of them shouted, but Sabine didn't stop, walking straight up to the front door.

"Your name, please," a young woman holding a clipboard said as she entered.

"Sabine Kumar."

"Miss. Kumar," the woman went down her list. "I'm afraid I don't have your name here."

"I'm sure it's a clerical error," Sabine said. "Please check again."

"Your name is not on the list, Miss Kumar."

"Perhaps my assistant forgot to rsvp," Sabine smiled.

"Just one moment," the young woman said and while she went behind the desk, Sabine grabbed a glass of champagne from the tray of a passing waiter and walked in.

"Hey!" the woman cried out. "Wait! You can't go in there...you're not on the list. Security...!" she said into the mike attached to her earpiece, "we have a problem. A crasher."

Sabine walked through the large front room of the gallery, disappearing into the crowd. Modern works graced the walls and stone sculptures of nude Indian Goddesses on plinths were scattered in the corners.

She saw two security men come in and talk to the assistant who was looking around frantically over the heads of people trying to find her. She took off her white coat and threw it over her arm, putting down her empty glass of champagne and helping herself to another.

She walked into the back room and suddenly there he was, leaning against a column. Tall and still handsome, JJ Singh was wearing a black suit, white shirt and a black turban with a diamond and emerald pin in the front of it. He had a glass of champagne in his hand and was smiling down at a young woman wearing a tight orange dress, high heels, and too much makeup, giggling and batting her eyelashes at him.

Sabine rolled her eyes and walked straight towards him.

"Hello JJ."

JJ looked shocked.

"Hey...what's going on?" the woman said.

"Excuse us," Sabine dismissed her.

"Sabine...darling!" he said, smiling as people turned to stare at them. "How are you? It's so good to see you...I've been thinking about you...and meaning to call you. It's just the days just slip away."

"1,825 days have slipped away," she said softly.

"Time flies, darling," he laughed. "But you look...you look...great!"

"I do?"

"Really...you look amazing."

"You know, JJ," she stood very close to him. "I wouldn't be too happy to see me, if I were you."

"Why?"

"Did you really think you were going to get away with it?"

"I...uh..."

"Karma can be a real bitch, JJ," Sabine got closer to him." Do you know that old saying?" her mouth was inches away from his. "Hell hath no fury like a woman scorned."

"Don't get too close, Sabine," he murmured.

"Yeah?" she said. "Or what?"

"I'll call..."

"You'll call the police?"

"Uh...yes..." he stammered. "I'll call the police."

"Is everything alright, sir?" the two security guards came

running up.

"Yes, yes," JJ smiled, putting his arm around Sabine's waist. "Sabine and I are old friends," he said loud enough for people to hear. "We were just catching up."

"Sir," one of the security men whispered to JJ, "her name was not on the list."

"It's no matter," he laughed. "I'm sure it was a mistake in the office."

"Very well, sir," the man melted away, whispering something into the mike in his sleeve.

"Let's have lunch," JJ said to her, a fake smile pasted on his face. "I'll call you."

"I don't have lunch with traitors," she murmured, tracing his jawline with her finger.

"What do you mean 'traitor?' he said. "I was the one who drove you to the airport and put you on the plane so you didn't have to go to jail here."

"You're the one who gave me up to the police when they questioned you about the Indore diamonds," Sabine said. "You told them you knew nothing about the sale or the robbery...that you were completely innocent..."

"I did not..."

"You told them I had brought you the diamonds, and asked you to organize the sale..."

"Well..."

"The diamonds were yours and you asked me to pose as the seller, remember?" Sabine said quietly. "And we...you and me...we organized the robbery..."

"I..." JJ started.

"You told the CBI that you felt defrauded and would testify

against me..."

"They were breathing down my neck..." JJ looked away.

"Hi JJ!" someone passing by said.

"You bastard..." Sabine shook her head. "You decided to save yourself..."

"I saved you from a jail cell at the Delhi Jail...can you imagine five years in a cell?"

"Sending me to Europe was you assuaging your conscience. But I still had to live looking over my shoulder.

"It was your plan, JJ...not mine," Sabine said. "And we were partners.

"You don't give up your partner, no matter what."

"I had no choice."

"Yes," Sabine's eyes bore into him, "you did."

JJ held her gaze but only for a moment.

"You know what happens to traitors, don't you?"

"What do you mean?" he said nervously.

In response, she ran her finger gently across his throat.

JJ gulped.

Sabine walked away, stopped and turned.

"It was good to see you, JJ," she said and smiled flirtatiously.

*

JJ opened the top button of his collar and put his hand on his neck, taking long deep breaths.

"Rusty!" he called to a man standing close by.

"Sir?"

"The woman who just walked away..."

"Yes, sir."

"Keep your wits about you with her..."

"Is she likely to come back tonight, sir?"

"No...but I want you to remember her face."

"I will, sir," Rusty said. "I will get a photo of her off the gallery cameras."

"And stay close to me," JJ cleared his throat.

"JJ! *Kya yaar*! How are you?" a man approached JJ.

Rusty went to stand in front of his boss.

"It's fine," JJ whispered. "I know him.

"Arun Singh!" JJ shook his hand . "Glad you could make it to my little opening."

Arun Singh was of medium height and a slim build with a protruding middle-age tummy. He had grey hair that had thinned and he teased it before combing it back and sprayed it with a hairspray. He was wearing grey pants, a white shirt with a blue paisley ascot tie and a blue blazer.

"Are you kidding, *yaar*?" he smiled, showing a very large set of teeth. "I wouldn't miss it for the world."

"That's nice of you to say."

"I've been trying to get in touch with you."

"Have you? I am sorry, it's been very busy."

"JJ, I wanted to talk to you..."

"About?"

"I don't want to discuss it here..."

"Listen Arun," JJ rubbed his forehead. "Is this about lending you more money?"

"Well...it's just that I have these projects," Arun cleared his throat. "And I just need a little help to get them over the hump and back in the running..."

"Arun..." JJ raised his hand. "I've lent you a lot of money and I'm still waiting for you to pay it back..."

"I just need a little more and these projects will be off to the races."

"How much are you talking?"

"About $50 million."

"50 million!" JJ said shocked. "I don't have that..." he looked around. "Not even close to that."

"I...uh..."

"It was good of you to come," JJ said. "Now, if you'll excuse me..."

*

"Wait here for me," Sabine said to her driver when he opened the door for her. She walked up a cobblestoned path through a garden towards large teak wood double doors. She was about to ring the bell when the doors opened.

"Well, well, well," a woman wearing loose beige linen pants and a man's style navy blue linen shirt smiled broadly. "Am I glad to see you."

Sabine stood for a moment before crossing the threshold.

"I'd have you know that it's evening," the woman said. "You don't need the sunglasses."

Sabine took off her glasses and walked in. "It's good to see you, Indi."

Indi threw her arms around Sabine hugging her warmly.

"Alright, alright," Sabine extricated herself from the embrace.

"I'm really happy to see you."

"Yeah well, no need to choke me," Sabine said. "This is a nice place," she walked into a round foyer looking around at the modern bamboo furnishings and artwork on the walls. "When did you move in?"

"Just after you left," she said.

"It's nice."

"The cook has the night off so I ordered in Chinese," she said as they walked arm-in-arm down a hallway. "Do you want a drink? Still drink Billecart-Salmon?"

"Did you really just ask me that?"

Indi pulled a bottle of Billecart-Salmon from an ice bucket.

Indi was really Indira Indiana Kumar, two first names because her parents had been unable to agree on which one when she was born in Bloomington, Indiana where her Indian father was a professor of Computing and Engineering at the University of Indiana and her American mother, an ex-model and perfect homemaker. Her Indian father wanted to name her Indira and her American mother Indiana. They finally settled on both and began calling her Indi.

She also shared her surname with Sabine. They were not related even though having the same name had served them on occasion in the past.

After her father retired from academia, the family moved back to Delhi, but life in the East was not for Indi's mother who insisted they return to the States, leaving the house in Delhi to Indi who by then, had gone into the world of fashion.

Indi had often wondered why her parents had named her after the state where she was born and not the city, but as Sabine often reminded her, 'Bloomington' was a bit of a mouthful.

At 5'9", Indi was just slightly taller than Sabine, darker in complexion but with finer features, a small nose, an alluring mouth, large brown eyes and short curly hair that took years off of her 50. A one-time model, she had a boyish figure and was still trim, occasionally doing shoots here and there for magazines and television.

"I brought you a present," Sabine delved into her bag and pulled out a red velvet pouch.

"Oooh!" Indi exclaimed, showing the perfect bright smile that lit up her whole face and had launched her modeling career.

She loosened the knot and pulled out a delicate necklace with a large diamond pendant in the shape of a pear that hung from a chain of smaller diamonds.

"Shit..." Indi raised her eyebrows.

"A little token of my friendship."

"Real?" Indi asked.

"Of course."

"Don't tell me you're still in the business..." Indi whipped around.

"What business?" Sabine shrugged again.

"Did you do this?" she pointed to the pendant. "Why?" she shook her head.

"Because it's what I'm good at," she said.

"And that's why you're back, right?" Indi said. "You've got your eye on something."

"If you don't like the pendant, then you're not going to like what I've got my eye on."

"Sabine..." Indi sounded exasperated.

"Let's go eat!" Sabine changed the topic. "I'm starving...and Chinese food and champagne is my favourite thing in the world, even in India."

Indi stared at her questioningly, but Sabine took her by the arm. "Come on!"

"So where were you earlier this evening?" the two women sat at an Indonesian teak table that was off to the side in a large space that served as living, dining and den space.

"I went to see him."

"Him?" Indi frowned. "Him who?"

"There's only one 'him.'"

"Oh my god!" Indi sat back, chopsticks in hand. "You mean 'him.'"

"'Him,'" Sabine nodded, smiling.

"Why would you do that?"

"I don't know..." Sabine said. "I wanted to look him in the eye and have him know that I knew what he'd done."

"What did he say?"

"Nothing, really," Sabine said. "But he got the idea."

"So why are you really back? Last I heard from you, you were in Paris...or Amsterdam."

"I wanted to see you, couple of other people."

"Bullshit!"

Sabine laughed.

"And...there's a party I think we should go to."

"Oh yeah," Indi asked. "Which one?"

"A party for Priya Chopra and Randy Singh."

"The Bollywood couple?"

Sabine nodded. "JJ's hosting it at his house."

"Why?"

"Why not?"

"You've got something up your sleeve, Sabine," Indi pushed her plate back and crossed her arms over her chest. "What is it?"

"I just thought it would be fun to see everyone," Sabine said.

"See everyone?" she said sarcastically. "Who do we know in Bollywood?

"Sabine...? What are you planning?"

Sabine took a long sip of her drink.

"Besides, that guest list is going to be so tightly controlled by JJ," Indi added. "How are we going to get in?"

"We'll come up with something," Sabine said confidently. "We always do."

"What's he got?"

"Ah! So now you're interested?"

"I don't know."

"Be careful, Sabine," Indi warned. "JJ's become a very big deal over the past few years...much more than he was and a very rich man who pays off all the right people."

"I know," Sabine said. "I've been following the news."

"He's not who he used to be when you and he were...partners."

"Stop worrying."

"I am worried," Indi said. "I just don't want you to do anything stupid."

"I'm not...I really just came back because I missed you."

"As I said before, 'Bull...'"

"It's jewels," Sabine interrupted.

"Of course, it is," Indi shook her head. "But they've got to be something special if you came back to India."

"They are...big beautiful diamonds, emeralds..."

Indi shook her head.

"Indi..." Sabine poured them both some more champagne. "This can set us all up for life.

"What are you going to do when you're 60?" she added. "Do you still want to be cheating at bridge or the bingo at the Gymkhana Club, never mind fixing hard drives?"

Indi looked away.

"You still look fantastic...but will you get any more modeling gigs at 60?"

"What do you have in mind?"

Sabine took a small newspaper cutting out of her pocket and slid it across the table.

"You're kidding," Indi exclaimed. "The Barodan necklace?"

Sabine nodded.

"But no one knows where it is," Indi said. "It disappeared before partition..."

"I know where it is."

"Where?"

"In a safe."

"And how do you propose to get it out?"

"They'll bring it out," Sabine said confidently.

"They? Who's 'they?' Whose safe?"

"By the way, I need some cash," Sabine ignored the question.

"What for?" Indi said, still staring at the cutting.

"I'm going to need to buy a few things."

"Like what?"

"I don't know...clothes...maybe a painting..."

"A painting?"

"You'll see."

"Why can't you just tell me?"

Sabine shrugged.

"By the way..." Indi helped herself to some more chili chicken. "Why are you staying at the Oberoi?" Indi asked. "You could stay here."

"Because he is going to look me up... and living well is the best revenge."

"How much you going to need?"

"Five...lakhs."

"That's a lot..."

"What do we still have?"

"The ruby is all that's left."

"Let's sell it." Sabine refilled her glass. "Is Gema still around?"

Indi smiled and nodded. "Of course, she's still around. Where's she going to go?"

*

"Detective?"

Detective Imran Khan was an attractive man in his mid-50's. Tall and slim, with a swarthy complexion, big brown eyes, a long nose and a moustache, and a full head of wavy salt and pepper hair, he wore a navy short-sleeved shirt over a pair of grey trousers.

He was seated at his desk in a small, cramped office at police headquarters in Delhi. He was looking over some files in an effort to clean out his desk, and was going through the drawers when the young officer walked in.

"What is it?" he answered, rifling through the manila folders.

"Sir...we just got a call from the Bureau of Immigration..."

"And?" Imran looked up at him over his small, silver wire-rimmed glasses.

"Two nights ago," the officer handed Imran a file, "one Sabine Kumar arrived in Delhi on British Airways flight 143."

"Sabine Kumar...?" Imran frowned and opened the file and scanned the few documents in it. "Are you sure?"

"Yes, sir.

"Immigration said there was a note in her file saying you wanted to be notified if she came back to India."

"I wonder why she's back," he adjusted his glasses behind his ears.

"Who is she, sir?"

"She's a very smart thief," he said. "About five years ago, she was going to be arrested in connection with an important jewelry theft, but she got away."

"How did we know she was involved?"

"JJ Singh, the millionaire collector, tipped off the commissioner at the time," Imran said. "We got to the airport, but the plane had already taken off."

"Where has she been all this time?"

"I don't know," Imran said. "We worked with the FBI and Interpol for a while, but she fell off the grid."

"Can't we just arrest her now?"

"No," he shook his head. "There's a statute of limitations on the warrant. It's expired. Too much time has gone by."

"What would you like me to do, sir?"

"Nothing at the moment...our Miss Kumar hasn't done anything wrong...yet."

"Yes, sir," the man stuck the manila folder under his arm and walked out.

After he walked out, Imran sat back and placed the tips of his fingers together, his eyebrows knit together, his expression pensive.

Suddenly, he pulled open the bottom cabinet and began fingering through until he got all the way to the end, picking out an old brown file, tied together with string: his first case after his promotion to Detective.

He opened it, and began leafing through: reports, notes, transcripts of interviews...all conducted by him. He pulled out a dog-eared photograph of a pair of diamond earrings: the famous Indore Pears that had been stolen from the home of Doctor Samir and Sonia Jaffrey five years ago. It was Sonia Jaffrey who had reported the theft.

He read through the transcript of the interview he did with JJ Singh who had sold them the earrings.

"How did you come to be in possession of the Indore Pears?"

"Sabine Kumar brought them to me."

"How did she get them?"

"I don't know."

Imran remembered pressing him, but JJ never said anything and despite Imran's gut feeling that he wasn't telling the truth, he'd been told by the police commissioner that JJ was off the hook. But how had Sabine Kumar gotten her hands on them? And somehow, Sabine managed to escape his clutches, her flight taking off just as the police had arrived at the airport. Someone had to have tipped her off? He'd immediately suspected JJ, but,

"Clearly it was the woman," Commissioner Chavan told him at the time. "Drop the case. You have the thief."

"Yes, and she is somewhere in Europe by now," Imran said.

"See what the boys at Interpol come up with," Chavan had said.

Imran had gotten in touch with the Interpol branch in Paris, and they'd promised to keep their eyes open.

A few months later, Imran called his colleague, François Marchand at the Sûreté in Paris.

"François...Imran Khan in New Delhi."

"*Oui! Comment vas tu?* How are things?"

"Good, good...listen man, I was wondering if you had anything on Sabine Kumar?"

"Imran, my friend, I have my hands full...the Panther has returned."

"Panther?"

François sighed. "He's a master thief," he said. "He was active for a long time in the 70s, 80s and 90s and then suddenly disappeared. We thought he'd died.

"But, he's either risen from the dead or someone imitating him has reappeared."

"Can it really be him?"

"If it is, he's in his 70s by now..."

"Hard to believe he's still active."

"I think it's more likely someone who knows him or his techniques.

"A copycat?"

"Likely someone close to him," François said. "Someone younger."

"Maybe he's become a mentor."

"But who?" he sighed.

"In his day, the man was a ghost," he added. "He got his hands on legendary jewels and we don't know how...somehow he was able to walk through walls, avoiding security cameras...nothing stopped him.

"It was almost as though people handed him their jewelry."

"You have no idea what he looks like?"

"Nothing...just shadows."

"That's a tough one."

"He's been on the Sûreté and Interpol's list for forty years."

"Well, keep me posted if you come up with anything on the Kumar woman."

"I will."

"Good luck."

"*Merci mon ami.*"

Imran frowned and reached for his keyboard and typed Indore Pears into Google. Perfectly shaped teardrop diamonds of almost the exact same size were bought in 1913 by the Maharajah of Indore at the house of Chaumet in Paris. At the time of partition, when all the Maharajahs were scrambling to keep their lifestyles unchanged, the diamonds were sold to Harry Winston in New York, who in turn sold them as earrings to a client of his in New York in 1953.

In the summer of 1975, the earrings were stolen from the Hotel du Cap in Cap d'Antibes and never found.

Imran sighed. He stared at the Google box on the screen of his computer and typed Sabine Kumar. Nothing came up. There were articles about people named Sabine and others named Kumar, but nothing on her. He shook his head. She had well and truly managed to stay off the grid, even in this day and age.

He scrolled the images tab, but again...nothing. Suddenly he stopped and scrolled back up, stopping at a small black and white photograph of a man in a tuxedo and a blonde woman in a gown and long opera gloves. He peered at the screen, clicked on the image and tried to enlarge it, but it was too small and it appeared blurry. There was something about the woman...she was beautiful, her dark hair waving around her. The caption read: 'Abi Kumar and Sabine Marceau arrive at the Oberoi for New Year's Eve Ball, Dec 31, 1975.'

Who was Abi Kumar? Imran wondered. He typed his name into Google. And there it was...an obituary in the Times of India...

Imran scanned the piece...tragic car accident on the Cote d'Azur...and the last sentence, *'Abi Kumar was the last Maharajkumar of Nawanagar.'*

Imran sat back, gluing the ends of his fingers together, frowning, deep in thought. Could it be that Abi Kumar the 'Panther' that the Sûreté had been after? Had he been behind the theft of the Indore diamonds in 1975? As the Maharajah, he would have been part of the international jet set...summering in the south of France, skiing in Gstadt...? He sat back up and stared at the photograph. Was it possible that he and Sabine Marceau had a daughter?

*

JJ Singh sat at his mahogany partner's desk in the luxurious library office of his sprawling Portuguese colonial style farmhouse on Cherry Lane in Chattarpur, New Delhi.

He was the kind of man whose charisma won over looks. In his mid- fifties, he was tall and still lean, attractive with an olive complexion, bold cheekbones, bright green eyes, a long nose and a trim, grey moustache and beard, in contrast to his thick, bushy eyebrows that were still black. A Sikh, he wore a black turban, without which, he was often mistaken for an Italian or a Spaniard. Today, he wore a perfectly cut navy suit and a white shirt that had quite obviously been made for him.

He thumbed through a sheaf of papers on his desk before hurling them across the room.

"Goddamnit!" he swore, pushing his chair back roughly as he watched them gently float to the ground. "Fuck!" he slammed his fist on his desk, getting up and going to stand at the window that gave out onto the pool and gardens, running his hand across his forehead. He paced around the room, stopping for a moment in front of a large fish tank, watching a turquoise and yellow fish swim around a mound of red coral. He reached for a small container of fish food and sprinkled some in. The fish immediately rose up and gobbled it all up, leaving nothing for the smaller orange fish that came out from behind a rock when it smelled the food.

He had just walked back to his desk when the phone on his desk rang. Before he could answer, the door opened.

"Sir...you cannot go in there," a voice sounded from the hallway. "Sir, I absolutely must insist...Mr. Singh doesn't see anyone without an appointment."

"I think he will see me," a man came in and shut the door forcefully, keeping his back to JJ.

Outside, angry voices mixed with the sounds of a scuffle.

"What the hell is going on?" JJ said.

"Hello JJ," the man turned and smiled.

He was of medium height, his complexion on the darker side, his eyes brown, a wide forehead, a long nose and a salt and pepper beard that matched his slightly long, wavy hair that was slicked back. He kept one hand in his pocket, the other one on the silver swan tip of the black cane he carried.

He was dressed in a tailored grey suit, a white shirt and a silk paisley pocket square that peeked cheekily out of his breast pocket.

"I see that you too have taken to bespoke clothing," he remarked.

"Rambo Singh..." JJ finally said. "What are you doing here?"

"It's been a few years and I thought we could catch up...by the way, that's a nice Jamini Roy in the hallway. Is it real?"

JJ ignored him. "I didn't even know you were in India."

"I've just arrived."

"Welcome back," JJ said sarcastically.

"You're living well, my friend," Rambo said.

"I've done alright," JJ said.

"I can see that, "Rambo looked around. "But... he pulled a cigar out of his breast pocket and ran it under his nose, inhaling deeply, "you have something of mine, something you stole to get all of this," he gestured around the room, lighting his cigar.

"I hope you don't mind," he gestured to the cigar after he'd taken a few puffs. "And I want it back."

"You got your money back..." JJ started.

"No, no," Rambo wagged his finger. "*My* money back, JJ," Rambo interrupted. "I want it back...every penny, plus interest."

"What are you talking about?

"Have you had a fucking lobotomy? Or do you just have a selective memory?" Rambo raised his voice.

"Have you forgotten that you worked for me? You ran my hotel business in Dubai...it was very lucrative..."

"It was lucrative because I made it lucrative," JJ said.

"You had a secret casino going in the hotel...membership only...booze, women, gambling...of course it was fucking lucrative."

"So what are you complaining about? You turned a blind eye and made a killing in the process.

"All you had to do was make it so no one raided us."

"I'm complaining about the goddamned money that disappeared one night from the vault...a night when you told me that you had big spenders coming in and that is why, we upped the reserve...I would never have kept that much cash on hand...you set me up, JJ.

"You knew how everything worked...even the security, so you came up with a plan, walked in, opened the vault and stole the money...and I was the idiot for trusting you with the keys to my kingdom."

"You got it back from the insurance..."

"Shut up!" Rambo slammed his cane into the floor and then pointed it at JJ. "The money you stole...all 35 million plus interest over five years...that's 50 million dollars."

"I don't have it. It's going to take me some time to sell..."

"You've got 4 weeks."

"4 weeks or what?"

"Don't make me tell you."

"What are you going to do, Rambo?

"You don't scare me."

"Really?" Rambo raised an eyebrow and walked over to the fish tank. Suddenly and without warning, he swung his stick, the handle smashing the glass. Water spilled out, drenching JJ and the fish lay on the carpet gasping to death.

"Only next time," Rambo wiped off a couple of drops of water, "it'll be you gasping, not the fish.

"4 weeks JJ," he repeated and walked out leaving JJ staring

after him.

Still soaking wet, JJ picked up the phone.

"Rusty...get in here."

Seconds later,

"Yes, sir..." Rusty came in, his eyes widening as he looked at a very wet JJ and the aquarium in shards. "*Sahib*...what happened?" he started cautiously.

Rusty Khan was a northerner, from Kashmir. Tall, broad and fair with light-brown hair and blue eyes, he was ex-Indian Army and JJ's right hand. He was casually dressed in a pair of grey pants, a light blue shirt and a dark blue jacket.

"Trouble," JJ said.

"I can see that."

"Karma is on my ass."

"Not sure I understand, *Sahib*?" Rusty said.

"It seems that everything I did five years ago is catching up to me."

"What happened?"

"Remember Sabine Kumar who came to the gallery a few days ago...she and I were partners...a deal went wrong, she got burned..."

"She got burned?" Rusty asked.

"I burned her."

"I see."

"And this guy, Rambo Singh...after Sabine left, things were getting hot for me here, so I went to Dubai and he gave me a job," JJ said.

"Rambo ran a hotel, a very luxurious five-star hotel and I came up with the idea of opening a members-only cigar club in the basement...that morphed into a lot more than the cigar club...it became a casino, big time booze and of course that led to the hookers...all Russian, Ukranian...you get the picture.

"Of course, the members, who paid a lot of money for their membership were all the elite Arabs, so if there was ever a raid...it would be bad.

"Rambo was crushing it...money was rolling in...millions."

"What happened?"

"I asked him for a piece of the business and he said no...he wanted to keep me as an employee."

Rusty nodded.

"So I went back to an old con...I got him to increase the money we had in the club safe, telling him we had big spenders coming.

"I fixed the cameras, robbed the money, walked out and took a flight back to Delhi with 35 million."

Rusty nodded. "And now he wants it back."

"He got it all back from his insurance...but yeah...now he wants it all back."

"Do you have it?"

"I don't," JJ said. "It's all gone. I set myself up in a new life...bought a couple of houses and the art collection...went legit."

"What can Rambo do?"

"He can make my life very difficult."

"How so?"

"Here in Delhi, he can talk to the CBI, tell them about how much I made in Dubai..." JJ said. "And they are waiting for even the slightest bit of info to come after me...and in Dubai itself, if word gets out, I'll be toast there and that's where I sell so much of this art...to people I met when I ran the club."

"What do you want me to do?"

"I don't know...yet."

"*Sahib*...why did Rambo wait so long to come after you?"

JJ opened his mouth to answer, but closed it.

"I don't know," he finally said. "But I'm sure we'll find out.

"In the meantime, get my butler in here...I need to get out of these wet clothes."

Chapter 2

Sabine got out of a taxi at the entrance to Old Khanna Market in an enclave of Sundar Nagar. Dressed casually in a pair of jeans with a long blue tunic and a shawl, she blended in perfectly with the crowds on the streets as she made her way around the square towards an old shop that sold Indian and Nepalese antiques.

She smiled at the toothless man who sat on a low stool out front and entered the dark shop, walking towards the back where she went up an old, creaky staircase at the top of which she pulled aside a curtain and walked into a room that didn't have much except a couple of mattresses covered with colourful pink and yellow patchwork sheets, embroidered with small mirrors and big maroon bolsters and a couple of pink pillows. The walls were painted pale green and there were large old black and white photos of a man wearing a suit and smiling, the frames hung with garlands of jasmine and roses. In the corner was a small clay altar with a statue of Ganesh surrounded by marigolds, burning incense and a small clay lamp filled with oil and a lit wick floating in it.

There was a door to the right that was slightly ajar.

"There is a flaw in this diamond," a pleasant, musical voice sounded.

Sabine chuckled when she heard the female voice.

"What are you talking about?" a shrill female voice retorted. "It is a perfect diamond."

"No, it's not," the first woman said. "It's yellowish...at very best it's a K diamond."

"You're lying! It's an H."

"No, it's not."

"Fine!" the shrill voice said annoyed. "I'll take my business elsewhere."

The door opened and a woman wearing a green sari, came out. She stopped for a second when she saw Sabine before rushing through the front door, her sandal heels clicking down the stairs.

Sabine pulled out her cellphone and sent a text. 'Can you come out?'

Moments later,

"You don't call? You don't write?" a woman wearing a long red embroidered tunic over a pair of red shalwar trousers came out. A classic Indian face, she had large almond shaped dark eyes, a small nose and thick lips. Her hair was long, cascading in small tight curls down her back.

"Hi Gema," Sabine smiled. "It's good to see you."

"And you..." Gema's eyes twinkled as she beamed back. "Where've you been?"

"Long story."

"Want some tea?" Gema put her arm in Sabine's. "Shall we go down to the chaiwallah?"

"Is it the same guy?"

Gema nodded.

"Does he still have samosas?"

"And they're still made by his wife."

Outside in the pale mid-morning sunshine of a January in

Delhi, the chaiwallah stood next to his cart parked under a large banyan tree in the middle of the square, shouting out the magical powers of his tea.

Gema bought glasses of tea and samosas and the two women sat at a stone chess table that was also used by the older shop-keepers to play backgammon on lazy afternoons, basking in the gentle rays that enveloped them.

"I was sorry to hear about your father," Sabine began.

"Thanks," Gema replied. "And I about yours...I read about it in The Times."

Sabine nodded.

"Are you in touch with your mother?"

"You know they weren't really married," Sabine said. "They only said they were because she was pregnant."

"She's still your mother," Gema shrugged.

"I wonder why Dad never married her?" Sabine wondered.

"Did you ever ask him?"

"I did...he said he did and she said no."

"You have your answer."

"I still think there was more to it, but anyhow, we're in touch once a year...we exchange Christmas cards."

"Where does she live?"

"Canada...after she left my dad, she remarried and moved.

"What about your mum?" Sabine bit into the samosa.

"Pain in the ass," Gema said. "All she can talk about is marriage and that there must be something wrong with me because I'm not married with 18 children...like my sister."

"Your sister has 18 children?" Sabine looked confused.

"No...she has 4," Gema said. "But you know what I mean."

"Does she still have anything to do with the business?"

"Thankfully, no," Gema replied. "Or she would make my life completely unlivable.

"I think my father knew that so, in his will, he left the business to me."

"Good."

The two women sipped their tea.

"What are you doing back here?" Gema asked. "Last I bumped into Indi, she said you were in Paris or something?"

"I've been in Europe," Sabine said, "mostly Paris with my father until the accident."

"You seen JJ?" she asked.

"I have."

"He's kind of a big deal now in Delhi."

"That's what I hear."

"Hobnobbing with all the rich and famous...I saw something on tv that he's having a big party for Priya Chopra and her new husband."

"I saw that too," Sabine said. "Listen," she added after a moment, "I need you to sell something."

"What is it?" Gema asked.

Sabine handed her a small brown paper bag.

Gema looked inside and looked back up at Sabine. "Burma ruby?"

Sabine nodded.

"Provenance?"

"1920's...Patiala necklace."

Gema rolled up the paper bag and put it in her pocket.

"How much do you want?"

"As much as you can get...and fast."

"Give me a couple of days," Gema nodded and tipped the young boy who came to collect their glasses.

"Why are you really here?"

"I have something I may need you for."

"You mean besides the ruby?"

Sabine nodded.

"What it is?" Gema asked. "You need to run some stuff through the store?"

"I need you to do your best work on something."

"No problem," Gema said. "How much time do I have?"

"Not a lot."

"What do you need me to do?"

"I want you to make a copy of something."

"What?"

Sabine pulled a newspaper cutting from her pocket and handed it over.

Gema stared aghast at piece of paper in her hands. "The Barodan?"

Sabine nodded.

"This necklace hasn't been seen in decades," Gema said. "Wasn't there something about it being stolen by the Maharajah's wife? The same one he bought it for?"

Sabine nodded. "The same."

"You came back for the necklace?"

"A little more than that," Sabine looked at her cellphone.

"But where is it?"

"Can you make me a copy?" Sabine got up off the stool.

"I can try," Gema nodded.

"You've got about four weeks."

*

JJ Singh pulled aside a painting in his office, revealing an antique grey steel safe behind it. He turned the wheel and on the third turn, it opened. Inside, was a velvet jewelry case, a wad of US dollars and the more colourful euros.

He pulled out the case and put it on his desk, staring at it for a few moments before he opened it. There it lay: the famous Barodan necklace, designed by the House of Richemont in 1928 for the Maharajah of Barodan. Six pounds of stones: Kimberley diamonds from South Africa the Maharajah had bought in London at an auction and Colombian emeralds he'd bought from the impoverished Ottoman sultan in Istanbul.

"Keep this…"

JJ was only in his late teens when his mother handed him a velvet pouch whilst she lay dying. "One day, it may come in handy."

"What is it, *umma*?" the young boy said watching his mother gasp for air as he took the pouch from her.

"It is all I have to give you…one day, your life may be in danger and this will save you."

"*Umma!*" JJ gasped when he opened the pouch. "Where did you get this?"

"I did it for my family, *beta*, I needed something just in case."

"But how did you get it?"

"I thought it would help us during partition, but it didn't," she said, not answering his question. "We were all separated, my brothers and my parents and I.

"After I got married, your father and I struggled…but I held onto it for some reason.

"Those years after Independence were terrible, Hindus and

Muslims killing one another...the looting, the rioting that continued well after 1947. ...but all that doesn't matter anymore.

"I thought I might need it when your father was killed in a riot, but my prayers were heard and God provided for us and I got a job in a school.

"This is now your secret. Promise me you will sell it only if your life is in danger."

"*Umma...*" JJ tried to get her to explain where she'd come upon the necklace.

But his mother never told him.

For a few weeks after his mother died, JJ would lie in bed looking at the diamonds and emeralds, wondering how his mother, a school teacher, had come upon such an exquisite necklace. With the necklace in his pocket, he went to various jewelers in Chhor Bazaar, but never had the courage to go in, terrified they might call the police.

He finally ended up at the library of the British Council and in the microfilm archives of *The Times of India*, he found an article about the jewels of the Maharajahs and the disappearance of the Patiala and Barodan necklaces around partition, with the reporter speculating that the heirs had privately sold pieces from their inheritance to survive in the new India.

When he read how much the necklace was worth, tears ran down his cheeks. In today's prices, the necklace was worth about 45-50 million in US dollars. His mother had left him a fortune.

JJ tried everything to find out how his mother had come by the Barodan necklace, but he'd never been able to find out and as time went by, the necklace became a symbol of his mother's love and her courage in face of the trouble she and his father had faced in the turbulent years after the partition of India.

JJ put it back in the safe, locking it.

"Get my lawyer on the phone."

"Yes JJ," said a male voice on the speaker phone.

"Sanjeev...how long will it take you to sell some of the artwork in the vault?"

"Well, the auction of Indian art at Christie's is in June and we just missed Sothebys."

"Shit."

"What about the house in Italy?"

"At least 3-4 months depending on how soon we have a buyer. The real estate market in Europe is soft."

JJ was silent.

"What jewelry can we sell?"

"The Jaipur pearls...the Mysore emeralds..."

"Sell."

"JJ," Sanjeev began cautiously. "Those are famous pieces...there'll be publicity."

"Find a private buyer," JJ said. "Call the Qataris...they'll jump on them."

"It's Eid...they're all on holiday," Sanjeev replied. "The Middle East is at a standstill. I'll get in touch with them in a week or so.

"What's going on?"

"I need liquid, fast."

"How fast?"

"Four weeks."

"What kind of liquid are we talking?"

"$50 million US."

"For the love of Ganesh," Sanjeev said. "I don't know that we can get it that quick...what kind of trouble are you in?"

"Trouble."

Sanjeev was silent for a moment. "I'll see what I can do."

JJ hung up and pressed the intercom button.

"Send Rusty in," he said.

Moments later, there was a knock on the door.

"Sir?"

"Rusty," JJ swiveled around in his chair. "Sabine Kumar..."

"Yes?"

"When did she arrive in Delhi?"

"According to my friends in immigration, she arrived a week ago on a British Airways flight from Rome."

"Rome?" JJ sat back, surprised.

"Yes, sir."

"Hmmm," JJ stroked his jawline. "Where is she staying?"

"The Oberoi, sir," Rusty replied. "The Eastern Star suite."

"Do you know what she's been doing?"

"Do you want me to keep an eye?'

"Yes."

"What about Rambo Singh?"

"Same flight..."

"Even more interesting...he came in from Rome too?"

"According to her itinerary, she went from Rome to London first."

"That makes sense," JJ got up from his desk. "Alright...now...I need you to do something...but we have to be very clever about it, and needless to say, very tight."

"Of course, sir."

"Get me Dev Anand from Lloyds on the phone."

Rusty picked up the phone on JJ's desk, dialed a number and handed it to him.

"Dev...*kya haal?*...Yes...all is well on my end...listen, I need a special insurance policy...it's a necklace...hasn't been seen in years...the Barodan...just bought it...no I'm not kidding...well, you know I'm having this party for Priya Chopra...she has asked to wear it, but it needs to be insured, just in case...you understand...good,   then   that's   settled...send   me   the paperwork...thanks *yaar*..." he handed the phone back to Rusty.

"Now," he pulled out his cellphone. "Priya!" he said cheerfully, "...listen gorgeous...how would you like to wear the Barodan necklace at the party?"

After he hung up, JJ stared silently at Rusty.

"The night after the party," he finally said. "You know what to do."

"I understand, sir."

*

Back in her suite at the Oberoi, Sabine sat at a small round table. The sun streamed in through a large window and she sipped some tea enjoying the silence.

There was a discreet knock at the door and she went to open it. There was no one outside, but when she looked down, there was a small brown envelope on the floor, addressed to her. She picked it up and went back to the table. Inside was a tiny flash drive. She inserted it into her laptop. There was one file that said JJ House. Sabine chuckled. It was good to have a fence.

Her phone beeped with an incoming message. '*Got it?*' She replied with a thumbs-up emoji.

"Now..." she mumbled to herself as she sipped a coffee.

"Where are all the security cameras?" She began studying what was on her screen.

"*Who runs his security*?" she went into google and typed in JJ Singh's name. The hits that followed were endless. She scrolled through the images. Photos of him at his gallery, at restaurants, parties...mostly with a woman by his side and a glass of whiskey or champagne in his hand. Wait! Who is this? She enlarged one of the photographs. Who is this man? She'd seen him at the gallery the night she went to see JJ. Who is he?

She launched an application that said 'Intelligence Bureau,' where she typed in a username and password. Seconds later, she was in the database of the Indian Domestic Intelligence Agency. She copied and pasted the man's photo, pressed a button and sat back, reaching for her tea cup. Scores of images flashed in front of her as the application searched for a facial recognition match. She got up and walked to the window looking out at the pool down below. A swim would do her no harm at all. Suddenly, a beeping sound. The database had found a match.

"Hmmm...Rustam Khan," she read off the screen. "Indian army...previously stationed in Kashmir...security specialist...JJ has an Indian Army guy in charge of his personal security...

"Alright...let's see if I can find you elsewhere..." she opened a couple of social media sites, but there wasn't anything, the man clearly liked his privacy. All she found was a photo of him playing cricket when he was still in the army.

Sabine sat back and put her hands behind her head, cradling it. She needed to hack into the security system of the house.

She picked up her phone.

"It's me."

"Yeah?"

"Do you know a good hacker?"

"This is India, Sabine...we're all about IT."

"Are you still in the game?

"What do you need?"

"I need access to JJ's security cameras."

"House?"

"Yes."

"I can do that," Indi said. "Why?"

"Good, then do it."

"Why won't you tell me why?"

"One thing at a time."

"Come on, Sabine!"

"Just get us in and I'll tell you."

"This is just like you...you get me interested and then I'm interested and then you back down."

"Indi...just do what you're good at..."

*

Indi hung up the phone with Sabine and flopped down on the sofa, letting out a cry of frustration.

"Everything alright, Indi *bibi*?" Laxmi came in.

"Yes, yes, Laxmi," Indi waved her away. "Sabine being difficult...again.

"I'd forgotten how crazy she makes me with all her selective sharing of information."

"*Bibi*?" Laxmi looked confused.

"I don't understand why she can't just tell me the whole story," Indi sighed.

"Sabine *bibi* is very secretive?" Laxmi asked.

"She always does this..." she added. "Getting a full plan out of her in one sitting is like pulling teeth."

"Pulling teeth?" Laxmi looked confused.

"Never mind, Laxmi," Indi smiled.

"I'll get you some tea, *bibi*," Laxmi said. "Tea always makes you think a little clearer."

Indi smiled.

Her phone rang and she looked at the caller id, 'Mum.'

"God..." she rolled her eyes.

"Hello, Mother," she answered.

"My darling daughter..." Violet Kumar drawled in a loud Midwestern American voice. "How are you?"

"Fine...how's things in Bloomington?"

"It's very cold this year."

"If you lived in Delhi," Indi said, "you wouldn't have to deal with the cold."

"I can't live there," Violet said. "Frankly, I don't know how you do it...especially when you could live in the States."

"Mother," Indi said. "I love coming to visit, but I prefer it here."

"There's so much more opportunity for you here, though," Violet said. "Even modeling, you could work with some of the catalogues."

"Why don't you do that?" Indi asked. "You used to model."

"That was another lifetime."

"You're still beautiful, mother," Indi said. "Slim, great skin...why not?"

"I suppose I could," Violet said. "Let's see...I'm exhausted, we had people for Thanksgiving, for Christmas and then your father and I had a New Years' Eve party..."

"You didn't go to the Golf Club on New Years' Eve?"

"We decided to do something different...and I'm glad we did, I suppose," Violet said. "But I don't know if I'll do it again."

"How's Dad?"

"He's deep into some paper or the other that he's writing."

"Dear daddy," Indi smiled thinking of her absent-minded academic father, his glasses always slightly askew on his nose. "How did he enjoy this big social whirl? Not exactly his scene..."

"I think he enjoyed himself."

"Mother!" Indi scoffed. "Dad enjoying being social?"

"Your father is much more amenable in his old age."

"Which means that you have become even more domineering..."

"How could you say that about your mother?"

"Because I'm your daughter..."

"And thank goodness my only one."

"By the way, Sabine is back," Indi said.

"Really? Where was she?"

"Hobnobbing around Europe."

"What a life!" Violet remarked. "What is she doing these days? Still dealing in art?"

"Yes," Indi was noncommittal.

"Why is she back?"

"I'm not entirely sure."

"How's your love life?"

"Mother!"

"What? I'm your mother...I can ask you these things."

"*Because* you're my mother, you cannot," Indi replied.

"You're so tiresome."

"I'm not...I just don't have anything to say."

"No boyfriend?"

"In case you've forgotten, this is India..."

"And people still date and get engaged and married," Violet said. "We're not living in the Victorian age."

"No... and I would have you know that people in the Victorian age were particularly randy."

"Anyway...nothing?"

"The Gobi Desert. Mother."

"Dear girl, that's such a waste."

"I have to say I'm very happy."

"How can you possibly be happy?"

"I'm not going to date someone just for the sake of it," Indi said.

"I hate to say this, but you're not getting any younger."

"I don't care what you say, but I'm never going to settle...he...whoever he is, is going to have to be great."

"But what do you do in the evenings?

"I know you've got your computer consults during the day, but the evening is when it must get lonely."

"For you, perhaps," Indi replied, "...but not for me.

"Besides, I have friends," Indi said. "And I occasionally go out."

"You're so like your father," Violet said. "He loves to be left alone with a book and a drink."

"I had to get it from someone," Indi replied. "And it definitely wasn't you, my dear social butterfly mother."

"But..."

"I can't handle the idea of being with anyone at the moment," she said.

"You're being silly," Violet said. "A broken heart cannot remain broken forever. It mends itself, wounds heal, scars fade."

"Perhaps...maybe I just need a bit more time."

"Don't take too long," Violet said. "Time doesn't stop for anyone."

"I know, mother."

"And you're not going to find anyone sitting at home."

"Stop nagging me," Indi said. "I'm almost 50."

"It's my job, dear, I'm your mother."

"I suppose."

"Have you heard from him?" Violet asked. "Do you know where he is?"

"He broke my heart, mother!" Indi exploded. "Why would I have heard from him?"

"I just thought that perhaps..."

"No," Indi said.

"Right," Violet took a deep breath. "I see I've stepped in it again. I suppose I'd better go."

"Give Dad my love," Indi said.

"Think about coming to the States, dear..."

"I must go," Indi interrupted. "Goodbye, Mother," she added and hung up.

She stared at the black screen of the phone for a moment before going into her contacts. She scrolled down the S's and stopped at Hari Singh. She clicked on the name.

There he was...smiling at her, a grey cotton scarf around his neck, his white shirt gleaming in the sunlight. She remembered the day she'd taken the photograph. She could feel her heart beating faster and the tears at the back of her eyes. She threw her phone down on the sofa and reached for her tea and took a sip.

"Oohhh!" she cried out. The tea was so hot that she spat it out and the cup tumbled, spilling the scalding liquid onto the white shaggy carpet, staining it caramel.

She stared at it, unable to move, her mother's words of time waiting for no one ringing in her ears,

On the second floor of a large white house in Golf Links, just behind the Oberoi Hotel, Mrs. Nina Singh, dressed in a pale pink sari with a lemon border was sitting in the covered veranda, staring absently at the vase of flowers on the coffee table in front of her. It was almost noon.

Just 60, Nina was on the short side and while she had always been plump, middle age had played havoc with her figure. Her face was oval shaped, her forehead wide, her dark eyes small, as was her nose and her lips were on the thin side. She had blue black hair that was cut short and she sported a diamond stud in her nose.

She was playing with the wedding ring on her left hand when,

"*Memsahiba*, would you like a cup of tea?" a maidservant's voice broke through her reverie.

She looked up at the older woman standing in front of her and smiled, shaking her head. "No thank you, Shanti," she said.

"Oh Shanti..." she said as the other woman turned to leave, "does the cook know that I have two friends coming for lunch today?"

"He does *memsahiba*," she replied.

"Good...and Shanti, I think I'll change, I'll wear my blue chiffon sari please."

"Yes, *memsahiba*."

Nina got up and walked to the windows and looked at the garden. The gardener was pruning some of the bushes, bees buzzed and birds chirped in this little oasis, whilst beyond the white wall that enclosed the garden, Delhi buzzed with the chaos of everyday life.

She crossed her arms across her chest and turned to walk back to the sofa she'd been sitting on.

"Oh!" she said, taken aback when she saw who stood at the entrance of the veranda.

It was her husband, Arun Singh. He wore a pair of black pants, a white shirt and a coral sweater, wrapped casually around his shoulders.

"Hello Nina," Arun said.

"What are you doing here?"

"I just wanted to tell you I am leaving."

"Why?" she sat down.

"In case you wanted to know where I was."

"If I wanted to know where you were, I would call my ex-best friend, Bunny."

"Nina..."

"And you would probably be right next to her...in her bed," Nina added.

"Nina...please."

"Why? Are you embarrassed?"

"Can we not be civilized about this?" Arun said.

"Civilized? Ha!" Nina scoffed. "That's rich."

"Look, I think we should try and keep this civil," Arun said.

"Civil?" Nina snorted. "Do you expect me to simply sit back and watch you and that slut make a fool of me?"

Arun opened his mouth to say something.

"Not a chance!" Nina interrupted. "I will not have everyone in Delhi looking at me with pity."

"No one will as long as we keep this under wraps."

"Under wraps?" she said. "I'm sure everyone already knows."

"They're all talking about it behind closed doors."

"But how?"

"Oh Arun..." Nina shook her head sadly. "She's been cozying up to you at every dinner party this season."

"I don't think so..."

"You are so blind!"

Arun looked away.

"After every dinner, I get a phone call telling me how she was all over you and how I ought to know what's going on."

"Look Nina..." Arun started. "I don't know what to say."

"You bastard!" Nina said in an eerily soft voice. "How could you? How could you have done this to me?"

"I didn't mean for it to happen..."

"That's such bullshit, Arun!" Nina raised her voice. "What do you take me for? Some feeble-minded woman?"

"Not at all...I think you're wonderful..."

"Stop!" Nina said. "You're just digging yourself into a hole...and besides, if you thought I was so wonderful, why the hell did you turn to another woman?

"What does she have that I don't?" Nina shot at him.

"Nina!" Arun said. "I've tried to tell you..."

"Yes, yes...tried to tell me that you're in love with her," Nina said sadly. "You know, if you'd gone and fallen for some twenty-year old, I'd almost understand that more than this...thing you have with that bitch."

"She understands me..."

"For the love of God!" Nina rolled her eyes. "You really are more pathetic than I thought...what was I thinking when I married you...? And why did I pick you? I had plenty of other offers."

She began pacing. "What did you add to my life? Nothing...you just pretended you were this aristocrat...the great-grandson of the Maharajah of Barodan and a rich successful businessman, but in truth, you were and still are, nothing...you didn't have a dime when we got married...and you still don't."

"I thought..." Arun tried to interrupt.

"Your title means nothing."

"But..."

"And all this," she stopped him gesturing with her hands, "this house, everything...it was all bought by my father...who helped you more than once...and what did you do with my dowry? Squandered it on some damned fool scheme of yours...?"

"I have tried..."

"You may have, but you've never been able to do anything, Arun," Nina continued talking over him. "And how you lie to people...all the stories you tell about this deal and that deal and this pathetic façade you put up of being a businessman. What do you have to show?

"Nothing!" she answered her own question. "And to think I sold everything to keep us going...and to finance your business plans.

"My entire inheritance...down the drain," she said sadly. "I have nothing left."

Arun stood silently and the two stared at each other.

"You are going to regret this, Arun Singh...I promise you."

"Are you threatening me?" Arun said, his nostrils suddenly flaring with anger.

"No threats, Arun, I am telling you that you will regret what you have done...you'll see."

"How dare you?" Arun puffed himself up.

"Go on!" Nina spat at him. "Get out! I don't want to see you here. This is my house..."

"But...but..." Arun stammered. "What do you mean?"

"Get out Arun!" Nina said. "You will hear from my lawyer."

"What? A divorce?" he spluttered.

"Of course!" Nina said. "Did you really think I was going to take this lying down?"

"But Nina," Arun tried, "that will be so public."

"You should have thought about that before you started up with her."

"Look, Nina...I'm sure there's a way we can work this out..."

"Get out Arun!" Nina repeated. "Or I will have you thrown out."

A run turned to walk away.

"You bastard!" she shouted.

Furious, Nina paced up and down the room, taking one deep breath after another to calm herself. But she couldn't. She picked up the vase filled with flowers and with all her might, threw it towards where Arun had been standing.

The vase shattered, the flowers lay in disarray and the water spilled all over the carpet. "You bastard!" Nina screamed again and collapsed on the sofa sobbing. "Why?" she said over and over amidst her tears.

After several minutes when she had calmed down, she saw the slight figure of Shanti hovering in the doorway. She sat up and sniffed. "What do you want Shanti?" she called out.

Seconds later, Shanti came in holding a tray with a mug of steaming hot, milky tea.

"Drink this, *memsahiba*," she said. "Everything always looks better after a cup of tea and a bath."

Nina nodded and slowly got up, leaning on Shanti, allowing her to guide her around the furniture and towards her bedroom.

"I didn't mean to lose my temper, Shanti," Nina said, wiping her tears.

"I know *memsahiba*," Shanti said soothingly.

"I really wanted to let it be amicable."

"Perhaps in time, it will be."

"I feel surprisingly relieved," she added.

"You needed to let him know how you felt."

"It feels good," she smiled wanly.

"You stood up for yourself, *memsahiba*," Shanti said. "And that is always a good feeling. You took your power back from him."

"I hope he's embarrassed and ashamed."

"Men are men, *memsahiba*."

Nina smiled.

"We still have to live, Shanti," Nina said. "How am I going to pay for all this? There's almost nothing left.

"Everything I had is gone...the jewelry, the houses in Goa

and in Kashmir...the apartment in London..."

"At least you still have this roof over your head."

"Oh Shanti...what am I to do?"

"Don't worry," she said. "Something will present itself."

Mrs. Rupa Patel and Mrs. Sonia Jaffrey, two society mavens, currently on good terms, walked up a short driveway towards a white three-story house.

Rupa, at 5'3" was of average height for an Indian woman. She was in an eternal battle with her weight, constantly trying new fads, always complaining about the 10 pounds she wished she could lose. Her complexion was dark olive, her eyes were dark, her nose short and her reddish-brown hair was shoulder length, always curled with lots of hairspray. She wore a pink sari and platform sandals to help her try to get to eye level with Sonia who was much taller at 5'6".

Sonia was slim. She was fair with grey eyes and light brown hair that was pulled back and attached with a clip at the nape of her neck. She wore a white sari with bright red poppies on it.

"The garden is looking quite lovely," she remarked.

"I wonder what's for lunch..." Rupa said.

"Do you always have to talk about food?" Sonia rolled her eyes.

"Mrs. Sonia," Rupa put her arm in hers. "Do you think we should broach the 'Bunny' story," she lowered her voice and looked around to make sure no one had heard. "I wonder if they are still friends?"

"Don't be silly, Mrs. Rupa!" Sonia scoffed. "Bunny's made a bee line for Nina's husband, for goodness sake. How can they possibly still be friends?"

The two women, slightly older than Nina, in their mid-60's, addressed one another using the prefix Mrs. as acknowledgement of their respective ages and social standing.

"Maybe Nina doesn't know?" Rupa suggested.

"If she doesn't know," Sonia retorted, "she is stupid, and Nina is not a stupid woman."

"Let's see," Rupa sniffed.

"Don't push her, Mrs. Rupa," Sonia wagged her finger.

"*Aray baba*," Rupa took her hand out of the crook of Sonia's arm. "Don't worry, I won't."

Sonia rang the doorbell.

"*Namaste memsahiba*," Shanti opened the door.

"*Namaste*," Sonia replied. "Is Nina *memsahiba* in?"

"Yes, she is expecting both of you," Shanti said. "Please come this way," she added politely. "Nina *memsahiba* is waiting for you in the veranda," she led the way.

"Rupa and Sonia *memsahibas*," Shanti said at the door to the veranda.

"Nina!" Rupa said, her arms outstretched as she went towards her. "Darling Nina," she hugged her. "How wonderful to see you! How beautiful you look..."

"My dear Rupa," Nina said. "How are you?"

The two women air-kissed one another on the cheek.

"And Sonia..."

"How are you, Nina?" Sonia said.

"What a lovely veranda," Rupa said as Nina pointed towards two armchairs opposite the sofa. "Don't you agree, Mrs. Sonia?"

Sonia didn't answer and sat down.

"What will the two of you have to drink?" Nina asked. "A

soft drink? Juice?"

"I should quite like a martini," Sonia said.

Rupa glared at Sonia. "I thought you said you were going to have some orange juice."

"I changed my mind," Sonia said. "Is that alright with you, Nina?"

"Yes, of course," Nina nodded to Shanti. "What about you Rupa? Martini? Gin and lime?"

"Well, if you both are going to drink, then I suppose I shall too."

"What will you have?" Nina offered.

"I'll have a gin," Rupa agreed.

Nina nodded to Shanti who disappeared quickly.

"So," she smiled, "how are you both?"

"Just fine!" Rupa replied brightly. "But Nina..." Rupa's voice dropped conspiratorially. "How are you? Is everything alright?"

"Yes," Nina looked perplexed. "Why?"

"Well...there are all these rumours," Rupa began while Sonia glared at her.

"Mrs. Rupa..." she said in a low voice.

"What rumours?" Nina said immediately.

"It's just that we haven't seen you much on the circuit this season...but Bunny, on the other hand, has been everywhere."

"But what are the rumours?" Nina insisted.

"Mrs. Rupa!" Sonia jumped in.

"No no, Sonia," Nina put a hand up to stop Sonia. "I want to hear what Rupa has to say."

"It's just that Bunny has been everywhere...with Arun..." Rupa finally said.

"I haven't been very social this season," Nina admitted, "because frankly I haven't felt much like it...but I obviously couldn't stop Arun."

"You and Arun were always the star couple at every event," Rupa added.

"Star couple..." Nina repeated sarcastically. "Maybe once..." she said and trailed off.

Rupa and Sonia looked at one another.

"Nina?" Rupa said.

"Yes...!" she replied quickly.

"You were miles away."

Nina wiped the corners of her eyes with a handkerchief. "Sorry, something in my eye," she added.

"Is everything alright, Nina?" Rupa got up and went to sit next to Nina on the couch.

"Why, yes...yes of course," she answered.

"But you're crying," Rupa said, concerned.

"I am not," Nina held her head proudly, trying to force away the tears glistening in her eyes.

"Nina!"

"It's nothing ladies."

"Take a sip," Rupa handed her her drink. "There...better?"

Nina drained the glass and put it back on the coffee table.

"Would you like some more?"

Nina nodded and Rupa quickly refilled the glass.

"Do you want to talk about it?" she added gently.

"Ladies, I have something to say," Nina hiccupped slightly.

Rupa leaned in.

"My marriage has fallen apart," Nina announced. "I'm filing

for divorce."

Rupa's eyes widened, her hand went to her mouth as she audibly gasped, while Sonia shifted in her seat and quickly finished her martini.

Silence reigned for a few moments as the two women digested the news.

"But...but..." Rupa finally stammered, "why?"

"Why?" Nina turned on her, her eyes glistening with tears. "Why? Because he has been, and continues to make a fool of me."

"How, Nina?"

"By carrying on with Bunny," Nina said sadly. "Did you really think I didn't know?"

Rupa sat back on the sofa, a triumphant look on her face. "See!" she mouthed to Sonia, wagging her finger as Nina blew her nose. "I told you!"

"Bunny Mehra?" Rupa put a sympathetic arm on Nina's.

"Yes," Nina acknowledged. "My former best friend."

"But how? When? Why?"

"Oh don't tell me you don't know!" Nina snapped. "The two of you always seem to know everything."

Rupa sat back chagrined.

"I'm sorry," Nina apologized.

"I don't really know how it started, or when," she began. "But it appears they are now living together."

"Living together!" Rupa said, a hand on her heaving chest.

Nina nodded sadly.

"Here in Delhi?"

"My dear Nina," Sonia got up and walked around the room. "This is the most awful news."

"Yes, it is," Rupa echoed.

"He's no longer living in this house?"

"No," Nina said. "I kicked him out this morning."

"But what's his reasoning?" Rupa asked. "What does he say?"

"He says he has fallen in love with her."

"In love?" Sonia snorted. "What does he know?

"He's a man, Nina," she added. "They don't know what they're talking about. They confuse lust with love all the time."

"Nonetheless," Nina said. "She has cast some sort of spell on him."

"I think it's about money," Sonia said defiantly. "I bet she's been dangling money in front of him as well as you know what..."

"What?"

"Mrs. Rupa!" Sonia said aghast. "Could you possibly be that naïve?"

"What? Money, right?" Rupa asked.

"Yes..." Sonia said, "and sex."

"Oh!" Rupa exclaimed.

Sonia rolled her eyes. "The papers are full of stories about how Arun's deals are not working out."

"And you believe what the press says?" Rupa raised an eyebrow. "I thought you told me to never believe the press," Rupa whined.

Sonia ignored her. "What do you think, Nina?"

"I don't know what to think."

"Maybe give it a little time, Nina," Rupa said gently. "Let him work it out of his system."

"Oh Rupa!" Nina turned on her. "Time? What time? It's not

as if Bunny is a 25-year-old who will tire of Arun when the next good-looking fellow comes along. She and I are the same age, for goodness sake."

Contrite, Rupa folded her arms across her middle. "That damned Bunny," she muttered.

"We've known each other since we were at the convent together," Nina said. "We've been friends for forty-five years, and this is how she repays me."

"Yes," Rupa wobbled her head. "This is unforgivable.

"But what are you going to do?" she wrung her hands together.

"I don't know," Nina sighed.

"Maybe you could find a..." Rupa started cautiously, "job?" she almost whispered.

"Job!" Sonia was aghast. "What job? Are you mad, Mrs. Rupa?

"Women like Nina don't work, nor us for that matter," she said haughtily.

"But...but...this is dire, Mrs. Sonia."

"At least you have your jewelry," Sonia said. "That will keep you for a while.

"Thank God our mothers had the sense to give us a few gems."

Nina didn't answer immediately.

"I mean," Sonia went on, "that ruby necklace is worth a fortune...and the diamond bracelet...isn't that a Cartier piece?"

Nina didn't reply.

"That should bring you several thousand..." Sonia said.

"The problem is," Nina finally said, "I don't have much left."

"What?" Sonia exploded. "What on earth do you mean?"

"I've been selling them off...to help Arun's business."

"Oh no...Nina!" Rupa said, a hand on her heaving chest.

"My goodness, Nina," Sonia said. "That is possibly the stupidest thing I've heard. Our jewels are our insurance. It's all we have."

"It's all I *had*," Nina said.

"But why?"

"Arun's deals kept going south," she said, "I had no choice."

"That's ridiculous!"

"Mrs. Sonia," Rupa interjected. "Arun was her husband and she loved him...she wanted to support him.

"There, there, Nina," she placed a soothing hand on Nina's arm.

"Love? Bullfeathers!" Sonia drained her martini and indicated to Shanti to bring another one. "Marriage isn't about love...it's a business. You do the man the great favour of marrying him and he, in return, has to support you...that is the way it is and has always been.

"The man takes care of the woman, end of story."

"Mrs. Sonia...you are so antiquated," Rupa replied. "This is 2019."

"Yes, and look what has happened...Nina has nothing having spent it all on that good-for-nothing."

The three women were silent.

"Is there nothing you can sell?" Sonia asked.

Nina shook her head. "I could sell this house, but then where would I live?"

"You could rent the top floor?"

"And have strangers live here?" Nina was shocked. "Not a chance.

"The whole house is interconnected and it would require some work to create apartments on the other floors," Nina said, "and I don't have the money."

"I wish you still had some jewelry," Rupa wobbled her head in that very Indian way.

"By the way, someone's selling a ruby from one of the Patiala necklaces," Sonia said.

"Really? How do you know?"

"Gema, my girl in Khanna Market, called me asking if I was interested," Sonia said.

"How much does she want?"

"5 lahks."

"That's a lot of money, Mrs. Sonia," Nina sighed and Rupa rolled her eyes.

"It's not a bad price if it really is a Patiala piece," Sonia said.

"Come on ladies," Nina got up. "Let's have lunch...the cook has made those kebabs you love."

"Ooooh!" Rupa rubbed her hands gleefully. "Yes, I've been waiting all week for those."

"By the way, have you heard about this lavish party JJ Singh is throwing for Priya Chopra?"

"Yes!" Rupa said excitedly. "I hope we get invited."

"Why?"

"I wouldn't mind meeting those Bollywood actors."

"Well...I'm sure we will," Sonia said. "After all, JJ Singh has to invite Delhi's high society..."

"JJ Singh will invite celebrities and rich people," Nina said, "and we are neither famous nor do we have any money."

"Sonia still does," Rupa said.

"Oh my dear ladies," Sonia sighed. "Being in high society

doesn't mean you have to be wealthy, it's about pedigree...we have class, elegance...

"And the nouveau riche simply don't."

"But Mrs. Sonia," Rupa said, "the only one out of the three of us who has a title is Nina."

"I don't have a title," Nina jumped in.

"No...but if circumstances were different, you would."

"None of us are royalty," Nina added.

"We may not be royalty," Sonia agreed. "But...all our families have roots in the aristocracy."

"You can be such a snob, Sonia," Nina said.

"He has to invite us...we run Delhi's society..." Sonia said. "Priya Chopra and all those Bollywood people can be so trashy.

"You watch...he will need to add a touch of class to his soiree."

Nina rolled her eyes.

"Oh Mrs. Sonia," Rupa wrung her hands.

"She'll never change," Nina said. "How long have we known her?" she added. "Over 50 years and she's been exactly the same."

"Has it really been that long?" Rupa asked as they sat down to lunch. "It feels like yesterday when we were all at the convent."

"Our families have known each other since the time of our grandmothers," Nina said. "They were best friends, then our mothers and now us."

"Time does fly."

"Do you regret not having children, Sonia?" Rupa asked as Shanti served the kebabs.

"Not really," she answered. "Samir is completely into his work as an academic and I...well...I've dabbled in this and that...and we've traveled...so, no."

"I'm quite excited about becoming a grandmother," Rupa said.

"Yes! How is Karan?" Nina asked. "How is he doing in Oman?"

"Well," Rupa answered.

"And his wife...?"

"What's her name?" Sonia asked.

"Mrs. Sonia!" Rupa said, offended. "You were at the wedding."

"Doesn't mean I have to remember your daughter-in-law's name..."

"Kareena," Rupa said. "Anyhow, she is pregnant and will give birth sometime in September."

"Congratulations, Rupa!" Nina raised a glass.

"Thank you," Rupa said. "And what about your two boys, Nina?"

"Roshan is in New York, running an IT firm and Naseer in Doha curating art exhibitions."

"Any marriages in the near future?"

"Roshan has an American girlfriend," Nina said. "He keeps threatening to bring her here over Christmas, but they still haven't made it.

"And Naseer...I don't know."

"No girlfriend?" Rupa asked.

"Apparently not."

"Is he..." Rupa started. "Well, you know..." she nodded conspiratorially.

"Do you mean to ask if he's gay?" Sonia said.

"Mrs. Sonia!" Rupa put a hand on her chest, aghast.

"It's very common these days, Mrs. Rupa," Sonia said. "No need to get all hot and bothered about it."

"It's just that...I'm...I'm not used to it."

"Honestly, Mrs. Rupa...you have to move with the times."

"He may well be gay," Nina said. "He hasn't said anything...yet."

"Do you suspect?"

Nina nodded. "He's 35."

"Tragic," Rupa shook her head from side to side. "And such a handsome boy."

Sonia rolled her eyes.

"Do they know about the split?" she asked.

"*Aray*, Mrs. Sonia," Rupa said, "have a heart. It's only just happened."

"The boys are both old enough," Nina said. "They'll be alright."

Chapter 3

Sabine hit the 'Face Time' icon on her laptop and moments later Indi's face appeared.

"Indi?"

"That would be me."

"Any luck getting into the security cameras?"

"That's a silly question," Indi said, "given how long we've known one another."

"How long have we known each other?"

"I've lost count," Indi replied. "Ten years...at least."

"Really, only ten years?" Sabine said. "It feels longer."

"I would say it's about ten years...let's see...my parents had moved back to the States," Indi said, "and I was broke, but too proud to tell them.

"I couldn't get a modeling job because I was in that mid-age, not young and not old enough...so I ended up working at that computer place..."

"That's right...I came in with my laptop and you fixed it."

"And I asked you if you knew of any jobs I could do to make a little quick money...remember?"

"That's right!" Sabine said excitedly.

"And what I meant were jobs involving computers..." Indi chuckled.

"Yeah, but at the time, I was hanging out at the Gymkhana Club fixing card games."

"And you invited me to be your partner at the bridge table

and we never looked back," Indi said. "It was a good four years and we made some decent money, not to mention the fun we had."

"We did," Sabine nodded.

"But then of course you met JJ."

"That's because you wanted out..."

"I did and I didn't," Indi said. "Hari was around by that time and honestly, I didn't want to be a card shark anymore.

"Anyway...why are we going down memory lane?" she added. "What did you want to know?"

"Are you in?"

"Of course...

"Sabine...what are you planning? Does JJ have this necklace?"

"Any chance I can see?" Sabine evaded the question.

Indi sighed. "I'm going to send you an invitation to remotely access my laptop. Accept, will you?"

Sabine laughed. "How did you get in?"

"It wasn't that hard...it was only a matter of figuring out the internet network, putting in some code and software and accessing it remotely," Indi said.

"What do you want to see?"

"Let's start at the gate," Sabine said.

"Cameras are all mostly outside."

"Nothing inside?"

"Just the reception hall and the kitchen."

"Let's take a look."

"Ok...here's the gate, front door...here's the garden, back garden, pool...

"Can you move the cameras around?" Sabine asked. "Change the angles?"

"If I do, they'll know they've been hacked."

"How can we get control of the cameras?"

"Well..." Indi said, "if they were to make any changes to the system, then we could go in and make changes undetected."

"I see," Sabine said.

"Sabine...what are you thinking?"

"Never you mind...pick me up later..."

"What time?"

"Around 1."

"In the afternoon?"

"No, morning."

"Where are we going?" Indi asked. "Actually...don't tell me."

*

"Sir?" a young policeman poked his head in the door.

Imran looked up.

"Sir, it's 8 o'clock," he said. "If there's nothing else, may I head out? I'd like to catch the 8:20 train, otherwise I'll have to wait for another hour, and I won't get home until 10:30."

"Of course," Imran nodded. "I'll see you in the morning."

"You should go home too, sir."

"I'll leave in a few minutes."

"I'm sure your wife has some delicious food ready for you to eat, sir."

"Yes..." Imran said.

"Good night, sir."

"Good night."

After he left, Imran looked back down at the reports he was

going over. But he couldn't concentrate. His tummy began rumbling. Why had that idiot mentioned food? He realized he hadn't eaten anything all day, apart from a samosa with his tea in the morning.

He turned to his computer to check if there was anything that needed his immediate attention, but there wasn't. Clearly, it was a quiet night. He sat back in his chair and after a few minutes got up, packed his satchel and walked out the door.

It was just 9 o'clock when he turned into a small, quiet street and came to a stop in front of a steel gate. He got out, opened it and drove the car in. He sat in the driver's seat for a minute, leaning his head back on the headrest. What was he going to do for the next three hours? Normally, he got home at midnight and went straight to bed, got up at 6 and went back to the office.

Taking a deep breath, he got out and, closed and locked the gate and walked across the small garden to the steps that led up to the apartment on the first floor.

There were only two apartments in the building. His elderly landlord lived on the first floor with his equally elderly wife. He saw the light on in their living room and, as he walked by, he saw them sitting at their dining table.

He slowly climbed the stairs, his legs as heavy as though he were a sailor walking the plank. He put his key in the lock and turned it slowly, opening the door wide. It was dark inside.

He shut his eyes and for a moment, he saw the lights on, and a cacophony of sounds, the television in the living room with some program or another and the radio in the kitchen and the sound of a woman singing as she made dinner. He saw her come out.

"*Aray*," he heard her say when he walked into the kitchen and put his arms around her waist as she made the rice for their dinner. "*Aap jaldi vapas aagay ho? You're back early?*"

"*Work was quiet today*," he replied.

"*Go sit at the table and I'll put the rotis on...*" she smiled. "*We can eat in 2 minutes.*"

*

He opened his eyes, but it was still dark. He reached for the light switch and turned on the light. The television was dark. Everything was still and silent.

He opened the window and leaning on the sill, took a deep breath. He looked at the neighbours' house and saw an entire family sitting at the dinner table: the children were fighting, the younger ones making a fuss about their food, whilst the mother tried to coax them to eat and the father trying to tell the mother to calm down. He took another deep breath, his nostrils flaring.

"I miss you," he murmured to himself, gulping, his forehead creasing, his fists clenched as he desperately tried to control the sadness that suddenly overcame him.

"Eat your food," the mother next door said to her little girl.

"But I don't like okra," the girl replied.

"Don't make such a fuss, girl," the mother said sternly. "Behave properly and eat your food."

"I don't like it," the girl whined.

"Eat your food, or you'll go to bed hungry..." the mother threatened.

"I don't want any..." she said in a small voice.

"Go to bed!" the mother ordered. "Now!"

"*Baba!*" the girl got up and ran to her father at the head of the table, climbing into his lap. "I don't want to eat the okra."

"*Beta*," he said softly, "eat the food your mother has cooked so lovingly for you."

"No..." the little girl whined.

"Alright...then go eat a piece of barfi."

"What?" the mother cried. "Are you mad? *Aap nay to kamaal kar diya*! How can you tell her to eat dessert if she hasn't eaten her food?"

"Let her go," the man soothed his irate wife. "She's only a child. Let her be a child."

Imran swallowed hard as he watched the family in front of him. He tried to control himself, taking long, deep breaths through his nose, but he could feel the sadness mounting.

He turned and went into the kitchen and opened the fridge. It was empty apart from two bottles of beer. He reached for one and went back into the living room, grabbing his laptop, taking it with him to the sofa, and turned on the television, letting the mindless chatter of an entertainment show fill the silence.

He opened his laptop and went into the archives of the CBI. He typed Sabine Kumar into the 'Search' box and waited. Moments later, a file popped up. There wasn't much in it, but the very existence of the file meant she was a person of interest for the Central Bureau of Investigation. He had just pulled up the files on JJ Singh when,

"*And next up, we have an exclusive interview with Priya Chopra,*" said the presenter. He watched the interview for a few minutes, before,

"What a load of shit," he reached for the remote and switched off the television.

He looked back at the laptop, but then suddenly got up, put his jacket on and walked out of the house and into the street.

He didn't come home until 2am and as he walked through the gate, tipsy from all the whiskey he'd drunk, he didn't see his landlady staring at him through the window, shaking her head sadly.

*

"What are you doing at the window?" the landlady's husband turned over in bed. "Spying on our tenant again?"

"That poor fellow," the landlady said. "He's bereft without his wife."

"We can't do anything about that."

"But he's such a lovely man," she turned and went back to bed, sitting up against the pillows. "He'd be such a catch for any woman.

"Good looking, good job..."

"Don't you be getting any ideas in your head."

"Maybe I could introduce him to my great niece when she comes to visit?"

"Begum...the last time you tried this matchmaking business, it was a disaster!" her husband turned over to the other side, punching his pillow before settling down peacefully.

"I just thought I would help."

"There's help and there's help," her husband said. "And I get the sense that our Mr. Khan doesn't want any help."

"You're probably right," his wife sighed.

"Go to sleep!"

After a few minutes, he was lightly snoring when,

"Can you believe they found the Barodan necklace?"

"Oh ho, Begum!" he cried. "A little peace..."

"It was just beautiful...all those diamonds..."

"Yes yes," he said. "Maybe you can have something like that in your next life."

His wife childishly stuck her tongue out at him. "I am happy the way I am."

He smiled and closed his eyes.

*

"Can I get you anything else, sir?" Aditya, the butler, picked up JJ's plate from the large dining room where JJ sat by himself at the head of the table.

"No, Adi," JJ said. "Thank you, though...I'll have coffee in my library."

"Very good, *Sahib*," Adi said. "I'll bring it through in a few minutes."

JJ walked out of the dining room and went down the hall towards the library office, stopping for a moment in front of a Jamini Roy painting of a dancing Gopini, a devotée of the God Krishna, in bright shades of burnt red and mustard yellow.

Every time he looked at the painting, he smiled. It had such a happy spirit. The dancer was giddy with life and love of her god, dancing with abandonment as would a young child.

In a strange way, that was how he remembered Sabine...a beautiful young woman, happy and carefree.

It was the painting that started it all. It was hers. The one they'd started the business with. They'd met, introduced strangely enough by Rambo and become partners, working together and lovers, living together, in an apartment in an old deco building in Vasant Vihar. They bought and sold paintings, driving up the prices with Sabine posing as a competitive buyer and made good money.

Why are they both back? He went into his library and sat down at his desk.

"Shall I put the coffee on your desk, sir?" Adi came in a few minutes later.

"Leave it on the coffee table, please, Adi," he replied.

"Very well...good night, *Sahib*."

"Good night," JJ replied and went and picked up his coffee cup and sat down at the edge of the sofa.

He'd asked her to marry him, but she'd turned him down saying she wanted to be free. He was devastated and hadn't spoken to her for a week.

But what a mess it would have been had they been married. Perhaps in the end, it was a blessing she'd said no.

There hadn't been anyone after Sabine...no one had quite measured up.

He wondered if she would ever forgive him. Probably not.

*

Rambo had only just come into his suite when his phone rang.

"It's me," he heard Sabine's voice.

"Everything alright?"

"Yes," she replied. "I just wanted to say 'thank you.'"

"For what? Nothing's happened yet"

"It's about to."

"Thank me when it's done and you have the Barodan in your hands," he reached for the remote and turned on the television.

"Speaking of, Priya Chopra is on television talking about the necklace."

"Why do you think he's making her wear the necklace?" she

asked.

"He's driving up the price for the insurance, it's going to be a very hot item on the neck of a celebrity," Rambo said. "But you should know that tactic."

"You think he's going to steal his own necklace?"

"Or," Rambo said, "if he gets lucky, somebody at that party will get drunk enough and buy it.

"Did you get the Jamini Roy?" he added.

"It's in my knapsack."

"Good...did my man let you borrow it or did you buy it?"

"I borrowed it," Sabine said.

"Which one?"

"Three Gopinis."

"One of my favourites," Rambo said, taking off his jacket as he spoke and loosening his tie knot.

"Rambo..." Sabine began cautiously. "Why did you wait until now to get your money back from JJ?"

"Because, my dear, in life, timing is everything...And I knew the day would come," he poured himself a healthy whiskey from a decanter and sat down in a large comfortable chair.

"You're very wise and philosophical this evening?"

"No," Rambo said. "Just old.

"Your father was all about timing, too," he continued. "If he didn't feel it, he didn't do it."

"Do you miss him?"

"Very much," Rambo replied. "We had a lot of years together...good years...we were a good team," he took a sip of his drink.

"Where were you tonight?"

"Out...to dinner."

"With anyone?"

"You're very nosy tonight," he smiled.

"Just checking," she said. "I have to make sure you stay on the straight and narrow."

"I don't think I've ever been on that road..." Rambo laughed. "It's never been straight, nor has it ever been narrow."

"I'm just looking after Soraya's interests."

"Mrs. Rambo knows me well, Sabine," he said. "I may look, but she knows I won't stray."

"That is comforting," Sabine said.

"If you must know...I had dinner with an old friend, luckily without his wife because I can't stand her."

"Plans for the rest of the evening?"

"A drink, a cigar and a good book."

"I'll talk to you later," she giggled.

"I know you will."

*

Nina had just finished a lonely dinner and as Shanti was clearing the table, she got up, poured herself a whiskey and went to sit in the small sitting area at the far end of her bedroom. She reached for the remote control and sat down on the sofa, her drink next to her and lit a cigarette, idly watching the news.

"Hello, I'm Priya Chopra..."

Nina picked up the remote and was about to change the channel when "...and stay tuned for my live interview with 'Entertain India.'"

"Yes everyone!" the presenter came back on the screen. "Priya is live with us from her home..." the camera cut to Priya sitting on a deck with the Arabian Sea glittering in the background as her new husband came into the shot to give her a peck on the top of her head, making Priya gaze at him lovingly. "And my goodness, that was Randy Singh, her husband...Priya will be talking to us about her wedding and the party that is coming up."

Nina gulped the whiskey and went back out to the trolley in the dining room and poured herself a little bit more. When she came back, the interview had begun.

"Tell us about your recent wedding," the presenter asked.

"Well, it was all a bit last minute," Priya giggled coyly. "We were on holiday in Rome and Randy proposed to me in the middle of the Spanish Steps... he got down on one knee and held out this red box," Priya related. "When he opened it, this was inside," she held up a hand from which shone a large diamond.

Nina rolled her eyes and took a sip of her whiskey.

"How romantic..."

"Yes, it really was," Priya nodded. "Later that day, we were going to meet Randy's friend JJ Singh, who has this beautiful home in Tuscany near Siena...and at dinner, JJ suggested we come join him for a few days and whilst we were there, we decided to elope.

"JJ organized everything...and we got married at his house a couple of days later...there was no one there except for us, the local mayor who married us, JJ and a couple of friends who flew in from London."

"What a story," the presenter commented. "But what did your families say?"

Suddenly, Randy, Priya's husband appeared in the shot and

sat down next to his wife on the sofa. "They were pretty angry..."

"Well, they were happy for us, Randy," Priya punched him playfully in the arm.

"Yeah...but more angry, I think," he held her chin between his thumb and forefinger and kissed the tip of her nose.

"My mother was upset," Priya put her head on his shoulder, "because she wanted a traditional, big Indian wedding with a cast of thousands, including her hairdresser and her jeweler..."

"But now, there are rumours of this party that JJ is throwing for you," the presenter said.

"Yes..." Priya said. "Actually...it was my mother who was growling at JJ for having facilitated the wedding, so to make amends, he said he would throw us a party."

"He's like our godfather," Randy interjected.

"So you are confirming this?"

"I am," Priya beamed. "It still won't be big, but there'll be more than we had at the wedding."

"Will there be a ceremony?"

"Yes, a small hindu ceremony...again, only family, and then the reception."

"And what will you be wearing?"

"That's my exit line," Randy interrupted, "If you girls are going to talk clothes..." he ran a loving finger along his wife's jawline and got up.

"You know...I don't know yet."

"But it's only a few weeks away..."

"I know, I know," Priya said. "I may just end up wearing something I have."

"You'll look gorgeous no matter what you wear."

"Oh, thank you," Priya said. "That's always nice to hear."

"What about the jewelry?"

"Well..." Priya giggled again. "It's funny you bring that up."

"Why?"

"Well, this is an exclusive," Priya began.

"We're all listening, Priya..."

"I will be wearing a necklace that disappeared 70 years ago..." Priya said. "It's called the 'Maharani,' and it was made by the House of Richemont for the Maharani of Barodan in 1928."

"The Barodan?" the presenter looked shocked.

Nina sat up.

"My goodness...this is news..."

Priya beamed her wide, toothy smile, tucking a lock of hair behind her ear.

"Have you seen it?"

"Well..." Priya chuckled.

"Have you tried it?"

"Maybe."

"How many diamonds?"

"A lot," Priya replied.

"But who has it?"

"I don't really know, but JJ called me and asked me if I wanted to wear it," Priya giggled. "How could I possibly say 'no.'

"As Randy says, he's like our godfather..."

After Priya went off screen, all kinds of images of the Barodan necklace flashed on screen with the presenter talking over them.

"The Barodan necklace was made in 1928 by the House of Richemont, a special commission from the Maharajah of Barodan

to be worn by him. He went to Paris with South African diamonds he had bought at auction in London and Colombian emeralds he had taken off the Ottoman Sultan's hands, arriving at the Richemont Shop on the Place Vendome with a large retinue of serv-ants and concubines who all hovered around him as he sat with Jacques Richemont.

"The Maharajah of Barodan paid 1.5 million francs for the stones and the setting, which in today's money amounts to about 35 million US dollars.

"The necklace was a masterpiece and became an iconic image of the wealth of the Indian Maharajahs, its disappearance around the time of partition only adding to its mystery.

"But 70 years later, it has reappeared and we will soon see this legendary piece on the neck of Priya Chopra...

"In other Bollywood news..."

Nina finished her whiskey, put out her cigarette and went to get ready for bed. As she pulled the soft cotton quilt up to her chin, she remembered her mother talking about the necklace and how exquisite it was.

"It was absolutely stunning," she heard her mother's voice. "And when Jacques Richemont presented the necklace to the Maharajah of Barodan, he looked at it, nodded and said that it wasn't for him, but would make a 'suitable necklace' for his wife!

"Can you imagine, Nina? Six pounds of diamonds and the most spectacular emeralds he'd bought in Colombia and he called it 'suitable!'"

"What happened to the necklace?"

"No one really knows, child," the mother said. "They say his Spanish wife stole it..."

Tears crept into Nina's eyes and she closed them tightly to stop the tears from falling. When she agreed to marry Arun, she thought that she too would be a Maharani, after all, the old Maharajah was his great-grandfather. And...that necklace could have been hers. How handy would it be today?

Why was I so stupid? I should have held on to a few things umma gave me...the girls were right. I should never have sold those jewels for Arun's ridiculous deals.

*

It was 1:30am when Sabine came out of her suite. She wore black pants and a black top, black sneakers and had a black leather satchel on her back. The hallway was empty. She walked down, past the elevators to a door that said 'Exit.' She opened the door and went down the seven staircases until she got to the second floor where she took an elevator down to the parking lot, slipped by the sleepy parking attendant, who sat snoring in a chair in a small booth at the entrance and out into the open air. She looked left and car beams turned on and off twice. She smiled and walked towards a small black Hyundai that was parked along a wall, somewhat hidden by tree foliage.

She walked over and got in.

"Why the cloak and dagger?" Indi asked.

"In case JJ's having me watched."

"Where to?" Indi started up the engine.

"Chattarpur," Sabine said without looking at her.

"Are you kidding me?"

"You said that for us to make changes undetected, they need to make changes,' Sabine said.

Indi sighed, her shoulders sagging.

"Just drive," Sabine said.

"What's in the satchel?"

"A painting."

"Of what?"

"Woman and child...it's a Jamini Roy."

"Jamini Roy?" Indi exclaimed. "Where did you get that?"

"I borrowed it."

"From whom?"

"A friend of a friend had it."

"And he or she let you *borrow* it...that easy?"

"Something like that."

"This feels a bit like old times," Indi said as she changed gears, "before you got involved with JJ."

"You've never liked him," Sabine rolled down the window and breathed deeply.

"Never have and never will.

"How did you meet him, anyway?" Indi asked.

"Rambo Singh introduced us."

"Rambo Singh...your father's best friend...how is he?"

"Incredibly well."

"Still dapper?"

"Oh yes!"

"How did Rambo know JJ?"

"JJ had a small art gallery and Rambo had bought a couple of pieces," Sabine said. "JJ was single and struggling and so was I, so Rambo thought it was a match made in heaven."

Sabine stared out the window.

"I always knew he was bad luck."

"I admit, I took a chance with him."

"And look what happened," Indi said. "You got screwed."

"Oh Indi," Sabine sighed. "You and I were making no money cheating at little card games."

"Perhaps not...but at least we had each other's back."

"That we did."

They drove along in silence for a few minutes before Sabine rolled her window down further and stuck her nose out. "That Delhi air...I have missed it."

"Why? It stinks!" Indi said.

"It smells familiar."

About 200 yards from the Singh compound, Indi stopped and pulled over and parked in a dark side lane. "I don't want to get any closer.

"The cameras will pick up the car and there's a guard post in front of the house," she said. "There'll be a security guard in there, watching the cameras."

"This is fine," Sabine said. "Wait for me here," she added, quickly smearing some black cream on her face.

"What are you going to do?"

"Don't ask me such questions," Sabine got out of the car, put the hood of her sweatshirt on her head and closed the door softly.

Indi watched as she disappeared into the shadows and then sat back and poured herself some coffee she had brought in a flask. She rolled up the windows and turned on the radio.

"And now for entertainment news on India Today," came the pleasant voice of a male presenter with a very English accent.

"*The famous Barodan Necklace has re-appeared after 70 years*," he said.

"What the hell?" Indi turned the volume up just a bit.

"*Actress Priya Chopra will wear it on the day of the party that is being thrown for her and her husband Randy Singh, by celebrity art collector, JJ Singh. As we know, the couple eloped a few months ago and were married in a civil ceremony in Italy.*

"*No one quite knows where the necklace has been all these years,*" the presenter continued. "*It was last seen on the neck of the fifth wife of the Maharajah of Barodan in 1948 before the Maharajah divorced her and sent her back to Spain. The Barodan family has long speculated that his Spanish wife stole it and took it back to Madrid...*"

Indi sat back in the driver's seat. "For the love of Ganesh...now I know what she's up to."

*

Sabine walked closely along the outer wall of the house, keeping in the shadows, crouching behind bushes as she approached a banana tree, sagging under the weight of its large green leaves. If she remembered correctly, the wall behind it was not that high and she could easily scale it using the trunk as a ladder. Just as she went over, she saw one of the security guards walking towards the guard post. She crouched down in the bushes until she heard the door to the little hut close.

She moved quickly, consciously staying beneath the cameras, padding along the flower beds that ringed the house until she got to the back patio. The manicured lawn stretched out in front of her and the pool gleamed in the moonlight. She stepped onto the patio and passed several French doors until she got to the main back door. She tried it. It was locked. She reached into the small pouch around her waist and pulled out what looked like a crochet needle and inserted it into the lock. Moments later, she heard a small click.

She went in and crossed the large round reception hall to the front doors. She saw the alarm panel flashing yellow. She pulled a keypad out of the same pouch and placed it on top of the one on the wall. The numbers and letters began whirring as the panel looked for the code. Seconds lighter, the light flashed green and Sabine sighed with relief and put the panel back in the pouch.

She turned down the hallway to the right and there it was, the Jamini Roy as she had been told. Working quickly, she took a ruler and measured four inches before she took a small nail and hammer that was covered with a cloth to minimize noise and gently drove it into the wall. She took the painting from her satchel and hung it next to it. She stepped back. Both paintings were perfectly aligned. She took a picture and sent it in a text message.

'*How do they look?*'

'*Perfect,*' came the reply.

She went back out into the reception hall, and through the back door back into the garden, making her way across the lawn to the small gate where she easily climbed over, landing with a thud on the ground.

When she reached the car, she threw the satchel in the back and got into the front with Indi.

The two stared at one another for a moment.

"Drive..." Sabine said.

"Where are we going?"

Indi turned on the engine and reversed down the lane as quietly as she could until they got to the main road.

"Listen, Sabine," Indi began, "the Barodan...Priya Chopra is going to wear it at the party JJ Singh is throwing for her."

"Did you know JJ had the necklace?"

"He showed it to me," Sabine finally said.

"And that's why you want to go to the party?" Indi sounded angry. "You want to steal it off the neck of one of Bollywood's biggest celebrities?"

Sabine looked at her sideways.

"Sabine!"

"What? I'm not deaf."

"Answer me, goddamnit!" Indi shouted.

"I have a plan."

"How did you get JJ to lend it to Priya?"

"I didn't do that."

"But you orchestrated it..."

"I came up with the idea."

"Look, Indi, that necklace means something to him," Sabine said.

"And is that why you're going after it?" Indi asked. "Because if that's the case, I'm out...you can't do a job in a job."

"Were you even in?" Sabine said.

"That's low, Sabine...even for you."

"Look, Indi...it's going to work..." Sabine said.

"Sabine, this is not like what we did before, you want to rob the biggest party in India."

"Not really...I want to rob a necklace that happens to be on the neck of someone at a party."

"You want to rob the Barodan necklace, a piece of jewelry that has been the subject of documentaries...in plain sight of everyone who is anyone...are you insane?

"Do you have any idea what the security is going to be like?

"And how the hell are we going to get in?"

"You know what your problem is Indi?" Sabine said calmly.

Indi shook her head.

"You worry too much."

"Yeah...I worry because I don't want to end up in a fucking cell."

"You won't.

"By the way, that camera in the entrance hall?"

"Yeah..."

"Can you delete about 10 minutes of recording?"

"You just went and hung a Jamini Roy in JJ Singh's house...why would you do that?"

"Because it's going to put JJ on edge to realize that someone walked in to his house, hung a painting and walked out."

"What does that have to do with anything?"

"It's going to force him to look at his security cameras, make changes to the angles...and that's when you can go in and make changes too, without being detected."

Indi took a deep breath and let it out slowly. "I need a drink."

"By the way, do you know Hanut Singh?"

"The designer? Yeah...I used to model for him, remember?" Indi said. "Wait! You think he's going to dress Priya?"

Sabine nodded. "And you will be his assistant and therefore, her stylist."

"Sabine..." Indi began to protest.

"But how do you know Hanut will dress her?"

"Because he will," Sabine said confidently. "He just did the outfits for her most recent movie.

"So tomorrow...call Hanut and get yourself in."

"Wait..." Indi put her hand up. "You always do this. You always push me into doing things?

"Have you ever thought about the fact that I may not want to do this?"

"Why would you not want to do this?"

"Sabine..."

"It'll be a lot of money in your bank account," she said. "You won't have to worry about money ever again.

"Besides, this is your jam, Indi...plus...when I was thinking this through, the only person I thought of doing this with is you...we're partners."

"You left me for JJ."

"Indi...that was different..." Sabine said. "Back then, our paths were diverging, we wanted different things...you wanted to get married...remember?"

"Yeah," Indi said. "And then I got dumped."

"Do you want to talk about it?" Sabine said.

"Now?" Indi stared at her surprised.

"Yes, why not?"

"Because it's the middle of the night and you just walked into JJ's house, hung a painting and came back out..." Indi said. "Maybe we should get out of here before someone finds us."

"Then drive," Sabine said.

Chapter 4

JJ came in the front door of his house and was walking down the hall to his office. Just past where the Jamini Roy painting hung. He stopped, turned and walked back.

He pulled out his phone.

"Get me Rusty," he said in an eerily calm voice.

"Yes, sir," Rusty came down the hall.

"There's a second Jamini Roy."

"Sir?" Rusty cocked his head.

"How many paintings do you see up here?"

"Two."

"That's right...there are two and usually there's only one."

"I see," Rusty nodded.

"Why are there two?"

"I don't know, sir."

"But how did this happen?" JJ asked. "How could someone have gotten into this house and put up another painting without anyone knowing about it?"

"I'll look at the security cameras now, sir."

*

"Indi darling!" Hanut Singh threw his arms up as he sashayed across his workshop towards her. Behind him was chaos as several women sat embroidering, several others were poring over a design on a drafting table, yelling instructions at someone to bring out mannequins.

"So good to see you!" he air-kissed her. "It's been much too long," he put his hand in the crook of her arm. "Where have you been hiding yourself?

"You look amazing!" he drawled, stretching out the 'a' in the word.

"Thanks, Hanut," Indi replied. "You look very good yourself."

"I need a little work, darling," he touched the apple of his cheek and pouted.

Hanut Singh was a prominent designer who dressed mostly actresses and celebrities. He was of medium height with a face that was so classically Indian that he could well have been a model for a Rajput miniature with his long moustache that was neatly waxed, swarthy complexion, big dark eyes, a small hooked nose, thin lips and dark wavy hair. He had a mole on one of his cheeks that he always stroked. He was wearing tight skinny black jeans and a flowy orange silk tunic with a Chinese collar.

"Seriously, you look fantastic..." Hanut said. "I don't know why you stopped modeling.

"You walked every major show and you were the star...in Mumbai, Delhi, Calcutta..." he added.

"Remember, we went to Dubai and Abu Dhabi and London!" Hanut rubbed his hands together gleefully. "Those were great times.

"You were supermodel material."

"I enjoyed it," Indi said. "And the money was really good."

"So what happened?"

"Age," Indi said. "I stopped getting the really good jobs," Indi said, "and I realized it was because I was too old for certain kinds of things, and too young for the older stuff..."

"That happens to all the girls."

"Also, my father really wanted to see me settled before they moved back to the States and I thought it was going to happen, but it didn't," she said.

"I'm sorry..." Hanut put an arm around her. "Tell me who it was and I'll tell him a thing or two."

"No one dumps my Indi!"

"You're sweet, Hanut," Indi said. "But I was hurt...and I've kind of been keeping myself to myself for the past few years, doing a few odd jobs to keep me afloat..."

"Like what?"

"You know...computer stuff."

"You can go back into modeling now, you know," Hanut said. "I'll introduce you to a couple of really good agents...soaps, talcum powder...makeup...look at your face, not a wrinkle," he added. "How old are you now?"

"I'll be 50 in a couple of years."

"We'll put it together.

"I'm so glad you called," he hugged her again. "I can't believe my assistant getting sick like that...and this is going to be such a crazy couple of weeks.

"I have less than three weeks to make Priya's reception gown...and...oh my god...Indi!" he stopped and waved his arms around frantically.

Indi looked at him, her eyes questioning.

He stopped and placed his hands on Indi's arms. "Do you know that she...Priya...is going to be wearing the Barodan necklace?"

"You mean *the* Barodan necklace?" Indi pretended surprise,

her eyes wide.

"Yes!" Hanut exclaimed gleefully.

"But that necklace hasn't been seen in years..."

"Well, it's apparently been found."

"But where?"

"Who knows!" Hanut sashayed around. "And who cares...it's just the most spectacular necklace in the world...and I have to design a gown around it."

"Oh...!"

"That's what I mean," he stood with his hand on his hips. "This is going to be intense, Indi...you better be ready.

"The eyes of the world are going to be on Priya and on my gown...just imagine the publicity...Vogue, Elle, Vanity Fair...

"This is going to make my career," he looked up at the ceiling, his arms outstretched. "I'm going to be just like Galliano, Dolce & Gabbana, Dior..."

Oh brother, Indi thought. "Hanut! That is fantastic. I am so proud of you."

"Indi...it all started with you," he said. "You were the first one to wear my stuff. You put me on the map."

"Hanut..."

"No, really!" he enveloped her in a hug. "You were there at the beginning and now you will be with me for the crowning glory."

"What's the plan?" Indi extricated herself from his grasp.

"Come!" he took her elbow, guiding her to a space at the far end of the atelier where there was a large board pinned with all kind of sketches, a table strewn with bolts of coloured fabrics, some embroidered and some not, and a mannequin wearing a makeshift necklace of coloured stones in front of a tall mirror with an ornate gold frame.

"First things first," Hanut pulled out all kinds of cuttings and photos of Priya in different outfits and pinned them on one side of the board, with a close up headshot of her that showed her neck and shoulders. "We have to pick a colour...what do you think?" he began draping fabrics on the mannequin.

"Red?" Hanut held up some red raw silk and chiffon. "Glam, right?"

Indi nodded. "But this isn't Bollywood, Hanut. It should be glam, but traditional...think about the necklace.

"White...more elegant."

"You've always had taste, Indi...the classiest girl on the runway."

*

Rupa and Sonia got out of a car and entered Khanna Market in Sundar Nagar walking silently towards a darkened shop at the far end that was opposite a chaiwallah.

"Mrs. Sonia, are you sure about this?" Rupa asked.

"Gema is the best in the business," Sonia said. "Not only does she have a great eye, she is also discreet."

"I cannot tell Mr. Patel," Rupa said sadly. "It will mean the end of everything."

"Don't worry," Sonia said.

"Why don't I know about her?"

"Gema only deals in very high-end jewelry."

Rupa stopped for a moment and looked at Sonia. "I think I've just been insulted, but I'm not sure how.

"Were you just being sarcastic?"

"Yes, I was, now come along, Mrs. Rupa," Sonia said.

"Gema is lovely, salt of the earth, humble...very talented, very much like her father," Sonia said as they walked. "Her mother was a piece of work, but thank goodness, Gema is like the father."

"She's got a great name...Gema...after all she's in the gems business."

"I rather think that was the idea."

"Who started the business?"

"Feroze Kaling, Gema's great-grandfather. He was apparently a real artist.

"He worked for the Maharajah of Patiala, evaluating the stones the Maharajah wanted to buy.

"They sent him to study at Cartier in Paris right around the turn of the century."

"Really?"

"It's because of him that the scouts and designers from Cartier still use Gema as their main source in India."

"And is Gema married?

"Her sister is, but Gema was always the quieter, studious one, always with her father, learning gemology.

"She says stones talk to her."

"How old is she?" Rupa asked.

"In her 40s."

"Odd that she's not married, isn't it?" Rupa added.

"Why?" Sonia replied. "I think it's terrific that she never succumbed to family pressure."

"What do you mean?"

"It's just that in India, you get to a certain age and there's so much pressure to get married," Sonia said, "and settle down and have children and a family life.

"But if that life doesn't speak to you, why should you go down that road?"

"It's nice to have a companion in life," Rupa said.

"Yes, it is...but I think in Gema's case, the right one hasn't come along and she didn't want to settle.

"You'll see...she's quiet, but you can tell she's got backbone."

"I just hope she can help me with this jewelry," Rupa said. "I feel terrible having to sell it...my mother would never forgive me."

"Chin up, Mrs. Rupa," Sonia said. "We've all done this at some point in our lives."

Rupa stopped and wrung her hands. "I don't know about this, Mrs. Sonia, I don't want to deceive Mr. Patel."

"It's either this or you tell him the truth."

"That may be worse."

"Do you want a cup of tea for some Dutch courage?"

Rupa shook her head sadly.

"Come on then," she gave her a gentle push up the staircase.

"Mrs. Jaffrey," Gema came out into the sitting area as they walked in. "*Namaste.*"

"*Namaste, namaste*, Gema," Sonia said. "This is Mrs. Rupa Patel."

"*Namaste*, Mrs. Patel," Gema said.

"Shall we go inside?" she went through a narrow rustic wooden door beyond which was a large room with a slanted ceiling that looked more like an old apothecary.

Along one wall, was an old, long chestnut wood chest with a glass case, a draftsman's table with a lamp near a large window that gave out onto the market square below and on the other side, was an antique Chinese silk screen. The area behind the screen was lit by the soft light of a large oval milk-glass globe that hung at the end of a long, braided silk cord that came down from the rafters.

In the middle of the room was a round table, a two-seater Victorian sofa and an armchair upholstered in purple velvet with a hexagonal chess table in the middle.

"Please sit down," Gema pointed to the sofa. "Would you like some tea?" she offered.

"Or a cold drink?" she pointed to a trolley that had a pitcher and some glasses on a tray. "Some fresh *nimbu pani*?"

"I would like a glass," Sonia said.

"Alright," Rupa nodded.

Gema poured them both some fresh lime and water and topped off the glasses with a sprig of fresh mint.

"This is delicious, Gema," Sonia said. "How did you make this?" she arched a questioning eyebrow.

"Fresh lime juice, sugar, water..."

"Very refreshing."

"Now, what can I do for you, Mrs. Patel?" Gema sat down in the armchair.

"Well," Rupa pulled a velvet pouch out of her purse. "I would like you take a look at these."

Gema took out a piece of felt and placed it on the table. "Put them on here."

Rupa placed three pieces of jewelry on it, two necklaces and a bracelet.

Wordlessly, Gema looked at them and picked up one after the other.

"I'll be right back," she said, "I need a special loop," and went through a door to another room.

Rupa, sitting up very straight at the edge of the sofa, shot Sonia a worried glance.

"Oh Mrs. Sonia," Rupa said in a tearful voice.

"Calm yourself, Mrs. Rupa."

"But what if...?

"Please, Mrs. Rupa," Sonia put a hand up to stop her from going any further.

Rupa got up, and began pacing. "What am I going to do, Mrs. Sonia?"

Sonia shrugged.

Rupa walked over to the Chinese silk screen and stopped in front of it. Made of black lacquered wood and a gold silk panels, it was a captivating piece. She stroked the smooth raw silk, tracing the figures woven into the fabric with her finger when a sudden sparkle caught her eye. She sidled up to the side of the screen and pushed it slightly so that she could see what was behind it.

"Oh!" she exclaimed, her hand to her chest.

There was a small table, strewn with photos from magazines and newspapers, a large board on which there were several photos and drawings of a necklace and the bust of a mannequin sitting on a plinth, wearing a necklace.

Rupa's eye caught sight of a newspaper cutting that lay on the desk. It was old and yellowed but the headline read '*Six pounds of diamonds: a suitable necklace for the Spanish wife of the Maharajah of Barodan,*" and below it was a photo of the Barodan necklace on the neck of the Maharani of Barodan.

Rupa looked back up at the necklace on the mannequin. Still

unfinished, it looked very much like the necklace in the newspaper. Rupa frowned. *What's this?* she wondered.

"Mrs. Sonia..." she turned and said, but just then Gema came back into the room.

"Mrs. Patel," Gema took a deep breath. "I'm afraid I cannot help you."

"But why on earth not?" Sonia jumped in.

"The craftsmanship of the pieces is lovely," Gema said. "But I deal in stones, and these are not ones I can use or re-sell."

"But why?" Mrs. Rupa said. "These pieces were my mother's, they are antiques...handed down to her from my grandmother."

"Mrs. Patel," Gema said. "As I said, the pieces are beautiful, but the work hides the quality of the stones."

"How much do you think she can get for them?" Sonia asked Gema.

"To be honest..." Gema said, "not much."

Rupa and Sonia exchanged a look.

"What about collectors of antique Indian jewelry?"

"You could get in touch with the big auction houses in London and New York and see if they have anything coming up," Gema suggested. "Or...closer to home, you could always try JJ Singh."

"JJ Singh!" Rupa exclaimed. "He's an art collector."

"He's a collector, Mrs. Patel...of all things," Gema said.

"But I can't go to JJ Singh and ask him to buy my jewelry," Rupa said.

"Mr. Singh is very discreet...but...if you want, I have another idea for you," Gema said cautiously.

"Yes!" Rupa sat up hopeful.

"Are the pieces insured?"

"No," Rupa said. "Why?"

"Because..." Gema started.

"Right," Sonia got up. "Thank you, Gema."

"I'm sorry I couldn't be of any more help."

"Thank you for telling me the truth," Rupa said. "I always thought they were worth so much more."

"Mrs. Sonia," Rupa asked as they walked out into the square. "Why did Gema ask if the pieces were insured?"

"Because if the pieces are insured for a decent amount, you could hide them and say you'd been robbed..."

"But...but..." Rupa spluttered, "that's insurance fraud."

"It has been known to happen," Sonia looked away. "Sometimes it is a last resort.

"Gema also makes the best fake pieces," she added. "She has clients all over the world."

"Really?"

"Yes...a lot of people want to sell their jewelry discreetly, but not admit to it," Sonia said. "You know what it's like in our society...

"So, they go to Gema, she makes a perfect fake and they sell the pieces and pocket the money..."

"You think some of our friends wear fakes?"

"Of course, Mrs. Rupa!" Sonia said. "Don't be so naïve."

"I don't think I could wear something fake."

"You wouldn't know a fake if it hit you."

"I would too," Rupa claimed. "I know my jewelry."

"Of course, you do," Sonia said sarcastically.

The two women picked their way across the square.

"Now what do I do?" Rupa said as they arrived at the entrance of the market. "I can't tell Mr. Patel."

"Don't worry, Mrs. Rupa," Sonia gave her a reassuring pat on the arm. "We will come up with another plan.

"As Gema said, you could go to JJ Singh."

"I can't."

"Why not?"

"He's the one I owe the money to...not to him directly, but to his man."

"Whatever for?"

"I've developed a love for horses."

"You've gone out and bought a stable?" Sonia said.

"No...but I may as well have."

"Who do you think you are? Queen Elizabeth...?"

"What do you mean?"

"The queen can buy horses, but you...you can't even drive, how on earth are you going to hoist your plump little self on a horse...and in a sari?"

"Mrs. Sonia, that is not a very nice thing to say about me."

"You're the one who's in love with riding."

"I never said anything about riding," Rupa replied.

"What else does one do with a horse?"

"Well Mrs. Sonia..." Rupa puffed her chest out like a peacock. "Horses are beautiful animals and when they run, they are magnificent."

"So you bought horses to watch them run?"

"Not exactly."

Sonia stared at her for a moment... "Oh," she said as realization dawned. "Oh!" she exclaimed again. "Are you telling me that...?"

"Yes, Mrs. Sonia, I bet on them," Rupa sniffed. "I'm not proud of it, but there it is."

"Well thank god it's just horses and not alcohol or something worse."

"Mrs. Sonia! I do not have a problem."

"Well you clearly do if you owe JJ Singh money."

"It's a little problem," Rupa squirmed.

"We have to sort it out before it gets any bigger."

"I so enjoy the races, though."

"Mrs. Rupa, you are incorrigible."

"I'm sorry...what am I to do?"

"Keep calm...and don't be so trigger-happy for the next few weeks."

"I see these beautiful, handsome beasts and I can't help myself."

"Mr. Patel is obviously not doing such a great job in the bedroom," Sonia mumbled.

"What did you say?" Rupa said.

"Nothing...now where is that driver?" she looked around. "He's always disappearing."

"By the way, Mrs. Sonia," Rupa said as Sonia waved to her driver who was parked a little further down the dirt lane. "Behind that Chinese screen in Gema's atelier was the Barodan necklace."

"What?" Sonia scoffed. "Are you feeling unwell?"

"Honestly, it was the Barodan necklace."

"The real one? That is impossible," Sonia said as the car stopped in front of them and the driver jumped out to hold the door open for Sonia.

"But I swear that is what I saw," Rupa got in after her.

"Mrs. Rupa, you are making no sense," Sonia said. "What would the necklace be doing there?

"I'm sure it's a copy," Sonia said.

"Why would she be making a copy? Why? And for whom?"

"Mrs. Rupa..." Sonia put a hand up.

"But why would she be making a fake?"

"Maybe she's making it for a movie Priya is going to star in?" Sonia suggested.

"Impossible!"

"Why?" Sonia was aghast.

"Because her latest movie, the one that just came out, is the one in which she plays a concubine..."

"Maybe Richemont commissioned it for something?"

"That's ridiculous."

"Fine! What's your theory?"

"I don't think the necklace exists at all and this is one big publicity ploy."

"Publicity ploy for what and for whom?"

"For Priya, of course...she's promoting her new movie."

"The necklace is apparently being lent to her by JJ Singh to wear at the party..." Sonia said.

"Even better!" Rupa said happily. "JJ is having a fake made because he doesn't really have the necklace, but he wants people to think he does.

"Or..." Rupa's eyes widened. "What if someone is trying to commit insurance fraud...? Like you said...?

"What you're saying makes no sense," Sonia said. "I've had a couple of fake pieces made because the originals were stolen.

"Or sometimes, people will have fakes made to take them to wear abroad if they're afraid of taking the real thing out of the bank."

"There's something very fishy going on, Mrs. Sonia," Rupa wobbled her head. "I can smell it."

"You are no Miss Marple, Mrs. Rupa..."

"But, but..."

"Stop! We are going to lunch."

*

"Hanut...I'm going out to get something to eat," Indi called out across the atelier.

He looked at her and gave her the 'peace' sign.

"Can I get you something?"

"Surprise me," he replied as he directed the women embroidering the yards of fabric before them.

As she stepped outside, Indi put on her sunglasses and walked to Le Bistro Indien, a small, quaint café restaurant not too far away. Luckily, the small table in the window that gave out onto the street was empty and she quickly slipped in and ordered a chicken burger and a glass of white wine.

"What's the network and password here?" she asked the waiter when he brought over the bottle of sauvignon blanc.

"Namaste," he replied.

"That's cute," she smiled.

As soon as he left, Indi opened up her laptop and got to work, creating an email from the India Cricket Board, announcing the sale of VIP tickets to the upcoming India vs. England games for the World Cup that were to be held on the cricket grounds in Delhi. She worked quickly, cutting and pasting the photo of the Indian Cricket team and below a link to buy tickets in which she installed computer code that when it was clicked on, would allow her remote access into the computer that opened the email.

She looked at it when it was done and then glanced at her watch. Two hours. Not bad, she congratulated herself.

"Another glass of wine?" she heard the waiter's voice.

"Why not?" she said and pressed the 'Send' button.

*

Sabine pulled up to the Singh property, parked to the side under a tree and got out, hoisted several garment bags over her shoulder and walked over to the guard post just inside the tall, white gate that was open.

She was wearing a three-piece black suit, white shirt and a black tie, had tied a Sikh turban on her head and added a beard, moustache and thick round glasses.

"I have some new suits here to deliver to Mr. Singh."

The security guard looked up.

"Your name?" he asked.

"Roshan...from Empire Tailors," Sabine said.

"You're not the regular Chinese guy."

"He had to go to Hong Kong."

The guard stared at her for a few seconds, expressionless.

"How lucky for him."

Sabine shrugged, indifferently.

"You're not on the delivery schedule today," the guard said, looking at his clipboard.

"No problem. I'll take them all back," she turned.

"Wait!" the guard called out when she was halfway back to the car.

She turned and he motioned her to come back.

"What?" she asked.

"Wait a minute...I'll call Singh *Sahib*'s butler," he picked up the phone.

"Adi..." she heard him say. "The tailor is here...I don't know...it looks like there's a lot...yes?...alright, I'll send the kid up to the kitchen."

"Go on up," the guard said. "Do you know where the kitchen entrance is?"

"I'll find it," Sabine nodded. "How hard can it be?"

"Watch that mouth on you, kid," the guard said. "The youth of today..." Sabine heard him say as she walked up the driveway, walking around the left to get to the kitchens. At least he said 'youth,' she thought.

The back door was open and Sabine walked in and looked around. There were cupboards and off to the side, a round table and chairs. "Hello?" she said. She put the garment bags on the table and went to peek around the side. There was a large modern kitchen at the far end of which was a door from which she heard sounds of pots and pans, someone chopping vegetables and a radio that was playing current Bollywood songs loudly.

She took her phone out of her pocket and looked at the plan of the ground floor. The reception hall where she was the night before was to the left and then out through the dining room. Just then, she heard someone come through into the main kitchen and put a tray on the centre island.

"*Aray...sub log kahan chalay gai*?" she heard a man's voice. "*Uff ho,*" he complained and she heard him pick up a phone.

"The *Sahib* asked for some tea," he said. "Can someone please come and get it? What do you mean I should serve it? I'm the cook, I can't leave the kitchen, I have things on the stove...soon, before it gets cold."

"*Kya yaar*...lazy idiots," he hung up.

"I can take Mr. Singh his tea," Sabine came around the corner.

"Take it then," the cook barely glanced at her as he waddled back to the inner kitchen. "Hurry up. It can't arrive cold."

"Yes, chef," Sabine said and picked up the tray going through the double swinging doors through the dining room to the round reception hall. It was beautiful in the daylight, with rays of the sun streaming in through the windows around the cupola. A man was sitting at a desk in the front. He looked up, nodded and looked back down at the screen of his laptop.

She went down the hallway, smiling as she passed the two Jamini Roy paintings and knocked at the second door on the right.

"*Ao*," she heard JJ's voice. He was on the phone.

"Sanjeev...any news on the pearls," she heard him say as she went in. "What the hell is taking so long, *yaar*? I need that fucking money."

Just as she was putting the tray down, the door opened and Rusty came in. JJ gestured him to sit down, but someone called to him from the hallway. "I'll be right back, *Sahib*," he went back out.

In the meantime, Sabine placed a small device under the rim of the coffee table and walked back out. She went through the reception hallway and saw Rusty talking to the man at the desk. She slipped by and went back into the kitchen.

She had just walked back in when,

"Where are those suits?" It was Aditya, JJ's butler.

"Here, *Sahib*," she said.

Aditya came around. "What are you doing hiding here?"

"I'm not hiding, sir," Sabine said. "I didn't know where to go."

"Where are the suits?"

"Here," Sabine opened the top bag.

"What is this?" Aditya pulled a sari. "This is not a man's suit."

"Oh!" Sabine looked shocked. "I must have picked up the wrong bag, *Sahib*."

"What about these others?" Aditya began opening bags. "None of these are men's suits.

"These are all women's clothes."

"I am so sorry, sir," Sabine quickly gathered everything.

"Next time, look at what you're picking up."

"Yes, sir," Sabine said and quickly walked out the door.

"Thank you!" she waved to the security guard and jumped into the car.

*

She drove away and when she was almost at the main road, she stopped. She pulled off the turban and peeled off the moustache and beard and looked at herself quickly in the rearview mirror. She pulled out her cellphone and sent a text.

'Ears are in.'

"Got it. We will have eyes soon."

She put her earphones in and launched an application on her phone. Suddenly, she heard JJ's voice loud and clear.

*

"Rusty," JJ said when he walked in. "Nina Singh is coming in this afternoon...let me know when she gets here."

"Yes, sir."

"*Sahib*...did you order any new suits from Mr. Cheong at Empire?"

"I don't think so...why?"

"Aditya is telling me that a man showed up this morning with suits for you."

"Send them back."

"Aditya was saying there was some mix up anyway."

"What's wrong with these people?" JJ rued to his papers. "No proper help these days."

*

Sabine giggled as she drove.

*

"What I really want to know is how that Roy painting ended up in the hallway?

"*Sahib*...I'm looking into it."

"We are supposed to have the most sophisticated security system in all of India," JJ said, "yet someone walks in here in the middle of the night, hangs a painting and walks out and no one can tell me anything about it."

"I understand, sir," Rusty nodded.

"I want a complete revision of the system," JJ said. "Especially with this party coming up.

"I'll do a full audit of the system and make the changes," Randy turned to leave.

"Wait a sec..."

"Sir?"

"Priya just emailed us...apparently the dress designer needs to see the necklace...for the love of God...fine. I'll reply telling her that it's alright but they should coordinate with you."

"Yes, sir."

JJ got up to open the safe.

"Here," he handed Rusty a velvet box. "Show it to the designer at the Gallery," JJ said. "And don't let it out of your sight."

"Yes, sir."

"And Rusty," JJ added over his shoulder. "Keep the necklace at the vault in the gallery until the day of the event..."

Rusty nodded, closed the door and went downstairs to his small office and opened up his email. There was the email from Hanut Singh asking when he could see the necklace, but there was another one from the India Cricket Board.

Rusty looked at the subject line: '*World Cup VIP Tickets to go on sale tomorrow. Click here and buy them now.*' His eyes flickered with excitement.

His finger hovered over the mouse for only a moment as he debated his decision, but then he pressed down and clicked 'Yes.'

*

Sabine screeched to a halt and dialed a number on her phone.

"Indi..."

"Yeah."

"They're reconfiguring the security system...Has he opened the email?"

"He will."

"JJ's moved the necklace to the vault."

"What does that mean?"

"Nothing".

Chapter 5

Nina took a deep breath and rang the bell. Moments later, it opened.

"I have an appointment to see Mr. JJ Singh," she said to the man who opened the door.

"Please come in, *begum sahiba*," the man stood politely aside as Nina walked in.

"If you would please wait here for just a moment," he said and disappeared.

As she waited, Nina looked around. The entrance hall was round with a vaulted cathedral ceiling from which hung a crystal chandelier that looked like it came from the ballroom of an old Venetian Palazzo as did the gilt and black mirrors. The marble on the floor was grey and black, the walls a soft shade of off-white. There was no furniture, only a stone sculpture of a classical Roman goddess on a plinth and a bright green banana tree in the corner. It was simple, yet grand. Beyond was the living room and through the French doors, Nina caught a glimpse of the glittering turquoise water of a pool and the bright green of the lawn.

"Would you come with me please, *begum sahiba*," the man re-appeared.

Nina followed him down a hallway.

"This is Mr. Singh's office," he led the way into an airy room that looked more like a library with its book-lined walls. In the middle was a large peacock blue sofa, two comfortable-looking deep purple armchairs and a coffee table. At the far end were doors that opened onto the garden.

"Mr. Singh is just finishing a phone call," the man said. "He will be here in a few minutes."

After he left, Nina sat primly down on the sofa. But she couldn't sit still. She walked over to JJ's desk, running her hands over the glossy marbled wood, before walking over to look at the books.

Suddenly she heard footsteps in the hallway and quickly ran back to the sofa and sat back down.

"Mrs. Singh!" JJ walked in a few minutes later, looking very dapper in a dark suit, open-collared shirt and a dark turban.

"Please...call me Nina," Nina said, sitting primly on the edge of an armchair, her hands intertwined in her lap.

"I just need to put something away," JJ went to a small painting next to his desk. Pushing it aside, he opened a safe with a key he pulled from his pocket. He rummaged in his desk, took out a brown paper packet, put it in and locked it.

"Sorry about that," he sat across from Nina on the sofa crossing his legs comfortably, stretching his arm across the back.

"Not at all."

"Would you like something to drink?"

"Uh...no, no...thank you," she replied.

"Very well...

"Now...to what do I owe this visit from the Maharani of Barodan?"

"Hardly a Maharani, Singh *Sahib*," she said.

"Well...if titles still existed, you would have it."

"Yes...but neither the title nor the name pays the bills these days."

JJ raised an eyebrow.

"Your husband was at the opening of my gallery a few days ago..."

"Was he?"

"He asked for my help."

"Of course he did," Nina said.

"Are you looking for the same?"

Nina looked away embarrassed.

"I'm sure this is difficult for you, Nina."

"Singh *Sahib*," Nina started and stopped.

"Well...it's a little awkward," she started again. "But the fact is that I do need a little help."

"Help?"

Nina nodded, squeezing her hands so hard that her knuckles turned white. "Yes...I...uh...need your help selling something."

"I see," JJ nodded, a smile playing around the sides of his mouth as he understood what Nina was getting at.

"I have filed for a divorce from Arun," she shifted her weight uncomfortably.

"Divorce?" JJ was surprised.

"Yes," Nina looked away. "It's an untenable situation."

"I see," JJ nodded.

"And so...I need money," she opened her purse and pulled out a dark green velvet pouch and handed it to JJ, who loosened the silk ties and opened it, pulling out a string of pearls.

"What do you think of those?"

"Yes...they are lovely."

"They were my grandmother's...a gift from the Maharajah of Jodhpur."

"Really?" JJ raised an eyebrow. "I have been thinking about starting a collection of the jewels of the Maharajahs," he twirled the necklace around in his fingers. "I have a piece or two, but I want to bring back some of the pieces that are scattered around Europe and America...and the middle east."

"What a wonderful idea!" Nina nodded eagerly.

"But..." JJ sighed and got up, walking around the library turning to face her, his hands in the pockets of trousers. "I cannot...not at this time.

"As you know, I have helped your family in the past...your grandfather in particular...and your grandmother after he passed away," he trailed off. "I paid her a nice sum of money for the shop in Vasant Vihar."

"Yes," Nina looked away as the hope on her face faded.

"Perhaps in a few months...?" he said. "Things may change...but at the moment, I cannot, I'm afraid. I am a bit overextended."

"I see," Nina put the pearls back in the pouch and got up.

She walked to the door and stopped.

"By the way, Singh *Sahib*," she turned. "The Barodan necklace that Priya is going to wear at this famous wedding reception..."

"Yes...?"

"Do you know who it belongs to?"

"To me."

"How did you find it?"

"It was in a private collection."

"That necklace should rightfully have been mine," Nina said. "It's curious how it ended up with you."

"Luck?" JJ suggested.

"Of course, isn't it always?" Nina said and walked out the door.

*

"Kamal," Rusty said.

Kamal Khan was the head of Pioneer Security and an ex-Army friend of Rusty's. Rusty had given him the job to map out the security camera matrix for JJ's house and Gallery, giving him a chance at having his own business after he went back into civilian life.

"Rusty, *kya haal hai*? How are you, sir?"

"Kamal...there has been a very serious breach of security at the house," Rusty said, walking around his small office with his cell phone.

"Allah!" Kamal exclaimed. "What happened?"

"A few days ago, someone walked in and hung a piece of art in the middle of the night," Rusty began.

"Is that a crime?"

"It's called trespassing"

"And just today, we had someone walk into the property posing as a delivery man from the tailor."

"My goodness," Kamal sounded as though he was sweating.

"Now, we have a very important event coming up..."

"Yes, Rusty *Sahib*," Kamal interrupted him. "I have heard. All Bollywood will be there."

"We cannot afford any embarrassments, Kamal...you understand."

"I do...we will go in and fix it..."

"When?"

"Immediately," Kamal said. "I will give you complete access

to the matrix."

*

It was just past 9am and Indi sleepily reached for her laptop as she sipped her tea in bed.

She opened a screen and saw a white wall, a desk and a chair, behind which was a door. Seconds later, Rusty came in and sat down in his chair, staring intently at the computer.

"Good morning, Mr. Khan," Indi smiled. She dialed a number on her cellphone.

"We're in. I'm staring at Rusty."

"Good girl!"

"There should be a new matrix," she said. "I'll start looking at it."

"Remember that every inch of that property is probably going to be recorded," Sabine said. "So we need to find a spot that's not going to be on camera."

"What are you thinking?"

"A place they're not even thinking about."

"Like?"

"Now that you can move cameras around, we can create a spot."

"I'm going to see the necklace later this morning with Hanut...I'll come to Gema's after."

"Don't pocket it or anything, would ya?" Sabine said wryly. "You'll put on 6 pounds and then you'll cry about being fat."

"Very funny, Sabine...do you hear me laughing?"

"Just saying..."

*

"This way please," a pretty young woman ushered Indi and

Hanut into a room with tall modern, French doors that opened onto an enclosed garden with a grey stone fountain in the middle, surrounded by grey and white galet stones.

"Thank you," Hanut said.

"Look at this place!" Hanut walked around. "This is beautiful...that fountain! Gorgeous."

"And the artwork," Indi added.

The door opened and a man walked in, carrying a velvet box.

"I am Rusty Khan," he introduced himself.

"Hanut Singh," Hanut shook his hand, "and my assistant, Indi Kumar."

Rusty acknowledged her with a polite nod.

Handsome man, Indi thought. Actually...very handsome.

"He's hot," Hanut whispered.

"Shut up."

"Shall we sit?" he pointed to a sage green sofa in the middle of the room and placed the velvet box on the coffee table.

"This...is the Barodan," Rusty announced and opened it.

Both Indi and Hanut stared, their eyes wide. Finally, Hanut reached for it, running his fingers over the stones, whilst Indi rummaged in her bag for a notebook and a measuring tape.

"What's that for?" Rusty asked.

"The choli blouse is being designed around the necklace," Indi said smoothly, placing her cell phone in the breast pocket of her jacket. "We need to measure it to see how far down it will reach on Priya's chest, so we can cut the fabric accordingly.

"Can I put it around Hanut's neck?" she asked.

"Sure."

"Holy shit!" Hanut swore as Indi got up and went around the back of the sofa and placed the necklace on his neck, fiddling with the clasp.

"What are you doing, Indi?" Hanut said. "I'm dying to see what this looks like."

"Just...one...quick...second," she said. "There!"

Hanut turned and gave her a questioning look.

"My oh my," Indi came around the front and looked at him.

Hanut's frown morphed into a huge smile. "Is it gorgeous?

"Look for yourself," Indi said and he got up to stand in front of an antique French mirror that was nearer the French doors.

"Stand right there," she added, standing next to him.

"I feel like a Maharajah!" Hanut squealed.

Rusty put his hands in his pockets and looked away as he tried to hide a chuckle.

"Look at the way these stones capture the natural sunlight," Hanut commented as Indi quickly took some measurements of the length, occasionally adjusting the cellphone in her breast pocket, especially just before she unclasped the necklace and put it back in the box.

"The necklace lives here, does it?" Indi asked Rusty, who nodded wordlessly as he closed the box and tucked it under his shoulder.

"You must have a vault here?"

He nodded again.

"Must be quite secure?"

"Of course, it is," he said with pride in his voice. "I will be personally handling security for the necklace.

"From the moment it leaves here to when it is returned."

"I'm sure Priya will appreciate a bodyguard," Hanut said.

"It's amazing," Indi smiled. "A necklace that hasn't been seen since partition and now...here it is...

"Where has it been all this time?"

"I don't know," Rusty replied.

"The world will once again be privy to its beauty on the neck of Priya Chopra," Hanut gestured around. "Everyone in India will be talking about it...everyone in the world will be talking about it."

"Yes..." Indi smiled, putting her hand under Hanut's elbow, guiding him towards the door.

"A whole generation of people who know nothing about what it meant to be a Maharajah will have their eyes opened," Hanut said.

"And they will," Indi said. "Thank you so much," she said to Rusty, gently pushing Hanut out the door towards the lobby.

"I don't think I've ever seen anything quite so beautiful," Hanut said as they got into the car. "Did you see the size of those stones?"

"Six pounds, Hanut," Indi pulled out her cellphone.

"What are you doing?" Hanut said.

"Oh...just some notes," Indi replied as she quickly sent a text, attaching a video she had secretly taken of the necklace, and especially the clasp.

'Nicely done,' came the response.

'The clasp could be a problem,' Indi typed. 'I'm on my way.'

*

Sabine was sitting on a bench with a glass of hot, milky tea in one hand and a samosa in a piece of newspaper under the large banyan tree in the small square park of Khanna Market.

"Why aren't you upstairs?"

"Gema has a client."

"Who is it?"

"Nina Singh..."

"Nina Singh?" Indi said. "How do I know her name?"

"Married to Arun Singh," Sabine started. "Soon to be divorced from Arun Singh."

"Arun Singh...the businessman?" Indi asked.

"Yeah," Sabine nodded. "But nothing he's done has ever come to anything."

"Is that why she's divorcing him?"

"Who knows?" Sabine shrugged. "But she went to see JJ...tried to sell him some pearls."

"And you know this...how?"

Sabine handed her earphones.

"Ah," Indi said. "What happened?

"He turned her away...said he didn't have any money."

"Really?"

"Apparently."

"I don't think he's broke," Indi said.

"Maybe he's saving for a rainy day?" Sabine suggested wryly.

"You're incorrigible," Indi shook her head. "He has money, maybe not to play around, but he's not broke...besides how is he paying for the party? That's got to be costing him a bundle?"

Sabine shrugged.

"By the way, where's my tea?"

"Chaiwallah!" Sabine called out to the man standing next to a cart on which was a canister filled with wood, on top of which sat a flat-bottomed copper cooking pot. "Chai and samosa please."

The thin old man, wearing a red and white checked turban,

smiled a toothless smile and obliged by bringing over a tray a few minutes later.

"This has to be the best cup of tea I've ever had," Indi said.

"Wait 'til you try the samosa," Sabine bit into hers.

"It's good," Indi nodded. "You know the necklace will have its own security team."

"Of course, it will," Sabine shrugged. "It should."

"It's going to be Rusty Khan, JJ's Head of Security."

Sabine nodded.

"Interesting guy," Indi said.

"What about andsome guy?" Sabine said.

"I wasn't going to say that," Indi started.

"I know...that's why I said it for you."

"Whatever...Sabine, he's going to follow that necklace around from the moment it goes on Priya's neck," Indi said. "The man is an ex-Army sniper...he's got eyes like a hawk."

Sabine nodded again.

"How the hell do you propose to get it off Priya?"

"Patience, my friend," a smile lurked around Sabine's lips. "All will be revealed."

After a few moments of silence,

"I was thinking," Indi started.

"Oh no!" Sabine interrupted.

"What does that mean?"

"It's just that you were thinking..."

Indi rolled her eyes.

"We've got into his security system," she began after a moment. "Why don't we just lift the necklace from the vault at the gallery."

"Are you nuts?"

"Why?"

"First of all, the vault is underground," Sabine started. "And, for that, we'll need a team and money...not just you and me.

"No...let JJ bring it to us."

"And you think you and I are going to be able to pull it off at the party?"

"Yeah..." Sabine looked at her. "I do."

"But how?" Indi asked.

"Actually, you are going to lift it right off her neck."

"Why me?"

"Because you're her stylist."

"So, what?" Indi said. "You want me to say, 'excuse me, Priya, but I need to take this off your neck?'"

"No...but we will create a situation in which you will be able to slip it off and hand it to me."

"What kind of situation?" Indi said.

"Where are you with the outfit?"

"It's coming together...why?"

"Priya is going to have a wardrobe malfunction," Sabine said. "You're going to snap the straps of her blouse."

"What?"

"She'll have to cover up," Sabine said. "And that's when you'll do it."

"Me?" Indi said. "Why me?" she looked confused. "My hands are not that good."

"Trust me...they are."

Sabine got up and went to return the empty glass to the chaiwallah.

"Come on! Gema's free!" Sabine said as they watched Nina

Singh walk across the park.

"Hey!" Gema said, coming towards them. "Thanks for the video and the measurements," she said to Indi. "It was impossible to tell from some of those old newspaper cuttings."

"How's it coming along?" Sabine said.

"Not bad," Gema pulled aside the Chinese silk screen.

"That's really good," Sabine inspected at the half-finished necklace around the neck of the mannequin.

"There is just one thing," Indi said.

Both Gema and Sabine looked up at her.

"There is a problem with the original clasp."

"Yes...?" Gema prompted.

"It's an odd-shaped fish hook," she replied. "Not that easy."

"Start practicing," Sabine said.

"Tea?" Gema pointed to a tray with a teapot.

"We just had some downstairs," Indi said.

"What's the plan, Sabine?" Gema poured herself a cup.

"Alright, let's start with things we already know," Sabine began. "In three weeks, JJ Singh is hosting a lavish party for Priya Chopra and Randy Singh at his house. Priya will be wearing the Barodan necklace and we are going to rob it.

"Hanut Singh is dressing Priya and Indi is already working with him; we have hacked into the security system at the house and Gema, you are working on a duplicate of the necklace.

"Last but not least we have to infiltrate the party."

"How are you going to do that?"

"Easy...the caterer," Sabine said.

*

"Indiiiiiiiii!" Hanut called out as Indi was adjusting some material on a mannequin.

"Hanut...I think this will look..."

"Quick! We have to go," he said. "Pack everything!"

"But where?"

"A fitting..."

"A fitting?" Indi asked. "With Priya? Where? Now?"

"Yes!" he nodded eagerly.

"But all we have is this muslin..."

"Let's go!" he rushed her as she folded fabric and various other muslins into a large case.

Outside, Hanut's car and driver was waiting and they both tumbled into the back seat.

"The Lodhi Hotel," Hanut instructed the driver.

"Nice..." Indi remarked.

"It's a secret," Hanut whispered. "She doesn't want the paparazzi to know."

When they arrived at the Lodhi Hotel, a young woman wearing big, heavy black-framed glasses, her hair pulled back in a sleek ponytail and a clipboard in her hand was waiting for them.

"I am Priya's assistant," she said. "Please come with me," she marched quickly down the hallway.

Hanut immediately started out, leaving Indi to awkwardly keep up, her hands full of folded fabrics and bags strapped on her shoulders.

"Here we are," the assistant said, opening a dark wood door that led into a large living room with a dining area at one end, and a courtyard with a couple of bright yellow sunbeds and a turquoise blue private pool.

Indi dropped the fabric on the taupe sofa and let down the bags off her shoulders, massaging them to get the circulation going again.

"Now...let's pull out the muslin of the skirt and the top," Hanut said. "I want to see how far we can plunge the neckline in order to show off this necklace."

"There you are!" Hanut swirled around when another door opened. "Priya dah-ling!" he swooned. "You are just so magnificent, my dear..." he air-kissed her on both cheeks. "Let me introduce you to my assistant...Indi Kumar."

Indi nodded hello.

"Indi...," she said. "What's it short for?" Priya looked her up and down.

"Indira Indiana," Indi replied.

"Interesting," Priya said.

In person, Priya was an extremely beautiful woman and, at 5'7", tall for an Indian woman, but just not quite model height. She had a smooth, café-au-lait complexion, large, almond shaped brown eyes, a small nose, high cheekbones in an oval face, large sensual lips and a big smile that lit up her whole face and was her trademark, both on screen and in the advertising she did for certain big brands. Fit and slim, she was still curvy with a large bust, small waist and rounded hips. Her dark hair was piled on top of her head in a messy bun and she wore a pair of loose white linen trousers and a fitted cropped pink t-shirt that said 'Madonna.'

"I feel as though I know you?" Priya said, lighting a cigarette, offering one to Hanut, who accepted.

"I don't think so," Indi replied, arranging the fabrics on the sofa.

"Hmmm...glass of champagne, Hanut?" Priya walked towards the dining area.

"Why not?" Hanut shrugged. "I'm sure it's 5 o'clock somewhere."

"I don't care," Priya popped the bottle, keeping her cigarette between her teeth. "It's 1 o'clock here and I feel like something bubbly."

She poured a glass for Hanut and herself.

Indi looked at Hanut, cocking an eyebrow. Hanut imperceptibly shrugged, silently mouthing, "You can have some of mine," pointing to his glass.

"What are we doing today?" Priya sat down in a large armchair, her legs swinging to the side.

"I want you to try this," Hanut handed her a small pile.

Priya disappeared through the doors.

"Hanut," Indi started. "That *choli* is small."

"Of course!" Hanut ran a hand through his curls. "It's meant to be. She has to look sexy."

"Alright, but that choli shows a lot of midriff," Indi said. "How's her tummy?"

"We will see," Hanut said. "She says she's been working out."

"I think you should lengthen it just a bit."

"Maybe we just add some chiffon and a row of those teardrop diamonds?" Hanut mused, stroking his waxed moustache.

The door opened and Priya came back out wearing a long white skirt and a small choli top, her champagne glass in her hand, her long dark hair now loosely tumbling down her back.

"I'm sure I know you," Priya said as Indi draped plain chiffon fabric around her.

"Indi was a model," Hanut said. "And one of my muses back in the early days."

"Ahhh!" Priya nodded. "So that's it...I knew it! I never forget a face."

After Indi was done, she stepped aside and Priya stared at herself in the mirror.

"And this is the necklace," she placed a chain around Priya's neck, "only it will be heavier and much larger."

Hanut was smiling, rubbing his hands gleefully, standing behind her. "And the fabric as you know is slightly golden and is being embroidered in gold, with an ornate border that will have a beautiful gold leaf pattern...

"I don't know..." Priya finally said and Hanut's smile died in an instant.

"What do you mean?"

"I just don't know about this..."

"Priya...this is only the pattern," he began stuttering. "It's a muslin...even the dopatta is a muslin."

"The top...the bottom," she wrinkled her nose.

"We can certainly change the bottom," Hanut went down on bended knee.

"It feels so plain."

"Darling..." Hanut got up and put his hands on her shoulders, looking at her in the mirror. "This will not be plain.

"Everything will have a train..." he said soothingly. "The lehnga, the dopatta, the choli will be off the shoulder with free flowing fabric...very medieval, very dramatic.

"As you walk, you will leave clouds of chiffon behind you."

"What happened to the duster coat?"

"I decided to add these long off the shoulder sleeves instead and diamante straps and diamonds along the neckline for extra glam...maybe even a few rosettes."

"Maybe it's the necklace," she said suddenly. "It's just too much. Let's just get rid of the necklace...I'll call JJ and tell him I don't want to wear it."

Indi's ears perked up.

"I want to look elegant and from what I've seen, this necklace is huge," Priya continued.

"Not at all..." Indi jumped in hurriedly. "You have to wear this necklace! It's one of the most famous necklaces in the world. It's all diamonds and emeralds."

Both Priya and Hanut turned to stare at her.

"Uhhh...what I meant," she added hurriedly, realizing how it must have sounded, "is that there is no one else who could wear this necklace...you want to look like a maharani...after all...right?" she stammered. "You have a regal presence, the way you hold yourself, carry yourself...this necklace could have been made for you."

A couple of seconds went by and then,

"Really?" Priya turned to the mirror. "You think so?"

"Of course!" Hanut standing behind her placed his hands on her shoulders. "You are a modern-day Maharani, Priya darling...only more beautiful."

"I don't know, Hanut...I'm just not feeling it."

"With my design and this necklace..." Hanut began.

"If the dress is going to be as ornate as the sketches you showed me, then maybe a simpler piece of jewelry...?"

"Honestly, Priya," Indi came to stand by her side. "There is no one else who can carry off this necklace except for you."

"Wearing my design," Hanut repeated, "you are going to be the talk of India...of the world...a bigger star even than Angelina Jolie...your photos will go viral..."

Good God, Indi silently rolled her eyes.

"You're sure about this necklace?" Priya turned to Indi who nodded.

"Isn't it just a little too big...almost man-ish?"

"It's six pounds of diamonds, Priya," Indi said. "And you have the neck and the presence that can carry it off."

Priya raised a questioning eyebrow.

Indi nodded.

"I am positive."

*

There was a gaggle of photographers at the entrance of the Lodhi Hotel when Sabine drove up. She got out of the car and was trying to make her way in when the heavy glass doors opened and the paparazzi began yelling and shouting, "Priya! Priya! This way! Over here!"

She stepped aside and waited as the movie star, dressed in a pair of jeans, a white top and espadrille platform shoes, and big sunglasses, walked down the steps towards a Range Rover with blackened windows.

Suddenly she was pushed and jostled and almost fell. Her sunglasses were askew on her nose and she stared up at Sabine who happened to be standing in front of her.

Sabine was about to help her up when one of her bodyguards scooped her up and led her to the waiting SUV that headed away as soon as the door shut, the gaggle of photographers running behind it, trying to get a shot through the smoked glass windows.

Sabine walked into the hotel and made her way to Indian Accent, the hottest restaurant in Delhi that was catering the reception at JJ's.

She wore a long, dark wig covering her shorter, light brown hair, her skin looked darker with the foundation and bronzer she'd used and black kohl to make her olive eyes look darker.

"I'm Ritika Stephen," a woman, wearing a dark pant-suit, her hair tied back in a bun, introduced herself to Sabine.

Sabine smiled.

"Thank you so much for coming in at such short notice," Ritika sat down at her desk, offering Sabine the chair in front of her. "This event is so last minute."

"Not at all," Sabine sat down easily, herself wearing a prim navy blue dress with pintucks down the front and a white collar and cuffs.

"This event has put a heavy toll on our staff and so I am glad you got in touch," Ritika said. "What I was looking for is someone to captain the VIP tables, although I think everyone at this event will be a VIP."

"I understand," Sabine said.

"My people are already spread a little too thin, and one more person will make all the difference," Ritika stared at the piece of paper in her hands. "Especially someone of your calibre.

"I will definitely need you on the day of the event," Ritika said, "but given all your experience, would you also be willing to coordinate the seating at the tables?" she asked. "All these dinner parties and events in Paris, London, Rome...must have been a fascinating experience."

"It was..."

"That's terrific!" Ritika said. "Let's get started," she got up. "I think it's best if you worked here, don't you think?"

"Of course."

"I'll be forwarding you the guest list so you can also look at nutritional requirements of the guests," she added. "Everyone is doing something different these days."

"No problem," Sabine smiled. "How many do we have?"

"200 exactly," Ritika said. "Mr. Singh wants 25 tables of 8."

"Very intimate."

"Happy to have you on board. Let me know if there is anything else you need."

*

"Boss," Rusty got in the driver's seat of JJ's shiny black Range Rover, "the painting that was hung in the hallway the other night..."

JJ turned to look at him.

"Could it have been a woman?"

"A woman?"

Rusty nodded, his eyes squarely on the road.

"And you're thinking..."

"Yes, sir, I am."

JJ silently stared out the passenger side window as Rusty drove them through congested Delhi streets, swearing as a cow began to cross a busy road and stopped in the middle, casually chewing the cud, but causing traffic to come a complete standstill until a policeman arrived on the scene and forced it to move to the side.

"Sabine and I were partners," JJ finally said. "I guess that's what you would call us," he added after a short pause. "We were partners until we weren't."

Rusty continued to drive in silence.

"We had a nice little thing going," he said. "When someone came in to buy a piece of art or a piece of jewelry, Sabine became the invisible 'other' buyer and we pushed the price up.

"If it was jewelry, Sabine would go in and get it back. She was good...like a ghost.

"Everyone kept their jewelry in their house, I knew their houses because they used to invite me to dinner, so I would tell Sabine.

"No one knew because people were too embarrassed to say they'd been robbed."

"No one filed a police report?"

"They did, but it never came to anything," JJ said. "The police had no idea it was Sabine. No one did. No one knew what she looked like and frankly, they probably couldn't image a woman as a jewel thief.

"But then one day, Sabine lifted the Indore pear diamond earrings from the woman we'd sold them to...she was a ballsy one and tipped off the police saying that it was me and they started to squeeze my balls...I had other problems back then with the CBI and so I cut a deal."

JJ lit a cigarette. "It was the hardest decision I've ever had to make."

"To give her up?"

JJ took a long drag, nodding as he let out the smoke and stubbed out the cigarette.

"But she got away?"

"I drove her to the airport and put her on the plane," he said. "I couldn't have lived with myself knowing she was in a cell at the Central Jail."

"Did you ever tell her you'd given her up?"

"She's a smart girl," JJ said. "She figured it out."

"Why do you think she's here now?"

"She wants the Barodan...she knows how much it means to me."

Suddenly his cellphone buzzed.

"Yes?"

"Rambo here."

"And?"

"You working on getting me my money?"

JJ didn't answer.

"Not a lot of time left, *yaar.*"

"I don't do well with threats," JJ said.

"This is no threat, JJ, " Rambo rung off.

JJ's nostrils flared and he pounded the dashboard with his fist. "Motherfucker!" he swore.

"Rusty...you got this, right?"

"Yes, boss."

"This cannot fail...I need the money. No one fucks around with this asshole."

"Yes, *sahib,*" Rusty said reassuringly.

"This son of a bitch could ruin me," JJ reached for a pack of Marlboros and took a swig from a flask he took from the side pocket next to his seat. "Rambo's hotel business is back on track and his clientele is the kind I need to fill my coffers."

*

"Hello, hello!" Gema was in the reception area of her atelier when Sabine and Indi came up the darkened stairs.

"What was so urgent?" Indi said.

"Come on!" Gema indicated they follow her. "You ready?" she said, her back to the silk screen in her atelier as Sabine and Indi stood facing her.

"Just show us, Gema!" Sabine said, exasperated, her arms folded across her chest.

Gema stepped aside, folding the screen, revealing a bust with the Barodan necklace hanging on it.

"Holy Mother of God!" Indi said.

Sabine stared at it silently and took it off the mannequin, holding it in her hands. "Even the weight feels right, Gema."

Gema nodded, smiling.

"That's amazing, Gema!"

"I think we all need a drink."

"All I can do is tea," Gema said and went to the window. "Chaiwallah!" she called out. "Send your boy with some tea and samosas."

A few minutes later, there was a knock on the outside door and a 10-year-old boy stood with a tray with a teapot and a plate of samosas.

While Gema busied herself finding cups, Sabine brought the mannequin with the necklace and placed it on the coffee table.

"To Gema!" Sabine raised a cup.

"To us," Gema replied.

"This has got to be your best work yet," Sabine said.

"It's not bad."

"What's the latest, Indi?" Sabine asked. "Where is Priya getting dressed?"

"Confirmed at the Lodhi," Indi said.

"So the necklace is going to come there first."

"Correct," Indi said. "And she will then make her grand entrance at JJ's around 8:30 – 9:00pm?"

"Alright...let's talk this through," Sabine said. "Priya is definitely wearing the necklace."

"She is," Indi said.

"Why? Was she not?" Gema asked.

"She thought it was a little masculine."

"Was she drunk?"

"Here is the seating chart I've put together," Sabine ignored her. "This is Table 1, Priya's table and this is Table 2, JJ's table."

"Look at all those celebrities..." Gema said. "Kareena Kapoor, Katrina Kaif, Aishwariya Rai...are you sure I can't go to this?"

"No," Sabine and Indi said in unison.

"I am sure," Sabine added, "that their new security matrix will have every inch of the driveway and the garden covered.

"So, we are going to create a blind spot between where Priya is sitting here," she pointed to the sheet of paper, "and the edge of the marquee.

"Indi...how much space do you need to lift the piece?"

"I don't know, Sabine," Indi shook her head.

"You're the only one who can do this."

Indi looked up and saw Sabine and Gema both staring at her.

"Alright, alright," Indi blew out a deep breath. "Probably 9 feet, give or take."

"And how long would it take to create that blind spot?"

"Moving the camera?" Indi pursed her lips. "About 10 days."

"That's perfect."

"But Sabine...how are we going to get the necklace out?"

"*We* are not going to get it out?" Sabine said. "Because you can be sure that JJ's guy and the insurance people will comb through the security footage looking for any hiccup."

"So who's going to move it?"

"Someone no one will remember."

"Come on...who can be that forgettable?"

"A waiter."

Chapter 6

Rupa sat at one of the bridge tables in the game room of the Gymkhana Club when a man approached the table. He wore grey slacks and a short-sleeved white shirt and his greying hair was slicked back.

"Hello Mrs. Patel," he said.

Rupa visibly jumped.

"Oh! Oh! Mr. Gupta...yes...well...you know, I've been meaning to get in touch..."she stammered, her heart beating against her rib cage, her mouth dry. "It's just that I've been very busy."

"It's a small matter of the money you owe me, Mrs. Patel..." he said, leaning on the chair next to her. "Actually, the money you owe Mr. Singh."

"Does he know it's me?" Rupa's face crinkled with worry.

Gupta didn't answer.

Instead,

"The money, Mrs. Patel..."

"I have it, Mr. Gupta," Rupa lied. "I'll be able to give it to you in a few days."

"If you have it, Mrs. Patel, then why not this afternoon?"

"Well...you see...it's...uh...it's...in the bank," she said. "Yes, it's in the bank, and you know, the bank closes in a few minutes," she looked at her watch.

"It's in the bank?" Mr. Gupta took his glasses off and cleaned them with a handkerchief he pulled from the pocket of his pants.

"Yes! Absolutely!"

"Tomorrow," Gupta said in a calm voice.

"Actually, I have to transfer some money from my account in Calcutta..."

"Mrs. Patel!" Gupta interrupted. "You have two weeks. And that is final. Otherwise, I will go to Mr. Patel, your good husband and tell him everything..."

"No!" Rupa's hand went to her heaving chest, in an effort to stop her heart pounding. "Now, Mr. Gupta," her voice quivered. "There is no reason to do that.

"I will get you your money back."

"In this lifetime, Mrs. Patel?" he sniggered. "Or in the next?"

"In this one, of course, Mr. Gupta," Rupa said, wringing her hands, as she always did when she was nervous.

"I want half the money now," Mr. Gupta said.

"I can give you a little money now," Rupa said.

"I will take *half* the money now," he repeated, "and the remainder in a month.

"Otherwise I go to Mr. Patel and the press."

"No! Mr. Gupta...please...a little more time."

"You have had plenty of time, Mrs. Patel," he put his sunglasses back on.

Behind Gupta, Rupa saw Nina and Sonia at the entrance to the game room, looking around for her. Damn!

"Mr. Gupta," Rupa squirmed. She desperately needed to get rid of him before the two other women saw him. "I will get you what I can...now I am sorry, but I have to go," she got up.

"You'd better start paying up, Mrs. Patel," Gupta's nostrils flared. "My patience is wearing thin."

Rupa scurried around, walking towards the bathroom, where she sat down in one of the blush pink armchairs in the boudoir, a large knot at the base of her throat and her tummy roiling.

"Mrs. Rupa!" she heard behind her. It was Sonia.

"Rupa!" Nina followed close behind. "What's the matter?"

Rupa looked up at both of them, her eyes glistening.

"Who was that oily man you were talking to?" Sonia wrinkled her nose.

"Oh ladies!" Rupa gulped. "I'm going to jail."

"What?" Sonia exclaimed. "What rubbish are you talking?"

"Mr. Patel is going to divorce me," she began to cry, "I'll have ruined his name, destroyed his standing in society.

"I will be humiliated and so very, very poor."

"Mrs. Rupa!" Sonia sat down in a chair across from her. "Calm down!" she ordered and handed her a handkerchief.

"Rupa," Nina gently put a hand on her arm. "Whatever it is, we will work it out. We're all friends and friends help one another."

"You can't help me," Rupa wailed dramatically.

"Is this to do with your horses?" Sonia asked, her voice cut and dried.

Rupa sniffed, nodding.

"And that man?" Sonia added. "Is he the one you borrowed money from?"

Rupa sniffed again in response and wiped the tears under her eyes, her mascara staining the white handkerchief.

"Oh no!" she looked at it and quickly got up to look in the mirror. "I look like a raccoon," she howled.

"Mrs. Rupa! Get a hold of yourself!" Sonia shouted. "You are in debt to a loan shark and you're worried about a little smeared eye makeup.

"Do you have any idea how dangerous those men are?"

"I didn't think it would go this far."

"How much do you owe him, Rupa?" Nina asked.

"Not much..." Rupa wrung the end of the sari pallu.

"How much?" Sonia repeated sternly.

"About five lakhs."

"Five lakhs!" Nina said shocked.

"Have you lost your mind, Mrs. Rupa?" Sonia shouted at her. "How did you let it get this far?"

"I don't know..." Rupa hung her head in shame. "I just kept thinking that if one horse made it..."

"Oh, Rupa!" Nina sighed.

"I know, I know," Rupa shook her head. "If only the jewelry I had was worth anything..."

"Well...you're going to sell what you have and it doesn't matter what you get for it," Sonia said. "You're going to have to give this guy something to show good faith.

"They're not called sharks for nothing."

"Alright," Rupa nodded. "But what I have doesn't even come out to a lakh."

"It doesn't matter."

"But what will I wear to the JJ Singh party?" Rupa asked, her eyes wet.

Both Nina and Sonia turned and glared at her.

"You'll wear paste," Sonia said.

"But people will know."

"No, they won't," Sonia said. "I've got some of Gema's

pieces."

"You?" Nina said. "You have paste?"

Sonia shrugged. "Yes, Nina...even I have paste."

"But why?" she asked. "Mr. Jaffrey's done extremely well."

Sonia didn't answer.

"How am I going to get the rest?"

"I wish I had the Barodan necklace," Nina said. "It would solve all our problems...set us up for life."

"Ladies..." Sonia got up and paced before stopping in front of the floor-length mirror to adjust her saree. "There may be a way."

"What? To get the Barodan?"

"Yes...why not."

"Are you mad?" Nina said. "And how do you propose to do that?"

"Exactly!" Rupa interrupted. "The necklace is going to be on Priya Chopra's neck in front of 200 people."

"I'm not suggesting we take it that night," Sonia said. "I suggest we go back the night after."

"Wait a minute, Sonia," Nina stopped her. "This is a bit much...we're sure to get caught."

"We won't," Sonia replied. "Who would suspect three middle-aged society matrons?"

"I don't know..." Rupa wrung her hands even more tightly.

"Why are the two of you shaking your heads?" Sonia said. "Both of you need the money."

"What about you?"

"Quid pro quo," Sonia said. "JJ Singh cheated me out of the Indore Pears he sold to Mr. Jaffrey and stole them back...besides you're my friends."

"So...you want to become a thief out of friendship?"

"Why not?"

"That's the stupidest reason I've ever heard for becoming a criminal!" Rupa exclaimed.

"Frankly, I wouldn't mind having a little nest egg of my own...something in Goa that I can rent out and have my own income."

"But Sonia...you...?" Rupa said. "You have a large allowance."

"It's better to be prepared...and now, having seen what's happening to Nina," she gestured with her chin, "it's good to be independent."

"I never thought I would hear you say so, Mrs. Sonia," Nina said.

"Still...becoming a thief just because you're bored is a bit much..."

"Shut up, Mrs. Rupa."

*

It was late in the evening and Indi and Gema were in Gema's atelier. The windows were all open and a late breeze sprung up. Outside, an almost full moon lit up the small park in the square below.

"Where's Sabine?" Gema looked up from the Barodan necklace she was finishing polishing.

"She'll be here," Indi had her laptop open and was reviewing the security cameras on JJ's estate, playing around with the angle of the two that were just outside JJ's office.

Moments later, Sabine came barreling through the door.

"Hi Ladies! Sorry I'm late," she said. "I was making last minute changes to the seating chart."

"Sabine," Indi looked up, "I was just thinking, why don't we just lift this at the Lodhi? Create a distraction...?"

"Stop trying to change the plan, Indi," Sabine said. "This isn't like playing bingo.

"What time are you going to the Lodhi...?"

"I'll be there with Hanut at 4."

"The invitation for the reception is for 7," Sabine looked at her notes, "so people will start arriving around 7:30-ish...as you said, Priya will arrive around 8:30 to let the other celebrities get face time with the television cameras and photographers...

"You and Hanut will come with her?"

Indi nodded.

"I will arrive at the Singh compound at 5 with the serving team to set up the tables," Sabine said. "The chef will come around 6.

"Do you have the security set up on your phone?" she asked. "Cameras and all?"

"I'm going to do that now," Indi said. "I just wanted to make sure that you were fine with all the angles."

"Let's look at the blind spot one more time," Sabine went around to look over Indi's shoulder at the screen of her laptop.

"Here it is," Indi showed her. "8 feet from the edge of Priya's table to the edge of the marquee."

"That's perfect.

"Once the necklace comes back to the kitchen, I will put it in the catering truck that will be parked outside.

"And Gema...!" Sabine called out to her. "You will be outside and when you see me put a trolley in the truck, you will go and retrieve the necklace and bring it back here."

Gema looked up and gave her a thumbs-up sign.

"Gema is the getaway driver?" Indi laughed. "She's not going to go very fast in that old Ambassador of hers."

"We don't need her to go fast," Sabine said. "We don't need the attention.

"And Indi, you'll hold on to the fake and pull it out at the right moment and have one of the security guards 'find' it."

Indi smiled and gave the thumbs-up sign.

*

Across town, Rupa and Sonia rang the bell at Nina's door.

"Mrs. Sonia, this is most worrying," Rupa said.

"Mrs. Rupa," Sonia said. "I simply must insist that you get yourself together.

"I'm the one who's going to save your roly-poly backside."

Rupa didn't answer as the door opened and Shanti, the maidservant, stood aside to let the two women in.

"Rupa! Sonia!" Nina smiled when she saw them both.

"Rupa here needs a drink," Sonia said as she air-kissed Nina, "quickly."

"Of course," Nina said, gesturing to Shanti.

"I think she will need more than a martini," Sonia said.

"Rupa?" Nina looked at her.

Rupa wrung her hands, her face contorted with worry.

"For goodness sake, Mrs. Rupa," Sonia said. "we haven't even done anything yet."

"Bring Mrs. Patel a whiskey," Nina said to Shanti. "And martinis for Mrs. Jaffrey and myself."

"I just don't understand how we are going to do this," Rupa walked around the room.

"Rupa," Nina said, "All you're going to do is go into the

downstairs bathroom and stay there until we tell you to come out."

"Where will the two of you be?"

Nina and Sonia looked at one another.

"Here," Nina handed Rupa a glass with some whiskey in it. "Drink this."

"Alright," Sonia drank a sip of her martini. "Let's review."

"I think," Nina said, "that we should wait until after the dinner, when everyone moves to the reception...I hear Shahrukh Khan will begin the festivities with a song and that will lead into dancing."

"He's only the biggest movie star in India," Sonia said. "Everyone will be there to see him."

"So, when everyone is engrossed in whatever he is doing onstage, the three of us will head inside," Nina said. "Rupa will go into the bathroom and, after a few minutes, Sonia and I will go to JJ's office."

"What if someone stops you?"

"If someone stops us, Sonia will pretend to be unwell and I am helping her to a bathroom because you will be in the guest bathroom."

"But why would you be going to JJ's office?"

"There's a bathroom in there," Nina replied. "I used it."

Rupa wrung her hands. "I don't understand.

"What about the safe, Nina?" she asked. "How are we getting into it?"

"Ah!" Nina's eyes gleamed. "I'm going to let you ladies into a little secret."

"Which is...?" Sonia prompted.

"Now...from what I saw the other day," Nina began. "JJ's is

an old Dixon Safe...the kind my grandfather had," she said.

"And you know the combination to the safe?"

"No," Nina went to get a laptop computer. "But I saw this on YouTube."

"We're going to crack JJ Singh's safe watching a YouTube video?" Sonia scoffed.

"No, no, no!" Nina said. "But as I was looking around, I found this short documentary," Nina pulled it up on her screen. "And what it says is that the safes Dixon made between in 1930 and 1932 were constructed with combination locks, but in case someone forgot the combination, or you lost your key, they would send you a new one..."

"So?" Sonia shrugged. "How are we going to get JJ's key?"

"If you let me finish..." Nina said. "My grandfather had several Dixon safes in all his shops...Dixon gave him a master key because it would take too long to send him another key all the way from England if he lost one.

"And I have the master key!" Nina said.

"How do you know it'll open Singh's safe?"

"Because the safe JJ has belonged to my grandfather."

"Wait a minute!" Rupa said. "How do you know?"

"After my grandfather died, my grandmother sold the shops and each one of them had a safe," Nina said. "And one of the properties is where Singh now has his gallery."

"So you think the safe in JJ's house used to at one point be in his gallery?"

Nina nodded. "I assure you his safe belonged to my grandfather. He was the only one in Delhi to have Dixon safes."

"Interesting..." Sonia began to smile. "Where's this key?"

Nina walked to a desk, opened the drawer and pulled out a large old black key. "Here it is!" she raised it up triumphantly.

"But how do we know it will fit?" Rupa asked.

"We will test it the night of the wedding when everyone is engrossed with Priya and all the other celebrities," Nina said. "And go back the night after."

"I think we have a plan," Sonia raised her drink. "Come on Mrs. Rupa..."

"I don't know about this..." Mrs. Rupa whined but raised her glass.

*

JJ poured himself a glass of whiskey and opened the French doors of his office and went out on the patio that led down onto the perfectly manicured lawn. The sun had long dipped behind the trees, the onset of night turning them into dark inky stains on a cobalt blue canvas.

He sat down in one of the large chairs and placed his drink on the small wooden side table next to him.

His cell phone rang.

"Yes?"

"It's Rambo."

JJ didn't reply.

"I'm just checking in."

"About what?" JJ said.

"A small matter of the 50 million dollars you owe me."

"As I have said," JJ said. "I'm working on it."

"Your time is almost up," Rambo said.

"Don't remind me."

"It amuses me to do so."

JJ's nostrils flared in anger.

"Anyhow...good talk, man," Rambo said, a smile in his voice before ringing off.

"Motherfucker!" JJ swore under his breath.

"Boss...?" he heard Rusty's voice in his office

"I'm outside," he called out in reply.

"I came to see if you needed anything," Rusty came and stood in front of JJ.

"Sit down," JJ said.

"Sir?"

"I said 'sit down,' Rusty," JJ repeated.

Rusty sank down in the chair across from JJ.

"Would you like a drink?"

"No, thank you, sir," Rusty shook his head.

JJ took a long, deliberate sip of his whiskey.

"Is the plan all set?"

"Yes," Rusty replied. "After the event...after the necklace is returned, the safe will be robbed...we will immediately file the police report and insurance claim...and a couple of days later, the police will be tipped off as we agreed."

JJ put the tips of his fingers together, his eyebrows knitted together as he thought.

"Make sure you keep a close eye on the guests..."

"Very good."

"And Rusty," JJ said. "Don't let that necklace out of your sight."

"I won't, sir," Rusty promised.

"Rusty...Sabine is very, very good."

*

The day of the party dawned breezy and cool with a touch

of balminess that reminded you that you were still in Delhi.

Rusty got out of the car in the Gallery driveway. He looked at his watch. It was almost two o'clock. He went inside and made his way down the marble stairs to the vault.

"Is Mohan here?" he asked one of the two burly security guards who stood in front of the golden grill beyond which was the door to the vault.

"He's inside the vault," the man replied.

"Ah! There you are Rusty," Mr. Mohan, a diminutive man with short, cropped curly grey hair, and a small, pinched face, wearing a navy blue blazer, white shirt and a red and navy striped tie came out carrying a navy velvet box under his arm.

He set it down on a wooden desk and sat down in a chair, cracking his knuckles before opening it.

"Mohan," Rusty rolled his eyes. "I don't have all day."

Mohan looked at him over his small, silver-framed glasses. "Don't rush me, Rusty," he said haughtily in a voice that was quite high-pitched. "Do you have any idea how much this necklace is worth?"

"I do," Rusty replied. "Can we please just get going?"

"Do you know the problems I have had with this necklace?"

"Why?"

Mohan began wiping his glasses with a handkerchief. "A necklace that is such a seminal piece from that era...the last piece made by Jacques Richemont before he died...one of the most important pieces from the Barodan Collection..."

Rusty sighed and crossed his arms over his chest, leaning against a column while Mohan put his glasses back on, adjusting them on his nose in a very precise way.

"Do you know how hard it was to value the necklace and

then get it insured?"

Rusty shrugged.

"It's worth over 50 million dollars," Mohan pulled out his jeweler's loop. "And if I were JJ, I would have gotten it its own dedicated security team," he looked Rusty up and down, his small, thin nose twitching like a beaver's.

"All you got, though, is me," Rusty said. "Now..." Rusty stood up and began pacing. "Can we get this moving?"

Mohan sniffed, rolled his head around and stretched his arms as though he were an athlete and finally put the loop to his eye and bent over the necklace.

Rusty rolled his eyes again as Mohan began, letting out murmurs of awe and squeals of glee as he painstakingly went over every stone in the necklace.

"For the love of Ganesh, Mohan!" Rusty finally exploded. "Are you done?"

Mohan put his hand up and his body tensed.

"Look, I really need to get this to the Lodhi."

Mohan didn't reply.

"Mohan!"

Mohan kept his hand in the air.

"Mohan!" Rusty approached the desk.

Finally, he looked up and took off his glasses.

"Take it," he sighed and sat back.

Rusty placed the necklace in the box, tucked it under his arm and ran up the stairs, taking them two at a time.

"Let's go," he jumped into the passenger seat. "We're late, so let's get a move on."

The Range Rover, with two uniformed security guards in the

back seat, careened through the busy Delhi streets, with the driver taking a few short cuts down alleys and back roads until they got to Humayun's Tomb and the Lodi Gardens in the heart of the area known as Lutyens Delhi, finally pulling into the driveway of the Lodhi Hotel.

*

Laden down with garment bags and two black canvas duffel bags strapped across her, Indi followed Hanut into Priya's suite.

"Darling!" Hanut said effusively throwing his arms open.

Priya was sitting in a tall director's chair wearing a bright pink Chinese silk dressing gown, her face turned towards the makeup artist who was painting her full lips a bright red, a glass of champagne on the dressing table.

"What do you think?" she mumbled without looking at them

"Think?" Hanut said as Indi put down her load, hanging the garment bags on a rolling clothing rack that stood next to the French window that led to the private pool.

"The lipstick, *yaar*?" Priya drawled. "Too much?"

Hanut walked around her, his index finger on his chin, looking at her from all angles.

"Hanut...it's not that hard," Priya rolled her eyes. "What do you think, Indi?"

Indi came over. "It's nice, but I think something more neutral, since your eyes are so smokey."

"Let's change it," Priya looked at the makeup artist.

Hanut glared at Indi who shrugged.

There was a knock on the door.

"Come in," Priya called.

"It's here," Priya's young assistant announced.

"Ah!" Priya jumped out of the canvas chair just as Rusty

came in, followed by the two guards who had been in the car with him.

"Finally!" Hanut said and went and sat on the sofa with Priya.

"You've never seen it...?" Indi stood next to Priya.

"No," she looked up.

"It's quite something," Indi said as Rusty placed the large titanium case on the coffee table and opened it with a key that was attached to his wrist.

Priya adjusted her dressing gown and sat up, a smile on her lips.

Rusty opened the box.

Priya's eyes widened and her mouth fell open as she stared at the necklace for several seconds. "Oh my God!" she finally uttered. "This is...this is..." she ran her fingers over the stones. "I am speechless..."

"I think we should try it on," Indi said. "May I?" she asked Rusty as Priya giggled and went over to the mirror.

"All yours..." Rusty replied, "...for today."

"I hope it fits," Indi said.

"There's always that jeweler friend of yours...the one in Sundar Nagar," Hanut said.

"Who?"

"I can't remember her name...Ginnie something or the other?"

"Gema!" Indi said.

"You should meet this woman, Priya," Hanut said. "She makes the most incredible fakes."

Priya didn't respond, instead got up and walked over to the dressing table, whilst Indi lifted the necklace out of the velvet case and placed it around her neck.

"Oooh!" she shivered.

"What do you think, Hanut?" Indi said.

"It's perfect."

"We should try it with the choli to make sure there are no adjustments," Indi said. "Those emeralds and that tear drop diamond on the end has to sit perfectly."

"Wow...I don't think I've ever worn anything like this."

"Six pounds of diamonds and emeralds, darling," Hanut said.

"Let's take it off and put on the outfit," Indi suggested, pulling at the clasp, but it wouldn't give.

"Ah..." Rusty walked over. "You can't do that.

"The clasp was replaced," Rusty came forward. "This piece now has fingerprint recognition," he placed his thumb on the clasp and pulled the hook out of the flat metal piece. "Only myself or Mr. Singh can take it off."

"Like an iphone?"

"Something like that."

"That's very clever," Indi smiled tightly. "We will be right back once Priya is dressed."

"And of course, I will be with Miss Priya all night," Rusty added. "I will go everywhere with her."

"Everywhere?" Hanut wrinkled his nose. "Darling..." he turned to Priya. "You're going to have a bodyguard."

"And I deserve it!" Priya flung her mane back and flamboyantly sashayed through the door into another room.

*

The Singh compound was a beehive of activity. Gardeners were trimming and pruning, while the garden was being turned into a nightclub. A very large white marquee with poles covered with flowing chiffon and garlands of white jasmine flowers and green magnolia leaves extended from the kitchen down to the swimming pool. Tables were being arranged, chairs were carried in and the servers were beginning to dress them with crisp, white tablecloths. Under another marquee, past the swimming pool, workers were putting down a dance floor around which, white sofas were arranged, with side tables, coffee tables and ice buckets for champagne. There was a full bar that a barman was starting to arrange and a stage for the band.

Sabine, carrying a clipboard, was walking around supervising the servers as they began putting down each setting and the correct glasses.

"Hey you!" she pointed to one of the younger servers. "Be careful with those glasses...they're crystal, not plastic.

"And you!" she walked up to a table and adjusted a knife and a fork. "How many times have I had to say one inch from the edge and this fork an inch and a half away from the plate?"

"Sorry, miss," the young man replied and went around fixing all the cutlery as Sabine watched.

Her cell phone buzzed with an incoming text.

'We're fucked.'

She frowned.

'Why?'

'The clasp.'

'What about it?' she replied quickly.

'The clasp has fingerprint technology embedded,' Indi replied. 'It can only be opened by JJ or his security guy, Rusty.'

Sabine took a deep breath and let it out slowly.

'Can you talk?'

'No,' came Indi's response. 'I'm in Priya's room with Hanut.'

'What finger is it of Rusty's?'

'Thumb.'

Sabine put her cellphone back into her pocket. Just then, she saw JJ come out onto the patio. She quickly fished out a pair of large black framed glasses that she put on and walked towards him, stopping a few feet away, pretending to inspect one of the tables, adjusting the floral centerpiece by a couple of inches.

From the corner of her eye, she watched him put his hands on his hips, looking around as he took in the transformation of the grounds.

"It's warm," she heard him say to someone as she sent a message. 'Text JJ please.'

"Can you get me something cold to drink?" JJ said to his butler.

Sabine watched him come out with a glass of water on a small valet tray.

JJ took it and sat down on one of the stone steps that led from the patio to the garden. He pulled his sunglasses out of his breast pocket and took a long sip of the water in his glass and put it down sighing deeply.

Suddenly his cellphone buzzed. He reached for it and took off his sunglasses. He snorted and put the phone back in his breast pocket, asking for another glass of water.

'Text him again,' Sabine wrote. 'Provoke him.'

Just as JJ took the second glass of water his cellphone buzzed again.

"You're such an asshole, Rambo!" he shook his head.

This time, he used the index finger of his right hand and responded to the text, leaving his glass on the small tray and walked back into the house.

Sabine smiled. She quickly walked over. "What is this doing here?" she said loudly so people could hear and picked up the tray with the glass and walked back through the kitchen and out to the truck.

"It's hot isn't it?" she smiled at one of the security guards who watched her coming out carrying a glass.

"Yes," he smiled.

"I'll be right back...I forgot something in the truck."

The guard nodded.

Once in the truck, Sabine opened a black backpack and pulled out some powder and a sheet of clear plastic.

She dusted some of the powder on the glass before placing a small piece of the plastic that crackled as she pressed it down on the glass. She peeled it off and looked at it closely with a magnifying glass that she also pulled out of her backpack. She pursed her lips and frowned. Because of the way JJ had held the glass, it was an almost full print, which could or could not work. She reached for her cell phone.

'Can you get Rusty's thumb print,' she texted.

'What?' came Indi's response. 'How?'

'Just do it.'

*

"Let's fit the lehnga first," Hanut said as Priya stood in front of the full length mirror wearing a long silk petticoat and a cropped t-shirt.

Indi took the long skirt with the train from the back of the sofa on which it lay and helped Priya on with it.

"Beautiful! Just beautiful!" Hanut effused.

"Your creation or me?" Priya said tartly as she took a sip of champagne.

Indi, standing behind Priya, adjusting the zip, stifled an unwitting giggle.

"Now the top," Hanut ignored Priya.

"It's tiny."

"It's meant to show off your waist."

Priya took off her t-shirt and Indi held out the top and Priya put her arms into it. Made out of chiffon and lined with silk, it was shaped like a bikini top to showcase Priya's ample bosom with thin velvet straps lined with diamonds.

"Hanut, light a cigarette for me," Priya said.

"It feels tight," Priya squirmed and wiggled about

"Here, let me do something," Indi said going behind her.

"Darling...it has to be a little tight," Hanut said. "Just look at that figure of yours."

"Are you sure I don't look fat?"

"Don't be silly...you've been hitting the gym, haven't you?"

"What are you doing back there, Indi?" Hanut said.

"How's that?" Indi popped back up and quickly zipped up the pouch around her waist.

"Better."

An hour later, Priya was ready, with no less than twenty yards of heavily embroidered material draped around her and behind her, and the three of them walked out of the bedroom back into the living room where Rusty was waiting.

Just as they were about to leave,

"There's something in this *choli* that's really uncomfortable," she said as Rusty put the necklace back on her. "It's digging into me."

"It's a thin whalebone like in a bra," Indi explained, "it's meant to give that very feminine, balconette shape."

From the corner of her eye, she glanced at Rusty. He looked too stoic. Good! He was embarrassed.

Priya wiggled around.

"Should we take it out?" Indi said.

"But that will spoil the shape of the bustline!" Hanut said.

"I have an idea," Indi jumped and reached into the small pouch she carried around her waist and pulled out a roll and put it on the coffee table.

"Should we go back into the bedroom?" Hanut sidled his eyes towards Rusty. "For privacy?"

"This is going to take a minute," Indi said hurriedly. "Hanut...you hold up the veil..." she bent down on one knee and reached up and pulled out the extra whalebone she had placed there when she put the *choli* on Priya.

"Oh!" Priya sighed with relief. "That's much better."

"Now..." Indi appeared from under the fabric pretending to look around. "Ah! Rusty! Can you pull off a couple of pieces of that tape for me," she pointed to the coffee table.

"Who? Me?"

"Of course, you!" Indi said. "There's no one else."

"Where is Miss Priya's assistant?" he looked around.

"Rusty, please!" Indi implored him. "We don't have much time.

"Give me a couple of pieces!" she urged.

Rusty gingerly picked up the roll of tape.

"Oh, come on!" Indi said.

He pulled at it with his nail and tore off a piece, holding it squarely on his thumb. "What is this?" he looked at it. "This is sticky on both sides.

"It's double-sided tape," Indi said. "We all use it when you can't wear a bra," she added.

Rusty looked away.

"It looks great and it's so comfy," she said and disappeared back under Priya's veil to fix the top. "And it keeps the breasts in place.

"A couple more pieces, please," she held out her hand and Rusty handed her a piece of tape with the perfect thumbprint.

Indi smiled. "Almost done here," she added carefully placing it into a small box and back into her pouch.

"I think we're good now," she emerged from under the yards of fabric that swathed Priya. "How does that feel?"

Priya nodded.

"Good," Rusty led the way. "Let's go.

"Bring the car to the front," he said into the small mike he had in his sleeve. "Is Randy in the car?"

In the elevator, Indi's cellphone buzzed.

'Did you get it?'

She replied with the thumbs-up emoji.

Chapter 7

The red-carpeted driveway of the Singh farmhouse was packed on both sides with photographers, journalists, television cameramen and reporters, corralled by the short hedges and security guards. Guests were dropped off at the gate and walked up to the house, smiling and posing for photos, some of the stars stopping to grant an interview.

"ETA 30 seconds," Rusty said into his mike.

The Range Rover pulled up in front of the gate. Rusty jumped out of the passenger seat and opened the door.

Priya had no sooner put a foot out of the car when the throng erupted. Cameras flashed, cameramen adjusted their lights on Priya and her husband, and the paparazzi began screaming their names, all of them hoping for the perfect shot.

Indi jumped out quickly adjusting the train of the veil while Priya graced the cameras with her million-dollar smile as she and her husband walked slowly along the red carpet, with Rusty behind them.

At the top of the driveway,

"Hello Priya...so good to see you...Tarek from Entertain India. "

"Oh! Tarek," Priya walked up to him.

"My dear," he said, holding her hands in his. "You look like a million bucks...."

"You'll have to add about 49 million to that number..."

"Is that the Barodan?" Tarek asked, holding his mike out for

Priya to answer.

Priya coyly ran her hands over her neck and décolleté. "Yes..." she batted her eyelashes.

"I don't actually have the words to describe it," he said. "Do you feel like a Maharani wearing it?"

"It's magical," Priya giggled.

"Here it is after disappearing for some 70 years..."

"What a wonderful coincidence that JJ Singh recently bought it."

"How on earth did you get him to agree to let you wear it?"

"I don't actually remember how it came about," Priya began to say.

"And there you are!" JJ Singh came down the few steps to where Priya and Randy were being interviewed.

"Mr. Singh!" Tarek said. "When did you acquire this necklace?"

"I've had it for some time," JJ replied.

"It's amazing," Tarek said into the microphone. "No one knew you had it.

"What made you pull it out of your safe tonight?" he held the microphone out to JJ.

JJ thought for a moment and then,

"She did..." he smiled at Priya.

"But Mr. Singh..." Tarek said and a couple of other journalists chimed in.

"And if you will excuse us please," JJ said, "I must get Priya and Randy to their guests," he linked his arms in theirs and led them away as the camera bulbs flashed again and another roar went up from photographers all vying for a front-page shot.

Inside,

"Rusty, where can I keep these two duffel bags?" Indi asked.

"Mr. Singh's office," he said. "Aditya, Mr. Singh's butler here will show you where it is.

"I have to follow the necklace..."

"And is that where Priya can freshen up?"

"Yes, I arranged it with Mr. Singh."

Indi nodded and followed the man who took the duffel bags and led her down a corridor.

"Here you are, Miss Kumar," he said politely and when he went through a doorway, Indi quickly took in the room. The floor to ceiling doors gave out onto the patio and the dinner marquee beyond.

"This is the dressing room," she heard him say. "And the bathroom is just through there," he continued.

"Thank you," Indi said taking a few quick steps to the dressing room door. "Can I use the bathroom quickly before I go back out?"

"I'll wait for you outside," he said politely.

Indi closed the door to the dressing room. There was no door or window.

She went through another door to a bathroom. There was a window here. She unlocked it and pushed it open, but it was one of those tilting windows that didn't open all the way, only a sliver.

Looking at herself in the mirror, Indi turned on a small earphone and placed it carefully in her ear, covering it with her hair, which made it completely invisible.

"Sabine, can you hear me?" she whispered.

"Yes."

"I'm on the property," she added. "Priya has arrived."

"Yes...I see her coming out now," Sabine replied and Indi heard applause break out outside and people yelling their congratulations over the music that was playing.

"Everything is in place," Sabine said. "We're a go."

Indi quickly dabbed on some lipstick, flushed the toilet to make some noise and walked back out to where the butler was discreetly standing near the door.

"Thank you," Indi said.

"I'll show you out."

"Why don't we just go through those doors?" Indi pointed to the French doors.

"They're locked," he said. "This is Mr. Singh's private office."

"But isn't this the area Priya can use if she needs to freshen up?"

"If she needs it, Rusty will show her in."

*

"We're late!" Rupa said looking at her watch as their car turned off the main highway onto the smaller streets that led to the Singh compound.

"*Oh ho*, Mrs. Rupa," Sonia said from the passenger seat in the front. "That's the third time you've said it."

"But we're going to arrive after the bride and groom."

"Have you forgotten that this is India? Everyone is always late."

"Yes..." Rupa began to retort. "But given what we are going to do..."

"Do shut up, Mrs. Rupa!" Sonia cut her off and Nina glared at her, indicating that she should not say anything in front of the driver.

"Neither one of you has said anything about my hair," Rupa whined, looking into her compact.

"You look like your mother," Sonia said sharply.

"What does that mean?" Rupa was immediately concerned.

"It's very old world."

"And you think those beachy waves of yours are modern?"

"Come on you two!" Nina jumped in before the situation escalated. "Your updo looks lovely Rupa and Sonia...the wavy look is very becoming."

"Humph," Rupa snorted.

There were a few moments of silence as the car swerved to avoid a couple of potholes, but bounced through one the driver didn't see.

"Sorry, *begum sahiba*," he apologized.

"Ufff! I just lost two inches off my chest," Rupa said.

Before Sonia could make any more acerbic remarks,

"Given all the money JJ has, you would think he would fix the road," Nina remarked.

Rupa nodded.

"You know ladies,' Nina gazed out the window, "this is the first big society event I'm going to without Arun."

"Yes, it's so sad..." Rupa leaned over and squeezed Nina's arm.

"Not sad at all," Sonia piped in from the front seat. "Arun Singh doesn't deserve you, Nina...

"Running off with your best friend? Who does that?"

Rupa sniffed. "There is something called 'forgiveness,' Mrs. Sonia."

"It doesn't apply to a man who cheats," Sonia said.

"Have you actually signed the papers?" Rupa asked.

Nina shook her head. "Not yet."

"Has he?" Sonia asked.

Nina nodded.

"What the hell are you waiting for?"

"I'll sign them," Nina said with resolve.

"Frankly, it's better that it's just the three of us," Sonia said. "We won't be bogged down with questions as to what we're doing or where we are going."

"How did you avoid Samir coming to this?" Nina asked Sonia.

"I just told him I was going with the two of you," Sonia wobbled her head.

"And he didn't make a fuss?" Rupa said.

"Mrs. Rupa," Sonia shook her head. "How many times do I have to remind you that you have to tell your husband what to do...it's not up to him to decide."

"What did you tell Feroze?" Nina asked Rupa.

"I didn't have to say anything," Rupa said. "He said he wasn't feeling well."

"That's the oldest trick in the book," Sonia snickered.

"Why?" Rupa's forehead crinkled. "Do you think he's lying?"

"I heard Samir talking to him and they were making plans to go play billiards and cards at the club and have dinner there."

"That Feroze...!" Rupa exclaimed. "Wait until I get a hold of him!"

"All he'll do is say that he was feeling slightly better and the boys came to pick him up..."

"Oh!" Rupa said wide-eyed.

"We're almost there," Nina said as the car turned the corner.

"My goodness!" Rupa exclaimed. "Look at all that press...and the lights."

"It is the party of the year," Nina said, as the driver stopped at the red carpet and three security men opened the front and back doors.

"Oh!" Rupa shielded her eyes at the glare of flashes and television cameras.

"Just one moment please, ladies," a woman holding a clipboard said. "We're running just a bit behind...Priya and Randy just arrived."

"What does that mean?" Sonia said haughtily.

"It'll be just a couple of minutes," the assistant said. "We just have to give the photographers ample time with all the arrivals, and we got a bit behind when Priya and Randy walked the carpet and right after them was Aishwariya and Abhishek.

"In the meantime, may I have your names?"

"Rupa Patel."

"Sonia Jaffrey."

"Nina Singh."

The woman went down her list. "Ah yes, there you all are..." she looked up at them. "Please go in.

"Enjoy the evening."

The three women smiled and together slowly walked up the red-carpeted driveway. A couple of flashbulbs went off with some of the photographers looking at their arrivals sheet to see who they were.

They got to the end and were walking into the main hall of the house when,

"Shouldn't we interview her?" Nina heard a male voice.

"Isn't she the wife of Arun Singh?"

"Who the hell is Arun Singh, *yaar*?"

"He came in earlier, remember? The one who told us he was the Maharajah of Barodan and that we should take his picture..."

"What Maharajah? He doesn't have a dime."

"But if this is his wife..." said another photographer, "then, who was the other woman?"

Nina stopped for a moment, stuck her chin in the air and walked on.

*

Inside, the round hallway, lit with large pillar candles, was filled with people looking at the works of art that hung on the walls brought in from the gallery especially for the evening, whilst an army of waiters, dressed in black pants and bandhgala jackets floated through the crowd carrying silver trays with crystal glasses brimming with champagne, others with caviar and all kinds of rich canapes.

"My goodness!" Rupa put a hand to her chest. "There's Shahrukh Khan! And Abhishek Bacchan...and look Kareena Kapoor...oh my! She's much shorter than she looks in the movies."

"Now, Rupa," Nina took her right arm and Sonia grabbed the left. "Concentrate," she added as they guided her around.

"Look," Nina pointed her chin in the direction of a door. "That is the guest bathroom..."

"How strange," Rupa replied. "Only one bathroom for 200 people and staff?"

"There are more, I am sure," Nina said. "But that is the one that you are going to lock yourself into for about 20 minutes."

Rupa sighed worriedly. "Ladies, I don't know..."

"It's too late to back out, Mrs. Rupa," Sonia pinched her.

"Oww!" she said, rubbing the top of her arm.

"I'm sure that if we went to jail, we would get preferential treatment."

"Shut up, Sonia," Nina said. "Can't you see she's scared enough already?"

They heard a tinkling of a bell.

"Ladies, if you would start moving towards the marquee," a waiter said politely, holding out a tray for their glasses of champagne. "Dinner will be served shortly."

"Can I take my champagne?" Rupa clutched her glass to her chest.

"Of course," the young man replied, bowing slightly, "but there is plenty at the table."

"I wouldn't mind a bit more of that caviar," Rupa looked greedily at the tray that went by. The waiter obliged and Rupa quickly put two blinis in her mouth. "Just delicious," she managed to say.

Sonia rolled her eyes. "Honestly, Mrs. Rupa, sometimes you say and do the stupidest things.

"No one would believe you're part of Delhi high society."

"Let's get to the table," Nina guided Rupa by the elbow towards the marquee.

As they took the couple of steps down onto the lawn,

"Nina!" JJ Singh raised his hand in salutation when he saw her. "And Mrs. Jaffrey and Mrs. Patel," he bowed slightly. "The grandes dames of Delhi... you honour my home with your presence."

"How nice to see you JJ," Nina replied and the two other women smiled.

"What a beautiful home you have," Rupa said.

"It's too bad you don't have anyone to share this with," Sonia said.

JJ raised a questioning eyebrow.

"I meant, a wife."

"Ah!" JJ laughed. "No luck in that department."

"I'm sure we can find you the perfect *sardarni*," Rupa said.

"Please ignore Mrs. Rupa, Singh *Sahib*," Nina said.

"Yes," Sonia added haughtily, "we are doyennes of Delhi Society, not matchmakers," she poked Rupa in the ribs with her elbow.

"Come ladies, let us find where we are sitting."

"Actually," JJ opened his arms, "you're all sitting at my table."

"Your table?" Rupa gasped.

"Why aren't you sitting with Priya and Randy?"

"The tables are adjacent," JJ said. "I'm only a couple of feet away."

"Oh!"

"Excuse me!" JJ flagged down a woman with short dark-hair who happened to be walking by.

It was Sabine.

"Sir?"

"Can you show these ladies to my table?" JJ said.

"Of course...this way please, ladies," the woman said and walked ahead of them.

"Now what?" Rupa whispered. "We are sitting at his table. How did that happen? Why?"

"Stay calm please, Mrs. Rupa," Sonia elbowed her sharply.

"Actually, it's quite shrewd of him."

"Agreed," Nina added. "JJ needs us to give him legitimacy in Delhi society.

"After all, we are still considered 'old money,' even though we don't have any."

*

As soon as she'd seated the three women, Sabine quickly walked away from the table and walked back towards the kitchen.

"All set?" she whispered.

"Yes, I am walking towards the table," Indi replied. "Rusty is with me."

"I see you...stand by."

"JJ hasn't recognized you, has he?"

"No," Sabine whispered. "You?"

"I haven't seen him yet."

Sabine pretended to be looking down at her clipboard as she walked by Indi, bumping into her.

"Oh!" she said. "I am so sorry," she apologized and walked on.

Indi slipped the small plastic bag Sabine had handed her into the pocket of the slim pants she wore.

"What was that?" Rusty looked back.

"What? That?" Indi looked perplexed. "Nothing," she answered her own question.

*

Meanwhile Sabine entered the kitchen that was whirring like a well-oiled machine. "We're at 20 percent special meals tonight," she said to the sous-chef.

He nodded.

"Come on people," she said authoritatively. "Let's go. Fire appetizers! ...Where's the gluten-free and the lactose-free for Table 1?"

*

"Hello everyone!" Priya walked over to a table in the middle of the marquee where Hanut was already seated, rising briefly as she sat down next to him.

"It's so good to see you all..." she addressed the table as Indi arranged her train behind her and stood off to the side with Rusty.

"You look beautiful Priya!" Katrina Kaif, another Bollywood star said to her.

"Oh my God! Thank you!" Priya said. "So do you," she replied taking a sip of the champagne that had just been poured for her.

"Cheers!" she raised her glass.

"Congrats Priya!"

As the conversation around the table got going, a very well-dressed man, carrying a black cane appeared at the top of the patio steps and seconds later, a couple of security guards came running across and put their hands on his arms.

"What's going on over there?" Indi said to Rusty.

"I'll be right back," Rusty said.

*

"Take your hands off me, please," the man said calmly as Rusty approached.

"Sir, your name was not on the list," one of the guards said.

"I was invited," the man adjusted the sleeves of his jacket.

"Your name please, sir," Rusty said, nodding at the guards

who went back through the house towards the front.

"And who are you?" the man asked.

"Rusty Khan," Rusty replied. "Mr. Singh's head of security...now your name please?"

"Rambo Singh."

"What the hell are you doing here?" JJ appeared behind Rusty.

"I'm here for the party," Rambo replied, pulling a cigar case out of his breast pocket.

"This is a private party," JJ said.

"I know."

"And that means, I have every right to kick you out, asshole."

"But I was invited," Rambo ran a cigar under his nose, inhaling the scent of the tobacco.

"Oh yeah?" JJ said. "By whom?"

"By the bride," Rambo said. "Here's my invitation," he pulled out a thick white card that had a note written on it: 'Dearest Rambo, can't wait to see you at the reception, love Priya and Randy.'

"I'm sure your office screwed up," Rambo smiled. "As usual."

JJ's nostrils flared and he took an angry step towards Rambo.

"Or maybe Miss Priya forgot to tell us," Rusty said, putting a hand on JJ's arm and pulled him aside.

"What the fuck is he doing here?" JJ said his fists clenched angrily.

"Sir, we don't want to make a scene," Rusty said.

JJ took a deep breath. "No," he hung his head submissively. "You are right.

"Besides, it does suit our purposes that he is here," he said staring meaningfully at JJ. "Do you know what I mean?"

"Alright, alright," JJ conceded. "Put him at a table where I can keep an eye on him."

"I'll put him at your table," Rusty said. "There's an extra seat."

The two men turned to see Rambo walk down the steps and over the lawn to the marquee, waving to Priya who waved back, motioning him to join her.

"Hey! You!" Rusty said to a young fellow carrying a tray. "I need another chair at Table 2, Mr. Singh's table."

"I just put one there, sir," he replied. "My supervisor, Miss Kumar already told me to do it. I'm just going back now with plates and glasses for the gentleman," he held out the tray in his hands.

"How did she know we were going to put him there?"

"I don't know, sir."

"Fine!" Rusty said. "Hurry up!" he added as he saw Rambo sitting down, shaking hands with everyone at JJ's table.

"Who is this supervisor of yours?" Rusty asked the young boy.

"She was just here," the young man said. "Perhaps she went back to the kitchen."

"Alright, alright, get on with it."

*

"What the hell is going on, Indi?" Sabine whispered into the microphone hidden under her shirt collar. "What's the delay."

"I don't know..." Indi replied. "It should have happened by now. I know I snipped the straps halfway."

"Main courses are coming out...the tray stand is in place."

"I see it," Indi said.

"Give it another minute," she added staring at Priya.

"Come on, come on, Priya! Just move around a little," she murmured.

*

"May I have a little more champagne?" Priya asked the waiter.

"Anyhow," she continued addressing the table, "and there we are at JJ's absolutely gorgeous home in Tuscany and we were walking back to the guest house after dinner...we were right by the pool that was beautifully lit, the moon was full and you could hear the crickets and wind in the cypress trees and...suddenly, he grabbed my hand and said 'Let's elope.'"

The whole table sighed.

"That's just so beautiful," Hanut wiped a tear from his eye.

"He'd already proposed in Rome," Priya showed off her ring.

"So romantic..." Katrina Kaif added. "Didn't you start cry-ing?"

For the love of God, Indi rolled her eyes, crossing her arms, careful not to ruin the two fingerprints she had on her thumb and forefinger.

"Not at all," Priya said. "We began laughing and hugging one another and then somehow I tripped and we fell into the pool," and she began moving her arms as she described the moment.

Suddenly, her eyes widened and she sat up straight.

"Are you ok?" Katrina said, concerned.

"Yes, yes," Priya said. "So, there we were," she began again, "and we're in the water and splashing around, fully clothed, making a hell of a racket..." she stopped and wiggled her chest from side to side and suddenly, one thin strap of her choli blouse snapped, followed by the other. Priya's eyes widened with shock as she looked down, quickly clamping her hands on her breasts, trying to keep her composure. She looked up, her eyes darting around the table embarrassed.

*

"Sabine..." Indi whispered. "We're in play."

"Oh my God!" Katrina Kaif's mouth fell open.

The table was silent, everyone staring at Priya, their gazes riveted on her chest.

Hanut quickly put his hands up to cover his mouth and froze as Priya tried desperately to hold up the two ends of the blouse, while she reached for the veil to cover herself up.

"*Jaani*," Randy got up and tried to help, but Indi had arranged the fabric in such a way that he ended up tugging at the free-flowing sleeves of the blouse, making everything worse.

"I'm going to need Singh's office," Indi whispered to Rusty.

"I have to tell Mr. Singh what has happened," Rusty said. "I'll be right back."

Indi nodded and rushed over to Priya, expertly moving the fabric of the veil around, placing it around her shoulders co-cooning Priya in it.

"Here, hold this over your left shoulder with your right hand," Indi whispered and handed some fabric to Priya.

"Are you sure?" Priya said nervously looking around. "What about the blouse?"

"I want you to almost hug yourself with the fabric," Indi said. "Like you're holding a shawl."

Priya nodded. "What about my left hand?"

"Nothing," Indi said. "Now, stand up.

"And smile as we walk," she guided her. "You look great. No one can see anything at all." "You're moving into the blind spot," Indi heard Sabine whisper. "Now, I'm just going to adjust this…" she said pressing down on the clasp with the fingerprint she had on her index finger. The clasp didn't budge. *Shit.* That was the print of JJ's index finger.

"Indi, you're in the blind spot."

"Priya…something is stuck," Indi went behind her and pretended to adjust the fabric at the back of her neck. She pressed down on the clasp with her thumb and suddenly Priya took a step forward, stretching and the necklace fell on the grass at Priya's feet.

In one swoop, Indi went down and scooped it up as Priya continued talking. Rusty's thumbprint had worked.

"Darling…hello! I'm so happy to see you! You look amazing," she said. "Everything looks beautiful, Priya," the person replied, "especially you. We have to catch up."

"Where are you going, Priya?" Shahrukh Khan, the highest paid star in Bollywood, called out. "I haven't even started singing yet."

"I'm starving, Priya…can't we just eat?" someone else laughingly said. "No!" she put a hand up and pointed at the person. "I'll be right back…No dinner until I get back and don't anyone eat my food!"

"We have to go Priya," Indi urged.

"I feel the back of the train tugging."

"Don't move," Indi said and went behind her and looked for what was stuck.

Indi looked around. "It's fine."

"Sorry," Priya looked back and smiled waving to someone.

"You're almost in view of one of the cameras," Sabine said in her ear.

At the edge of the marquee, Indi slipped the necklace between a gold charger plate and a dinner plate on a large round tray that was on a stand.

"What happened?" Rusty re-appeared.

"The straps of her blouse snapped," Indi said. "They were too delicate."

"Shall we?" Priya said.

"I was waiting for you," Indi replied and they walked onto the grass with Indi holding up the train of the veil and the lehnga, and Rusty next to her.

When they reached JJ's office,

"Give us a moment, please, Rusty," Indi said.

"I have to stay with the necklace."

"Can't you see that she's half naked?" Indi said.

"Indi..." Priya said in a quiet voice.

Indi ignored her.

"Look, Rusty, she's going to have to take everything off, so that I can drape everything back on again."

"It's my job to stay with the necklace."

"Indi!" Priya said more forcefully.

"What?" Indi turned on her heel.

Priya let the veil drop from her shoulders, clutching the choli blouse over her breasts.

Rusty's eyes widened. "Where's the necklace?" He walked to the French doors and looked on the patio.

"I don't know," Priya said.

"Oh my God!" Indi's hand went to her mouth. "It must have

fallen off as we walked across the lawn.

"What should we do?"

"You didn't feel it fall off?" Rusty said.

"No," Priya said. "I was a little bit more concerned with the blouse falling off and exposing myself to all of Bollywood."

"You stay here," Rusty said and ran through the French doors.

"I can't believe this," Priya said walking into the dressing room. "How could this happen on my fucking wedding day."

"Have a glass of water," Indi poured her a glass from a crystal jug.

"I don't need water, I need a shot of whiskey.

"This is going to ruin me," Priya cried. "Can you imagine the publicity?"

"It won't..." Indi said.

"I don't give a shit about the necklace...I'm worried about having exposed myself."

"Don't be...you've worn less in your movies."

Priya shot her a look.

"How could the necklace have fallen off? Didn't they replace the clasp with some new thing?"

"Maybe it just gave way."

"But how could it?" Priya clutched the veil around her chest, leaving her shoulders bare. "Didn't they need some kind of special fingerprint?"

"They'll find it.

"In the meantime, let's get you dressed," Indi said evasively. "You can't walk around like this."

"Can you fix the blouse?" Priya took it off.

"I'm not going to fix it."

"What?"

"I have another one," Indi pulled a hanger out of a black duffel bag.

"That's amazing!" Priya exclaimed. "How did you know?"

"Just prepared," Indi shrugged.

*

When she saw Priya step onto the lawn, Sabine, hurried, winding her way around the tables towards the tray stand. Just as she walked by JJ's table,

"Miss!" she heard someone say.

Ignoring the voice, she walked on.

"Miss!" said the sing-song voice a bit more forcefully.

Suddenly, she heard JJ's voice.

"Here...excuse me..."

She turned.

"Can I help you, sir?" she said, bending down but keeping squarely behind his chair so that he could not look at her without getting up and turning around.

"Would you please get us another bottle of champagne?" he asked.

"Of course, sir," Sabine said, inwardly fuming. Damn! She had to get to that tray. Servers were already putting down dinner plates covered with cloches.

Looking around, she saw one of the wine stewards,

"Hey you!" she signaled to him. "What are you doing? You're not paid to stand around?

"Get over to Mr. Singh's table, right now."

"Sorry, Miss Kumar," the man was contrite.

When Sabine arrived at the spot where the tray stand had

stood, she stopped dead in her tracks. The tray was empty, and she saw a server put a plate down in front of JJ.

Shit. Where were the plates on the tray?

The same server was walking back to her.

"Miss Kumar," he bowed slightly and went to pick up the now empty tray.

"Where are the plates that were on this tray?"

"Miss?"

"Where are the plates that were on this tray?" she repeated.

"I just served them."

"You served them?" she said in a low, angry voice. "To whom?"

"To Mr. Singh's table, Miss Kumar," he wobbled his head apologetically.

"You were assigned to Table 3," Sabine said. "What were you doing serving Table 2?"

"I was helping Siddharth."

"And where is Siddharth?"

"He had to go to the bathroom."

"So you decided, on your own," she emphasized, "that you would take over his table? Without checking with me?"

"I just thought the food would get cold..."

"Do you know what a cloche is?" Sabine asked angrily.

The server wobbled his head and smiled embarrassedly.

"Do you?" Sabine shouted.

"You don't...a cloche is the dome on the plate that keeps the food warm."

"Miss Kumar, I am very sorry."

"Who did you serve those plates to?"

"Table 2."

"Yes, but whom?"

"I don't know, Miss Kumar," he said apologetically. "Everyone has food."

Sabine glared at him angrily.

"Miss...am I in trouble?

"Miss, please...I really need this job," the young man pleaded. "My wife is pregnant..."

"Get back to the kitchen," Sabine said, exasperated.

"Please, Miss...I didn't know..."

"Go!" she ordered.

She waited until he'd left.

"Indi, we have a problem," she whispered in her mike, waiting for a reply.

"Indi...?" she said again.

"Where are you? We have a problem..."

She looked over towards JJ's table. Everyone had a plate with a cloche covering it.

Damn! Damn! Damn! She grimaced. Which five got the plates that were on that tray?

*

Rusty ran to JJ's table.

"Sir, we have a problem..." he whispered in his ear.

"Excuse me a moment," JJ said to Nina and turned to Rusty.

"What is it?"

"Sir, the necklace..."

"What's happened to it?"

"It's gone."

"What?" JJ exploded.

"Sir, somewhere between the table and your office, it must

have fallen off."

"Find it before it leaves the premises," JJ ordered. "And keep an eye on Rambo."

Rusty nodded.

"Have you seen Sabine?"

"No, sir."

JJ gestured for him to get on.

"Seal the exits," Rusty said into the microphone and hurried away, back across the garden towards JJ's office.

*

"What is going on, Mrs. Sonia?" Rupa whispered as security guards surrounded the marquee.

"I'm not sure."

"Well, something is happening," she said. "Look at all those security guards."

"First Priya walks out of the dinner and next we have all these guards," Rupa said. "I tell you, Mrs. Sonia, this does not bode well."

"Have another drink, Mrs. Rupa," Sonia filled her glass.

Rupa hiccupped as she downed half a glass of champagne quickly.

"At least we have something to eat," she added. "I was about to faint from hunger."

"I wonder what's for dinner," she was about to lift the gold cloche cover on her plate.

"Biryani," Sonia said. "It's the chef's speciality."

"How do you know?" Rupa looked astonished, taking her hand off the dome.

"Mrs. Rupa," Sonia snorted. "Do you read?"

"Well of course I do!" she said, offended.

"If you did, then you would have read it on the menu that was under the napkin when we first sat down."

"Oh..." Rupa looked embarrassed as she looked around, hoping no one had heard. "I suppose I didn't."

"Mrs. Sonia," she began a few moments later.

"What is it now?" Sonia turned away from the conversation she was having with Nina.

"Why aren't we eating?"

Sonia rolled her eyes. "Because we are waiting for these covers to be taken off."

"Why can't we just take them off?"

"And where are you going to put it?" Sonia said acerbically. "On your head?"

Rupa wobbled her head.

"Mrs. Rupa...this is a formal dinner," Sonia explained. "The covers will be taken off at the same time for everyone."

"Quite theatrical," Rupa remarked.

"Mrs. Rupa...we are Indian," Sonia said. "We love drama...just look at our movies...three hours long and tearjerkers."

"I see..." Rupa said.

"Look how beautiful this crockery is," Rupa said. "And the gold chargers...very tasteful, I must say," she ran a hand around the gold-rimmed plate.

Sonia gave her a wry look.

"My goodness!" Rupa exclaimed.

"Now what's the matter?" Sonia asked.

"Look!" Rupa gestured. "There's Arun Singh."

"What?" Sonia looked around. "Where?"

"Over there..." she inclined her chin. "He's sitting with Bunny."

"I can't believe JJ invited Bunny," Sonia said.

"It's worse that he's sitting with her," Rupa said. "You'd better tell Nina."

"Wait!" Rupa put a hand to her chest. "Mrs. Sonia...he's coming this way," Rupa gasped. "Tell Nina! Hurry!"

*

"Nina..." Sonia turned to her right.

"What is it?"

"Don't look now, but Arun is making his way over to the table."

Nina visibly stiffened. "Is she with him?" she asked.

"No...but she's here."

"This is just awful."

"I know," Sonia squeezed her hand. "How dare JJ invite him to the party...especially since you told him about the divorce?"

"It's going to happen, Sonia," Nina said. "We do move in the same circles."

"He has balls coming to this table...he can see you sitting here."

"It's so typical," Nina said. "He wants people to see him sitting here," she added. "Look at this table...Kareena Kapoor, Ambani, JJ Singh...it's the kind of table Arun would give his right arm to be included in."

"He should go back to where he came from."

"Why don't you say something to JJ?"

"I can't make a fuss, Sonia," Nina said. "Besides, where's he going to sit? The table is full."

Just then, several people got up and a game of musical chairs ensued. Kareena Kapoor's husband excused himself and got up, while Kareena and Mrs. Ambani exchanged seats, with Mrs. Ambani to JJ's right and Kareena between Rambo and Mukesh Ambani, the richest man in India.

*

"JJ!" Nina heard Arun's voice as he approached the table.

*

"Arun...good to see you," JJ shook his hand.

"JJ *yaar*, I was wondering if I could talk to you," Arun said in a low voice.

"Arun...dinner's been served," JJ said. "I'm a bit busy."

"How about later?"

"Arun...if this is about more money."

"JJ!" Someone called out. "How are you, *yaar*?"

"Excuse me, Arun," JJ turned to someone who approached him.

"I'll just wait here for you," Arun looked around embarrassed when he caught Rambo's eye.

"Rambo Singh!" he said. "I didn't even see you...how are you?" he sat down in an empty chair next to him.

"Fine."

"It's been a while hasn't it?" Arun said. "Where are you these days?"

"I live in London now."

"London? Really? Things must be good?"

"Very good."

"Do you still have your hotel business?"

"Yes...I now have several all around Europe and the Middle East and am thinking now about the Far East, perhaps even

North Africa."

"How ambitious!"

"You may as well go big when you can."

"Of course if you have the money, it's easy," Arun said. "You must have a bottomless fund?"

Rambo stared at him stonily.

"How long are you in town?" Arun asked.

"Probably another week or ten days."

"I was wondering...can we meet?" Arun asked. "I have a couple of projects here in Delhi that might be of interest to you."

"What projects?"

"They're excellent real estate deals," Arun said. "I'm a bit short on capital...so...I...uh..."

"I don't know, Arun," Rambo said. "I'm not investing at the moment," he added and turned towards Kareena.

"Ah..." Arun sat back, stretching his legs out, crossing one foot over the other, as he put one hand in his pocket and with the other rubbed his forehead.

"Excuse me, but I think you're in my chair," a good-looking man approached Arun.

"I am sorry," Arun apologized. "I was finishing a conversation with my good friend, Rambo, here," Arun got up. "We haven't seen each other in ages."

"Arun Singh," he held his hand out. "Maharajah of Barodan."

"Arvind Kapoor," the younger man shook his hand.

"I thought perhaps if no one was sitting here, I would join you all for dinner."

Arvind Kapoor smiled.

"Well Rambo...it was great to see you," Arun put a hand on

Rambo's shoulder. Rambo looked at the hand on his shoulder as though it were a fly he was about to swat.

"I'd best be going," Arun said.

As he turned to go, he tripped, lost his balance and fell rather ungracefully, almost taking the dinner plate and cloche with him as he fumbled.

Arvind Kapoor immediately went to help him. "Are you alright?" he said offering his hand to help Arun back up.

"I'm fine, I'm fine," Arun smiled, looking embarrassed about the fall. "Thank you, though," he got to his knees and put one hand on the chair and the other on the table to haul himself back up.

"Don't forget your phone," Arvind Kapoor bent down to retrieve the iphone.

"Thank you," Arun said and put it back in his pocket, patting it. "I'm always losing them."

"You're sure you're alright?" Arvind asked.

"Never better," Arun smiled and walked around the tables back to where he was seated.

*

"What a clown!" Nina remarked. "That man can't put one foot in front of the other without falling...it's like everything else he does."

"Clumsy indeed," Sonia added. "Besides that, why the hell did he have to introduce himself as the Maharajah of Barodan?" Sonia said to Nina.

"Because it makes him feel important," Nina replied. "Especially in a crowd like this where everyone is someone."

"I am getting hungry now," Sonia said. "This biryani smells

exceptionally good.

"Where is Priya?"

"You know actresses," Nina replied. "They're always late."

*

Meantime, Priya and Indi were about to walk out when Indi saw Rusty walking quickly towards them.

Damn! Indi thought. She had the fake necklace in her pocket and needed to be outside to drop it on the lawn and "pretend" to find it.

"Alright, Miss Priya...what happened?"

"I don't know," Priya said. "It could have fallen off outside, in here...I have no idea."

Rusty's ear-piece buzzed.

"Yes," he replied, "shut it down. Create a perimeter and don't let anyone in or out.

"No!" he replied to a question. "No one moves. Not even to go to the bathroom."

"Oh come on!" Priya replied. "Let's not get dramatic. You'll find it."

"Do you know how much the necklace is worth?" Rusty said.

Priya rolled her eyes. "I know...but I think you're making a mountain out of a molehill."

"Can we go back out to the dinner?" Priya asked.

"Not until we've searched everywhere...and everyone."

"This is ridiculous," Priya said. "It'll take hours...and I'm starving."

Suddenly his earpiece buzzed again. "Stay here," he said to Indi and Priya. "I'll be back."

*

"Mr. Singh," Randy bent down to whisper. "We have to

clear the marquee. It must be in here."

"Rusty, are you sure?" JJ whispered back. "Do you know the people who are here?"

"Yes, sir."

"What's the plan?"

"I want to move everyone into the reception marquee, have a team search them there and another team search here and the grounds and a third the staff."

"Bring me a microphone and I will make the announcement," JJ nodded and got up.

He walked over to the other side of the table.

"Do you have anything to do with this?" he bent down, whispering in Rambo's ear.

Rambo didn't answer at first, his gaze inscrutable. He took a deep drag of his cigarette and blew it out.

"With what?" he put his cigarette out in a small silver box he carried.

"I'm asking you again," JJ said. "Did you have anything to do with this?"

"With what?" Rambo repeated.

"Because if you did..."

"Here's the microphone, sir," Rusty said.

"Ladies and Gentlemen," JJ cleared his throat.

Rusty's earpiece buzzed. "We found it."

"Sir," Rusty muted the microphone. "It's found."

"Where?" JJ asked.

"Where?" Rusty asked his team, nodding as he got the answer.

"In the grass outside your office," he told JJ.

"Stay there," Rusty said. "I'm on my way."

"Ladies and Gentlemen," JJ cleared his throat. "...Welcome to this *darbar*..." he smiled.

"Hear, hear!" someone shouted out and the sounds of glasses clinking filled the air.

"Thank you," JJ raised his glass and took a sip of champagne. "I hope no one here is offended by my saying this is a *darbar* because no one here is a maharajah or head of state..."

Nina and Sonia looked at one another and smiled.

"I bet Arun is devastated..."

"...but it is a ceremonial gathering to celebrate Priya and Randy.

"And thank goodness it no longer has any political connotations!"

Everyone laughed.

"Thank you all for coming tonight," he added as servers surrounded the tables. "I hope you are all ready for a fantastic evening.

"I am told Priya is on her way back and I know we are all hungry...so without much further ado...let us begin."

As soon as he sat down, servers who had silently filed in and taken their places behind the guests, lifted the domed covers off the plates in one highly-coordinated gesture.

*

Rusty arrived back at JJ's office where Priya, Indi and one of Rusty's men stood with the necklace in his hand.

"Where exactly was it?" Rusty asked him and the man walked a few feet from the patio onto the lawn and pointed.

"Alright," Rusty said and came back.

Indi took the necklace and put it back on Priya, adjusting her veil and train as she walked regally out the doors towards the marquee.

She quickly tidied up putting everything back into the duffel bag and was about to zip it up when she saw her cellphone in it. Damn! It must have fallen out of her pocket.

She looked at it. There were five messages from Sabine all saying 'Urgent.'

Shit!

She looked up to see Rusty and Priya halfway across the garden.

Just then, another message came in.

'*We have a problem*,' it said.

Indi was about to reply when she saw Rusty looking at her. She put the phone in her pocket and rushed to join him as Priya wound her way back to her seat.

Chapter 8

After dinner, the band began warming up and people moved into the second tent on the far side of the pool, some standing by the bar, most sitting down in the comfortable white sofas around the edge of the dance floor.

Nina, Sonia and Rupa walked over together.

"What should we do?" Rupa asked. "Should we sit?"

"We could," Nina said.

"Don't be silly!" Sonia said. "It will be much more conspicuous when we all decide to get up."

Suddenly, the lights on stage went on and band began playing a few riffs.

"Is everyone ready to dance?" Shahrukh Khan's voice was heard offstage.

A roar went up from the crowd that was now mostly on its feet.

Seconds later, the star appeared on stage and another roar went up, followed by thunderous applause.

Nina looked over to Rupa, nodding imperceptibly.

"I think I would like to powder my nose," Rupa said quite loudly.

"You don't have to scream it," Sonia said. "You're not competing with him," she motioned her chin towards the stage.

"But Nina said that I should say it loudly," Rupa argued.

"God help me," Sonia shook her head.

"I would also like to freshen up," Nina said.

"Shall we all go?" Rupa wobbled her head, enthusiastically.

Sonia rolled her eyes. "Can you not be normal?"

"Let's go," Nina put her hand in Sonia's arm.

They had no sooner taken a few steps when they came face to face with JJ.

"Ladies! Where are you going? Shahrukh has just taken the stage," he pointed.

"Yes..." Nina smiled. "We were just going up to the house. Rupa needs to..." she cleared her throat, "powder her nose."

"There's no need to go all the way there," JJ said. "The guest house is much closer...

"Come, let me get someone to show you," he motioned to a young man, who rushed over.

"Show these ladies please to the guest house," he instructed.

"Thank you, JJ *sahib*," Nina smiled graciously.

"Not at all," he said. "I hope you are enjoying yourselves?"

"Oh immensely!" Rupa smiled broadly.

"Good," he bowed slightly. "Now if you will excuse me..."

"Would you follow me please?" the man said. "It's this way to the guest house."

Just as they had taken a few steps,

"Oh!" Nina stopped. "You know, I just remembered something.

"I've left something in the car," she announced.

"What is it?" Rupa asked.

"I'm just going to go and get it."

"Why don't you call your driver and have him bring it?" Rupa said.

Nina glared at her.

"It's my cellphone," she said hesitatingly. "I left it in the car, so I can't call him."

"We can send someone," the man who accompanied them said.

"No, no," Nina said quickly. "You go ahead. I'll be right back."

"How could she have left her cellphone in the car?" Rupa said as Nina walked away.

"Oh, Mrs. Rupa..." Sonia sighed. "Sometimes I despair of you." She pushed her in the direction of the guest house.

*

"I'll be right back," Indi whispered to Rusty, shortly after Shahrukh took to the stage.

"Where are you going?"

"I need to eat something."

"What if something happens to her outfit?"

"Nothing will."

"Alright," he nodded, "but don't be long."

Indi rushed across towards the kitchen, pulling her cellphone out.

'*Where are you?*' she texted Sabine.

'*In the kitchen...come to the den next to the library. The next door in the hallway.*'

Indi walked into the hallway off the reception hall. It was empty. She headed towards the den and knocked softly. The door opened and she slipped in. Dark, apart from the dimmed lights from the sconces, it was a large room that also gave out onto the garden, this one with a floor to ceiling arched window and comfortable sofas and chairs arranged in front of a large panel that, when opened, revealed a very large television screen.

"Sabine?"

"I'm here," she came out of the shadows.

"What the hell happened?" Indi asked.

"All it took was one minute and one trigger-happy server," Sabine said. "As I was heading to the tray, JJ stopped me and asked for more champagne.

"The tray was right there...I was going to have it picked up by one of the servers and brought back to the kitchen...but the server served the plates."

"Shit," Indi paced around the small room. "To whom?"

"Any one at JJ's table."

"I thought you'd choreographed that."

"I had."

"Now what?"

Sabine took a deep breath and let it out slowly. "I honestly don't know."

"Do you think we can get it back?"

"God knows who has it," Sabine ran her hands over her face. "There were 9 people at JJ's table."

"Who were they?" Indi came over to look at the list on Sabine's clipboard.

"JJ, Rambo Singh, the three society doyennes, Nina Singh, Sonia Jaffrey and Rupa Patel, Kareena Kapoor, the actress and her husband, and Mukesh Ambani and his wife.

"One of them ate their biryani with a 50 million dollar necklace hidden under their plate...that's expensive rice.

"Wait! Did you check the plates when they were cleared?"

"Of course," Sabine said.

"And nothing?"

Sabine shook her head. "One of them has it."

Suddenly, they heard a noise in the library next door.

Sabine put a finger to her lips and went to the sliding door that separated the two rooms, opening it a sliver.

"Who is it?" Indi whispered standing behind her.

"Someone just came into JJ's office."

"Who is it?"

"I don't know...it's a woman...she's wearing a sari...her back is to me..."

"What?" Indi said.

"I can't see her face...but she's dressed like she could be a guest."

"What's one of the guests doing in there?"

"I don't know...but we are going to find out," Sabine said. "You stay here."

Outside, the Shahrukh Khan concert was in full swing, loud and raucous with big bangs from all the theatrics and fireworks that accompanied his shows.

Masked by it, Sabine was able to slide open one of the doors and crawl into the library, moving quickly in the darkened room to hide behind one of the large sofas. The only light was the ambient light from the marquees outside, but it wasn't much as they had been lowered for the concert.

Sabine peeked her head around the arm of the sofa. There indeed was a woman, in what looked like an emerald green sari with a heavily embroidered gold border and a gold sari blouse, standing behind JJ's desk, wearing gloves. She pulled a key from her small handbag, moved a small painting aside, revealing an old safe and inserted the key in the lock. When she heard the lock click, she pushed the heavy lever to the right, opened the door a sliver, closed it, put the painting back in place and quickly walked out the door all the while having kept her back to Sabine.

Sabine stayed there for a moment, shocked at what she had just seen.

"What happened?" Indi asked when Sabine slipped back into the den, a perplexed look on her face.

"I don't know," Sabine said, her expression still incredulous. "A woman opened the safe and closed it."

"Are you kidding me?"

"No."

"What did she take?"

"Nothing."

"Who was it?"

"No idea, I couldn't see."

"Shit..." Indi swore. "Now what?"

"I'm confused," Sabine frowned.

*

Nina's heart was pounding and her mouth dry as she slipped out into the hallway and into the large reception hall where they'd had cocktails.

She had just put one foot outside when,

"Can I help you, *begum sahiba*?"

"Oh...I forgot my cellphone in the car and went to get it and I was looking to freshen up before going back to the party."

"You'll find everything you need in the guest house beyond the marquee," the man said politely.

"Ah yes...well thank you," Nina smiled tightly and walked away.

As she walked down towards the dance floor, she saw Arun and Bunny walking quickly back up to the driveway. She looked at her watch. They were leaving early. It was unlike Arun to leave a party like this at midnight. Frowning, she quickly made her way down.

*

The man watched Nina step onto the patio and with his cell-phone quickly took a photograph.

'She was just in the reception hall,' said the caption he added to the photo he sent to Rusty.

'Do you know why?'

'Said she was looking to freshen up.'

'Name?'

'Nina Singh.'

*

It was late morning when JJ, wearing a pair of jeans and a shirt went out onto the balcony off the master suite and sat down in one of the chairs under the awning. A few minutes later, Aditya appeared with a tray that he placed on the coffee table in front of him.

"Good morning *Sahib*," he said handing him the newspaper. "Shall I pour your tea?"

"Thank you," JJ replied. "One can hardly tell there was a big party here last night..."

"The crew just left," the valet said. "They were at it since 6 am when the last guest left."

"Where is Rusty?"

"He went to the Lodhi to pick up the necklace...he should be back any minute now."

"Have him come up when he does," JJ said. "Anything interesting in the papers?"

"The party is the talk of the town," Aditya said.

JJ opened the paper to the Society section and there was a large photo of him greeting Priya and Randy with the article being mostly about the Barodan necklace.

He smiled.

Just as the valet was leaving, there was a knock on the door and Rusty walked in.

"You have it?" JJ asked.

"Yes," Rusty held out a box.

JJ opened it. "Put it back in the safe."

"Yes, sir."

"You know what to do?" JJ asked.

Rusty nodded.

"Sir..."

"What is it?"

"Last night," Rusty pulled out his cellphone. "Mrs. Nina Singh was in the main hall during the concert," he handed JJ his phone.

"What was she doing there?"

"She said she was looking for the bathroom."

"How odd," JJ frowned. "I remember sending her and her two friends down to the guest cottage.

"What do you think?"

"Hard to tell."

"Do you think she went into the office?"

"Possible."

"But what could she want from there?"

"Something from the safe?" Rusty suggested.

"How could she open it? She'd need the combination or the key," JJ shrugged, "and she doesn't have either."

"Besides there was nothing in there."

"I don't know, sir."

"Do we have her on the security cameras?

"In the reception hall, yes," Rusty nodded.

"Well keep it in your back pocket...we may need a Plan B if the other doesn't work."

"Yes, sir."

*

In her suite at the Oberoi, Sabine paced the room, deep in thought.

Her phone rang and she grabbed it.

"Yes..."

"What happened?" asked a male voice.

It was Rambo.

"Every server was assigned a table," Sabine said. "Every table had two trays. One for the women and one for the men."

"The server assigned to Singh's table had to go to the bathroom and this one decided he was going to take matters into his own hands."

"I thought you'd planned for everything."

Sabine sighed. "I had," she said, "but clearly not."

Rambo was quiet.

"What's next?" he said after a moment.

"You didn't see anything, did you?" Sabine asked.

"Well..." she heard him take a few puffs of his cigar, "it didn't come to me."

"What about Kareena Kapoor?" Sabine asked. "She was on

your right?"

"I don't think so...she was originally on my left and then switched with her husband."

"Ambani...?"

"No."

"And Arun Singh?"

"He sat down, asked me for money which I refused and left because Kareena's husband came back."

"And Mrs. Ambani?"

"Doubtful."

"That narrows it down to JJ and the three society women."

"Do you know the women?" he asked.

"I do," Sabine nodded, "especially Sonia Jaffrey and Nina Singh."

"So...it won't be hard..." he puffed on his cigar.

"Now that we've narrowed it down...no."

Sabine spread open a large sheet of paper and looked at a map of the tables and the placement of the tray stand. She took three plates from the room service tray and put them in her hand. "Now...if I were the server, I would have served the women first...starting at the head of the table and moving clockwise.

"And if that is the case, she cocked her head looking at JJ's table...that would mean Nina Singh...Sonia Jaffrey and Rupa Patel.

"After that..." she kept tilting her head. "...Kareena Kapoor and Mrs. Ambani."

She stood up and put the plates back on the tray.

Sabine hung up and dialed another number.

"Yeah...it's me...can you meet me at Gema's? And bring your laptop...we need to find this damned necklace, and we need to find out who was in JJ's office last night."

*

Nina was reading the newspaper when the phone rang.

"Nina, it's Sonia," she heard Sonia's voice. "I'll pick you up around midnight."

"What about Rupa?" Nina asked.

"We'll pick her up together...now don't forget, we have to look the part."

"Alright...but Sonia, are you sure we can pull this off?"

"Yes."

Nina sat back against the pillows of the sofa. She wrinkled her nose and went back to reading the paper. Suddenly, she closed it and put it down next to her, her expression pensive.

*

Across town,

"I don't understand," Gema shook her head. "How could this have happened? How could the two of you have lost the Barodan?"

Both Indi and Sabine shrugged. "Things happen."

"Yes, but the plan was so perfectly mapped out."

"It didn't take into account my being stopped by JJ to serve champagne to his table."

"I'd factored in extra time, but I never thought to add in a do-gooder server and an idiot wine steward.

"I don't believe the friend was in the bathroom...I think he was smoking pot."

"Maybe they both were?" Indi suggested.

Sabine shrugged.

"Now what?" Gema asked.

"I think we have to go back in," Sabine leaned forward.

"Go back in?" Gema questioned. "Why? Isn't that bad luck?"

Sabine ignored her comment. "Priya returned the necklace today," she said. "So it will be back in the safe."

"Sabine, are you forgetting that the necklace that Priya returns today is a fake?"

"Yeah...my creation," Gema added proudly.

"Yeah, but JJ doesn't know that," Indi said.

"Look, we have to go through everyone at the table," Sabine explained. "Our suspects are JJ and the three society women...the rest would probably have returned the necklace if they'd seen it."

"What if no one saw it and the necklace went back to the kitchen after dinner."

"It didn't come back," Sabine said. "I checked every plate that was cleared."

"So you're saying that JJ might have it, and if so, we'll find two necklaces in his safe?"

"If he was served the necklace," Sabine said, "he'll know the one Priya sent back was a fake and he will simply toss it out."

"Won't he know it was you?"

"Of course he'll suspect...but what's he going to do?"

"You've lost me..." Indi said.

"And me too," Gema added.

"It's simple," Sabine began and Indi and Gema looked at one another. "There will be one necklace in the safe tonight, and it will either be the real or the fake.

"Whatever it is, we lift it," she added. "There's a 50% chance that it's the real thing."

"And if it's the fake?" Indi questioned.

"If it's a fake...well," Sabine shrugged. "We keep looking."

"So you want to go back into the Singh compound, get into his office, open the safe and just walk out with the necklace? That easy..."

"We've done it before, remember?"

"You're mad," Indi said. "We're going to get caught."

"No..." Sabine started in a very deliberate tone. "We are not," she added confidently.

"How do you even know that the necklace is going to go back into the safe at his house?"

"Because the Barodan is a necklace JJ wants to keep close to him."

"And do you have the combination to the lock on the safe?" Indi asked.

"No, we'll crack it."

"I don't know..." Indi shook her head. "This is just bad karma."

"It's a cloudy night," Sabine looked at the weather app on her phone.

"What does that mean?"

"No moonlight."

"Indi, did you look at the footage?" Sabine asked. "Who was in JJ's office that night?"

"Oh..." Indi turned her laptop around to face the other two. "Here she is coming into the reception hall," she pointed to the screen, "...and here she is talking to one of the guards."

"Can you zoom in on her face?"

"Yes," Indi pressed a couple of buttons.

"Interesting," Sabine smiled. "It's Nina Singh."

"But she didn't take anything, right?" Indi said.

"Maybe because it was empty?" Gema suggested.

"She didn't open the safe to even see," Sabine said. "The lock clicked, she pulled the lever and right back down."

"I wonder what she was looking for."

"This is getting more and more interesting."

*

It was just past midnight and very quiet, the silence broken only occasionally by the usual sounds of the night, the howls of the stray dogs in the distance, cats as they stalked vermin, crying babies and crickets in the bushes.

A dark figure moved stealthily across the reception hall and entered JJ's library office. Moments later, a heavy clunking sound was heard throughout the house.

Aditya, who was fast asleep in his room off the kitchen, stirred. His eyes opened. He swung his legs out of bed and put them in his slippers and got up, rubbing his head. He walked into his bathroom and looked at himself in the mirror. He was about to slip off his pajamas when he heard another loud click.

He thought about going out to investigate, but the call of nature beckoned and after he'd done his business, he went straight back to bed.

*

About an hour later, a car without headlights trundled softly past the front gate of JJ's farmhouse, the tires crunching over the sand and pebbles, coming to a stop about a quarter of a mile away. A figure got out and the driver parked the car very close to the compound wall hiding it under the leaves of a ficus tree that grew over the wall. The driver got out and joined the other figure and the two dressed in dark clothing ran along the compound wall until they came to a small lane. They turned down it and a couple of hundred feet away, they came upon a small gate. One of the figures placed a panel over the combination keypad, activating it with the push of a button. A series of numbers flashed as the machine looked for the combination to the gate and a couple of minutes later, there was a small click and the gate opened.

"Where the hell did you find that?" a voice whispered.

"Come on," another voice answered and the two figures turned right and ran around to the back of the house, moving quickly and silently across the garden staying out of sight of the cameras.

They ran up onto the porch outside JJ's office and stopped at the French doors.

One of the figures pulled the ski mask down to her chin. It was Indi.

"How do we open these doors?" she whispered loudly.

The other figure pulled her mask down. "Shhhh," Sabine said.

From the pocket of her sweatshirt she took out a wallet and went down on her knees to insert an instrument into the lock. She struggled a bit, but the lock finally gave and the window opened.

"We have to get to the alarm.

"Quickly!" she opened the door that led out into the hallway.

They went down the hall and were in the large entrance hall.

Indi silently pointed to a panel at the door. It was flashing yellow.

"It's about to go!" Indi whispered.

Sabine ran and quickly fitted the panel on to it. "Come on, come on!"

Suddenly the panel flashed green and the two women sighed with relief. They went back to JJ's office where Sabine quickly made her way to the safe, while Indi kept watch at the door. "Hurry!"

"I'm going as fast as I can," Sabine moved the painting that covered the safe. "Shit!"

"What's the matter?"

"It's an old-school safe."

"What does that mean?"

"It means that I have to crack the combination the way they do in the movies...I can't use the panel. It's not electronic."

Indi sighed silently. "Get on with it."

Sabine put her ear to the safe.

"What's going on?" Indi said after a few minutes.

"I need one more number."

"Hurry up," Indi said. "I'd like to sleep in my own bed tonight."

Suddenly the chime of the doorbell rang through the house.

"What the..." Sabine jumped. "What's going on?"

"I don't know," Indi opened the door a sliver. "Wait! Someone's coming!"

"What?" Sabine said in a loud whisper.

"Someone just walked across the hall."

*

Outside, a sleepy Aditya walked to the alarm pad and punched in the code.

"Yes," he opened the door.

"I'm Mrs. Singh," a woman said. "Nina Singh, and this is Mrs. Sonia Jaffrey and Mrs. Rupa Patel...we're friends of Mr. Singh..."

Suddenly, the alarm went off, loud clanging bells that filled the entrance.

Aditya quickly punched in a code and the noise immediately stopped.

"I am so sorry," he said. "I must have punched in the wrong code by mistake.

"How can I help you, *begum sahiba*?"

"We are very sorry to disturb you at this hour," Nina said, "but we were on our way back from a dinner party that wasn't far from here and our car has broken down."

"Oh..." the man said.

"We were hoping you could help us," she pleaded.

"Uhhh...yes," he mumbled.

"We were at the party last night..."

"Oh yes, of course!" Aditya perked up. "I'm so sorry, *begum sahiba*..." he apologized. "I'm half asleep. Please come in...I'll get Mr. Khan.

"Mr. Singh is fast asleep, but would you like for me to wake him?"

"Not at all," Nina waved a hand. "I'm sure Mr. Khan can help us with the car."

"Of course," Aditya said.

"Shall we wait in Mr. Singh's office?" Nina walked down the hallway.

"Of course..." the butler hesitated. "Or you could perhaps wait here until I get Mr. Khan."

"Unfortunately, my friend, Mrs. Rupa Patel, here, doesn't

feel at all well," Nina pretended to hold Rupa up, "do you Rupa?"

"Ohhhhh..." Rupa swooned. "I must sit down...I must."

"Let me show you..."

"I know the way to the office," Nina said and put one hand under Rupa's elbow while Sonia took the other.

"Let me at least turn on the light for you," Aditya led the way to JJ's office.

Aditya opened the door and flipped the switch just inside the door and light flooded the office.

"I will be back shortly," he said.

"How could JJ have slept through all that noise?" Rupa said softly.

"Perhaps he takes a sleeping pill?" Sonia suggested.

"Shut up you two," Nina said. "Now let's hurry. We don't have much time," Nina pulled an old black key out of her handbag.

"Look!" Rupa said. "That window is open," she got up to go investigate.

"You stay right there," Sonia instructed. "You're supposed to be drunk."

"Drunk?" Rupa looked shocked. "I am not drunk."

"Just pretend."

"But I've never been drunk, how am I supposed to act?"

"Just be yourself, Mrs. Rupa," Sonia said. "That'll do."

"Stop it, you two!" Nina inserted the key and opened the safe.

"Well...?" Sonia smiled in anticipation.

"It's empty."

"Empty?"

Nina nodded.

"Where the hell is the Barodan necklace?"

The three women looked at each other.

"Nina!" Sonia suddenly said. "Hurry! Someone's coming. Close it...quickly!"

*

"What the hell is going on?" Rusty walked quickly with Aditya at his heels.

"There are three women in Mr. Singh's office," he said, trying to keep up. "They were all here for the party last night and they said their car broke down and one of them isn't feeling well."

"Why the hell didn't you turn off the alarm before you opened the door?"

"I did, Rusty *Sahib*," Aditya said.

"Did you alarm the house on your last rounds, before you went to bed?"

"I did," Aditya assured him. "I must have just punched in the wrong code."

"You go get some tea and I'll deal with these women,' Rusty ordered. "I wonder if I should wake Mr. Singh."

"He took a pill before he went to bed tonight," Aditya said.

"Thank goodness," Rusty said and walked into the office.

*

"Ah! Mr. Khan," Nina said.

"How can I help?"

"We are so very sorry about this," Nina said, "but as you can see, our friend, Rupa, here is not well."

"Noooooo," Rupa moaned on the couch. "Not well, not well..."

Rusty looked at her. "Aditya will be back with some tea in just a moment.

"Now, where is this car of yours?" he asked. "And why don't you have a driver at this hour?"

"Well..." Nina and Sonia looked at one another.

"He disappeared," Sonia declared.

"Disappeared?"

"Yes..." Sonia nodded emphatically. "He drove us to the dinner and when we came out, he was gone."

"Really?" Rusty said. "Where is the car now?"

"It broke down in front of your gate."

"I see."

"Would you be able to take a look to see what's wrong with it?"

"Why don't we just leave it there and I will drive you all home?" Rusty said.

"That's very nice," Nina said. "Are you quite sure?"

"Whose driver was it?"

"He was mine," Nina said.

"I hope you sack him," Sonia said.

"If he ever comes back..." Nina agreed.

"Here is the tea," Rusty said.

"Actually, I would much rather get going," Nina said. "We should get Rupa back into her bed."

"Ohhhhhhhh," Rupa moaned on cue.

"Alright," Rusty agreed. "Aditya, please pull the Range Rover out."

"Yes," the butler nodded.

"Well, I suppose I could have a cup of tea..." Rupa said.

"It'll only make you worse," Sonia brushed her hand away from the tray. "Shall we go?" she got up. "Come on Mrs. Rupa, I'll help you up," she said.

"Owwwwww..." Rupa squealed. "You pinched me."

"I did no such thing."

"Let's go ladies," Nina said.

Aditya cleared away the tea tray after they left, took one look around the room to make sure it was in order, turned off the light and closed the door.

*

"Sabine...?" Indi whispered.

"Yes...?" Sabine emerged from behind one of the brocade curtains.

"Did I really see what I just saw?

"Three society ladies playing cat burglar?"

The two women stood in the dark, two shadows against the soft light that came in from one of the lanterns on the porch.

"Well...I guess they did our work for us...the safe was empty."

"Where the fuck is that necklace?" Sabine swore, her hands on her hips. "We don't have it, it appears JJ doesn't have it, nor do the aunties...so who does?"

"Priya?"

"I don't know...why would she steal it?"

"It's a big necklace, Sabine," Indi said. "Those diamonds would turn anyone's head...even Mother Teresa."

"Don't be disrespectful."

"I'm not, but you know what I mean."

"This is crazy..."

"I think we should get out of here."

"Yeah."

"I bet they put the alarm back on."

"We can turn it off."

*

The following morning, Aditya went to turn off the alarm, but instead he armed the system. He frowned. He was sure he had armed the system after the ladies left. He punched the code in again and the system flashed green. Suddenly, he heard shouting coming from JJ's office.

Chapter 9

"What the hell?" JJ bellowed when he opened his safe.

"Sir?" his assistant poked his head in the door. "Is everything alright?"

"Get Rusty in here!" he shouted.

"What has happened, Singh *Sahib*?"

"Get out!" JJ screamed. "Get out of my sight or I'll sack you this very minute."

"Yes, sir," the man said. "Sorry, sir..." he apologized.

"Go!"

The assistant scrambled away, leaving the door slightly open.

JJ went to stand by the French window and crossed his arms over his chest.

"You asked to see me, sir?" he heard Rusty's voice behind him.

"The Barodan...it's gone..." JJ walked to his desk and collapsed into it. "I went to open the safe this morning and it was empty.

"Get the police...

"Apoorva!" JJ yelled out.

Apoorva appeared at the door.

"Yes, sir."

"Get me Anand at Lloyd's on the phone...now."

"Yes, sir," Apoorva's worried eyes darted from JJ to Rusty and back.

"Now!" JJ hollered.

"Yes, sir," Apoorva said.

"In this fucking lifetime, not the next."

"Of course, sir," Apoorva mumbled. "Sorry sir."

"And shut the door behind you."

As soon as Apoorva left, JJ looked at Rusty. "Get the ball rolling," he nodded.

Rusty acknowledged him silently, turned on his heel and walked out the door. Outside, as he walked into his small office, he pulled out his cellphone.

"Detective Imran Khan, please," he said.

"Yes?" Imran answered.

"It's Rusty Khan," he announced himself.

There was a moment of silence.

"Rusty Khan!" Imran exclaimed. "The same Rusty Khan I was in the army with?"

"One and the same."

"How are you, man? I haven't heard from you in a while...last I heard you were in the military police escorting heads of state around Delhi."

"I'm in personal security now."

"It's not a bad gig if you can get it," Imran said. "Who're you working for?"

"JJ Singh..."

"You're kidding!"

"No...why?"

"Nothing," Imran replied. "I was looking at an old file and his name came up.

"Catch me up...you married?"

"Listen man, we can catch up some other time, but right now, I need your help..."

"What's going on?"

"We've had a robbery," Rusty said.

"Rusty...I'm in Major Crimes now," Imran said. "I'll send you over to the guy who took my place in Theft."

"Imran, the Barodan Necklace was stolen."

"What?"

"The Barodan...

"You mean the famous one..."

"Yes," Rusty said. "Mr. Singh lent it to Priya Chopra for the party held in her honour and it was stolen last night from Mr. Singh's safe at the house."

"The house?" Imran repeated, incredulous.

"Unfortunately..."

"Have you called the insurance?"

"That's the next phone call."

"I'll make a call down to Theft," Imran said.

*

He had only just put the phone down and was looking up a number when it rang again.

"Khan here," he answered.

"Detective, please hold for Commissioner Chavan..." a voice said.

Imran frowned. What did the police commissioner of Delhi want from him?

"Imran!"

"Commissioner..." Imran acknowledged.

"How are you?"

"I'm fine, sir...thank you," Imran balanced the phone receiver on his shoulder. "What can I do for you?"

"There was a robbery at the house of JJ Singh..."

"Yes," Imran sighed. "I heard."

"Good...good," the commissioner cleared his throat. "Well then you're on it."

"Commissioner, you do realize that I'm a major crimes detective, not petty theft."

"Imran...you're the best I've got and I need you to handle this," the commissioner said. "Singh is an important guy."

"Sir, I will look into it, but I think this is one for Singh's insurance company."

"Imran...my balls are being squeezed on this one.

"Get in there, find out who did what and put the damned case to bed....it'll be an easy close," he said.

"And Imran...no press. This has to be as discreet as possible," he added before hanging up.

"Goddamnit!" Imran swore.

*

He hung up and dialed Rusty.

"I'll be there as soon as I can," Imran said.

"Thank you," Rusty said.

"Don't touch anything...my forensic team may be there before me," he said. "Let them start dusting for fingerprints."

"Copy that."

"Anything else taken?"

"Not as far as we know."

"Fuck..." he swore and was packing up his satchel when a young police officer appeared at his door. "What's happening, boss?"

"Never you mind...what do you want?" he slung his satchel over his shoulder.

"Just wanted to tell you that Rambo Singh is in town."

"For the love of Ganesh!" Imran swore. "When did he arrive?"

"And he is staying in the same hotel as Sabine Kumar."

Imran glared at him.

"And you couldn't have told me this before?"

"I'm sorry, I only just got the information, sir," the officer said.

"Rambo Singh has been a person of interest for us for a long time...he and JJ Singh were associates at one time," he signaled the sign of quotation marks.

"I see...should I do something about it?"

"If you want to be a good police officer, do your goddamned homework and don't ask me stupid questions.

"I'll be on my mobile," Imran walked out, leaving the officer staring after him, a puzzled expression on his face.

*

Indi and Sabine were sitting at the table in Gema's atelier, looking at camera footage from the night of the party.

"The two of you have been sitting there for hours," Gema remarked from across the room.

Indi and Sabine didn't reply, staring intently at the laptop.

"Hey!" Gema said.

Still no response.

"Hello?" Gema walked over to them.

"What is it?" Sabine said without looking up at her.

"Aren't you hungry?"

"No," Indi and Sabine said in unison.

"Thirsty?"

Sabine shrugged.

"What's wrong with the two of you?" Gema exclaimed. "You're not hungry, you're not thirsty...you haven't even gotten up to pee."

Both Sabine and Indi glowered.

"What are you? Camels?"

"I suppose I could drink something," Sabine finally gave in.

"Well..." Gema began walking away. "I was going to cook something for us," she said. "If you would like to join me in the kitchen?"

"What do you have to drink?" Sabine scraped her chair back.

"Whiskey, beer...white wine in the fridge."

"Let's open the wine," Sabine said.

"Cook?" Indi perked up. "What were you thinking?"

"What do you feel like eating?" Gema came back with a bottle and three glasses.

"What about those chicken burgers you make with the spicy yoghurt cucumber slaw?" Indi said. "Those are bloody outstanding!"

"Sounds yum!" Sabine took a sip of the wine and screwed up her nose.

"Just drink the damn thing," Gema said. "I can't afford to buy all those expensive wines you two like."

"What is it?"

"It's sauvignon blanc from New Zealand," Gema said. "And I like it," she said, putting her nose in the air.

"I'll have a beer," Sabine said.

"Go get it yourself," Gema said.

"Don't be offended, Gema," Sabine smiled affectionately.

"You guys are such snobs," Gema sniffed.

"What's the beer?"

"It's Kingfisher," Gema replied. "Good Indian beer."

"God!" Sabine rolled her eyes.

"We're in India, remember," Gema said. "Indian beer is what you get here."

"I'll stick to the wine."

Suddenly Indi sat up and put her glass down.

"What's going on?" Sabine ran back to the table.

"Shhh!" Indi said turning up the volume on the laptop and they heard Rusty's voice crackle.

"Who's he talking to?" Gema came around. "You still have that little bug in his computer?"

"Shut up!" Indi said.

The three of them listened carefully:

"Mr. Singh wants you in his office...he has Mr. Anand on the phone."

"Who's Anand?" Gema asked.

Sabine shrugged.

"Let's see if we can find out," Indi sat up and began typing. "I'll go through Rusty's emails."

"OK...here we go," she announced. "Dev Anand is with Lloyd's of London."

Sabine frowned and came around to look over Indi's shoulder. "See what you can dig up on him," she said.

Indi quickly pulled up a newspaper article. *"Sir Charles Harrison, the CEO of Lloyds of London announced today that he has appointed Dev Anand as the head of their new Indian operation based in Mumbai...Mr. Anand has worked for Lloyds for over 20 years...* blah, blah, blah."

"Alright..." Sabine got up and paced. "So if JJ is filing an insurance claim, either he knows the necklace Priya returned is a fake or he's committing insurance fraud and has 'stolen' his own necklace."

"If he's stolen his own necklace, does he know it's a fake?"

"Probably not."

They were all silent.

"Let's go back over that camera footage," Sabine said, as the cigarette smoke swirled around her head, "there has to be something in there."

*

"Yes, Mr. Singh...now don't worry...we will sort this out immediately...yes, sir, I will put my best man on it immediately...thank you, sir..." he was about to put the phone down when he heard JJ's voice.

"Yes, sir...we will be sending you a cheque for the lithographs that you reported stolen from the house in Tuscany, that will be sent from our London office...yes...no, we will not let you down on the Barodan...thank you, sir...yes...goodbye."

Dev Anand, in his office at the swank new headquarters of Lloyds of London in Colaba, overlooking the Arabian Sea, put the phone down and covered his face with the palms of his hands.

He took a deep breath. "Ohhhh," he sighed audibly as he blew it out.

He sat there for a moment, staring at his phone before picking it up.

"I want to see Hari Singh in my office...now."

A few minutes later, there was a knock at his door.

"Come in," he said, without looking up.

"You wanted to see me?" a voice said at the door.

Dev looked up. "Ah! Yes! Hari...come on in."

In his mid-50's, Hari Singh was unusually good looking. The son of an Indian father and an English mother, he was over six feet tall, well-built and athletic with sandy brown hair that was slightly long, a short beard and moustache, peppered with grey, and green eyes. His complexion was fair but tanned owing to the amount of time he spent outdoors playing cricket and a boyish innocence that made women from London to Mumbai swoon. He was wearing a grey suit with a white shirt, a grey and black patterned cotton scarf wrapped around his neck and Converse sneakers on his feet.

"You wanted to see me, boss?" he came in and sat down in the black leather chair, casually crossing one leg over the other, showing grey and white argyle socks.

"We have a problem..." Dev started.

Hari cocked his head questioningly.

"I just got off the phone with JJ Singh," he took a deep breath, "and it appears the Barodan necklace has been stolen."

"Stolen? He was robbed..."

"That's what stolen implies," Dev rolled his eyes.

"Was anything else taken?"

"Just the necklace."

"Well...I suppose that's unfortunate," Hari remarked wryly.

"It'll be even more unfortunate if we have to dish out 50 million US dollars."

It was Hari's turn to take a deep breath.

"Do you know what happened?

"Apparently he took the necklace out of the vault to lend it to Priya Chopra on the night of the reception he hosted for her and her husband..." Dev said. "She returned it the next day and he put it in his safe at the house. When he came into his office, the safe was open and the necklace was gone."

"How old school," Hari said sarcastically.

"What does that mean?"

"Just that it sounds like an Agatha Christie novel...you know, house safe broken into in the middle of the night...a famous necklace stolen and the safe left open..."

"Singh..." Dev warned. "No sarcasm please."

"So it was a safe, not a vault that was broken into?"

"It was the safe at his house," Dev confirmed.

"Do you know what kind of safe?"

"No."

"Anything else in the safe?"

"Don't know."

"Is the police involved?"

"I don't know, but I'm sure they are."

Hari nodded silently.

"I don't need to tell you that we have to find this necklace..."

"Was this a set up?"

Dev shrugged.

"Fraud?"

"You're on the next flight to Delhi this afternoon and you're going to find out," Dev said. "You'd better get going."

Hari got up and walked back to the door.

"Oh...Hari...not a word to the press at all."

"Of course not, sir," Hari nodded.

"You're my best investigator, Hari," Dev added. "Find that goddamned necklace."

*

Imran drove up the driveway of JJ's house, his car backfiring all the way. "Fucking car!" he kicked it when he got out. He walked up to the door, the gravel crunching under his feet.

"Rusty!"

"Hey man," Rusty shook his hand warmly. "I'm sorry we have to reconnect under these circumstances."

Imran nodded. "I hope nothing has been touched."

"Of course not...no forensic team yet..."

"They're right behind me," he said. "They will need to dust the area for fingerprints, take photographs etc."

The two men walked through the entrance hall towards JJ's office.

"Nice house," Imran said. "I assume you have security cameras."

Rusty nodded.

"Where is Mr. Singh?"

"He had a meeting."

"Alright," Imran said as Rusty led the way into the office. "Tell me what happened..."

There was a quick knock on the door and Apoorva, the assistant, poked his head in.

"There are two more policemen here," he said before opening the door wide.

Imran nodded. Two men came in carrying duffel bags, which they put down and saluted Imran.

"Where's the safe?" Imran asked.

Rusty pointed to the right of the desk. "That's it there," he said pointing to the old fashioned grey steel safe that was slightly open.

"Get to work," Imran told the two officers, "fingerprints...anything you can get...I need photos and videos."

"Sir," they acknowledged the order, cordoning off the desk and the area behind it.

"Tell me what you think happened," Imran asked Rusty as he flipped open a small notebook.

"All I know is what Mr. Singh told me this morning..."

"Which is what exactly?"

"That he came into his office this morning and sat down behind his desk and then noticed the painting was askew and the safe door was open."

"Was the necklace the only item taken?"

"There was nothing else. It was the *only* item in the safe."

"I see," Imran scribbled in his notebook. "No cash? No other jewelry?"

Rusty shook his head. "Everything is usually kept at the vault at the Gallery," Rusty said.

"So why was the Barodan necklace here?"

"We took it out of the vault for Miss Priya and the day after the party, I picked it up and he put it in the safe."

"What does Mr. Singh keep in that safe?"

"Honestly, I don't know."

Imran pursed his lips, nodding as he looked around.

"Anything guys?" he walked around the desk as the two officers were carefully brushing around the sides of the safe.

They shook their heads in unison.

"This is a really old safe," Imran remarked as he walked up to it and stuck his nose inside it. "It's lined with felt."

"Yes, it's very old," Rusty concurred.

"Where did he get this?"

"It was in the gallery when Mr. Singh bought the property," Rusty said. "He had it pulled out and installed here.

"I think it's English..."

"Yes..." Imran murmured as he pulled on a pair of gloves and ran his fingers along the top and sides. "From the 20's or 30's..." he confirmed.

"I'm wondering how the robber opened this safe..." Imran pulled off the gloves and came back around. "He either had the combination or the key.

"Who has the combination to the safe?"

"Mr. Singh," Rusty said.

"And key?"

"He does."

"His assistant doesn't have the combination?" Imran asked. "Or you?"

"I do not," Rusty said.

"Right..." Imran walked over to the French windows. "I assume the thief came through these windows," he opened them wide.

"Sir?" the two men heard a voice behind them.

It was the butler.

"What is it, Adi?" Rusty said.

"Sir...Apoorva told me the police were here..."

"Detective Imran Khan," Rusty began the introduction, "Aditya Kapoor, Mr. Singh's personal butler."

The two men shook hands.

"Sir, I think I heard something last night," he said.

"What do you mean?" Imran frowned questioningly. "What kind of sound?"

"I'm not sure," Adi replied. "It was the middle of the night and I was half asleep, but it sounded like a clunky sound, like a big lever of some kind."

"Like this?" Imran went behind the desk, closed the safe and opened it.

"Yes," Adi nodded.

"Around what time would you say this was?"

"Probably around 1," Aditya stood with his hands folded. "Maybe..." he thought for a second, "but I can't be sure."

"And you heard the sound just once?"

"I think so."

"Well that would make sense since the thief or thieves left the door to the safe open," Imran said. "If there'd been two loud noises, it would mean the thief pulled the lever back down to lock the safe."

Imran stroked his chin.

"Anything?" he asked his officers.

"Nothing," one of them said.

"We will get these back to the lab, but most of the fingerprints are of Mr. Singh," the second officer said, his laptop open in front of him. "There's a second set of fingerprints, but it is his assistant's."

"Are they on the safe?" Imran asked.

"No," the man replied. "Just around the desk."

"What about the safe?"

"Only Mr. Singh's."

"Can we take a look at the security footage?" Imran asked Rusty.

"Of course," Rusty replied.

"There's a fingerprint here," the officer said just as the two men were walking out. "But it's only a partial one. I don't know what we will get from that."

"Keep looking," Imran said.

"I assume you've called the insurance company?" Imran said as they walked to Rusty's small office near the kitchen.

Rusty nodded. "They are on their way."

"Let me know who the investigator is."

"So..." Rusty turned on his computer and went to the security footage, pulling up all the cameras around the house from the night before. "Here we are."

"Let's narrow it down from 1 to 3am," Imran said, "since that is what the butler said."

Rusty fast forwarded until the time-code stamp said 1am.

"Look!" Imran said. "What's that?"

Rusty peered at the screen. "I don't see anything."

"It's moving," Imran pointed to a dark shadow in the bushes. "And there it is entering the library office...and the time is 1:09am..." Imran scribbled in his book. "The butler was right."

Rusty stared at the screen in silence.

"And there's the shadow again, slipping out of the library," Imran chewed on the end of his pencil. "This guy knew what he was doing...he knew where all the cameras were...the footage gives us nothing."

"Could this have been an inside job?"

"You mean one of the staff?" Rusty asked, a look of mild surprise on his face.

Imran nodded. "Doesn't this have the earmarks of an inside job?"

Rusty took a deep breath as a response.

"What about the alarm? Did that go off?"

"It went off when the three ladies arrived..." Rusty forwarded the tape. "That's Begum Patel, Singh and Jaffrey," Rusty said. "Their car broke down and I drove them home."

"Their car broke down?" Imran looked skeptical. "At 2:30 in the morning?

"Where was their driver?"

"Apparently disappeared."

"I'll need the names of everyone who works here, please," Imran added.

*

Hari Singh was walking off the plane when his phone rang.

"Yes?" he answered.

"It's your boss," he heard Dev Anand's voice.

"Yes?"

"Did you find the necklace yet?"

"Boss, I just arrived in Delhi," Hari shook his head, incredulous. "I'm still at the airport."

Dev cleared his throat. "Alright...your police contact is Detective Imran Khan...I'll text you his number.

"Singh...I cannot tell you how important it is you find this necklace..." he began.

"Boss, please," Hari said, "I heard you the first time."

"Do your best," Dev said and rang off.

Hari put his phone back in his breast pocket and walked towards the exit of the airport, where he hailed a taxi.

"Hotel InterContinental please."

As the taxi headed towards Delhi, Hari looked out the window...

I wonder where she is now, what she's doing...what she looks like...

He pulled out his phone and scrolled through his photos until he found a collage taken in a photo booth in a street fair. He closed his eyes for a moment and took a deep breath. He still missed her.

*

"This is a lovely room, sir," the young porter said when they got off on the 6th and topmost floor of the very unpretentious Hotel Intercontinental near Connaught Place in downtown Delhi. "You will see...it has a beautiful view of the city and your own private terrace."

"Here we are!" he opened the door with great flourish and stood aside to let Hari in.

Hari smiled to himself as he walked in. The room was small with a slanted ceiling and tall French-style doors that opened onto a ledge you couldn't step onto unless of course you were planning on jumping. Luckily, it had a railing and it did allow a view of the rooftops of the buildings in front.

"Beautiful, isn't it?" the young man grinned proudly.

"Yes, it's fine, thank you," Hari dug into his pocket to pull out a few rupees. "Thank you."

As soon as he'd left, Hari took a deep breath and looked around. The website said 'simple' and that is exactly what it was, except for the marigold orange paint on the wall behind the bed and the matching bedspread. And it was clean, which was important.

Apart from the bed, there was a desk and chair and an armchair, floor lamp and side table next to the French window. The postcard on the side table said 'Please enjoy Delhi.' Hari picked it up and smiled. It looked like something out of the 60's.

He unpacked and hung his two shirts, jacket and pair of pants in the tiny closet and washed up. He looked at his watch. It was past 10. He wondered what to do about dinner and picked up the house phone before putting it back down. He put on his jacket and took the elevator downstairs.

"Is there a restaurant nearby that's still open for dinner?" he asked the already sleepy night receptionist.

"Yes, sir...there's a restaurant called Le Bistro Indien, just a few blocks away," he said. "You can walk there."

"Thank you," Hari said and stepped out into the slightly chilly Delhi evening, pulling up his jacket collar and tightening the maroon and black striped scarf he wore around his neck.

*

"Reservation, sir?" the hostess asked.

"No...just a drink at the bar and something to eat."

"Of course," she smiled. "We're open until midnight."

He sat down in the corner and leaned back against the wall. "I'll have a Johnny Walker black on the rocks please," he said to the bartender. "And a menu, please."

"Yes, sir."

As he sipped his drink, another man walked in and sat across from him on the other side of the bar. "Johnny Walker Black, rocks," he heard the man say.

The man raised his glass to take a sip and as he was putting it down, caught Hari's eye. He inclined his head acknowledging

Hari, who did the same.

Several minutes later, two plates came out, one was served to Hari and the other to the man across the bar.

Hari took a bite of the spicy roast lamb...it was delicious...just what he needed.

"How is it?" the man across the bar asked.

"It's great!" Hari replied.

"Roast lamb?" he asked.

"Roast lamb," Hari nodded.

"You got the best thing on the menu."

"I think I'll be here every night!"

The man nodded.

"Would you like to join me?" Hari said.

The man looked up at him for a moment, then shrugged and got up to move around sitting a couple of stools away from Hari as the barman moved over his plate and drink.

"You live in Delhi?" he asked when he sat down.

"I'm here for a little work."

"Where're you from?" he took a bite of his food.

"Bombay."

"Ahhh the big city," the man smiled. "We're just provincials here."

"I actually lived here for a while."

"Why'd you move down to Bombay?"

"Long story...a bad break up."

"Sorry to hear."

Hari signaled the bartender to refill his drink. "Can I buy you a round?" he asked the man.

"Thank you," the man nodded.

"What about you?" Hari asked. "You live here?"

"Born and bred."

There was a pause as the two men sipped their drinks.

"Are you married?"

"Widower," the man admitted.

"I'm sorry."

The man shrugged.

"What brings you to Delhi?"

"I'm an insurance investigator..."

The man nodded.

"You?"

"Detective...Major Crimes, Delhi Police."

"I thought about going into the police force when I got out of the army," Hari said.

"You were in the army?" Imran said. "So was I."

"Coincidence," Hari smiled.

"What did you do in the army?"

"I was in military intelligence," Hari said. "You?"

"Criminal investigation."

Hari nodded. "Tough job...going after your own."

Imran nodded.

"So why didn't you make the transition?" he asked.

"After the break up, I went to London...my mother is there...and got into the insurance business and when the company was opening an office in Bombay, I came back."

"Who do you work for?"

"Lloyd's of London," Hari answered.

The man nodded and asked the bartender to refill their glasses. "My turn," he said to Hari.

"Thanks man...by the way, my name is Hari Singh," he put

his hand out.

"Imran Khan..."

The two men shook hands.

"Wait a minute!" Hari said. "Are you working the case of the Barodan necklace at the Singh party?"

"Yeah...!" Imran looked surprised.

"That's why I'm here," Hari said.

"You're kidding!" Imran said. "What are the odds?"

Hari laughed.

"How did you find this place?"

"I'm staying at the Intercontinental," Hari said.

"I live a few blocks away from here, but in the other direction," Imran said. "This is my local."

"I've got a meeting tomorrow morning with JJ Singh," Hari said.

"Keep me posted."

"Have you talked to him?"

"Not yet," Imran replied. "He wasn't there when I went, but my guys dusted the area for prints."

"Anything."

"Not a thing," Imran said. "I think it's an inside job."

"Why do you say that?"

"The thief knew everything, the code to the alarm, to the safe...he knew where the cameras were..."

"Shit."

"Yeah...this isn't going to be easy for you."

"I think I know that.

"How did you get on this case anyway, if you're major crimes?"

"I used to be in Theft...but I don't know," he shook his head.

"JJ Singh is an influential man...he must've called someone."

"Listen man, I'm going to go," Hari said, pulling out his wallet.

"Yeah," Imran said. "Me too."

"We'll obviously be in touch," Hari put a note down on the bar. "Good to meet you," he held his hand out and shook Imran's.

As he walked out, he pulled out his phone, scrolling down his contacts. He stopped when he came to 'Indi.' He hesitated for a moment before bringing up her profile. There she appeared, smiling at him, her long hair tied up in a loose bun, locks waving around her face, her eyes gleaming mischieviously. He remembered taking that photo. They'd been at her house and she had promised to cook for him. Sitting in the kitchen, they'd opened a bottle of wine and she'd completely forgotten about the food in the oven that had burned. They'd ended up ordering in... his finger hovered over the green 'call' button. Should he? What if she is married?

Just then a young couple walked out of the restaurant. The man gallantly held out his arm and the woman smiled putting her hand in it. He looked so proud to have her next to him and she looked at him, placing a lock of hair coyly around her ear. They giggled and laughed and Hari wistfully watched as he opened the car door for her, helping her in, giving her a quick kiss before she got into the passenger seat.

After they drove away, Hari put his head down, his shoulders sagging as he put his hands in his pockets and walked into the cool Delhi night.

Chapter 10

"By the way," Sabine strode in when Indi opened the door, rubbing her eyes, "I haven't asked you..." was all Indi heard as she walked down the hallway.

"So? How are they?" Sabine asked when Indi finally caught up with her in the living room, yawning.

"How's who?"

"Your parents..."

"Do you know what time it is?" Indi flopped down on the oversized white armchair, curling into it, hugging the throw pillow and closing her eyes.

"Of course, it's 8am."

"Yes," Indi nodded, her eyes still closed. "8am."

"I don't know why you're still asleep."

"You may not need sleep, Sabine," Indi mumbled. "But most of us do."

"Shall I make some coffee?" Sabine put her bag down and headed to the kitchen.

Indi could hear cabinets being opened and closed and finally heard the kettle whistle. She heard the clatter of cups and saucers and finally the jingle of spoons against china.

Sabine set the tray down on the coffee table. "It's tea," she says. "I couldn't find the coffee."

Indi gave her a wry look. "Why couldn't you wait for the *ayah*?" she said referring to her housemaid. "She usually comes in at 9 or 10."

"So how are your parents?" Sabine sat back and sipped her tea.

Indi yawned and reached for the cup of tea Sabine had placed in front of her, grimacing as she took a sip.

"There's no sugar in this," she says. "And where's the milk?"

"It's green tea."

"First thing in the morning, I like black tea, sweet with lots of milk."

Sabine shrugged.

"My parents are fine...still in Indiana," Indi pushed the cup away.

"I don't understand why you don't go and live in the States?"

"Because I like my life here."

"But there's nothing here," Sabine said, "and *no one*."

"I keep busy," Indi defended herself.

"What about Hari?"

"Hari who?"

"Hari Singh, you idiot."

"Wow!" Indi slumped back in the armchair.

"Why are you wearing pajamas with elephants on them?" Sabine said. "Aren't you a little old for them?"

"I like them...they're comfortable."

"Yeah...and flannel," Sabine giggled. "What are you? Two?"

"What is today? Let's pick on Indi day?"

"I'm sorry," Sabine said.

"Whatever..." Indi pulled her feet up and tucked them under her.

"Seriously, though...no news of Hari..."

"We broke up, remember?" Indi said.

"I do remember…" Sabine said. "I just thought that perhaps he might have tried to get back in touch."

"Well, he didn't."

"So weird,' Sabine said. "I was convinced he was going to propose."

"I don't want to talk about it," Indi said. "It was years ago and besides, it's water under the bridge.

"More importantly…what are you doing here this early?"

"JJ doesn't have the real necklace, so it has to be one of the aunties," Sabine said. "The only question is what was Nina doing in JJ's office the night of the party?

"She couldn't have been looking for the necklace because it was on Priya's neck."

Indi agreed.

"But then all three of them came back the night after…why?"

"Clearly, they were going after the necklace," Indi said.

"But, as we know, someone else beat them and us to the punch."

"Hmmm," Sabine pondered.

"What if the night of the party, Nina was on a reconnaissance mission?" Indi proposed. "She had a key…it's not as though she cracked the combination."

"What do you mean?"

"The night of the party, she was checking to make sure the key worked," Indi said. "And they all went back the day after to lift the necklace."

"Indi *Memsahiba*?" a delicate voice was heard in the hallway behind them.

"Lakshmi!" Indi called out. "I'm in the living room."

"*Namaste, Memsahiba*," Lakshmi put her hands together

when she came in. "And *namaste* Sabine *Memsahiba!*" she smiled, showing her broken front tooth.

"*Namaste* Lakshmi," Sabine smiled back.

"Can I get you some breakfast?"

"Please make me some tea, Lakshmi," Indi sighed gratefully.

"Some toast?"

"Yes, some toast and butter and marmalade."

"Very good, *Memsahiba*," Lakshmi replied. "Will you come to the table? Or shall I serve it here?"

"Here," Indi replied. "Thank you, Lakshmi."

After she left,

"You want to know why I stay in India as opposed to going to the States?" Indi said.

"Why?"

"It's because of her."

"Because of your maidservant?"

"Because she makes my life so easy," Indi sighed happily. "She wakes me up, serves me breakfast, irons my clothes...reminds me of stuff...and she's as loyal as they get.

"I could never have that in the States."

"You could," Sabine said, "if you really wanted."

"Not without paying a small fortune."

"No, I suppose not," Sabine agreed. "It's a completely different lifestyle."

"And I like this one."

"Alright..." Sabine sat forward, "let's stay on topic, please.

"We've established the aunties were after the Barodan...but what's the motive? Money? Has to be."

"What if it's not about money?"

"What about revenge?"

"What do you mean?"

"Well, in the case of Nina Singh..." Indi suggested, "maybe she's bitter that she's not really a Maharani..."

"Could be," Sabine mused. "Let's stick to the money trail."

"Alright, alright," Indi relented. "Let's take them one by one," Indi munched on her toast. "All of them are wealthy women...they went from rich fathers to rich husbands...they don't 'need' the money...

"I mean...take Sonia, for example," she continued. "She's grown up around money, has never wanted for it, never had to earn it...but even though her husband is rich, how much does she have? What kind of allowance does she have? Or maybe she has an inheritance?"

"But even so, wouldn't it go into the husband's account?"

"I guess...although I would like to think that Indian women have moved forward in that regard."

"Alright, I'll take a look at them," Indi sighed. "What are you going to do?"

"I'm going to stay right here, combing all that security video footage."

"Again? We've only done it half a dozen times."

"I could've missed something," Sabine said.

"Yes," Rusty opened the door to the Singh farmhouse.

"Hari Singh," Hari held out one of his calling cards. He was dressed in a navy suit with a white shirt and a dark striped tie. "Lloyds of London."

"Mr. Singh has been waiting for you."

"I just arrived last evening."

"This way please," Rusty went ahead of him.

"Hari Singh, Lloyd's of London," he announced before he moved aside to let Hari in.

"Thank you for coming so promptly," JJ Singh came around his desk to shake Hari's hand.

"Not at all, sir," Hari said. "It's a pleasure to meet you."

"Please...have a seat," JJ pointed to one of the armchairs in the sitting area. "Would you like some tea?"

"Thank you," Hari nodded.

JJ picked up a phone and pressed a button.

"You rang, sir?" Aditya, the butler appeared.

"Please bring some tea, Adi."

"Yes, sir."

"Rusty," JJ pointed to the armchair next to Hari. "Join us."

"Rusty is my right hand," JJ explained, "and also my head of security."

Hari opened his satchel and pulled out a file and a small notebook.

"Now, just to make it clear," he cleared his throat. "I am not the police. I am not here to find the thief.

"I am either looking for fraud or the necklace. Apart from that, it's none of my business."

"You won't find the necklace here," JJ sat down on the sofa, "nor will you find fraud."

"People have gone to great lengths to defraud Lloyds," Hari said.

"Mr. Singh," he began.

"Please call me JJ..."

"If you will call me Hari..."

JJ nodded.

Hari flipped open his notebook.

"Now, I understand that you decided to lend the Barodan necklace to Priya Chopra to wear at a party you hosted for her...?"

"Yes," JJ joined the tips of his fingers together.

"Why?"

"What do you mean, 'why?'"

"I mean," Harry crossed one leg over the other, "why did you decide to lend Ms. Chopra the necklace?"

"She and her now husband were at my villa in Tuscany where they eloped and got married," JJ recounted, "and when we all came back to India, her mother wanted to have a reception and I offered to have it here..."

"You haven't answered my question," Harry said.

"I thought it would look good on her."

"You insured the necklace quite recently," he looked down at his notes. "In fact, just about a month before the party."

"So?"

"Was it previously insured?"

"I own an awful lot of art and different valuable pieces, Hari."

"But," Hari looked up at him, "you decided to call us to insure the necklace once you'd promised Priya that she could wear it..."

"Well..." JJ began.

"That was not a question," Hari interrupted him.

JJ pursed his lips.

"When did you come into possession of the necklace, sir?"

"I bought it at an auction, I believe."

"Sotheby's?" Hari read from his notes.

"I think so."

"I have their catalogue from last September where you did indeed buy a couple of pieces, but the Barodan necklace was not in that auction," Hari said.

"It's public knowledge that the Barodan disappeared 70 odd years ago...so how did you come upon it."

JJ took a deep breath.

"I was mistaken," JJ took a deep breath. "Actually, the Barodan was a private transaction. I bought it from someone who needed the money and wanted the sale kept quiet."

"But once you bought it, did you not think of insuring it?" Hari pressed. "After all, it's valued at 50 million dollars."

"I thought I had put it in with the other pieces I bought at Sothebys."

"I see," Hari said. "Do you know where the person you bought it from came upon the necklace?"

"I didn't ask."

"It is, of course, the real piece," Hari looked at his notes, "made by Richemont in the '20's for the Maharajah of Barodan's fifth wife.

"When did this private sale take place?" Hari asked.

JJ's nostrils flared with frustration and he got up and walked to the window.

"What I need from you is to find the damned thing or pay the claim," he said angrily.

"I'm just trying to get all the information I can to carry out a thorough investigation, Mr. Singh," Hari said.

"As I said, I am not a member of law enforcement," Hari said, "so how the thief came in, how he opened the safe, whether or not he had the security codes, keys...that profile will be built by the police detective in charge of the case.

"His name is Imran Khan..."

"Yes," Rusty said, "we have already had some dealings with him."

"Now, from what I understand," Hari said, "the theft happened the night after the party?"

"That is correct."

"When did the necklace come back?"

"I went to pick up the necklace the morning after the party," Rusty said.

"And you brought it back here?"

'Yes of course," Rusty said. "I brought it to Mr. Singh and he put it in the safe."

"I see," Hari scribbled in his notebook. "Do you have a guest list from the party?"

"Yes," Rusty nodded. "It's in my office."

"Why would you look at that?" JJ asked.

"It's entirely possible that whoever stole the necklace was at the event..."

"Hari," JJ smiled, "the people who attended were movie stars, celebrities, millionaires and even a billionaire...why would they need to steal the Barodan?"

"You never know, sir..." Hari got up and put his hand out to shake JJ's. "You just never know.

"Thank you for your time and I will be in touch."

"Hari," JJ said as Hari was walking out. "I told your boss that I didn't want the press finding out about this or any of this going public."

"I understand and it won't."

*

"Can I also get the security footage from the night of the robbery?" Hari asked Rusty as they crossed the entrance hallway towards his office.

"Yes."

"Has Detective Khan seen it?"

"He has."

"And did he see anything?"

"He saw what I saw."

"And what was that?"

"A shadow."

They walked into Rusty's office.

Hari looked around as Rusty cleared his desk of a pile of papers.

It was a small office with a large bay window that gave out onto the garden sparsely furnished with only a desk and two chairs.

"Where do you control your security system and cameras from?" Hari asked.

"It's through here," Rusty punched in a code on his phone and a wall slid open to reveal a bank of television monitors, each one with a different view.

"Very state of the art," Hari remarked. "How do you control these cameras?"

"This computer here," Rusty pointed to a desktop, "or my laptop."

"I assume we can watch the footage on your laptop?"

"Or on my phone," Rusty sat down in one of the chairs.

"What would you like to start with?"

"Let's do the night of the event since Detective Khan has already seen the night of the robbery."

"Have a seat," Rusty pulled a chair over for Hari and turned on his computer.

*

Around the same time, Indi was sitting in her living room with her feet up on an ottoman, her laptop open in front of her and a mug of steaming hot coffee on a coaster next to her. She was concentrating on reading her screen and was taken aback when a small window appeared on the top right corner of her screen.

"Hey!" she said to Sabine who was sitting with another laptop on the sofa in front of her.

"Yeah?" Sabine looked up.

"Rusty's on his computer."

"What's he doing?"

"I'm not sure yet," Indi hit a few keys on her laptop.

"It looks like he's pulling up footage from the night of the wedding."

Sabine put her laptop down and came and sat next to Indi.

"Sabine...exit the footage, would you," Indi said. "We don't want him to realize we are looking at the same thing."

"Is he alone?"

"I don't see anyone," Indi replied... "yet."

*

"When did you last see the necklace?" Hari asked as Rusty began to pull up security footage.

"When Priya left at the end of the party."

"About what time was that?"

"Around five in the morning."

"When you went to pick it up..." Hari paused for a moment as he stared at the screen, "did she hand it to you?"

"No...it was with her assistant," Rusty said. "Miss Priya was asleep."

"Wait!" Hari said. "Stop right there!"

"Where?" Rusty peered at the screen.

"There!" Hari pointed. "What's going on? What's Priya doing? And who's that woman with her? What is she doing?"

Hari leaned forward to look closely at the image.

*

"What the hell?" Indi jumped backwards in the chair.

"What?"

"Sabine..." she stuttered.

"What's going on?" Sabine came over holding a glass of fresh lime juice and soda.

"Sabine...I think I just saw Hari."

"Hari? Hari who?"

"Hari Singh..."

"Your ex?"

"That's right."

"Are you feeling alright?" Sabine put her palm on Indi's forehead.

"It's not funny."

"You're dreaming, Indi."

"No...Sabine, I swear it was him," Indi said. "He is sitting next to Rusty."

"Why?" Sabine sat on the arm of the chair. "What's he doing there?"

"I don't know...look! Look!" Indi screeched pointing at the screen of her laptop. "It's him."

"Shit!" Sabine swore. "It *is* him. I thought he went back to England."

"So did I," Indi curled up on the couch, holding a cushion to her chest as though it were a shield.

"Can we try and find out what they're looking at?" Sabine asked.

Indi leaned over the arm of the sofa, stretching to reach the keyboard.

"Indi," Sabine said. "You don't have to lean away...they can't see you.

"You'll get a crick in your neck or something."

"Oh yes," Indi shook her head, "you're right. I'm just a bit shaken up."

"There was a problem with Priya's outfit," they heard Rusty say.

"Damnit!" Indi puffed her cheeks up. "They're looking at the wardrobe malfunction."

"So?"

Indi looked at her, her eyes filled with worry. "Sabine...he'll see me."

"But why is he there?"

Just then,

"How long have you been with Lloyds of London?" Rusty asked.

Sabine and Indi looked at each other.

"Oh my God..." they both said at the same time.

"He's the insurance investigator."

*

"Can you play that back?" Hari said. "The so-called malfunction?"

Rusty pressed the 'play' button and the security camera footage showed Priya clutching the top of her blouse and tugging at the fabric of her veil.

"Pause it for a second," Hari asked. "Do you know what happened?"

"The strap of the blouse she was wearing snapped."

Hari looked at him. "You're kidding."

Rusty shook his head.

"Let's keep going," Hari said.

The footage continued, showing Priya's husband getting up and trying to help her.

"Wait...stop!"

"Who's this?" he pointed at the screen. "She's standing next to you."

"That's the designer's assistant," Rusty said.

"What is she doing?" Hari peered at the screen.

"She helped Priya," Rusty said. "We had to go to Mr. Singh's office, which is where Hanut Singh...the designer...had left some stuff."

"What stuff?"

"I honestly don't know...clothes, I think," Rusty said. "And needles, thread...some makeup...you should talk to him."

"There's something about that woman..." Hari looked back at the screen. "She looks so familiar."

"Can you play that again?"

Rusty rewound and hit play.

Hari watched the footage. Suddenly he sat back and rubbed

his temples with his fingers, inhaling deeply and holding it so that his cheeks puffed up.

"You ok, man?" Rusty asked.

"Yeah..." Hari looked back at the screen. "Do you know the name of the designer's assistant?"

"Yeah..." Rusty pulled out his phone and went to his contacts. "Here...Indiana or Indira Kumar," he said. "Strange name...anyhow, they call her Indi."

Hari slumped, his head bowed, his hands intertwined in front of him as he stared at the floor.

"Do you know her?" Rusty asked.

Without looking at him, Hari nodded. "Very well."

"Indi Kumar used to be a big time model," he added.

"She's a beautiful woman," Rusty agreed.

Hari gave him a wry look.

"Was there anyone else with Indi?" he asked.

"Only Hanut Singh, the designer," Rusty replied. "Why?"

"Hanut Singh was the designer..." Hari nodded knowingly.

"You know who he is?"

Hari nodded. "No other woman with Indi?"

Rusty shook his head. "Why?"

"Because Indi's best friend is a woman called Sabine Kumar...they're not related."

"Sabine Kumar..." Rusty repeated.

"Do you know her?"

"She showed up at a gallery event we had a few weeks ago," Rusty revealed.

"So she's back in town..." Hari mused. "This makes this so much more interesting."

Rusty didn't answer.

"Do you know her?"

"Not personally."

"You know her history?"

"I don't think so."

"Sabine Kumar is someone that has been on our radar in Europe for a few years," Hari said.

Rusty sat back pensively, joining the tips of his fingers as his eyes narrowed. "Why?"

"A few years ago, she was the Delhi Police's main suspect in the robbery of the Indore pear diamonds...somehow, she managed to get out, and for the past few years, we know she's been somewhere in Europe, but we haven't been able to pinpoint her whereabouts."

"Really?" Rusty said. "I was still in the army."

"She had a partner...but we don't know whom."

"And you think it's Indi Kumar?"

"I don't want to think it is," Hari said. "But...it may be."

*

"What are we going to do, Sabine?" Indi asked as she cut into a potato and mince patty and added some hot mango chutney to it before putting it in her mouth.

"What do you mean?"

"If Hari realizes it's me on the footage, which, by the way, he will," Indi said, "he will start looking for you...and worse...me."

"Not necessarily."

"Of course necessarily."

"Why?"

"Because he knows that we are friends..."

"Well it doesn't matter," Sabine helped herself to a bite of lunch from Indi's plate.

"What do you mean?" Indi moved her plate towards herself.

"Don't you think they're still looking for you?" Indi said. "It wasn't just the Indore pears, Sabine," she added. "What about all those other jobs?"

"My dear Indi," Sabine reached across the table for another bite of the potato patty. "This is really good," she said as an aside.

"Why are you ignoring the question?" Indi said.

"Indi..." Sabine put a bite in her mouth. "...we genuinely don't have the necklace."

"But can't they come after you for the Pears?"

"No," Sabine shook her head. "Warrants are only valid for five years."

"You sure they can't come after you?"

"Positive," Sabine assured her. "Besides, they don't have any proof that I was the one..." she reached for another bite. "This is really good."

"Can you get your own damned food?" Indi said.

"Such a grump," Sabine rolled her eyes. "Let's get back to work...what have you found on our three society matrons?"

"There's a few things..." Indi swallowed the last of what was left on her plate and took a tall glass of water with her back to the living room and sat down in front of her laptop.

"Our matrons have secrets."

"Everybody does, Indi."

"OK..." Indi pulled up a shot of Nina. "Nina Singh...forty-three years ago, when she was 20, she married Arun Singh the current scion of the House of Barodan, but broke...he was only 15 when the title was taken away from his father in 1971 and the family, along with all the other royal families was stripped of its' privileges.

"As we know, Nina has recently filed for divorce."

"That's quite a move for a woman like her."

"Why?"

"Because women like that never get divorced...no matter what," Sabine said. "Different generation."

"She's not that much older than we are, Sabine," Indi remarked.

"We're not the same, Indi," Sabine said. "We grew up differently."

"I have to say, though, India has come into the 21st century."

"Yes, but India still has traditions and women like Nina Singh stay very close to those traditions."

"I suppose," Indi said. "Anyhow, she has filed for divorce, citing infidelity as the cause."

"Nicely done," Sabine nodded. "Who was the mistress?"

"Bunny Mehra."

"Bunny Mehra and Nina Singh were best friends," Sabine said.

"You're kidding," Indi laughed. "He ran off with his wife's best friend...that's rich.

"Interestingly, Nina is the one who had the money," Indi continued. "Arun, as we know, was as poor as a church mouse when they married."

"So Nina provided all the funding for Arun's real estate deals?"

"Truth be told, it was Nina's father," Indi said. "He provided the initial capital and then after he died, Nina gave Arun her inheritance.

"Of course, all of those deals have pretty much gone south."

"Is Nina broke?"

"Hard to tell..." Indi went back to her laptop. "I was able to get into her bank account," she said. "It's low ... but she may have money hidden away in a shoebox."

"But if they are divorcing," Sabine mused, "what kind of money is Arun going to be able to give Nina?"

"If his financials are anything to go on...not much."

"So she has motive," Sabine put a pencil behind her ear.

"Moving right along," Indi pulled up a photo of Sonia Jaffrey.

"Sonia Jaffrey is married to Samir Jaffrey.

"She is the classic case of the young girl who was born into the right family and then married well," Indi said. "From what I can tell, the marriage is sound..."

"Sonia may know that JJ was behind the staged robbery of the Indore pears that she'd bought and took the Barodan necklace as quid pro quo."

"It's possible," Indi shrugged.

"The last one on this very short list is Rupa Mehra.

"Rupa is definitely one naughty girl."

"Really?" Sabine raised an eyebrow.

"I'm not sure," Indi said. "But maybe...

"For one, she's been all over town trying to sell a few pieces of jewelry..." Indi stared at her screen. "Including going to Gema."

"Are they any good?"

"Gema said the craftsmanship was decent, but the quality of the stones wasn't great."

"Where else has she been?"

"A couple of the guys in Chhor Bazaar," Indi got up and walked around.

"What did they say?"

"Pretty much the same as Gema."

"I don't understand, though," Sabine put one foot up on the chair, hugging her knee. "Why does that make her naughty?"

"She's just another so-called society woman trying to sell some jewelry."

"Well...it turns out that our Rupa has gotten herself into quite a bit of debt, and her allowance doesn't cover it."

"How?"

"Rupa has a gambling problem," Indi revealed.

"This is interesting."

"Yeah," Indi nodded.

"How do you know this?"

"Laxmi's cousin works for Rupa."

"That's nice..." Sabine said. "All in the family."

"Anyhow, Rupa has gotten deeper and deeper in and has been borrowing money from one of the sharks."

"Who?"

"Gupta..."

"What a slime!" Sabine exclaimed wrinkling her nose.

"Yes...but Gupta now works for JJ."

"What?"

"Yes, apparently JJ's corralled them all...Gupta, Sen, all those guys...they work for him now."

"So Gupta is putting the screws into Rupa..." Sabine nodded.

"Rupa definitely needs the money because when Gupta threatens, he means it."

"Also according to Laxmi's cousin, she's too scared to tell her husband how much debt she has..."

"Ok...which makes Rupa desperate," Sabine said. "Which also means," she added, "that if the necklace was on the plate that was put in front of her, she would've kept her mouth shut."

Indi and Sabine stared at each other for a moment.

"Mrs. Rupa Patel," Sabine turned the laptop towards her, staring at the headshot of Rupa smiling, her eyes wide with anticipation as she stared at a plate of sweets offered to her.

"What do you want to do?"

"If Rupa has the necklace, it must still be in her house," Sabine mused. "See if Laxmi's cousin knows anymore or can find out where Rupa keeps her jewelry in the house."

"Wait..." Indi whipped around and stared at Sabine, her face tense.

Sabine cocked an eyebrow.

"No, no, no, no, no," Indi shook her head, understanding. "Are you really thinking about breaking into Rupa Patel's house?"

Sabine didn't answer.

"You're going to get us caught."

"No, I'm not."

"I don't want to go to jail, Sabine."

"You're not, I promise."

"What is your obsession with this necklace?" Indi asked.

"It's a very special necklace, Indi," Sabine replied, her chin stubbornly inclined.

"Sabine...there's something you're not telling me," Indi said.

"Why are you so stuck on it?"

"You know Indi," Sabine started, "when I had to go on the run, I left with nothing...no friends, no family, no money...just the clothes on my back."

"I understand..." Indi began.

"No, you can't say that because you have no idea what it's like..." Sabine said. "None whatsoever."

"Is this necklace really worth it?" Indi asked.

"Yes...it is."

"Sabine...don't try to pull anything on me...I'm no rookie."

"I'm not."

"Why can't you just tell me?"

"There's nothing to tell."

"Then why do I get the sense there is..."

Sabine shrugged.

"Look, if you're trying to frame JJ for what he did to you," Indi said, "I want no part of it."

"My agenda is not going to matter."

"And you're sure we're not going to get caught?"

"I'm sure."

*

Le Bistro Indien was still quiet when Hari walked in.

"Are you open?" he asked the hostess.

"Not quite yet," she said. "The kitchen won't open for another hour."

"What about the bar?"

"The bar is open," she smiled. "Would you like one of the little lounge tables?" she pointed to a small round chair surrounded by two brown leather porter's chairs. "Or would you prefer a seat at the bar?"

"The table, please," he said looking at the rounded chair that reminded him a bit of a confessional in a church.

"What shall I ask the bartender to get you?" she asked.

"A beer, please," Hari replied.

"Kingfisher?" she offered.

"Perfect," Hari nodded.

Half an hour later, Hari put his laptop in his satchel and reclined back into the porter's chair so that all that was visible of him were his legs. He took the final sip of his beer and leaned forward to put the empty bottle on the small coffee table in front of him. He gestured to the bartender for another one and sat back, allowing the sensation of tranquility and privacy afforded by the chair's raised, rounded hood and enclosed sides.

"Thank you," he said when he saw a hand place the bottle of beer on the table in front him.

"Would you like to take a look at the menu, sir?" said a female voice, followed by a soft, leather-bound book that she held out.

That voice...Hari's heart skipped a beat. Could it be? "Thank you," he said and accepted it, too scared to see who it was.

"I'll give you a few minutes to take a look," she said.

He heard her heels tick as she walked away.

Hari put the menu in his lap and took a deep breath. He sat forward and looked out. There was another man sitting in one of the other porter chairs near him and the bartender was polishing glasses. He put the menu back down on the table and reached for his beer. Maybe he was dreaming. It wasn't her. It couldn't be. Or could it?

Just as he had calmed down,

"What may I get for you?" he heard the voice before she reappeared, this time in front of the porter chair.

His stomach knotted.

Tall and svelte, the woman was beautiful. Her long wavy hair, her almond-shaped brown eyes and thick eyebrows...Her face was oval, her cheekbones were chiseled and prominent, her complexion olive, and her lips sensual. She wore a 60's-style black swing dress with short sleeves and low-heeled black shoes. She wore no jewelry apart from a simple chain around her neck and slim charm bracelet.

"Sir? Is everything alright?"

"Uh...yes," Hari said, shaking his head. "I'm sorry...it's just that you remind me so much of someone else."

"What can I get for you, sir?"

"A whiskey please...a double."

*

Imran was sitting in the small, cramped office of the superintendent of the Lodhi Police Station, tapping his fingers on the desk as he scrolled through the footage of all the people arriving at the wedding on the computer screen in front of him.

A young officer came in with a cup of tea and put it on the desk.

"Do you have a cigarette, officer?" Imran asked.

"No, sir, I don't smoke," the man said.

"You don't?" Imran looked shocked.

"Go find me a cigarette," Imran said. "I can't sit here watching all these people without a cigarette."

"Yes, sir," the man said hesitantly.

"What is it?"

"You can't smoke in here, sir."

"What? Why not?"

"We're not allowed to smoke inside the police station."

"For the love of...." Imran began to swear before he stopped and looked at the screen. He stopped the video and rewound. "Who is this?" he peered at the screen.

"Can you send Ajay in here?" he said to the officer.

"No cigarette, sir?" the young man asked.

"Just Ajay, please," Imran glared at him.

Seconds later, another young policeman came in. "Sir," he saluted.

"I need a few screen grabs," he said and turned the video monitor towards the man.

"Very well, sir," the man said. "Do you have the time codes?"

Imran silently handed him a small piece of paper. He kept watching the footage for a couple of minutes before getting up and walking out of the office into the main area of the station where all the officers had their small cubicles. As he waited for the young officer to print him all the screen grabs he'd requested, he sent a text to Hari, 'Interesting photos. Where are you?'

'Le Bistro.'

Hari was on his laptop when a manila folder was tossed onto the table in front of him. He sat up and saw Imran gesturing to the bartender.

"Two whiskies, please," he said.

"What did you find?" Hari said.

"You look like your favourite cat just died," Imran said, looking him up and down. "What happened?"

"I thought I saw my ex," Hari said flatly.

"It wasn't her?"

"No."

"And you're in this shape?" Imran said. "What's going to happen when you really see her?"

"I don't know whether to feel relieved or disappointed that it wasn't her."

"It must've been pretty bad...the break up, that is..." Imran remarked.

"It wasn't pretty," Hari admitted. "But it was my fault."

"When was the last time you saw her?"

"When I walked out on her, about five years ago," Hari said.

"But enough about that...what are we looking at?" he picked up the manila folder. Inside were various shots of a man wearing a velvet sherwani jacket as he entered the gate, walked up the driveway before disappearing into the garden.

"Who does this look like to you?"

Hari looked at the photographs one by one.

"I don't recognize him," Hari put the photographs back on the table. "He just looks like another guest."

"This," Imran picked up the photos and waving them around, "looks very much like a guy by the name of Rambo Singh..."

"Rambo Singh...?" Hari said, reaching for the photos again.

"Rambo Singh is loaded, had a very successful hotel business in Dubai and JJ Singh worked for him, and they were very close...purportedly," Imran started. "But then, suddenly, JJ was back in Delhi, opening up his art gallery and reinventing himself as a celebrity."

"What does this have to do with the necklace?"

"From what I've been able to dig up," Imran said, "Rambo and JJ fell out over money and it is rumoured that JJ stole millions from Rambo and that is how he set himself up in business in Delhi."

"You think Rambo is somehow involved in the disappearance of the necklace?" Hari asked.

"With revenge being the motive, I wouldn't discount Rambo at all," Imran said. "I just have this hunch that he's somehow involved."

"How did Rambo make his fortune?"

"No one really knows," Imran said. "About forty years ago, a series of very high-profile robberies took place in Delhi," Imran said. "But the police were never able to get the thief."

"What kinds of robberies?"

"A lot of very rich people were robbed...money, jewels, art..."

"I think I've read about this, but what does this have to do with Rambo Singh?"

"He was the police's prime suspect," Imran said.

"Really? Why didn't you arrest him?"

"Never had enough to get him," Imran said.

"Interesting."

"I was going through the files, and the detective on the case said that he was positive Rambo had a partner."

"A partner?"

Imran nodded.

"Any leads on who?"

"None," Imran said. "He was a ghost...not a single trace, not a fingerprint, nothing."

"Who do you think it was?"

"I don't know...but there was one guy Rambo Singh hung out with a lot..."

"Yeah? Who?"

"A guy called Abi Kumar," Imran said.

"Abi Kumar?" Hari questioned. "Why do I feel like I've heard the name?"

"Abi Kumar was the Maharajah of Nawanagar..."

Hari frowned.

"And...I think he was Sabine Kumar's father," Imran said as the bartender put a couple of whiskies down in front of them.

"Really?" Hari nodded. This is all beginning to make sense, he thought.

"Rambo lives in London...but I was told that he's back in town," Imran added.

*

Rupa adjusted the pallu of her sari as she walked quickly down the hall to the dining room where she surveyed the table with an eagle eye, adjusting one of the forks to exactly an inch from the edge, and tucking a flower into the centerpiece to avoid it drooping. She picked up the silver bell that had been placed next to her seat at the head of the table and rang it.

"Yes, *memsahiba*," a man servant dressed in white cotton pants, a white tunic and a black sleeveless *bandghala*-style jacket, appeared a few seconds later.

"Ah Kabir!" Rupa swung around. "There you are...make sure there is some white wine nicely chilled and some of that sparkling wine and beers of course."

"Yes, *memsahiba*," Kabir replied.

"And do we have any vodka?"

He nodded.

"Mrs. Sonia may want a martini...we shall see," she said as she headed towards the living room. "And make sure there are some cashews and almonds in the den...and chips," she added. "We will have drinks there. It's such a beautiful day."

And indeed it was. The sunlight streamed through the large windows that gave out onto the garden that was filled with palm trees swaying in the breeze, large green bushes and banana trees and bougainvillea climbing the white walls at the edge of the deep green lawn. Unlike Rupa's traditional personality, the room, with its teak floors, covered with old Central Asian hand-woven rugs, had a very contemporary feel to it, with taupe sofas, black chairs with gold leaf backs and large silver Japanese lamps and books lining one entire wall, the others dotted with paintings by contemporary, young Indian artists.

Rupa loved this room, especially the corner next to one of the large windows that had two black marble sculptures of Indian goddesses set on white marble plinths.

Rupa walked around nervously wringing her hands together, a worried expression on her face. She kept looking at her phone, but there was nothing yet.

She was just about to put the phone down when it rang.

"...uh...hello?" she said gingerly.

"Mrs. Patel..." said a cheery male voice. "Mr. Gupta here."

"Y...y...yes?"

"This is just a friendly reminder that your deadline is coming up."

"Mr. Gupta...I need a little more time."

"You've already had two extensions, Mrs. Patel..."

"I know that I can get it all back to you, Mr. Gupta...there's this one horse running tomorrow and I've got a tip from my bookie..."

"The money, Mrs. Patel," Gupta interrupted her.

"Or else...you know the consequences."

"I...I...that is to say Mr. Gupta..." Rupa swallowed. "I've just had a bit of bad luck and some bad tips..."

"That is not my problem," Gupta's voice sounded sterner and Rupa shivered.

"Please..." Rupa began.

"No more time," Gupta said and hung up.

"Gosh..." Rupa's eyes teared.

She heard the front doorbell ring and quickly dried her eyes, surveying herself in the large bronze mirror on one of the walls when,

"Mrs. Sonia Jaffrey and Mrs. Nina Singh," Kabir announced.

"Ladies!" Rupa was overly cheerful as she welcomed her friends with air kisses. "How lovely you both look. That's an exquisite sari, Mrs. Sonia..."

"This old rag...it's 100 years old," Sonia said caustically.

"Oh, just take the compliment, Sonia," Nina admonished her.

"Thank you," Sonia shrugged her indifference.

"Do come and sit down," Rupa pointed at the chair next to the sofa.

"I'd rather sit on the sofa, Mrs. Rupa," Sonia said.

Rupa obliged and sat down in the chair leaving the sofa for Nina and Sonia.

"What will you all have to drink?" she offered, as Kabir stood respectfully off to the side. "Martinis?"

Sonia and Nina both nodded and Kabir nodded silently and

melted away to fetch the cocktails.

"How are you both?"

"Did you take some sort of happy tablet this morning?" Sonia's eyes narrowed as she peered at Rupa. "Or did you win big at the races yesterday?"

"No, no..." Rupa replied. "Just happy to see you both."

"You're a terrible liar, Mrs. Rupa," Sonia said.

Kabir reappeared at the door with a tray that had individual cocktail shakers and a bowl of green olives on toothpicks.

"I'll ring when we are ready for lunch, Kabir," Rupa said.

"Is everything alright, Mrs. Rupa?" Sonia asked.

"Yes, yes..." Rupa stuck her nose in her glass.

"You are looking a little worried."

"Oh ladies..." Rupa broke down. "Just before you came, I got a call from Gupta...I don't have much time left to return what I owe him.

"I've been thinking about selling the couple of pieces I have left..."

"I thought you sold those."

Rupa shook her head.

"Then what's the point?" Nina said.

"I have this tip on a horse in the seventh race tomorrow..." Rupa began.

"Ok...stop right there!" Sonia interrupted. "Have you gone completely mad, Mrs. Rupa?"

"I'm just trying to get the money together..."

"By betting your last few pennies on a horse race?"

"I don't know what else to do," Rupa wrung her hands together.

"I think you're going to have to come clean to your husband," Sonia said.

"Oh no!" Rupa wailed. "He will divorce me...I can't be a divorcee in Delhi society..."

"I'm going to be a divorcee in Delhi society," Nina said.

"How will I live?" Rupa cried. "I can't get a job...I don't know how to work."

"You could do something socially acceptable like volunteer work or fundraising."

"But that doesn't pay anything...ohhhh!" Rupa wailed. "I'm going to jail and Mr. Patel will divorce me.

"I'll be so, so poor."

"Look..." Nina took a deep breath, "let's not get quite so dramatic. Nothing has happened yet."

"I can't lose all this," she gestured around the room just as Kabir came back in.

"Bring another round of drinks, please," she said to him.

"Yes, *memsahiba*."

"I can't believe JJ Singh's safe was empty," Sonia said after he'd left.

"Both nights," Nina nodded.

"That son of a bitch," Sonia swore.

"He must need the money."

"Not as much as I do."

"What on earth did he do with the Barodan?" Sonia said.

"Speaking of," Rupa said. "Do you remember we saw it at Gema's?"

"What?" Sonia said.

"Remember that day you took me to Gema's to see if we

could sell those couple of pieces," Rupa reminded her. "And I saw the Barodan necklace..."

"What do you mean 'saw the Barodan necklace?'" Nina jumped in.

"I saw the necklace, Nina," Rupa insisted.

"She's talking through her hat," Sonia said.

"I am not, Mrs. Sonia," Rupa said indignantly. "I know what I saw."

"Why would Gema have the Barodan?" Nina wondered out loud.

"Nina...I don't think it was the real one," Sonia said. "Gema makes copies and this was most certainly a copy."

"No, no," Nina replied. "But why would Gema have been making a copy? And for whom?"

"Oh," Sonia cocked her head. "I see what you mean."

"And who would have commissioned the copy?"

"Wouldn't that be JJ?" Rupa asked.

"Yes...but why?" Nina narrowed her eyes. "Unless..."

"Unless what?"

"When I went to see him to try sell those pearls from the Maharajah of Jodhpur..."

"You have pearls from the Maharajah of Jodhpur?" Rupa's eyes grew wide.

"Shut up, Mrs. Rupa!" Sonia admonished her. "Continue, Nina."

"I wanted to sell him the pearls, but he turned me down, saying he was overextended."

"What does that mean?" Rupa asked.

"It means that he doesn't have as much money as he claims to have," Sonia glared at her. "Honestly, compared to what he spent on that party, buying the pearls off of Nina would have been a drop in the bucket."

"But why would he be making a copy of the Barodan, unless he's planning on selling it?" Nina asked.

"Or insurance fraud?" Rupa said.

The two women looked at her, surprised.

"What?" Rupa shrugged. "Didn't you tell me that, Sonia?" she added.

Sonia rolled her eyes. "Alright, I did," she admitted.

"So was Priya wearing a fake necklace at that party?"

"Could be," Sonia said. "And the real necklace has been quietly sold or JJ stole his own necklace and is committing insurance fraud."

*

"Can we talk about about Sabine Kumar?" Hari asked Imran, sitting across a desk from him in his office at police headquarters.

"She's a person of interest for the CBI," Imran pulled on a file drawer that screeched open. "About five years ago, she was implicated in the theft of some very important diamonds that were stolen from Samir and Sonia Jaffrey.

"I was the investigating detective," he added. "Sonia Jaffrey tipped us off saying that she thought JJ, who had sold them the diamonds, was also the thief.

"When we got JJ in to talk to him, he told us that Sabine Kumar, was the one who had come up with the whole scheme...that she'd brought the diamonds to him and asked him to set up the sale with the Jaffreys and gone in to steal the diamonds back."

"What happened to the diamonds?"

"We never got Sabine," Imran said. "She got out of the country, with the diamonds, I assume.

"After that, she fell off our radar in Delhi."

Hari nodded. "She didn't stop."

"Yes? What has she been up to?"

"She's been roaming around Europe," Hari began. "There were a couple of things recently in London and Rome..." Hari began. "Both cases were Lloyd's, which is why I know about them," he said. "But I wasn't directly involved in either."

"Well...she's back in town."

"Really?"

"Arrived a few weeks ago," Imran nodded, handing him a manila folder. "And staying at the Oberoi, down the hall from Rambo Singh's suite."

"Interesting," Hari perused the file.

"From what we know, she's been keeping to herself."

"Are you sure?" he asked. "Sabine Kumar never keeps to herself."

"As far as we know."

"Do you know if she has seen a woman called Indi Kumar?"

"I don't know," Imran looked puzzled. "Who is she? Sister? Cousin?"

"Best friend."

"What's her story?"

Hari took a deep breath.

"Indi used to be a model...she is extremely smart and I know she has been Sabine's partner-in-crime."

"What do you mean by 'partner-in-crime?'" Imran asked. "We don't have a file on her."

"No...you wouldn't...she was always in the background,"

Hari said. "Computers, logistics..."

"And you know a lot about her..." Imran looked at him over his reading glasses.

"I do," Hari said.

"Care to share?"

"Not really," Hari said. "Suffice to say she was the bad breakup."

Imran nodded understanding.

"It wasn't pleasant...towards the end, that is, when I found out about Sabine and this other side of her life."

"And that is why it ended?"

"There was more," Hari admitted, "but yes, that had something to do with it."

"Life isn't easy."

"Listen, man," Hari said, "I know this may be crazy, but I think Sabine Kumar has something to do with the disappearance of this necklace."

"How? Why?"

"I saw some footage of the wedding and Indi was there...and if she was there, you can be sure Sabine was too."

"But wait," Imran put a hand up. "The necklace wasn't stolen until the night after the party."

Hari shrugged.

"You think it was stolen the night of the party?"

"Maybe."

"You're going to need more than a hunch."

Hari silently nodded.

"But if the necklace was stolen on the night of the party,"

Imran scratched his chin, "then what was stolen the night after?"

"I don't know...but for now, let's say it was stolen the night after," Hari said. "I do think, though, we have to begin by looking at the event and everyone who was there."

"Do you think that someone at the party was casing the house?"

"I do.

"I've asked for a copy of the footage," Hari got up. "I'll go through it.

"Let's see if we can find her on the footage at JJ's party."

*

Sabine, dressed completely in black got out of the car and tightened the hood around her head. "I'll be back in 15 minutes," she bent down and whispered to Indi, who was in the driver's seat.

"It's a small hotel-type safe in her dressing room inside a cupboard."

Sabine gave her the thumbs-up sign, and Indi sat back in the seat, her stomach in knots.

Suddenly, she saw headlights coming down the lane in her rearview mirror. She slid down in the seat and waited. The car passed her by and stopped in front of the gate to the Patel House

*

The driver jumped out and came around the side and opened the passenger door. A smallish man got out and opened the gate and went in. Indi peered at him. It was Mr. Ramesh Patel. What the hell is he doing here? He was supposed to be in Bombay.

Indi grabbed her phone and sent a text. Seconds later, she heard a muted sound. Damnit! Sabine had left her phone in the car.

Chapter 11

Rupa tossed and turned, stabbing her pillow, turning from one side to another, trying to fall asleep. She opened her eyes and looked at the small clock on her bedside table. 1am. Damn. She'd been trying to fall asleep for two hours. Thank goodness, Ramesh was away on business. She swung her legs onto the floor and sat up, her hair tied in a plait and reached for her dressing gown at the bottom of the bed.

She yawned and slipped her feet into a pair of house slippers and walked out into the living room where Kabir had left a lamp on.

She went into the kitchen, turned on the light and opened the fridge and took out a jug of milk and poured some in a small pan to warm it up. Just then, she heard a creaking sound. She stopped, cocking her head. There it was again, this time a bit more forceful. She put the jug down and cautiously went back outside into the darkened dining room, holding a rolling pin out in front of her like a sword.

She walked down the hallway to her bedroom and slowly opened the door. The far side of the bedroom with the windows that gave out onto the balcony and the garden was in darkness, the only light being a small lamp on her bedside table that she had switched on. She walked around. Nothing looked like it had been disturbed. She was sure she'd heard the sounds coming from her bedroom.

"Owwww!" she suddenly heard a muffled groan. She walked

back out, down the hall and around the dining table when she heard a scuffling sound. She stood rooted to the spot. There was someone in the house. She ran to the entrance table...her keys were in the little plate she always left them on. She reached for her cellphone and dialed 100 for the local police. She got an engaged signal. *What?* She stared at the phone incredulous. She walked to a room that was on the far side of the entrance hallway and saw a light under the doorway and the shadow of a figure moving around.

She quickly went back to the kitchen and out the back door where directly to the right, she knocked on Kabir's door.

"Kabir! Kabir!" she said. "Wake up!"

"Who is it?" she heard his sleepy voice.

"What do you mean 'who is it?' Rupa said annoyed. "It's me...Rupa *memsahiba*."

Moments later, Kabir opened the door wearing a pair of pants and a shirt, looking disheveled. "Yes, *memsahiba*," he said.

"There's a *chhor* in the house?"

"*Chhor, memsahiba?*"

"Yes, you idiot!" she said, "now come with me and bring something to hit him with.

"He may have a gun or a knife...luckily I was up or he would've killed us all in our beds."

Together, they walked back towards the room, Kabir holding a cricket bat. The light was still on. Suddenly, they heard the sound of water running.

"*Memsahiba*...it sounds like he's having a bath."

"What *bakwaas* are you talking?" Rupa said. "Why would a *chhor* have a bath?"

"Maybe he thought he was dirty?"

"Oh!" Rupa rolled her eyes. "Don't be stupid!" she prodded him with her rolling pin. "Now, go in!" she ordered.

"Me? *Memsahiba*?" Kabir said. "Maybe we should call the police?"

"By the time they come, we'll all be dead!" Rupa pushed him towards the door. "Now get in there."

Kabir pushed the door open and at that same moment, a male figure was wrapping a towel around his middle.

"*Chhor*!" Rupa screamed. "*Chhor*!" she began brandishing the rolling pin. "Thief! Thief!"

Kabir froze, staring at the man who was so stunned that he let his towel fall to the ground.

"Kabir! Call the police!" Rupa shouted.

"*Memsahiba*," Kabir began.

"What are you doing? Go call the police!" she yelled.

"*Memsahiba*..." Kabir averted his gaze from the naked man. "It's *Sahib*."

"What?" Rupa turned to look, her eyes growing wide. "Ohhhhhh!" she watched her husband pick the towel up and try to cover himself with it.

"Ramesh! You scared me to death!" Rupa said. "What are you doing here?"

Ramesh grinned as he looked at his wife in her dressing gown, the rolling pin up in the air.

"I got the last flight out...but it was delayed," Ramesh began chuckling. "I didn't want to disturb you, so I thought I would sleep in the guest room."

"I thought you were here to rob us!" Rupa said.

"I am sorry, Mrs. Patel," he said affectionately.

"Would you like some hot cocoa?" she sat down in an armchair. "I was just going to make some."

He nodded, smiling.

*

Sabine came out from behind a curtain in Rupa's bedroom just in time to hear Rupa's high-pitched screech. She froze in her tracks for a moment, but when there was no movement, she walked to the door and peeked out, smiling as she saw what was happening on the other side of the hallway.

Quickly, she went into Rupa's dressing room. There were two cupboards, both locked. She reached into the pouch at her waist and pulled out a long needle-like instrument and inserted it into the first lock. It opened. Men's shirts. She pried open the second that screeched a bit, making her wince. Inside were sari blouses, petticoats and saris all hung meticulously. Rifling around, she found the safe in the back. She opened it easily. Inside were passports, some cash and a leather jewelry case that had a few pieces in it but no Barodan.

Just then, she heard sounds of footsteps down the hallway coming towards the bedroom.

"Why wouldn't you sleep in your own bed, Ramesh?" she heard Rupa.

Moving fast, she ran to the window, opened it and went out onto the balcony.

"Mrs. Patel, you left the window open," she heard a male voice. "That is a clear invitation to thieves."

"I didn't leave it open," Rupa replied.

"Yet, it's open," Mr. Patel's voice sounded closer to the window.

Sabine climbed over the railing and clung to a creeping plant as Ramesh Patel stood on the balcony looking around. "It's such a beautiful night, Mrs. Patel," Ramesh said. "Look at that crescent moon."

"What are you getting all romantic for?" Rupa giggled. "Talking about the moon and all that stuff..."

"Why not, Rupa?" Ramesh called back to her as he took a deep breath of the night air.

Sabine glued herself to the wall.

"Come inside, Ramesh," Rupa said. "You'll catch cold."

Sabine heard the window click. She breathed a huge sigh of relief, slithered down, landing softly on the grass below.

*

"Anything?" Indi asked as she jumped into the passenger seat, pulling the hoodie off her head.

"Nothing."

"Honestly, if she had it, she would've tried to sell it and we would've heard, don't you think?"

"Maybe...depends where she tried to sell it."

"I tried texting you about the husband...he went in a minute or so after you."

"I know, and thank goodness he did, otherwise I would have walked in on Rupa having cocoa in her living room," Sabine looked up at Rupa's balcony just in time to see the light go out.

"I wonder what they're doing," she said suggestively.

"Stop!" Indi started the car engine. "I don't want to think about it...the visual is enough."

"What? You don't think they do the wild thing?"

"Shut up Sabine!"

"Maybe she's doing the right thing so she can get the money

she owes Gupta," Sabine chuckled.

"God!"

"You're such a prude," Sabine teased her.

"I am not.

"Seriously, though, now what?" Indi put the car in gear.

"We wait," Sabine said. "Whoever has it is going to blink."

*

Hari was sitting in the conference room of the Singh Gallery, his legs up on the table as he scrolled through the footage of the party. Next to him, he had a large board on which there were photos of a handful of people, shots of Priya seated at her table during the dinner and shots of JJ at his table along with a handful of notes he had pinned next to the photos.

"How's it going?" Rusty came in.

"There's a lot," Hari replied.

Rusty sat down in one of the chairs.

"Who set up the security cameras?" Hari asked.

"A company called Pioneer Security."

"Who designed the matrix?" Hari asked. "In other words, who decided on the angles?"

"They did," Rusty said. "The guy who started the company is a good friend of mine from army intelligence."

"Do they also do the gallery?"

Rusty nodded. "They have a pretty sophisticated system," he said. "Here at the gallery, the art is recorded from multiple angles, and so is the art at the house."

"What about the rest of the house?"

"The rest is pretty standard."

"Do you think anyone could have gotten into their system?"

"I highly doubt it," Rusty said.

"Now," Hari sat up, tapping a pencil on a yellow pad, "You told me you had eyes on the necklace the whole time?"

"From the moment it came out of the vault.

"I was the one who took it out and took it to the hotel."

"What about during this wardrobe malfunction of Priya's?" Hari hit a button on his laptop.

"It's as I told you."

"So..." Hari said, "from here...where Priya gets up from her table and covers herself with her veil or gown or whatever, all the way to ... here...at the office," he stopped the tape, "you did not have a physical eye on the necklace."

"I...guess not," Rusty sounded contrite.

"When did you realize the necklace had fallen off?"

"When we were in Mr. Singh's office and Priya took off the *dopatta*."

"What did you do?"

"I locked the place down and had a team combing the area from the marquee to the office."

"Where was Indi Kumar during this time?"

"With Priya."

"You are sure?"

"Yes."

Hari pursed his lips.

"Now...who is this?" he fast forwarded to images of a woman coming out of JJ's office and walking through the reception hall.

"Mrs. Nina Singh," Rusty said. "She is married to Arun Singh, from the Barodan family.

"She was sitting to Mr. Singh's left at his table."

"But what was she doing in Mr. Singh's office?"

"When my man approached her," Rusty said, "she said she got lost looking for the bathroom."

"But why was she in Mr. Singh's office?"

Rusty shook his head.

"There's no camera in his office?"

"No."

"But he has a safe," Hari said. "So why no camera?"

"That safe is an old safe that was in the gallery when he bought the building," Rusty said. "It's impossible to get into..."

Hari got up and looked at his mood board and wrote 'Why?' on a sticker and put it under the headshot of Nina Singh.

"Listen...I'm going to have to talk to Priya," Hari said. "And Nina...I'm going to have to ask her what she was doing in Singh's office."

*

Dressed casually in a pair of white cotton pants, a long white tunic with a stone grey shawl wrapped around his shoulders and a black karakul Kahsmiri hat, Rusty got out of a taxi at the entrance to Sundar Nagar. Pulling the shawl closely around him, he walked into the small square park, looking left and right. It was a couple of minutes past 10 and the shops were just getting going.

"That miserable bastard is late!" he swore when he saw that the shutters were still down on the shop he was going to. Looking around, he was walking across the patch of green towards a café that was just opening when he heard the creaking wheels of a hand cart and the shrill shout of a man calling out his wares.

"Chai! Fresh chai! Fresh samosas...come all...the chai is hot!"

Rusty turned and took a few big steps over to the banyan

tree in the middle of the square where the chaiwallah had parked his cart, climbing on top of it, sitting cross-legged on a cushion as he stirred a very large kettle of tea, a wooden tray of glasses next to it.

"That's a pretty big kettle," Rusty remarked.

"It has been in the family for a long time," the man grinned, showing his toothless gums. "I remember my great-grandfather making tea in six of these kettles for the whole kitchen at the British viceroy's house before partition."

"Where are the other five?"

"Around town...we are five brothers, all chaiwallahs."

"Let me try your tea, chaiwallah," Rusty smiled.

"And a *samosa, sahib*?" the chaiwallah asked. "They are very good. My wife makes them."

"Oh alright," Rusty said and took the potato-filled pastry in a piece of newspaper and sat down on one of the stumps of the tree to enjoy it.

"Chaiwallah!" he heard a female voice.

"Gema *bibi*..." the chaiwallah replied. "The usual?"

"*Haan*," she replied. "*Kya haal*, chaiwallah? How are you?"

"*Bas*," he wobbled his head, grinning, "*sub theek thaak!*"

Just then, Rusty noticed the shutters of the shop he'd come to visit go up. He drained his glass, and put it back on the cart. "Thank you, chaiwallah," he said.

"Come back, sahib!" the chaiwallah called as he walked away. "I am here every day, even before the shops open."

Rusty saluted him, smiling.

"*Namaste*, Rusty *Sahib*," the man who opened the door wished him.

"*Namaste*, Mahesh."

"Sorry I'm a bit late, the scooter didn't start."

"Never mind...I've brought the piece," Rusty said, taking his shawl off. "I need you to cut it and make 8 pieces of jewelry."

"Yes, *Sahib*."

*

"Who is that?" Gema asked as she blew on the hot tea to cool it.

"I don't know," the chaiwallah replied. "These eyes aren't the same as they used to be."

"He must be a customer for one of the shops."

"He was waiting for Mahesh Bharany to open," Gema said as she watched him knock at the door of a shop at the far end of the square. "No one waits for Mahesh to open unless they've got something important they're trying to get rid of."

Gema quickly pulled her phone from her pocket and snapped a quick shot just as Rusty walked into the shop and shut the door.

"Damn!" she said when she looked at it. All she got was his back and his shawl.

Priya and Hari were sitting at the dining table in Priya's hotel suite.

Priya was wearing a black velvet top with a plunging neckline, showing off her ample bosom.

"Thank you for seeing me at such short notice," Hari rummaged around in his satchel and pulled out a file.

"I can't believe the necklace has been stolen," Priya looked chagrined. "Would you join me in a glass of champagne?" she placed her perfectly manicured hands on her shoulders.

"It's...uh...a bit early for me," Hari replied, looking at his watch. "But please don't let me stop you."

"Really? I've got French champagne," she batted her eyelashes flirtatiously.

"I don't think there's any other kind."

Priya sat back looking mildly chastised.

"I'd like to go through the day of the party," Hari's pen hovered over his notebook.

"JJ's guy arrived with the necklace," Priya began.

"Was that Rusty Khan?" Hari asked.

"The tall, good-looking guy..." she said saucily, "he almost looked European..."

Hari nodded.

"Yes, he brought it," Priya said. "We tried it on...I took it off...then I got dressed...then they put it back on me...then..." she frowned as she thought back.

"Who was here with you?"

"My whole design team...hair, makeup, clothes."

"Alright, go on..."

"There was a problem with my blouse and Indi fixed it."

"Indi?"

"Indi's Hanut's assistant...she's great! I *love* her!" Priya made a little heart with her fingers next to her left breast.

Hari stifled a chuckle behind a pretend sneeze.

"Then we went to the party, we walked the red carpet, then we mingled at the reception, then we sat for dinner and then just before the main course, my blouse ripped...you know maybe it was just too tight and then once I started eating...because I hadn't eaten anything in about three days..."

"Just go on," Hari stopped her.

"My husband tried to cover me, but he was useless, so Indi came to my rescue and draped the dopatta veil over me or else... it would have been beyond embarrassing...you understand?"

Hari looked down at his notes.

"We had to go back to JJ's office so she could fix it, but when we got there, the necklace was gone."

"What do you mean, 'gone?'

"I don't know," Priya shrugged. "It was not on my neck."

"What do you mean?"

Priya rolled her eyes. "I mean, it was not on me."

"It fell off?"

"Yes, and everyone freaked out."

"Where did it fall off?"

Priya shrugged.

"But then obviously, they found it?"

"Yes," Priya said. "It was in the garden."

"So it fell off when you were walking to the office?"

"Probably."

"And after that, it stayed on throughout the entire party?"

"It did."

"You didn't return the necklace until the following evening...where was it until then?"

"Well..." Priya flicked her mane of hair and began twirling a lock around her finger, "the party didn't end until dawn and everyone was exhausted..." she clarified and Hari nodded.

"We came back here and...you know...got into bed..."

"Where was the necklace?"

"Around my neck."

"You slept with it on?"

Priya shifted her weight in the chair and sort of nodded.

"You slept with it on?" Hari repeated.

"Yes."

"Why?"

"I wanted to see how I felt sleeping with such an expensive necklace...I need to be able to draw on different emotions from memory for my craft as an actor."

Hari scribbled in his notebook.

"Plus, you know...it was...umm," she hesitated.

Hari cocked an eyebrow prompting her.

"Ummm...it was a big turn on for Randy."

God! I don't need to hear this. "I see," Hari looked squarely at his notepad.

"Tell me..." Hari opened his folder and pulled several photographs out. "This woman... Indi Kumar..."

"She was my...stylist..." Priya said cautiously.

"Do you know if she was ever alone in Mr. Singh's office?"

"I don't think so."

"Was she with you the whole time?"

"Yes, she helped dress me in JJ's office," Priya said.

"What about this woman?" Hari slapped another photograph down on the table.

Priya cocked her head first from one side and then to the other, staring at a photo of Sabine.

"No," she finally said, chewing the gum she had in her mouth, loudly. "I don't think so."

"Sabine Kumar...professional thief and con artist..."

"Oh!" Priya's eyes grew wide.

"She managed to escape a few years ago after stealing the Indore pear diamonds from a private collector, but we couldn't prove it.

"She's been living in Europe and only just came back to Delhi a few weeks ago.

Priya was riveted.

"Her best friend and one-time partner is Indi Kumar."

"Oh my God!"

"Did you see Sabine at the party?"

Priya shook her head.

"If Indi was there, it is likely that Sabine was too, but no one seems to have seen her nor does she appear on any of the cameras."

"Could Sabine have been there, but disguised?" Priya suggested.

"Disguised?"

Priya nodded. "Sometimes when I go out and I don't want to be recognized, I wear a wig...and lots of makeup.

"And if she was there to look over the place to see how she was going to get in and rob the safe, she would've definitely not come as herself."

Hari nodded, scribbling in his notebook.

"I don't know, but if I were a thief in a movie, I would disguise myself to get in somewhere."

"It's a very interesting case," Hari sat back, cradling the back of his head in his hands.

"Hmmm..." Priya murmured staring at the photos. "Am I a suspect?" she asked.

Suddenly, the muffled sound of a cell phone ringing was heard.

"Oh sorry," Priya got up and took her phone out of the bag

and looked at it, frowning as she did.

"Everything alright?" Hari asked.

She took a couple of moments to reply. "Yes!" she swung around, smiling her big, toothy movie-star smile. "Everything is wonderful.

"I'm sorry I can't be of more help," she said.

"Well, I won't take up any more of your time," Hari gathered up his papers. "Thank you."

Priya smiled as he walked out.

*

As soon as he left, the smile died, replaced by worry as she furrowed her brow dialing a number. "Yes...I'm working on it...I need a little more time.

"Hello...? Hello?"

The line was dead.

Priya stared at her phone for a moment and dialed another number.

"Hello...yes, it's me...I need to sell a little jewelry...someone very discreet...alright, but please get me a name quickly."

She rushed into the bedroom of her suite. In the dressing room, she pulled a small suitcase from the cupboard. She opened it and inside was a short salt and pepper wig and a pair of large sunglasses. She removed her makeup and changed into a simple white sari. Staring at herself in the long mirror, she put on her sunglasses. Yes, she looked like a widow. She took a small brown paper packet out of a drawer and walked out into the living room. Her phone beeped with an incoming message.

'Gema Kaling, Khanna Market.'

'Is she discreet?' Priya texted back.

'Yes.'

Priya opened the door to her suite and after looking right and left to make sure it was empty, she quickly padded to the elevator where she made a call.

"Have the Maruti brought to the front," she said.

Just before she walked into the lobby, she took the sari pallu and draped it around her shoulders.

Walking with her head down, she sailed past the paparazzi who were all waiting outside and got into the small nondescript car.

"Sundar Nagar *chalo*," she said to the driver. "Khanna Market..." she stared out of the darkened window watching one of the photographer's light up a cigarette. What if he knew where I'm going? she thought.

Sitting in the driver's seat of a black Range Rover in the driveway of the Oberoi Hotel, Rusty sent a text,

'Is she in her room?'

'Walking out the door.'

Rusty sat back and waited, watching the main entrance. Moments later, Sabine, wearing a pair of jeans and a loose white cotton shirt, walked out and got into a white Mercedes that was waiting for her.

As soon as the car disappeared from sight, Rusty drove around the back to the service entrance. He parked the car on the road and took off the jacket of his suit, replacing it with a white jacket with a Nehru collar. He walked up to the door that said 'Service' and slipped inside, walking quickly down a hallway towards the lifts.

"Hey, you!" a man shouted.

Rusty glanced over his shoulder but did not respond.

"You! I'm talking to you!" the voice continued.

Rusty had just pressed the button for the lift when a short, rotund man waddled over to him.

"You! Are you deaf?"

"Were you talking to me, sir?" Rusty said.

"No, I was talking to you father," the man said, looking at his jacket. "Of course I was talking to you.

"What's your name? And why isn't it on your jacket?"

"It's Rakesh, sir," Rusty said. "I've just started today."

"Rakesh...Rakesh what?" he stood with a pencil poised over a sheet of paper on his clipboard. "Goddamned clock-in machine isn't working either today."

"Rakesh Malhotra."

The man scribbled it down. "What are you? A butler?"

"Yes, sir."

"Good...because that idiot Sen didn't come to work today," the man swore. "Next time I see him, he's sacked."

He looked at his clipboard. "You'll be on the 10th floor today.

"Do you have a card for the lift?"

Rusty pulled one from his pocket.

"Good, at least they had the sense to give you one.

"Since you're going up there, take this trolley for housekeeping, and if they need help, make sure you help," he wagged his finger at Rusty. "We're very short-staffed today."

Rusty pushed a trolley filled with sheets and towels into the elevator and pressed the button for the 10th floor.

Just as the door was almost closed, some chubby fingers appeared in the crack and the door slid back open.

It was the small, pudgy man.

"Just make sure that no one is in Miss Kumar's suite when you go in," he said. "She's very funny about us going in if she's there."

"Yes, sir."

On the 10th floor, Rusty left the trolley off to the side in the hallway and walked to the end where he rang the bell of the Eastern Star suite.

"Service," he said politely, keeping the back of his head to the camera he knew was behind him.

He rang the bell again. Still no answer. He took a key out of his pocket and opened the door.

"Service..." he called out, walking into the entrance hallway. Without waiting, he went through the bedroom to the dressing room. He opened the top drawer of the chest of drawers and pulled a velvet pouch out of his breast pocket and placed it under some carefully folded t-shirts.

He walked back out of the suite, keeping his head down, and walked down the hall to the Western Star Suite at the other end.

He rang the doorbell and when there was no answer, he went in. Just as he was placing another velvet pouch in the drawer in the dressing room, he heard the door open. He quickly hid behind the door, listening to the footsteps that came into the bedroom. Shit! he grimaced.

He carefully poked his head out. He could see a man, wearing a dark blue robe lying on the bed.

He pulled out his cellphone and sent a text.

Moments later, the phone on the side of the bed rang.

"Yes...a package you say? ... yes, alright, send it up."

The man got off the bed and went into the bathroom.

Rusty opened the door and slipped through the bedroom and out the front door, closing it as quietly as he could behind him.

He was waiting for the service elevator when suddenly, about 100 feet away, the main elevator door opened and Sabine came out. Rusty whipped around, keeping his back to her and his head down. "Come on...come on," he looked at the service elevator inching its way upstairs. Just before he got into the service elevator, he looked back, but Sabine had already disappeared into her suite. As soon as the doors opened, Rusty jumped in and pressed the ground floor button. In the elevator, he sent a text.

'It's done.'

'Both?' came the reply.

'Yes.'

*

When Sabine got off the elevator, she glanced to the right and saw a man, dressed as a butler come out of Rambo's suite. He looked vaguely familiar. Who was he? she wondered as she walked down the hall towards the Eastern Star. She knew she'd seen him before, but where? She hadn't really gotten a good look at his face before he'd turned, his back facing her.

She pulled out her cellphone and sent a text.

'Everything alright in the West?'

'Yes...and in the East?'

'I'll let you know in a few if anything is wrong.'

'Why do you ask?'

'I just saw a man coming out of your suite and he looked familiar, but I didn't get a good look at his face.'

'I don't know, I was in the shower...probably the butler leaving *my suits.'*

'Yeah...probably...anyhow, just thought I'd check.'

*

Back in the Western Star suite, Rambo picked up the phone and dialed.

"Reception," answered an efficient voice. "How can I help you, Mr. Singh."

"Aren't you sending up my package?'

"Package, sir?"

"Yes, I got a call a few minutes ago about a messenger being here with a package."

"No sir...I'm afraid there's no one here."

"I see."

"Perhaps one of my colleagues got it wrong," the receptionist said. "I apologize for the error, sir."

"Thank you," Rambo said and hung up. He walked around the suite, but nothing seemed amiss.

He shrugged...perhaps it had been a genuine mistake.

Chapter 12

Indi looked at herself in the bathroom mirror. She poked the apples of her cheeks, frowned and then smoothed out her forehead with her fingers. Her phone on the sink rang. It was Sabine. "Hey!" she answered putting the call on speaker phone. "I'm thinking about getting some work done. Maybe the crows feet around my eyes..."

"I'm in traffic."

Indi rolled her eyes. "Well, it is Delhi."

"Any news?"

"None so far."

"You got any food?"

"I have a cook, remember," Indi brushed one of her eyebrows and tweezed off a hair. "And a maid...that's why I live in India...I've got staff."

"You're such a goddamned snob...I'll be there in a few."

"Some filler in my cheeks..." Indi started. "What do you think? ... Hello? Sabine? You there?

"That brat!" she swore. "She hung up on me."

A few minutes later, the doorbell rang.

"That was quick..." Indi opened the door. Her mouth fell open and she immediately shut it.

The doorbell rang again.

"Go away," she said.

"Indi..." Hari's voice came through the door.

Indi leaned against the door and shut her eyes tightly to stop the tears.

"Come on Indi!"

"What are you doing here?" she said.

"Open the door."

Slowly, Indi opened the door a sliver.

"Are you going to let me in?" he said.

She shut the door again. Quickly she ran to the mirror and looked at herself. Her hair was messy, she wasn't really made up, and damn! Why was she wearing that oversized white shirt? It made her look so fat. God!

The doorbell rang again. She walked to the door resignedly. He knew she was home. She opened the door wide, smiling.

"Why, Hari!" she said brightly. "What a surprise! What brings you here?"

"If you let me in, I can explain."

"Come on in," she stood aside to let him in. "I don't have a lot of time," she added. "I have an appointment."

"How have you been?" he looked around the entrance hallway.

"Fine," she replied. "You?"

"Yeah," he turned around and looked her up and down. "Good.

"Beautiful house."

"Thanks," she folded her arms across her chest. "What do you want, Hari?"

"I'm here for work."

"You? Work? That's rich."

"Listen...I'm here because the Barodan necklace was stolen..."

"The what necklace?"

"Come on, Indi...you know what I'm talking about...it's one of the most famous necklaces in the world."

"So?" she shrugged.

"So..." he sauntered over to her. "I want to talk to you about it."

"Why?"

"Well, you were Priya Chopra's stylist."

"I was the assistant to the designer of her outfit."

"Whatever...but you were with her from the time the necklace was placed around her neck, and when she had her unfortunate wardrobe malfunction."

"She was wearing the necklace all night..."

"Yes, but it was stolen after she returned it."

"What do you mean?" Indi's eyes grew wide.

"What's wrong with you?" Hari said. "Am I not making sense?"

"The necklace was stolen after she returned it?" Indi pretended to sneeze, trying to stifle a giggle.

"Yes, stolen from JJ Singh's safe in his office at his home."

"Wait...you're joking?"

"No, I'm not."

"So that's why you're here?"

"Yes..."

"You're investigating the theft of the necklace from JJ Singh's office safe?"

"For God's sake's, Indi...yes!" Hari rolled his eyes.

"That's hilarious."

"Why?"

"I don't know why I said that," she said.

"I want to talk to you about the night of the party?"

"Why?"

"Because I think someone at the party was casing the joint."

"And you think it was Sabine and me...?"

"I didn't say that..."

"But that's what you think..." Indi walked over to the entrance hall table and quickly sent a text.

'Hari is here.'

'I'll be there soon.'

"Look, Indi," Hari sighed. "I know this is awkward..."

"Oh really?"

"I don't need the sarcasm," he said.

Indi stuck her chin up defiantly, shifting her weight from one foot to the other.

"You look really good," he said after a few moments of silence. "I love the short hair."

"Thank you," she crossed her hands over her chest.

"Listen...I'm just looking for the necklace, Indi," he said. "I don't care who took it, who has it...I can just say that I found it in the bazaar..."

"I don't have it."

"I know Sabine is in town..."

Indi nodded. "She doesn't have it."

"She doesn't?"

"No."

Just then the front door opened and Sabine burst in.

"Sabine!" Indi said.

"You alright?' Sabine asked Indi. "Hari..." she acknowledged him.

"Sabine...thanks for calling," Hari said. "I was going to call you..."

"Wait! You called him?" Indi exploded.

Sabine nodded sheepishly.

"Can I have a word with you...in private?" Indi marched off in the direction of her bedroom.

"I'll be right back," she heard Sabine tell Hari.

"Are you flipping kidding me?" she turned on Sabine once the door was closed. "Have you lost your mind? *You* called *him*?"

"Indi...calm down."

"I will not calm down," Indi threw her hands up in the air. "I am supposedly your best friend and partner and that guy out there is my ex who dumped me...and in a pretty bad way."

"I thought you dumped him," Sabine looked confused.

"Whatever...but how dare you call him...and have him come to my house without even telling me?"

"I really thought I was going to be here," Sabine said apologetically.

"But what are you thinking asking him here, besides giving me the shock of my life?"

"I'm sorry I didn't tell you."

Indi took a deep breath.

"He looks good," Sabine said.

"Shut up...I don't want to hear it."

"I asked him here because what better way to find the necklace than help out the insurance investigator," Sabine said.

"You do realize that he has no idea that the necklace Priya returned is a fake?

"And," she added quickly, "He also thinks that whoever stole the necklace the night after the party was casing the joint the night of the party...

"And he thinks it's us," Indi said.

Sabine pursed her lips.

"Do you think JJ robbed his own safe?"

"Yes, but he robbed the fake.

"Come on! Let's see what Hari knows," she added. "Now, you ready?"

"How do I look?"

"You look good," Sabine said. "Maybe a little makeup?"

"I was thinking that."

"I'll go and offer him a cup of tea."

Indi went into the bathroom and pulled out a small makeup case.

"Don't go overboard," Sabine said. "You're not going to walk the runway or anything."

"Get out!" Indi said.

"Just saying."

Indi raised an eyebrow.

"I'll go and offer him some tea."

"Fine...just don't ask him to stay for dinner or anything."

"You look well, Sabine," Hari said when Sabine came into the living room.

"So do you."

"It's been a while."

"A few years."

"Thanks for calling, by the way..."

"I didn't do it."

"No tea, no chit chat, no catch-up."

"You think I robbed JJ's safe, but I didn't."

Sabine stared at him, her hands on her hips.

"Yet," Hari walked around and came to face her, "you come back to Delhi after all this time...to do what exactly?"

"I came back to hang out and catch up with Indi."

"And it's a coincidence that the Barodan necklace that hasn't been seen in 70 years reappears and turns out that it belongs to JJ Singh..."

Sabine shrugged.

"Sabine...I just want the necklace..."

"I really don't have it, Hari, I promise you."

"I don't get it," he shook his head. "So why the hell are you here?"

Sabine didn't answer.

"Does JJ know you're in town?"

"Yes."

"Come on Sabine! Help me out."

"If you must know, I thought about it," Sabine said. "I did," she nodded. "It one of the most beautiful necklaces of that era.

"But how was I going to lift a necklace off the neck of one of the biggest Bollywood celebrities at a party celebrating her wedding to another big Bollywood actor, at the home of one the country's wealthiest ..." she stopped for a moment, "...men?" she finished.

"Because that's exactly the kind of challenge you love," Hari said.

"Maybe," Sabine shrugged.

"Were you at the party?"

"I was not checking out the house..."

"So what was Indi doing there?"

"She was the designer's assistant."

"There was some problem with Priya's dress..."

"... in front of 200 people."

"And the necklace apparently fell off on the grass around JJ's office."

"So?"

"Indi was with her..."

"So was JJ's bodyguard."

"I don't get it," Hari rubbed his temples. "Something here doesn't make sense...the clasp on that necklace was fitted with fingerprint technology...it couldn't have just fallen off."

"What's that got to do with anything?" Sabine said quickly. "You told me the necklace was stolen the day after the party."

"Yes...but still, how could the necklace have fallen off in the garden?" Hari mused.

"I just can't help feeling that someone at the party was somehow involved," he said, clenching his fist. "It can't just be some random guy who walks into Singh's house, knows exactly where to go, knows the necklace is in the safe, knows the combination, grabs it and walks away..."

"Maybe JJ orchestrated this?" Sabine suggested.

"You'd like that wouldn't you?" Hari said. "The guy who gave you up gets done for insurance fraud...scores are settled, the world is set right again."

Sabine's expression was noncommittal.

"You're still here," Indi came back into the room.

Sabine shot her a look. "I'll be right back."

"Where are you going?" Indi turned towards her with her

back to Hari. "Don't leave me here," she mouthed.

Sabine walked out and Indi turned back around.

"Indi *bibi*," Laxmi appeared. "Shall I bring some tea?"

Indi nodded.

"*Namaste* Laxmi," Hari said.

"*Namaste, Sahib*," Laxmi replied without looking at him and scurried away.

"I guess she doesn't like me much either," Hari said.

"She does work for *me*, remember..." Indi said.

An awkward silence ensued.

"Hari...I think you should go," she finally said. "Coming here was not a good idea."

"It wasn't mine."

"Whatever...you should still go."

"You've done well, Indi," he gestured around. "This is a beautiful house...all this great art..."

"Oh for goodness sake!" she jumped up and walked around, her arms folded tightly across her chest. "Just stop with the small talk."

Hari got up and took a couple of strides to where she was standing near the window.

"Indi," he said softly. "I only accepted Sabine's invitation because I really wanted to see you."

Indi's eyes began to glisten and she turned her back to him.

"I've had a lot of time to think and...I was wrong," she heard him take a deep breath and let it out slowly. "I should never have let you go...I am sorry."

Indi's chin began to tremble and she could feel the tears at the back of her eyes. Controlling her emotions, she squared her shoulders and whipped around. "Yes, well you should've thought about all that before."

Still holding her arms defensively across her chest, she stared at him.

"Indi...I want us to start over..." he began.

She opened her mouth to protest, but he stopped her. "Please, just hear me out.

"I was wrong about a lot of things," he put his hands in his pockets. "I was lost...my professional life was down the drain, I was drinking too much...and I took out all my frustration on you and on our relationship

"And then when I found out about what you and Sabine did, well..." he sighed, "I didn't deal with it so well...and that will be something I regret until the day I die.

"You never even bothered to talk to me about it," Indi said.

"I..."

"You walked out on me," Indi cried. "You went out one day for cigarettes and never came back."

"Indi...I honestly did not know what I was doing."

"Yes, well, I had to move on," she threw at him.

"Really? Who is he?"

"What is it to you? What do you care?"

Hari stared at her, swallowing. "Does he make you laugh?" he asked.

"He doesn't make me cry."

He looked away, nodding and walked to the window.

Indi shifted her weight from one foot to the other. She knew she'd hurt him... there was no one in her life, but he deserved it, she stuck her chin out defiantly.

"Listen Indi," he finally turned around, his hands in his pockets, "I just want to make sure that you're ok...and that you're not involved in some hairbrained, crazy scheme of Sabine's."

"Again...why do you care?"

"I don't want to see you get into trouble."

"Don't worry," Indi scoffed. "I can take care of myself."

Hari's shoulders sagged.

"Remember what I told you a long time ago...?"

"Always make sure you know what you're doing?" she chewed on her bottom lip.

"Do you?"

"Of course she knows what she's doing," Sabine came back into the room. "Have you gotten anything off the security cameras on the night the safe was robbed?" she changed the topic.

"Just shadows," Hari said. "The guy knew what he was doing and where all the cameras were. He never shows his face."

"Who are your suspects?"

"Right now," Hari sighed, "all 200 people at the wedding, anyone of them could have been giving the house the eye...all those celebrities, millionaires..." he shrugged.

"Although..." he stopped for a moment before continuing. "There is a woman whose name is...let's see...," he flicked through his notes, "...who was seen in the hallway of Singh's office..."

Sabine and Indi exchanged a quick glance.

"Her name is...ah! Here it is...Nina Singh," he looked back up at both women. "And apparently, the night after, she and a couple of her friends showed up claiming their car had broken down?

"Know anything about her?"

Sabine shook her head. "What was she doing in the hall-way?"

"Apparently looking for a bathroom...that's what she told one of the security guards.

"Do you know her, Indi?"

"She's one of those society women," Indi said.

"Did you see her at the dinner?" he looked at Indi. "Since Sabine was not there..." he added with a touch of sarcasm to his voice.

Sabine shrugged uncaring and flopped down on one of the armchairs.

"She was at Singh's table," Indi replied.

"Are they friends?"

"I don't really know."

"It says here she's married to Arun Singh," Hari looked back at his notes, "who inherited the Barodan title."

"So what?" Indi asked.

"I don't know...just talking out loud," he took a sip of his tea. "I'm going to see her now."

"Good luck with that," Sabine said and Hari gave her a wry look.

"I'd best be going," Hari drained his cup of tea and got up. "It was good to see you, Indi," he said. "And you too, Sabine."

Indi nodded wordlessly and watched him as he walked to the front door.

"You ok?" Sabine said after they heard the door close.

Indi took a deep breath and let it out slowly. "I think I need a shot of something."

"Whiskey?" Sabine suggested as she walked over to the

drinks trolley.

"Sure."

"Indi..." Sabine poured some whiskey for the two of them, "we've been focusing so much on the people at JJ's table," she handed her a glass, "that we've neglected to look at the people at Priya's table...the tray was in between both tables...the plate could have been served to someone at her table."

"Sabine, she had the biggest Bollywood celebs at that table..."

"So...do you think none of them would lose their heads over the sight of the Barodan?"

"Like Priya..."

"What do you mean?" Sabine asked.

"You should have seen Priya's eyes when she first saw the necklace," Indi said.

"6 pounds of diamonds could do that to you.

"Let's take a closer look at her."

"Do you think she could have somehow switched the necklace before us?"

"Perhaps?" Sabine said.

"Alright," Indi reached for her laptop. "What about the fake piece?"

"Forget about that...that's for JJ to find out he's been had."

*

Outside, Hari's phone rang. It was Imran.

"Hey...what's going on?" Hari answered.

"Where are you?"

"I'm on my way to see Nina Singh..."

"When you're done, come to headquarters."

"What's happened?"

"I don't know, but one of the guys got a strange phone call

and I want you to hear it."

"What's it about?"

"Something about having information about the Barodan necklace..."

"Who is it?"

"Hard to tell."

"Where was the call made from?"

"Burner phone."

"Alright...I'll be there soon."

*

JJ climbed into the back seat of the Range Rover and Rusty shut the door behind him. He was walking around to the passenger door when his phone rang. He looked at the phone and frowned.

"Yes," he answered.

"It's Mahesh, the jeweler."

"Make it quick," Rusty said. "I'm about to get in the car with the boss."

"I have to see you."

"I can come by tomorrow."

"No, now...it's important."

"What is it?"

"I'll tell you when you get here."

"Sir...I have to run over to Sundar Nagar," Rusty poked his head in the car.

"What is it?"

"I just got a call from Bharany...he wants to talk to me."

"What about?"

"I don't know," Rusty replied. "Wouldn't say."

"Keep me posted."

*

"Hari Singh," Hari announced himself when the door opened. "I have an appointment with Mrs. Nina Singh."

"Yes, the *Memsahiba* is expecting you," Shanti said and stood aside to let him in. "This way please, *Sahib*," she led the way down the hall.

Hari took the couple of steps down into the living room with the covered veranda beyond.

"Hello," he heard a female voice behind him.

He turned around.

"I'm Nina Singh."

"Mrs. Singh," Hari inclined his head. "Thank you very much for seeing me at such short notice."

"Of course," she pointed to a sofa. "Would you like some tea?"

"Thank you," he nodded.

"Shanti, *chai* please," she turned to Shanti who nodded and disappeared.

"Now," she looked at Hari, "what can I do for you?"

"It's about the Barodan necklace," Hari began.

"Yes...?" she prompted.

"I'm sure you knew of its existence?"

"It's a legendary piece of jewelry, Singh *Sahib*," she replied. "I remember my mother telling me about it."

"What happened to it, exactly?"

"I don't know what the truth is," Nina said, "but it disappeared when the old Maharajah divorced the wife he'd had it made for and sent her back to...uh...Spain, I think," Nina cocked her head. "Yes, I believe she was a Spaniard."

"Did she take it with her?"

"It is possible, of course," Nina said, "after all, it was hers."

"But isn't it true that all jewels were part of the Maharajah's vault and pieces were handed out to wives and concubines, according to their status, to wear and to return."

"Yes...I believe that was the case."

"So, if the woman in question walked away with it," Hari said, "she stole it."

"Those were very complicated times in India, Singh *Sahib*," she added. "It was partition...the British were leaving, Nehru was taking over, India was united and the Maharajahs were being sidelined...it was the birth of a new country...not to mention the trouble with Pakistan and the mass exodus of Muslims."

"Yes," Hari nodded. "What do you think happened to the necklace?"

"I don't know," Nina sighed. "After the old Maharajah died, shortly after partition, his sons began selling off everything, properties, furniture..."

"Why?"

"They were desperately clinging to their old way of life," Nina said. "My father-in-law didn't know how to work...they didn't know how to pay for simple things...they needed money to survive in the new India."

"Could it be that one of his sons sold it and blamed their father's wife?"

"Possible."

"Were you surprised when the necklace suddenly reappeared?"

"Of course!" Nina said. "Like everyone..."

"Did you know that it belonged to JJ Singh?"

"No."

"Do you know how he came to it?"

"I don't."

"Do you feel the necklace belongs to you...?" Hari suggested.

Nina didn't answer.

"After all, you are the wife of the current Maharajah."

"Arun doesn't have any officially recognized title," she said.

"No, but he is the son of the last Maharajah."

"What are you getting at, Singh *Sahib*?" Nina drained her cup of tea and put the saucer down on the coffee table.

"The Barodan necklace has been stolen."

"What?" Nina looked shocked.

Hari nodded, his eyes narrowing.

"When?" Nina asked.

"JJ Singh was robbed the night after the party and the necklace was taken out of the safe," Hari said.

"Robbed?" she repeated. "Was anything else stolen?"

"Apparently only the necklace."

"Who robbed him?" Nina said.

"That's what we are investigating," Hari said.

"What does this have to do with me?"

"You were at the party for Priya Chopra," Hari looked at his notebook.

Nina nodded.

"And...you and two other women appeared at Mr. Singh's doorstep on the night after the party, saying you had car trouble...the same night JJs' safe was robbed."

"Are you suggesting that I..." Nina sat up.

"I'm not suggesting anything, Mrs. Singh," Hari said calmly.

"I'm simply stating the facts."

Nina pursed her lips angrily.

"What happened that night?"

"I don't see what this has to do with the robbery?"

"Also...if I may..." Hari flipped a couple of pages in his notebook, "you went into Mr. Singh's office in the middle of the party," he looked up at her. "Why is that?"

"It was personal."

"Mrs. Singh, I'm afraid I need a better answer than that."

She stared at Hari stonily.

"Mrs. Singh..." he prompted.

"I was looking for the bathroom if you must know."

"Why?"

"What do you mean 'why?'" she replied. " Why does one normally look for a bathroom?"

"It's just that all guests were directed to the guest house at the bottom of the garden," Hari said. "And I believe JJ did send you that way..." he stopped for a moment.

"So why did you go into his office?"

"I had left something in the car and I went to get it, and on the way back, I thought I might as well make a quick stop in the bathroom," Nina said.

"But why his office?"

"Because I knew there was a bathroom there."

"I see," Hari said. "So, you'd been to the house before?"

"Only once, for an appointment with JJ."

"What was that about?"

"That is none of your business," Nina replied angrily.

"I'm afraid it is, Mrs. Singh," Hari said, "because you are on a short list of suspects."

"That's ridiculous!" Nina scoffed.

"You see, we think that whoever stole the necklace was at the party the night before," he revealed, "and came back the night after...and given that you were on camera coming out of Mr. Singh's office," he handed Nina his phone. "Here you are walking down the hallway to the reception hall where one of the security men stopped you..."

Nina sat back.

"And you went back the night after with the unlikely story of a broken down car," he continued.

"It was not an unlikely story..." Nina tried.

"And you told JJ's head of security that the driver had disappeared...no, Mrs. Singh," Hari said. "You are one of the prime suspects in this.

"And you have motive..." he continued. "You recently filed divorce papers and it is well known that your husband has no money..."

"I'm afraid I must ask you to leave, Singh *Sahib*," Nina got up and rang a small silver bell on the side table next to her.

"Thank you for your time," Hari said.

"Shanti, please show Singh *Sahib* out," she said when Shanti appeared.

As soon as he'd left, Nina went to the candlestick telephone and dialed, her hand shaking. "Sonia, I think we may be in trouble," she said.

"Why? What happened?" Sonia asked.

"The insurance investigator was just here and he thinks I'm the one whole stole the Barodan."

"Well, you didn't."

"But we tried."

"We may have tried," Sonia said, "but the fact is we don't have it."

"What if they think I stole it and sold it?"

"Let them try and prove that."

"Are you sure they can't get me?" Nina's voice trembled. "They have me on camera coming out of JJ's office the night of the party."

"You told them you were looking for the bathroom, right?"

"Of course."

"They can't get you for using the toilet."

"No...I suppose not."

"But we were there the night after..."

"Nina...did we try? Yes," Sonia answered her own question. "But listen to me carefully...we don't have it."

"Alright," Nina took a deep breath.

"Don't worry," Sonia said.

*

Hari dialed a number as he walked out of Nina's house. "Come on, man...pick up," he murmured. But the call went into voicemail.

"Hey, it's Hari...call me when you get this."

*

"*Sahib!*" Rusty heard a man call out as he rushed across the small park towards the Bharany shop on the far side. "*Chai, Sahib?*"

Rusty glanced towards his right and saw the old chaiwallah smiling at him, holding up an old cloudy glass. "Some other time," Rusty called out.

"I've just made the samosas," the man pointed to a small frying pan in front of him.

"I'll be back," Rusty nodded.

"The best samosas in all Delhi."

Rusty raised his hand in salutation just before walking through an unmarked door that led into an old shop in which all four walls were outfitted with dark wooden shelves and cubby holes of all kinds. Around the room there were antique glass cases filled with all kinds of jewelry, from necklaces to earrings, rings, bracelets and heavy ankle bracelets.

"Can I help you, *sahib*?" a young man came out from behind a thick grey curtain.

"I'm here to see Mahesh," Rusty said.

The young man peeked behind the curtain and seconds later an older man came out, beckoning Rusty with the crook of his finger.

"So what is so important?" Rusty sat down in an old wooden chair across a desk from Mahesh Bharany, a thin, wiry man in his late 60's with a dark complexion and salt and pepper hair.

"Rusty..." he leaned his elbows on the velvet pad in front of him.

"What is it, Bharany? Spit it out!"

"I...uh..."

"I don't have all day," Rusty said.

"Rusty...it's about the necklace you brought me to cut the other day..." Mahesh looked nervous.

"What about it?"

"It's...it's not real," he finally blurted out.

"What?" Rusty sat forward.

Mahesh shrugged.

"What do you mean it's not real?"

"Rusty...the necklace is a fake. The diamonds are not real. They're cubic zirconia...

"Very good quality I have to say and very easy to fool the human eye."

"What the hell are you talking about?" Rusty got up out of his chair and leaned forward on the desk.

"Look," Mahesh shifted his own chair back, trying to put as much space between him and Rusty, "don't shoot the messenger...I was as shocked as you are."

"You didn't realize it when you cut the pieces?"

"No," Mahesh put his hands in front of him as if to stall Rusty. "I only cut the pieces you wanted...but then when you asked me to sell the stones, I looked at the pieces closely to determine a price and realized they are not worth very much at all."

"Has anyone had access to the stones?"

Mahesh shook his head. "They have been in my safe."

Rusty paced around the room, running his fingers through his hair. "This means, the necklace that was returned was a fake..."

And suddenly he whipped around. "So who the hell has the real thing?"

Mahesh sat at his desk, his hands intertwined, a very worried look on his face.

"Who uses this quality of cubic zirconia?" Rusty asked.

"Anyone who specializes in good quality fakes," Mahesh replied.

"Give me some names."

"Here in Khanna Market, there are two..." Mahesh stammered.

"Who?" Rusty shouted.

"Uh...uh..." Mahesh cowered.

"In this fucking lifetime!" Rusty moved even closer to Mahesh.

"Me...and Gema Kaling."

"And you swear to me you never made this necklace?"

"I swear it...on my mother's head."

"Who's Gema?"

"She has a shop on the other side of the park."

"You'd better be telling me the truth," Rusty's eyes narrowed as he looked at Mahesh.

"I am, Rusty *Sahib*," Mahesh trembled as Rusty's hand tightened around his collar.

Rusty let him go and he fell back in the chair.

"Give me the rest of the necklace," Rusty ordered.

Hands trembling, Mahesh opened his safe and pulled out a blue velvet box.

Rusty opened it and stared for a moment at the pieces.

"*Sahib*..." the same young man who had shown Rusty in, poked his face from behind the grey curtain.

"What is it?" Mahesh answered.

"There's a woman to see you," he said.

"Which woman?"

"The widow...who was here the other day."

"Yes, yes," Mahesh shooed him away. "Tell her I am busy and she should come back.

"Just another woman peddling junk."

"Very well, *Sahib*," he said.

Straightening out his jacket, Rusty closed the box, put it under his arm and walked out.

He was striding across the park when,

"*Chai, Sahib?*" he heard the chaiwallah.

"Some other time," he said. "Actually...do you know a jeweler named Gema?"

"Yes, *Sahib*," the chaiwallah nodded. "She is over there," he pointed to a window on the first floor of a building behind him. "But she has a customer now."

"How do you know?"

"The chaiwallah knows everything, *Sahib!*" the man smiled, showing his toothless gums as usual.

"Do you know who is with her?" Rusty pulled a 500 rupee note from a bill fold and dangled it in front of the chaiwallah.

"I have never seen her before," the chaiwallah replied. "But she is a widow."

"A widow...?"

"Yes...she went into Bharany's and came back out and went there."

"How do you know she is a widow?"

"She was wearing a white sari," the chaiwallah's eyes followed the rupee note that Rusty swung from side to side.

"You'll have to give me more than that."

"I don't know, sahib," he shook his voice, chagrined. "Her head was covered with the pallu of the sari and she wore big glasses."

"Did she look like either one of these women?" Rusty showed him a photo of Sabine and one of Indi.

The chaiwallah's gaze flickered for a moment, but he shook

his head.

"What about her?" he pulled up a photo of Priya.

"*Aray, Sahib,*" the chaiwallah grinned. "That's Priya Chopra...of course I know her, she's the most famous actress in all of India...who doesn't know her?"

"Has she been here recently?"

"If she had been here, Sahib," the chaiwallah wobbled his head, grinning from ear to ear. "I would have run away with her..."

Rusty threw the money on the cart and walked away, dialing a number on his phone.

"What is it Rusty?"

"Sir, there's a problem with the necklace," Rusty said when JJ answered.

"What's the problem?"

"It's a fake."

"A fake?" JJ repeated loudly. "What the hell do you mean?"

"The necklace that was returned by Miss Priya was a fake."

"But how...?" JJ said. "She had it for less than 24 hours...could she have had a copy made in that time?

"Besides, how did she take it off?"

"Anything is possible, sir."

"Who the fuck has the real piece?" JJ swore.

"I don't know, sir."

"Whoever has it, is going to pay with his balls."

"Yes, sir."

"Where are you now?"

"At Khanna Market in Sundar Nagar."

"There is only one person who could have made a fake that good," JJ said.

"Gema Kaling," both men said in unison.

Suddenly the line crackled and JJ's voice sounded scrambled.

"Sir?" Rusty said walking around. "Sir...I lost you..."

"Rusty!" JJ's voice came back through loud and clear.

"Yes, sir."

"Get to the Oberoi now...the pieces you left for Sabine and Rambo...you have to get them out.

"If the police find them and have them looked at, they will know the necklace that was stolen was a fake...Hari Singh and Imran Khan cannot know that a fake necklace exists or I'll never get the insurance money...and worse, they'll start looking at me.

"We will deal with Priya later."

"I'm on my way, sir."

*

As soon as he left, the chaiwallah pulled out a small phone and sent a text.

'*Bibi*, a man was looking for you.'

'Who?' came the reply.

'I don't know.'

'Is he still there?'

'No, he is gone.'

'He showed me pictures of your two friends, Sabine *bibi* and Indi *bibi*.'

'Do you know who he was?'

'I have seen him here before. He's been to Bharany's a couple of times.'

'Thank you, chaiwallah.'

'*Namaste, bibi*.'

*

"Call me when you get this," Imran heard Hari's voice on his phone. He put the phone back in his pocket.

"What time is it?" he asked the bartender.

"Past 11 o'clock, sir," the man said.

"Double whiskey," Imran said, gulping it down as soon as the glass appeared in front of him.

"Another double," he ordered.

He was staring into his whiskey when a man slipped onto the stool next to him.

"Hey," Hari said. "Johnny Walker, rocks," he ordered from the bartender. "I've been trying to get a hold of you since this afternoon.

"I figured you'd be here."

"Oh yeah?" Imran raised an eyebrow.

"I texted and called," Hari said.

"I didn't get the message."

"How long have you been here?"

"Not long," Imran shook his head. Hari noticed his eyes were glassy and his speech slurred.

"How much have you had to drink?" Hari asked.

"Why?"

"Because it's unlike you to ignore me," Hari said. "We are on the same case."

"Today's my day off," Imran said.

"Oh!" Hari said. "I'm sorry...I didn't realize..."

Imran put his head down on the bar.

"What's up, man?" Hari asked.

"Today's just a really bad day," Imran shook his head, lost in thought.

"Is everything alright?"

"No."

"Have you had bad news?"

"No."

Hari nodded and reached for his drink.

Finally, Imran raised his head, his eyes dark and glassy with grief.

"Five years ago, today..." he managed to say, "...I lost my wife..."

"Oh man," Hari said, "I am so sorry."

"She died, giving birth to our child," Imran stared into his drink. "Neither of them survived."

Hari nodded.

"Life is passing me by..." Imran continued, "this existence of mine... it's not a life. I breathe, so I am alive...but I don't live.

"I miss her, Hari, and I loved her with all my heart," Imran drained his glass of whiskey. "And you know...the saddest thing is that I never told her."

"Why?"

"Because I thought she knew," he said. "But then suddenly, she was gone and she never knew how I felt."

"I'm sure she knew," Hari said.

"But I wanted to tell her...it was just so stupid," he clenched his fist, "I couldn't say the words...my stupid upbringing.

"I wish I had spent more time with her," he continued. "I was obsessed with making a name for myself in the police force, and I worked long hours.

"She would complain that I was working too hard, but I never heeded what she was saying.

"And now I am where I want to be, but I can't share it with her."

"How could she have died in childbirth?" Hari asked. "This is the 21st century...women don't die in childbirth..."

"Hema did," Imran said. "We had wanted children for a long time...she was desperate to be a mother and I a father. But it never happened...and so we continued, happy just with one another.

"And then one fine day, she got pregnant...we were ecstatic...but it wasn't meant to be."

"Some things just aren't, man," Hari said. "No matter how hard you try."

"I'm half a person without her," Imran said. "I'm no longer complete, all I do is work..."

"You've got to keep going," Hari said. "As hard as it is, you have to."

"I'm sorry," Imran suddenly looked up. "You needed something?"

"Don't worry about it," Hari said.

"News on the necklace?"

"It can wait."

"You sure?"

"Yeah...let's talk about it another time..." Hari insisted. "Want to have some dinner?"

"Thanks man," Imran said gratefully. "I could really do with the company today."

Chapter 13

Upstairs in her atelier, Gema looked at the woman sitting in front of her. She looked vaguely familiar, but it was hard to tell, her dark sunglasses covered most of her face and her head was covered with the pallu of a white sari.

"How can I help you today?" Gema said.

"I'm in a predicament," the woman's chin trembled. "My husband passed away and left me in terrible debt."

"I'm very sorry."

"Thank you," the woman wiped tears from her eyes. "I have to sell some jewelry to pay off the people he'd borrowed money from."

"How did you find me?"

"My friends say you are very well connected especially with the French jewelry houses," she said.

Gema didn't reply.

"They say you are the main source of stones for Cartier, Richemont...

"You come very highly recommended."

"May I ask from whom?"

"Uh..." the woman hesitated. "I can't remember the name exactly...

"I must say, my memory just isn't what it used to be..." she wrung her hands. "It was someone I met..."

"Are you from Delhi?" Gema asked.

The woman shook her head. "Chennai."

"What is your name?"

"Mine?"

"Well...yes..." Gema replied, raising an eyebrow.

"It's...uh...Padma..."

"I see...well, Padma *Sahiba*," Gema said, "may I have a look at what you would like to sell?"

Padma opened her purse and pulled out a brown paper bag and from it a velvet box that she handed to Gema.

"That's a beautiful bracelet," Gema remarked.

"That was given to me on my wedding night by my husband," she wiped the corners of her eyes with a handkerchief.

"Would you mind if I took a closer look?"

"Please."

"Where did he get this?"

"It's...uh...I think he inherited it...from his mother."

Gema took it with her to her desk near the window where she laid it on a velvet pad, going over it carefully with her loop. She turned it over and looked at it closely. The stones were perfect.

Gema sat back up, took the loop out of her eye and came back to where Padma was sitting.

"Well...?" Padma stammered. "Is it worth anything?"

"Yes...it is," Gema replied. "It's worth quite a lot."

"Oh! God be praised," Padma sighed deeply, placing her hands together in prayer. "How much can you get for it?"

"I will make some calls."

"Do you have any other pieces?" Gema asked. "Did your husband inherit anything else?"

"Well...yes, a few other pieces."

"Are you interested in selling them?"

"I'd like to see what we can get for this," Padma said. "How soon do you think you can sell them?"

"Stones of this quality...it won't take long."

"I'm in a bit of a hurry," Padma wobbled her head. "The bills have piled up...I'm sure you understand."

"I understand," Gema said. "I will do the best I can."

Gema accompanied Padma to the door, waving goodbye as she went down the dark flight of stairs. She walked back into her atelier and went to the window and watched her pulling the pallu of her sari close around her head and walking quickly towards the dusty lane at the edge of the park.

Gema reached for her cellphone.

'We need to meet,' said the text addressed to Indi and Sabine.

She stared at it for a few moments and then hit the 'Send' button.

*

Hari and Imran sat in a police car as it barreled its way towards the Oberoi Hotel.

"I'm feeling really weird about this," Hari said, looking out the window.

"It's a tip and we have to follow it up," Imran replied.

"Yes, but we don't know who the guy was and whether it was legitimate."

"Look man, I don't know how you insurance guys work, but this is an open police case and we have to check out every tip we get."

"We're just going to waltz into the Oberoi and ask to search these two suites..." Hari shook his head.

"We have a warrant," Imran patted his breast pocket. "What are you so worried about?"

"I'm not worried."

"You look it."

"I'm not worried," Hari snapped. "OK?"

"Alright, alright…" Imran spread his hands apart. "No need to get yourself in a lather."

Hari's nostrils flared as he took a deep breath to control himself and they rode the rest of the way in silence.

"Gentlemen, welcome to the Oberoi, New Delhi," the doorman opened the door for them.

They were met in the lobby by a short bald man.

"I am Mr. Vivek, the general manager of this eminent establishment," he bowed deeply, handing them a card each.

"Imran Khan, Delhi Police," Imran flashed his credentials.

"Hari Singh, Lloyds of London."

"May I ask what is going on?" Vivek asked, his hands linked, his eyes twitching under his wire-rimmed glasses.

"There was a robbery at the home of Mr. JJ Singh," Imran said.

Mr. Vivek cocked his head. "*The* JJ Singh?"

"Yes, the Barodan necklace was stolen," Imran said.

Mr. Vivek put a hand to his chest as if to stop the shock Imran's words had elicited from spilling out.

"And you think it is here in the hotel?"

"We received a tip that pieces of it could be found in two of your suites."

"Which ones?"

Imran flicked open his notebook, "the Eastern and Western

Star," he read his notes.

"That's impossible!" Mr. Vivek said. "We have some very esteemed clients in those suites."

"I don't care if it's the Prime Minister of India," Imran said, "I have a warrant to search them."

Vivek wrung his hands. "Would you allow me to find out if this is a convenient time for them?"

"You have 2 minutes," Imran said.

"You really think there's something to this tip?" Hari asked as Vivek scurried away to the reception desk.

"We'll see, won't we?" Imran shrugged.

"This way please," Vivek came back, gesturing they follow him to the lifts.

He pressed the Penthouse button, shifting around nervously, adjusting the cuffs of his sleeves and fixing his tie pin as they went up in silence.

"Shall we start in the Eastern Star?" Vivek went ahead of the two men to the left. He rang the bell and when there was no answer, opened the door, knocking politely. "Miss Kumar...? Hello?" Vivek walked in cautiously.

"Oh come on!" Imran muscled his way in. "This is ridiculous...we have a warrant.

"Let's go, boys," he ordered four officers who had come upstairs separately.

"Miss Kumar? Are you here?" Vivek said again. "Please be careful," he said as the men began opening drawers, pulling books off shelves and rifling through closets as Imran and Hari stood watching.

Suddenly, a woman opened the door. "Oh!" her hand went to her mouth as she saw all the policemen.

"Who are you?" Imran said.

"I am the maid for this suite," the basket in the woman's hands shook.

"What are you doing here?"

"Putting some clean laundry back for the guest."

"Let me take a look," Imran said, approaching her, placing his hand on the linen napkin that covered them.

The woman put the basket behind her. "They are lady's undergarments."

Imran looked embarrassed. "Very well, go ahead," he said.

The woman disappeared into the bedroom, coming out several minutes later, an exasperated look on her face.

"That took long enough."

"I had to refold everything," she said. "These men had made a mess," she addressed Vivek.

"The place is clean, boss," one of the officers came up to Imran.

"Let's go to the other suite," Imran said.

"Call housekeeping," Mr. Vivek instructed the maid, "and make sure everything is spic and span before Miss Kumar returns."

They were walking down the hallway towards the Western Star Suite when a tall man wearing a butler's jacket came out.

"Hey!" Imran shouted and picked up his pace.

But the man ignored him and disappeared around the corner.

"Stop!" Imran began running, with the officers following close behind. "Police!"

By the time they got to the service lift, it was already going down.

"Who was that?" Imran demanded.

Vivek trembled. "One of the butlers..."

"What was he doing in there?"

"Presumably what our butlers do," Vivek replied, "look after our high priority guests who pay a lot of money to stay in these suites," he added pointing back and forth down the hall.

"We will have to talk to him," Imran said.

Vivek nodded and pulled out his phone. "Who is the butler in the Western Star Suite?... Send him upstairs, please."

As the officers poked around, a woman appeared.

"Mr. Vivek..." she began politely.

"Yes, Miss Anita," Vivek replied. "This is our head of house-keeping," he said to Imran and Hari.

"May I speak to you for a moment?" she said.

Vivek nodded and walked over to the side while Imran and Hari watched.

"He looks animated," Hari remarked as Vivek gesticulated furiously and Anita wrung her hands, looking worried. "I wonder what they're arguing about."

Moments later, Vivek came back.

Imran raised an eyebrow silently questioning him.

"It appears that the butler for the Western Star Suite is out today," Vivek said. "Something about a sick child..."

"So who was the man we saw coming out of the suite?" Imran asked.

"I'm afraid we don't know," Vivek looked away, embarrassed.

"You must have security cameras?" Hari said.

"Miss Anita is looking into it now."

"How could he have gotten by hotel security?"

Vivek shook his head, spreading his hands.

"What was he doing in this suite?"

"I don't know."

"Nothing here either, boss," one of the officers came up to Imran.

"Out of curiosity, who is staying here?" Imran asked.

"Mr. Raminder Singh."

"Really?" Imran narrowed his eyes. "And the other one?"

"Miss Sabine Kumar."

"Even more interesting...does either one of them have anything in the hotel safe?"

"Nothing."

"Alright," Imran sighed. "That was a bit of a wild goose chase," he walked out of the suite.

"Miss Anita," Vivek said as he followed Imran, "please make sure the suite is put back to normal by the time Mr. Singh returns after lunch."

Anita nodded and pulled out her phone.

"Keep us posted on who that man was," Imran said as the three men shook hands in the lobby.

"I will," Vivek said. "I'm just glad we didn't find anything."

"It would have been most embarrassing for the hotel."

Imran nodded and he and Hari walked towards the entrance. "Isn't it curious that Rambo Singh and Sabine Kumar are both staying on the Penthouse floor?"

"Why?" Hari said. "It just means they can both afford it."

"I guess," Imran said. "Still curious though..."

"Look!" Hari said as they got outside. "There's Rusty...Singh's man.

"Hey Rusty!" he waved.

Rusty looked around and waved back.

"How's it going?" he walked over, his hand out. "What are the two of you doing here?"

"We got a tip that perhaps parts of the necklace were in the two penthouse suites," Hari said.

"Oh yeah...?" Rusty nodded. "And...?"

"Nothing."

"What are *you* doing here?" Imran asked him.

"Mr. Singh has a couple of business acquaintances staying here," Rusty replied smoothly. "I came to drop off the gallery catalogues."

"Anything on the necklace?" Rusty asked.

Imran shook his head.

As they spoke, the doorman opened the door to a car and a well-dressed man got out. He carried a cane with a silver swan as a tip. As he walked past them, he nodded to them all.

"Isn't that...?" Imran scratched his head.

"That's Raminder Singh," Rusty said.

"Yes..." Imran nodded. "I haven't seen him in a few years.

"He's looking older than I remember him."

"He was at the party the other night," Rusty said.

"I heard he was back in town...it appears the whole crew is back for a little reunion."

"What do you mean?"

"Rambo Singh, Sabine Kumar, JJ Singh..."

"I must get going," Rusty said. "Traffic is going to be horrendous at this time of evening.

"Keep me posted," Rusty mock saluted them both and walked away.

*

Rusty was waiting at the end of the driveway for the Range Rover to pull up when his phone rang.

"Did you get both pieces?" It was JJ.

"I got one," Rusty said.

"Which one are you missing?"

"The one in Sabine Kumar's room."

"Fuck!" JJ swore heartily.

"She must've found it, boss," Rusty said.

"Goddamnit..."

"Alright, we're going to have to contain this," JJ said.

"I'm getting in the car now," Rusty said. "I'll be there soon."

"Miss Kumar," Mr. Vivek came running over to her as she walked through the lobby.

"Mr. Vivek," Sabine smiled. "I'm afraid I must fly, I'm late for an appointment."

"I just needed to tell you that...well...when you were out earlier, the police came by..."

"They did?" Sabine looked surprised.

"It's just that..." beads of sweat appeared on Vivek's brow.

"Yes...?"

"They had a warrant to search your suite..." Vivek closed his eyes tightly, hoping that he would somehow avoid the wrath he was sure was about to descend upon him.

"Oh yes..." Sabine said calmly. "What were they looking for?"

Vivek opened his eyes very slowly, first one and then the other.

"They were looking for pieces of a necklace that was stolen from the house of JJ Singh," Vivek whispered.

"And they thought they were going to find them in my suite?" Sabine said.

"Absurd, I know," Vivek shook his head.

"Well, obviously they didn't find anything," Sabine shrugged.

"They didn't," Vivek agreed. "But I wanted to let you know."

"Thank you, Mr. Vivek. You are very kind."

"It is my pleasure, Miss Kumar," he added quickly. "I was with them the whole time and I had housekeeping go in and check on everything..."

"Well, they did a fantastic job because I didn't even notice that anyone had been in.

"Now, I'm afraid I must fly..."

*

"Look at this!" Sabine threw a small silk pouch down on Gema's worktable.

"What is it?" Gema stared up at her.

"Open the damned thing!" Sabine exploded.

"I have some great pills that will calm you down," Gema pulled open the pouch and pulled out a pair of diamond ear-rings. "My, oh my..."

"Take a look at them, would you please?" Sabine said.

Just then Indi walked in.

"Sorry...traffic," she said. "What's going on?" she looked at the two other women.

"Sabine here is in a state."

"Sounds very Bollywood."

"I'll get us something to drink," Indi said.

"Tea would be nice," Gema put her jeweler's loop in her eye and bent over the earrings.

Indie disappeared into the kitchen, returning a few minutes later with a tray set with a teapot, three cups, milk, sugar and a pound cake.

"Everyone want a cup?"

"Please," Gema said without looking up.

Finally, she sat up, took off her loop and came to join Indi and Sabine at the round table in the middle of the room. She sat down and took a sip of her tea and broke off a piece of cake.

"The stones are cubic zirconia," she finally said. "And I am 98% sure that they are the stones I used to make the fake Barodan."

There was silence around the table.

"That son of a bitch!" Sabine exploded. "Bastard!" she took her teacup and threw it against the wall smashing it to smithereens.

Gema and Indi exchanged looks.

"Gosh!" Gema said calmly. "Am I glad that wasn't an expensive teacup."

"I'll replace it..." Sabine shook her head. "I am sorry."

"What just happened?" Indi crossed one leg over the other.

"Don't the two of you see what's going on?" Sabine threw her arms in the air. "God! It must be so dull in your brains..."

"Just explain, Sabine."

"Someone placed these earrings in my suite and then called the police to tip them off that they were there...

"Whoever that was," she put her hands on her hips, "was trying to frame me...yet again."

"JJ...?" Indi suggested cautiously.

"Of course, who else?" Sabine shouted.

"Who put the earrings in your room?"

"One of his guys..."

"Probably Rusty," Gema said.

"How do you know?"

"I've seen him at Bharanys across the park a couple of times this week."

"So now we know that JJ orchestrated the robbery of his own safe," Sabine started, "in fact Rusty is probably the one who stole the necklace...

"He filed an insurance claim, hoping for a quick resolution and a check with which he can pay off his debt to Rambo Singh *and* keep the fucking necklace...*and* frame me again in the process. He was going to hit the jackpot."

"He had what he thought was the real necklace cut ..." Indi said.

"Yes, but Bharany could have put it back together, right Gema...?"

Gema nodded, helping herself to some more cake.

"But then Rusty finds out from Bharany that it's a fake, so he has to rush to get the little gift he left for me before the police gets to it..."

"But why?"

"Indi..." Sabine rolled her eyes.

"What? I don't get it...."

"Because if the police had found the earrings," Sabine said, "yes...they would have arrested me, but they would have also found out that the earrings were fake and therefore the necklace was fake and JJ was trying to defraud Lloyds of London."

"How did you get the earrings?"

"I found them at the back of the drawer totally by accident this morning," Sabine said. "I went downstairs for a cup of coffee and when I came back up the police were in there. I borrowed a maid's clothes, went in and got the earrings."

"Why save JJ's ass?" Indi asked.

"Because the real necklace is still out there...and he's going to be looking for it too..."

"Do you think he may lead us to it?"

"Maybe..."

"Listen you two...I had a visitor this morning...an older woman, a widow, who wanted to sell a diamond bracelet..." Gema began.

"So?"

"The stones were beautiful...but the setting was a real work of art," Gema said, "the workmanship was definitely not Indian..."

"What are you saying?" Indi said.

"Do you think it was from the Barodan?" Sabine pounced.

"It could be...but those Maharajahs had a lot of these kinds of diamonds...they would go to Paris with crates of stones and have Cartier or Richemont set them."

"What did this woman look like?"

"I couldn't really tell...grey hair, big sunglasses, white sari..."

"Who recommended her?"

"She couldn't remember."

"Let's think about this," Sabine grabbed a piece of paper and a pencil. "If the bracelet was made from the Barodan..." she wrote down the names of the women at JJ's table. "But what if that idiot server served Priya's table instead? Who were they? Indi...take a look," Sabine pointed to her laptop.

"JJ had the three Aunties, Mrs. Ambani and Kareena Kapoor... and at Priya's table, there was...Katrina Kaif, Mrs. Shahrukh Khan..."

"Also..." Gema started cautiously.

Indi looked up. "What?"

"There was one thing about the woman..."

"Go on."

"Well..." Gema grimaced, cocking her head to one side.

"What, Gema?" Sabine rolled her eyes.

"Her hands..."

"What about her hands?"

"They didn't match her face..."

"What do you mean?"

"Her hands were...young-looking..." Gema said. "You know...there weren't any veins, or spots or any signs that this woman was in her late 60's...her hands were kind of 30-ish..."

Both Indi and Sabine looked at her.

"Priya..." they all said in unison.

"What if she got the Barodan on her plate?"

There was silence for a moment as they all realized what they had said.

"You really think so?" Gema finally said.

"I wouldn't be surprised," Sabine shrugged. "She's an actress...if anyone can play a widow, she can.

"Indi...see what we can find out about her..."

"I'm on it."

"There was also a rumour going around that Bharany had some beautiful stones he was looking to unload," she added.

"But that was probably before he realized they were my cubic zirconia pieces.

"I would have loved to see his face when he realized it..." she giggled.

"Hmmm," Sabine nodded.

"What's the matter?" Gema said. "You're miles away."

"There has to be something in that footage from the night of the event," Sabine reached for her laptop.

"Sabine...you've looked at that footage..."

"I know, but now I want to dissect every move Priya made that night."

*

Rusty walked into JJ's office and put a blue velvet box on the leather blotter on the desk.

JJ looked up at him over a pair of silver-framed reading glasses.

"You sure Sabine has the other piece."

"I am."

"You're going to have to get it back," JJ said.

"It's not in her suite," Rusty said.

"Then she has it on her."

"Yes, sir."

"Take care of this, Rusty," JJ said. "I can't have any loose ends that tie me to this fake necklace.

"The insurance guy has got to believe the necklace that was stolen is real."

"I understand, sir."

JJ took a deep breath. "What about the real necklace? Where is it?"

"Miss Priya...?" Rusty suggested.

"You think Priya had a copy made between the time she left this house at 5am and when you picked it up at 11am, 6 hours later?"

"It's possible..."

JJ opened the box and calmly stared at pieces of the necklace. Suddenly he picked up the box and threw it across the room like a frisbee, watching it hit the wall and the pieces rain down onto the carpet, some of them landing under the sofa.

"Goddamnit!" he pounded his fist on the table. "How could this happen?" he raised his voice.

He came out from behind the desk and picked up one of the stones from the floor and walked over to the French doors, staring at it in the light. He threw it down on the floor and with the heel of his shoe, crushed it to smithereens. "That is what will happen to the person who stole my necklace."

He walked back to his desk and sat down, the tips of his fingers together.

"Do you remember when you told me at the party that Priya had lost the necklace?"

"Yes, sir."

"That is when they switched the necklace."

"Who, sir?"

"There is only one person who could have pulled something like this off."

"But Sabine wasn't at the party," Rusty said.

"Maybe she was...

"For now, I need that insurance money to pay Rambo Singh...so I need that piece back from Sabine..."

Hari sat in the conference room at police headquarters, his laptop open in front of him, concentrating on the screen. He blew out a deep breath and got up to walk to the easel in the corner near the window. The easel was divided in half: the left was the day of the wedding party, photographs of JJ, Sabine, Indi, and Nina Singh and the seating charts for JJ's and Priya's table. On the right was a map he made of the grounds of the house and the house itself and detailed photos of JJ's library office. He cocked his head, crossing his arms, deep in thought.

"Anything?" he heard the door open and Imran walked in.

"Not really," Hari replied and came back to sit at the large oval table.

"And that tip led nowhere..." Imran said.

"I wonder who made that call," Hari put his feet up on the table. "It has to be someone familiar with the case," he added, "someone who knows the necklace has been pinched...but who?"

"And someone who wanted to point the finger at Sabine and Rambo Singh," Imran added.

"Yes," Hari nodded, "but that begs the question as to why we didn't find anything?"

"There's a lot of pranksters out there."

"There are..." Hari agreed. "But the tip was very specific, so it had to be someone who wants us to think that Sabine or Rambo were the thieves.

"Did they get cold feet? Something went wrong and they backtracked...but what and why?"

Hari got up and went to the easel, staring at it.

"Let's take the robbery in isolation," Hari put his hands in his pockets. "The necklace arrives in the morning," he began. "JJ puts the necklace in the safe at the house.

"That night at 1:00-ish, the butler hears something, presumably, from what he described, was the sound of that old safe being opened.

"The thief gets in and out without being caught on any of the cameras, so he knew where they were and to turn his back or slide under them, he knew the alarm code, and the combination to the safe..."

"The thief knew an awful lot," Imran said.

"Yes, he did," Hari agreed.

"Inside job?" Imran leaned forward, his elbows on the table.

"It has all the earmarks."

"Insurance fraud..." Imran let the phrase hang in the air. "In that case, the pointing to Sabine and Rambo makes sense."

"You think Singh needs the money for something?" Hari scratched his head. "If so, he orchestrated this so-called robbery and has the real necklace hidden away somewhere?"

"Could Singh be that stupid?" Imran pulled a cigarette out of his breast pocket.

"He's not," Hari said, "which is why I think there is more to this story."

"What are you thinking?"

"I think that whoever stole the necklace was at the party the day before," Hari said. "They checked out the whole house, put the plan in place and executed it the night after."

"What if the necklace was stolen at the party?" Imran suggested

"And replaced with a fake?" Hari pursed his lips. "But how?"

Imran ran the cigarette under his nose.

"But...if somehow that happened and a fake was returned to Singh?" Imran said. "And Singh, if he orchestrated the robbery, would have stolen the necklace not knowing it was a fake.

"Except how can we prove that the necklace that was stolen was a fake?" he added.

"We would have to find the real one," Hari sat down.

"If the necklace *was* stolen on the night of the party, how the hell would you get the most famous woman in India to simply take off one of the most famous necklaces in the world and put on a fake?" Imran mused. "In front of 200 of the good and the great of India."

*

"Look!" Sabine said, playing the footage of Priya's sari blouse strap snapping.

"Come on Sabine!" Indi said. "We've seen this a hundred times over."

Sabine ignored her. "And here she is, getting up, and there you are wrapping the gown and the *dopatta* around her..."

"I was there, remember..." Indi said.

"Ok...but here!" Sabine paused it. "Here you pass by the tray, you put the necklace on the charger...but then look...she stops...why?"

"I think that's when someone called out to her and said something."

"All we see is her back, but she's right in front of the tray," Sabine said excitedly. "What happened here?" she asked. "She looks like she said something to you and here you are bending down..."

"She said she thought she'd caught her train on something,

so I checked."

Sabine sat back, stretching both arms on the back of the sofa, a big smile on her face.

"What?" Indi said.

"She could have grabbed the necklace from the charger..."

"Don't be absurd, Sabine!" Indi said. "How would she have known it was there?"

"Maybe she saw you?" Gema suggested. "And distracted you saying that something was caught."

"There is no way," Indi rebuffed her. "She was so caught up with her blouse coming apart...besides, even if she did grab the necklace, where would she have put it?"

"She could have somehow hidden it under all that fabric she was wrapped in and put it somewhere in JJ's office," Gema suggested.

"I don't think so," Indi said. "I would have seen her do it."

"What about when she changed her blouse?" Sabine suggested. "Did she go into the bathroom?"

"No," Indi said. "There was no one in the room but us, so she changed in front of me.

"Besides, I had to hook up the blouse and drape everything back on."

Sabine got up and began pacing.

"I feel an idea coming on," Indi looked at Gema.

"Did you find out anything on Priya yet?" Sabine asked.

"I'm digging...there may be something," Indi replied.

Sabine opened her mouth to say something when there was a loud knock on the front door.

All three women turned to look at it.

"Are you expecting anyone?" Indi looked at Gema.

Gema shook her head and quickly got up and went to the window. There was no sign of the chaiwallah.

There was another knock at the door, this time a bit louder.

"I guess, I'd better go see who it is," Gema said. She went through and the two women heard a hushed male voice.

The door to the atelier opened to reveal Gema standing next to JJ Singh.

"Gosh...full house," JJ remarked. "How did I get so lucky?"

"What do you want?" Sabine sprang up.

"Can we talk...please?" he asked.

Sabine nodded to Indi and Gema and they left the room.

"I don't have it," Sabine went to the window and watched her two friends as they walked over to a small café and sat down at a small table outside.

"If you don't have it, who does?" JJ asked.

"I honestly don't know," Sabine replied.

"I know you had your eye on it."

"Of course, I did."

"Why? Because you need the money or was it to get back at me?"

Sabine didn't answer.

"You still have something that belongs to me," JJ said.

"Really?" Sabine kept her back to him. "And what could that be?"

"It's a small piece," JJ said. "Perhaps you found it in your hotel suite..."

"I see..." Sabine sniggered. "How do you know it was in my suite?"

JJ pursed his lips.

"Is it because you put it there?" she asked. "Tell me, JJ," she added, "why did you put it there?

"Was this going to be history repeating itself? Are we playing the 'let's frame Sabine' game again?"

"Sabine...give me the piece..."

"I don't have it, either."

"Yes, you do," JJ said quietly.

"Just give it back to me and I'll be on my way."

"You son of a bitch!" Sabine cried. "How dare you think you can come here and ask me for anything?"

"The piece is not real, Sabine...why would you hold on to it?"

"Ah..." she smiled broadly and walked in a small circle around him.

"You think I'll go to the police with it and then they will know there's a fake in circulation...and you won't get your insurance money..."

"Why are you doing this?"

"Why? You're asking *me* why? That's rich!

"You know...you were able to stay in this city, keep going, but I...I had to leave...I had to leave this country in order to rebuild my life," she said in a quiet, even tone. "And you are the one who pushed me onto that plane...When I got to London, I had nothing, not even a dime..."

JJ looked down at his hands.

"I have worked too hard," she said quickly, "to build myself back up and I'll be damned if I allow you to ruin my life again..."

"Sabine...I had no choice...it was either you..."

"It was either me or you," she finished his sentence. "And you chose '*you*'...as usual."

"Wouldn't you have done the same?"

"No...I would not have given up my partner, not ever."

"You were always so beautiful when angry," he said suddenly taking Sabine by surprise.

"Why don't you just go, JJ?" Sabine frowned.

"Because I want that piece..."

"Who do you think stole that necklace?" Sabine asked.

"If I knew, I would have gotten the necklace back by now," he said, "and you and I would not be having this conversation...."

She didn't retaliate.

"We had something really good together, JJ," Sabine said. "It's too bad that you went and fucking ruined it!" she raised her voice.

"I really just came to get that piece..."

"You could have sent your crony for that."

"I could have," JJ nodded, "but I wanted to see you."

"I don't believe you," Sabine said.

"Believe it," he said, "or don't believe it...you're the only one who ever stayed in my heart and in my head."

"I think it's time you left," Sabine crossed her hands across her chest.

He got up to walk away, stopped at the door and turned. Sabine pulled out a black velvet suede pouch and threw it at him. He caught it in his right hand and looked inside. He looked back at her and nodded.

Chapter 14

"You ok?" Indi put two glasses of steaming tea on the table and a packet of digestive biscuits.

Sabine looked up from her laptop. "Why?"

"Because of him."

"What him?"

"Him...JJ."

Sabine shrugged.

"He got to you, didn't he?" Indi opened the packet and put a few biscuits on a plate.

"Where's Gema?"

"She went to show the stones that widow brought over for her to a buyer," Indi said. "But don't change the subject."

"What do you want me to say?"

"I don't know...I'm just making sure that you're alright."

"Of course, I'm alright!" Sabine said. "What are you? My mother?"

"No," Indi said gently. "I'm your friend."

Sabine looked away.

"Is there anything I can do?"

"Find me something on Priya."

"You really think she has the necklace?"

"Who else?"

"Alright then..." Indi sighed. "But Sabine...if you need to talk..."

"About what?" Sabine glared at her.

Indi sighed, opened up her laptop and sat down. "It's not fair," she said.

"What?"

"You lecture me about Hari coming back," Indi started, "yet when I bring up JJ..."

"It's two different situations," Sabine interrupted.

"Why?"

"I don't want to talk about it..."

"Why do you do this?"

"Do what?"

"We are friends," Indi said. "Some may even say we are best friends, yet you shut me out of so much."

"JJ almost sent me to jail!" Sabine said. "If I hadn't been able to slip away, I'd have rotted in some cell somewhere in the Central Delhi jail..."

Indi looked at her hands.

"I know it wasn't the same, but we were both betrayed," she finally said. "In different ways, but it was still betrayal, no matter what shape it takes."

Sabine stared at her silently.

"And just so you know, this friendship of ours means more to me than any piece of jewelry."

Sabine sighed. "I am sorry.

"We've been through a lot you and I and we've always been there for one another..."

Indi smiled.

"Now, what's the story on Priya?"

Indi sighed. "So, yes...it turns out that Miss Priya Chopra could have a secret..."

"And what is it?"

"She's kept her private life under tight lock and key...but," Indi said, "there's a brother..."

"So?"

"The brother may be in some trouble..."

"What kind of trouble?"

"It seems he owes quite a bit of money..."

"But why? For what?"

"From what I can tell, he's had a few businesses," Indi scrolled down her screen, "but none of them have ever worked..."

"Such as?"

"E-commerce, travel, a bunch of restaurants and bars in Bombay and Goa," Indi looked up. "And from what I can see, as of last year, he owes a lot of people and banks some pretty serious money."

"Yes, but how much?"

"A few million."

"Is that enough to give our little Bollywood actress motive?"

"I'm sure she loves her brother."

"Enough to steal a necklace worth 50 million?"

"Maybe they're splitting it?" Indi suggested.

"Possible," Sabine twirled a pencil around between her fingers. "Anything else on him?"

"Let's see..." Indi began typing. "Well look here..."

"What is it?" Sabine sat up. "What have you found?"

"Young Chopra had a brief partnership with none other than Rambo Singh."

"Rambo Singh?" Sabine frowned. "Really?"

"Perhaps the brother owes Rambo money in addition to all

the banks and other people...?

"Maybe all this was his idea?" Indi suggested.

"What idea?"

"That Priya steal the necklace as quid pro quo for what the brother owes him?"

Sabine raised an eyebrow.

"That's why he was at the wedding?" Indi said. "To make sure she got the necklace...and just maybe," she continued, "Priya grabbed the necklace from the charger and handed it off to Rambo and got it out that way?"

"I don't think so...but," Sabine narrowed her eyes, "if the brother owes Rambo money and he doesn't pay it back," Sabine said, "he's skating on some very thin ice."

"Even more reason for Priya to lift it," Indi added.

"Maybe."

"What are you thinking?"

"I think it's time we had a little chat with Priya," Sabine replied.

"But how are we going to get her to talk?"

"That's easy."

*

Indi heard the church-like chime of the doorbell and looked up from her book. It was the first night she'd had alone in some weeks and she'd decided to spend it in a comfy chair, with a mystery novel, Miles Davis and a glass of wine.

The bell rang again.

"Where is Laxmi?" she muttered, struggling a bit to get up from the oversized armchair. "Laxmi!" she called out. "The door!"

Exasperated, she was putting on her slippers when she heard Laxmi open the door. "Thank God," she slipped back into her spot in the chair and opened her book to where she'd left off.

"Indi!" she heard Sabine call her name.

"I'm in here," she replied.

Moments later, Sabine walked in.

"What are you doing here?" Indi said.

"Aren't you happy to see me?"

"Yes..." Indi replied. "I just thought I'd have a quiet evening."

"You still might," Sabine helped herself to a glass of wine and sat down in front of her.

"It's never quiet when you're around."

On cue, the doorbell rang again.

"That's what I mean," Indi sat forward.

"Indi *Sahiba*?" Laxmi appeared in the arched doorway.

"Yes?"

"There's someone here to see both you and Sabine *bibi*." Laxmi began to giggle as she wrung her hands.

"What's wrong with you?" Indi looked at her puzzled.

"Nothing, Indi *Sahiba*," she looked away.

"Would you please tell me what the hell is going on?" Indi turned to Sabine.

"Don't look at me...she works for you."

"Laxmi...?"

Suddenly a woman appeared behind Laxmi and walked into the room.

"Hello Indi..."

"Priya!" Indi was shocked "What brings you here?" she managed to smile.

"I invited her," Sabine admitted.

"You invited her? Here?" Indi looked at her. "Why am I always the last to know about our plans?" she shook her head. "Please come in...what would you like to drink?"

"I'll have a glass of whatever you're having," Priya sat gingerly at the edge of the sofa next to Sabine.

"Thanks for coming," Sabine began.

"Sure," Priya shrugged. "But what was so important that we couldn't talk about it on the phone?" she pushed a lock of hair behind her ear.

"We wanted to talk to you about the Barodan necklace..." Sabine began.

"What about it?" Priya took a sip.

"Do you have it?" Sabine asked directly.

"What?" Priya spluttered.

"I assume you know the Barodan necklace was stolen?"

Priya nodded, wiping her mouth delicately with a napkin. "I spoke to the insurance guy...he was kind of hot."

"What the...?" Indi began.

Sabine glared at Indi.

"Did you take it?" she turned to Priya.

"Me?"

"Yes, you..."

Priya did not answer.

"You know the insurance investigator is on to you," Sabine said deliberately slowly.

"Me?" Priya said, placing a hand dramatically on her chest. "Actually, he's onto the two of you."

"What are you talking about?"

"He told me all about the two of you...your past...your history...you're kind of legendary," she said to Sabine.

"You see, I'm not the airhead actress you probably think I am," she said. "Because the minute he showed me a photo of you, Sabine," she added. "I knew who you were...you see, I never forget a face...I saw you at the Lodhi...I stumbled as I was coming down the stairs and you were right there.

"And at JJ's, I saw through the wig and the makeup..."

"Yup," Sabine let out a deep breath. "Well..."

"And I saw the necklace on the plate," she added. "When I leaned over to say hello to Shahrukh Khan, it was right there...

"I knew Indi put it there," she got up and walked around the room.

"How do you know?"

"Sorry to say, but I also know bad acting..."

"What?"

"Why did you ask JJ Singh's guy to show you how to take the necklace off?

"And it was a little strange the blouse straps snapping...I know I'm a big girl, but seriously...and by the way, when you unhooked the necklace, I felt it...six pounds around your neck is pretty heavy...

"And last but not least...the way you just happened to have found the necklace in the grass..."

"Did you take it?" Sabine asked. "From the plate?"

"I didn't."

"Why not?"

"You need the money..." Indi added.

"That's ridiculous...do you know how much I make per movie?"

"Still...50 million is 50 million."

"For goodness sake..." Priya began.

"Maybe you needed it to help out your brother?"

"What do you mean?" Priya said, suddenly defensive.

"Come on Priya!" Sabine crossed her arms across her chest. "No need to act so coy...we know all about your brother and his debts."

Priya did not reply immediately. "My family is my problem...it's personal."

"We know you went to Khanna Market in Sundar Nagar..."

"So? Am I not allowed to go shopping in Delhi?"

"You went disguised..."

"Do you have any idea how hard it is for me to move around? I am a celebrity in case you'd forgotten."

"And you were selling some very impressive diamonds."

"Are you having me followed?"

"No."

"Then how?"

"Because you went to see Gema..." Indi started.

"And we've known one another for years," Sabine finished her sentence.

Priya opened her mouth to say something and quickly closed it.

"Where'd you get those diamonds?"

"Why?"

"Did they come from the Barodan?'

"No."

"Then?"

"I don't have to explain myself to you," Priya said indignantly.

"Actually, you do," Sabine said.

"Or what?"

"Or..." Sabine began.

"Alright, alright," Priya said. "Look...my brother is in deep debt," she admitted. "He owes money to a few banks, people...and Rambo Singh."

"That's not good."

"No," Priya shook her head, "It's not."

"You need money...a lot of it," Sabine said.

"I do," Priya nodded.

"How did you find out about my brother?" she added after several moments of silence.

"When you do what we do," Sabine said, "you need to know everything about everyone."

"And what do you do?

"Are the two of you really what the insurance investigator says you are?

"Jewel thieves?" she added, twirling a strand of hair in her hands.

Sabine and Indi looked at one another.

Indi sat back in her chair and Sabine took a deep breath and let it out slowly.

"So, if you don't have the necklace...?" Sabine started.

"Who has it?" she looked at Indi.

"I thought you had it," Priya stood up and helped herself to more wine. "And in fact, if you hadn't gotten in touch with me, I was going call you..." she smiled.

"Why?" Indi asked.

"Because...I want in," Priya said.

"We'll discuss it and get back to you," Sabine said.

"Three shares of 50 million is a heck of a lot better than two shares of...nothing," Priya smiled sweetly. "Not to mention a little time behind bars."

*

Hari sat at a small desk in his hotel room at his computer when his cellphone rang.

"It's Imran."

"How's it going?"

"I was going to ask you the same."

"I'm writing my report."

"Are you going to give Singh the money?"

"We're going to have to."

"I'm downstairs," Imran said. "Want a cup of tea?"

"Sure."

When Hari walked off the lift, Imran was standing near the door.

"Come on!" he said.

"Where are we going?"

"There's a little café around the corner," Imran led the way. "When are you headed back to Mumbai?"

"I have to finish up here first."

"Well...I have to say...it's been interesting working on this case."

"Yeah," Hari said. "There just wasn't enough to go on."

"You still think your old girlfriend was somehow involved?" Imran opened the door to the café.

"Unfortunately," Hari nodded. "And I also think the necklace was stolen the day before...the thing is I don't know how.

"And it was replaced with a fake and the fake was stolen from Singh's safe the day after..." Hari finished.

"I just can't prove any of it."

"I'm sorry we couldn't be of more help," Imran apologized as they sat down at the bar. "Two teas please," he gestured to the barista.

The two men sat sipping their tea, idly looking up at the television that was on silent.

"Hey...look at that!" Imran pointed to the screen. "Isn't that Nina Singh? And that must be her husband? Arun Singh...it's about their divorce...

"And who's that?" Imran asked as the picture of another woman appeared on the screen with a caption that said 'Did she wreck the marriage?'

"Obviously the other woman," Hari said.

"That Arun Singh is a weird one," Imran said. "Some kind of real estate guy, except nothing he ever did amounted to anything."

Hari shrugged.

"He was in the papers a lot at one point about some development in Vasant Vihar," Imran said. "I was going to buy an apartment there, but then construction stopped.

"Hey!" Imran said to the barista. "Can you turn that up, please?"

The barista looked around for the remote, but by the time, he turned up the volume, the presenter was on to the next bit of local news.

"It was probably nothing," Imran said.

"Probably..."

*

"Have you seen the paper?" Sonia stormed into Nina's living room early the following morning.

"Goodness, Sonia! What has happened?" Nina put her teacup down and watched as Sonia threw the newspaper across the room. "Calm down..."

"Take a look!"

Nina opened the paper and in the society pages in the middle was a photograph of her ex-husband, Arun and her ex-best friend, Bunny Mehra.

"How could he?" Sonia sat heavily down on the sofa in front of Nina. "How could he flaunt it in your face like this?"

"I suppose it was bound to happen," Nina said sadly.

"I know...but so soon?" Sonia said. "You aren't even properly divorced yet...are you?"

"He has signed the papers," Nina admitted.

"Just because he's signed the papers, he feels entitled to go around town with that hooker on his arm?"

"Let it go, Sonia," Nina shook her head.

"I don't know why I'm getting myself all riled up," Sonia said, "especially since you don't care."

"It's not that I don't care," Nina said, "and thank you for look-ing out for me...but I don't know what purpose it will serve.

"It's a done deal," she added. "It's not as if we will be getting back together."

"Did you read the rest of the article?"

"No."

"It says that Bunny has invested in Arun's company...that

they are business partners...so all his various real estate projects around town are back on track."

"Really?" Nina picked up the paper again. "How?" she frowned.

"Why? What do you mean?"

"Bunny doesn't have any money...well not that kind of money."

"I thought Bunny was loaded," Sonia said. "She's always going on and on about this house and that house and trips to London and Dubai and jewelry and private planes."

"None of that means she has any serious money," Nina said. "After all, I have this house and a few pieces of jewelry and I may even go to Dubai in a couple of months for a break, but I don't have real money."

"She's always talking about how well she did from her divorces."

"She does have a couple of houses that she rents out," Nina nodded agreement. "That's her income."

"So, what's all this about investing in Arun's projects?"

"It's just the papers," Nina shrugged. "Do we really believe what they say?"

"No...," Sonia said. "But they can't invent them out of nothing."

"True," Nina agreed. "Who knows? Perhaps this is Arun's way of assuaging his conscience, justifying his behaviour...maybe they are business partners as the article suggests."

"That's rubbish, Nina," Sonia scoffed. "And you know that."

Suddenly, the phone rang out in the hall and Shanti answered it. She appeared at the door moments later.

"Nina *Memsahiba*," she said politely.

"What is it, Shanti?"

"There is a woman who would like to speak to you..."

"Who is it?"

"Sabine Kumar..."

"I'd heard she was back in town..." Sonia said.

"Who is she?"

"She used to work closely with JJ Singh," Sonia said.

"Do you know what she wants, Shanti?"

"She didn't say."

Nina got up and picked up the candlestick telephone.

"Hello?" she said, turning towards the window so that Sonia could not hear her.

"What did she want?" Sonia said when Nina came back.

"She wants to talk to me."

"What about?"

"She said that it was a delicate matter and could only talk to me face to face."

"What could it be about?" Sonia said. "What could she know?"

"I don't know," Nina wrung her hands.

"What did you say?"

"I asked her to come here."

"When?"

Just then, the doorbell rang.

"That would be her," Nina said.

"That was quick," Sonia said, "almost like she was standing outside."

Nina took a deep breath.

"Mrs. Singh," Sabine came into the drawing room. "Thank

you for seeing me."

"You know Mrs. Jaffrey?" Nina introduced them.

"I think we may have met."

"May I offer you some tea?" Nina said.

"Yes, thank you," Sabine accepted the armchair Nina pointed to.

"Now, how can I help you?"

"Mrs. Singh..." Sabine began, "the Barodan Necklace has been stolen."

"Yes," Nina said. "I had a visit from JJ Singh's insurance man."

"And what did you tell them?"

"Well, I was shocked to say the least," Nina put a hand to her chest. "How could it just disappear like that?"

"I agree," Sonia added. "After all, Priya was wearing the necklace all night...how could it have been taken off her neck in front of all those people."

"Mrs. Singh..." Sabine began, "you were in JJ's office on the night of the wedding..."

"Yes," Nina cleared her throat.

"What were you doing there?"

"I...uh...was looking for the bathroom and got lost."

"Well...you see...I was in the office as well," Sabine admitted.

"Wait...you were in the office?" Nina repeated, incredulous. "Where?"

"On the far side," Sabine said.

"Why?" Sonia asked.

"It's a long story."

"We have time," Sonia said. "Don't we Nina?"

Nina nodded.

"And the night after the party," Sabine ignored Sonia's question, "yourself, Mrs. Jaffrey here and Mrs. Patel returned to JJ's office."

"And don't tell me," Sonia drawled, "you were there again."

Sabine took a deep breath. "Yes," she said. "And I saw you opening the safe."

"And what were you doing there?" Sonia asked. "Probably the same thing we were," she answered her own question. "You were after the Barodan, weren't you?"

Sabine nodded.

"It was you, wasn't it?" Sonia began. "...the private seller of the Indore Pears...and the one who put them back in JJ Singh's hands?"

Sabine didn't answer.

"You know I could have you put in jail," Sonia said.

"And I could do the same," Sabine returned.

"What do you want?" Nina interrupted.

"I want us to join forces to find the necklace and we can share the proceeds," Sabine said. "I know you need the money."

"There's three of us," Nina said. "Sonia, Rupa and myself."

"What are you saying, Nina?" Sonia interjected. "We are not going to ally ourselves with thieves."

"There's myself, my partners Indi and Gema and...Priya Chopra," Sabine said.

"Priya?" Nina said. "Why is she in this?"

"Because somehow," Sabine added, "she figured out that Indi and I were involved."

"What about JJ?" Sonia asked.

"JJ is going to get the money from his insurance," Sabine said.

"Three of us, Indi, Priya and myself will find the necklace," Sabine said. "And the three of you will sell it."

"But how?" Nina looked worried.

"Where?" Sonia asked.

"That is for us to figure out," Sabine drained her cup of tea. "Thank you for the tea. I'll be in touch."

"There's seven of us now?" Indi exclaimed.

"That's just over 7 million each," Sabine said.

"I can live on that," Gema said.

"That works for me," Priya added. "That's enough to get my brother out of debt."

"But where are we going to look for this goddamned necklace?" Indi said.

"Look," Sabine stretched out on the sofa. "When the thief goes to sell it, we will know about it."

"But how...?" Priya asked.

"Gema will know."

Everyone looked over at Gema.

"I will?" her eyes opened wide.

"You'll see," Sabine said confidently.

"What do we do now?" Priya asked.

"We wait," Sabine reached for her phone.

*

A woman wearing black shalwar pants, a long white tunic, a black dopatta covering her head and big dark glasses got out of a cab at the entrance to Khanna Market and walked across the garden towards Bharany's.

"*Memsahiba!* Chai!" the old chaiwallah sitting on his cart under the banyan tree called out to her.

She didn't reply, instead walked towards the shop in the corner, opened the door and went in.

"I'd like to see Mahesh Bharany," she said to the young man behind the counter.

"One moment please."

"I am Mahesh Bharany," an older man came out from behind a curtain.

"I would like to sell some jewelry," she said.

"May I see the pieces, *Begum Sahiba*?"

"Yes," the woman replied. "Is there somewhere private?" she looked around the shop.

"This way," Mahesh said, and pulled aside the curtain. "May I get you some tea?"

"Yes, please," the woman accepted.

Mahesh nodded to his assistant who went out the front door, jingling the doorbell attached to it.

"Let's take a look," Mahesh indicated a chair for the woman to sit in.

She took a small pouch out of her bag and laid it on the felt mat on the table. Mahesh pulled a loop out of a drawer before placing the pieces in front of him. He turned on a small lamp, placed the loop on his eye and bent over the jewelry.

"Your *chai*, sir," the young man came in with two glasses of tea. "*Memsahiba*," he put one down in front of her.

Several minutes later, Mahesh looked up. The young man was still there, his eyes wide as he stared at the piece.

"What are you still doing here?" Mahesh said. "Out! There's people in the shop," he shooed him out when the doorbell rang.

"*Memsahiba*," Mahesh took the loop off his eye. "May I ask

where you got this piece?"

"It belonged to my husband."

"These stones are exquisite," Mahesh said. "I assume it was a brooch?"

"Uhhhh...yes, probably."

"Or it could have been a *sarpech*? A turban pin?"

"It's possible."

"May I ask, *Memsahiba*, which family your husband belonged to?"

"Why?"

"This is clearly from the collection of a Maharajah."

"I'm selling the stones, not the history."

"I see," Mahesh put his loop back on.

"And I'm sure the stones are flawless."

"They are," Mahesh agreed. "But you could get more if we knew the exact provenance."

"How much can you get for these, as is?" the woman asked.

"Well, they are certainly worth quite a lot," Mahesh sat back. "These are the kinds of stones that will fetch a lot of money from some of the big jewelry houses in Europe."

"Thank you," the woman smiled.

"I will get in touch with my contacts," Mahesh said. "How can I reach you?"

"Here is my cell phone number," she scribbled a number on a piece of paper.

"What is your name, *Begum Sahiba*?"

"My name...ah...yes...it's Pooja."

"Mrs. Pooja...?" Mahesh prompted her for a surname.

"Mrs. Pooja Khanna."

"Very well, Pooja *Sahiba*..." Mahesh got up. "I will be in

touch."

*

"Sabine," Gema looked at the screen on her cellphone.

"What is it?"

"Mahesh Bharany just had a visitor..." Gema said. "A woman selling stones."

"So?"

"Apparently the stones are the kind he thinks would interest Cartier."

"Really?" Sabine sat up. "Who's the woman?"

"Some woman called Pooja Khanna."

"Pooja Khanna....? Indi?"

Indi reached for her laptop.

"Could these be the Barodan stones?"

"It's possible."

"How do you know all this?" Priya chipped in.

"The chaiwallah texted me."

"The chaiwallah? How does he know?"

"Chaiwallahs know everything," Sabine said. "Or didn't you know?"

"No," Priya shook her head. "I didn't."

"The chaiwallah downstairs makes it his business to know about everything and everyone," Gema said. "His son works at Bharanys."

"I get it," Priya laughed.

"Indi...any luck?" Sabine asked.

"Nothing yet,' Indi said. "Do you know how many Pooja Khannas there are in Delhi?"

"How many?"

"A couple hundred."

"I'm a little hungry," Priya started.

"So am I," Indi raised her hand.

"Why don't I make lunch? I'm a pretty good cook," Priya said.

"You?" Sabine looked at her in disbelief.

"Yes, me...just because I'm an actress, doesn't mean I can't cook.

"I learned from my mother," she added.

"Why don't we all go to the kitchen?" Gema said. "Indi can work there and I have some fresh lemonade with mint."

"Look at these baby eggplants," Priya pointed to a small colourful basket on the counter. "These look beautiful," she picked up one of them and felt them in her hands. "These would be delicious and some *daal* and rice."

"Sounds good to me," Gema looked around at the other two women.

"Where's your new husband?" Sabine asked, sitting down at the small table, whilst Gema poured everyone something to drink.

"He had to go back to Bombay," Priya began chopping some ginger and garlic. She made a paste of the two with a pestle, adding ground cumin, coriander and turmeric and Kashmiri chili powder to the rustic mortar. "New movie."

"I guess that's going to happen a lot."

"The life of an actor..." Priya heated a couple of lugs of oil in a frying pan and gently placed the eggplants stuffed with the spice mixture in it, occasionally turning them, smelling the spices as they came alive.

"Oh...there's my phone," Gema walked out of the kitchen.

"I'm going to call Mahesh and see if I can find out anymore."

"How did you get into acting?" Sabine asked.

"I actually started modeling," Priya reached for a couple of dried red chilies and chopped them, adding them to the oil as well as a palmful of fresh coriander stems, turning the heat down so they wouldn't burn. "And that led to the Miss World contest and after that, acting offers."

"Hey...did you see this?" Indi turned her laptop towards Sabine.

"What is it?"

"Read it," Indi urged. "It's about Arun Singh...Nina Singh's husband."

Sabine began reading. "Look at this..."

"What does it say?" Priya dipped a small teaspoon in the *daal* to taste for salt, adding a pinch more before turning down the heat on that too.

"Apparently, his real estate projects that had shut down because of lack of money are back on track," Indi said.

"Come to think of it...he was on the front page of 'Hello' with some woman going into a club in Mumbai," Priya began to wash the rice.

"And I bet that woman was not his wife, Nina," Sabine said.

"Her name was something like Manny or Munney..." Priya sautéed some ginger and garlic and whole red chilies.

"It was Bunny," Indi held up a copy of the magazine.

"That's it," Priya finished off the eggplant with a sprinkling of chili powder, turmeric, cinnamon, and fresh coriander.

Moments later, the kitchen was awash with the fragrance of

the basmati grain, mixing with the pungent spices of the eggplant and the stir fry of cumin seeds and green chili and garlic
that Priya poured over the boiled lentils.

"That smells absolutely delicious, Priya," Sabine said. "And
here I was doubting your culinary talent."

Priya smiled, placing the eggplants on a bed of *raita* yoghurt
to which she had added some garam masala, cumin powder and
fresh grated cucumber.

"What about a couple of *rotis*?" she offered as she came back
to the table, pulling her hair back, tying it tighter behind her
head.

Indi nodded.

"Why don't you start before it gets cold?" Priya suggested.
"And I'll get the *rotis* in a couple of minutes."

"Let's wait if it's only a couple of minutes," Sabrina suggested. "And call Gema!"

"Call me for what?" Gema walked into the kitchen. "That
eggplant smells amazing."

The four of them sat down at the table. "Mahesh says the
stones from this Pooja Khanna could be the Barodan."

"Gema, I have an idea," Sabine said as they began to pass the
food around.

"Ganesh help us all," Gema sighed.

"Why don't I pose as a buyer from Cartier?" Sabine said. "Invite her here, you inspect the stones and we see...

"And Indi, in the meantime, could try and find out who this
mysterious Pooja Khanna is."

"Will you be able to recognize the stones?" Indi asked.

"If she brings the emeralds, yes," Gema said.

Chapter 15

"Mrs. Khanna?" Gema said politely when she opened the door.

The woman nodded. She wore a white shalwar pant and a white embroidered tunic, and a heavily embroidered black Kashmiri shawl that was draped so as to cover her head and a lot of her face. She wore very large dark sunglasses that covered from the middle of her forehead to just below the apple of her cheeks.

"What can I offer you?" Gema said. "Something cold? Or some tea?"

"Some tea, I think," she replied.

"Please come in," she said. "Let me introduce you to one of the brokers for Cartier."

"This is Miss Kumar," Gema said.

"Oh!" Pooja exclaimed. "You're Indian."

"Yes," Sabine replied.

"I didn't know that."

"I work mostly in Paris," Sabine said. "And I come to Delhi often to source stones for the designers."

Pooja looked surprised.

"May I see what you have?" Sabine asked.

Pooja pulled a pouch from her bag and handed it to Sabine who passed it to Gema. "Gema is our local expert."

"Is this what you showed to Mahesh?" Gema pulled out her loop.

Pooja nodded.

Gema bent over the stones.

After a few minutes, she handed Sabine the loop.

"Well?' Pooja looked at the two of them.

"Beautiful," Sabine said. "Where did you get the piece?"

"My husband's family," she said. "Unfortunately, the time has come to sell some of what he inherited."

"I understand," Sabine nodded.

"Do you have any more where these came from?"

"Oh yes," Pooja said, smiling broadly. "So you think I could do well from these?"

"I think you could do very well indeed," Sabine said.

"How much could I get for this?"

"Well, I will have to speak to my superiors in Paris," Sabine shrugged in that very Gallic way, "but I would not hesitate to say at least four, five million euros."

"My goodness!" Pooja exclaimed. "That is very good news indeed.

"How soon can I sell?"

"Are you in a rush?"

"It's just that I need some money soon...for an investment I made."

"I will try and get you the answer shortly," Sabine said.

"Well?" Sabine asked after Pooja had left.

"They definitely look like they could have been taken from the Barodan," Gema said. "Same era and the work on the setting is very deco and European.

"Those stones were not set in India."

"I agree," Sabine said. "If I were a betting person, I would say they are the diamonds from the strand that goes around the neck."

"How does she have them?"

"Who the hell is this Pooja Khanna?" Sabine ranted, pacing up and down the atelier.

"How old do you think she is?" Indi came into the room.

"It was really hard to tell."

"Do you think she's a local or from Bombay?"

"I wish we'd taken a photo," Gema said.

"Aren't you lucky that I took one?" Indi smiled and pulled up a picture she had secretly taken.

"You're a genius!" Sabine said.

"I am?" Indi looked at her skeptically. "Because I took her photo?"

"Can you send that to Priya and ask her if she knows who she is?" Sabine said. "If she's party of Bombay society, Priya will know."

"Got it," Indi said.

"Now, Gema," Sabine said, "let's get in touch with Mrs. Khanna and ask her for her bank details."

"Why?"

"Just get them...and then we let Indi work her magic."

*

"I don't think I've ever seen her before," Priya said when Indi handed her her iphone.

"Are you sure?" Sabine said. "Look again."

"I'm positive."

"Who the hell is this woman?" Sabine ran her fingers through her hair.

Indi took her phone back and stared at the photo. She frowned. "I feel like I've seen her before.

"She kind of looks like a typical aunty...you know?" she crinkled her nose. "Look at those sunglasses...they're huge."

"I think they're huge because she doesn't want anyone to recognize her," Gema said.

"I guess..." Indi shrugged. "I wonder if Nina Singh or her friends know her?"

"They might," Sabine said. "Let's ask them...."

"What's the plan for now?"

"We are waiting for those bank details of Mrs. Khanna," Sabine said. "Actually, I have an appointment...I'll be back."

"What appointment?" Indi asked. "Who are you meeting?"

"See you!" Sabine slung her bag over her shoulder. "Oh Indi!" she turned. "Can I borrow your car?"

"Can I say no?" Indi said.

"No."

Indi pulled a bunch of keys from her bag and handed them to Sabine.

"I won't be long."

*

"Thank you very much, sir," the front desk clerk said, handing Hari back his credit card. He turned and picked up his beaten suitcase.

"Hello Hari," he heard a female voice. He dropped his suitcase when he saw Sabine standing in the lobby.

"Well, well...this is a surprise."

"Are you leaving?"

"It certainly looks that way, doesn't it?"

She nodded.

"What do you want?"

"Are you going to pay JJ the money?"

"We have to," Hari said.

"I'm sorry."

"Don't be," he said. "It happens. I'm a big boy. I know when I've failed."

"I suppose."

"Look, I know you had something to do with it," Hari said. "I just can't prove it."

"I don't have the necklace, Hari," Sabine said. "I swear it."

Hari didn't reply.

"What time is your flight?"

"I have a little time."

"Do you want to have a coffee?"

"Why?"

"Come on! Leave your bag here and let's go around the corner."

"I don't understand, Sabine."

"I just thought that now the whole story is over, we could catch up a bit."

"About what?"

"Oh I don't know...Indi?"

"Why? That was over a long time ago."

"Perhaps not, Hari..." Sabine said.

"What do you mean?" Hari said as they walked over to the coffee shop. "Look, I was stupid. I wasn't thinking straight and it seems I did the terrible thing of breaking her heart."

"I think she still loves you, though."

"What makes you say that?"

"Call it a hunch.

"And I know you still love her."

"Why are you doing this?"

"Because I think the two of you are really good together and it's a damn shame that you're not."

"Is she with someone else?"

"No...she's still in love with you, Hari..." Sabine said. "Didn't you listen to me?"

"What do you think I should do?" Hari gestured to a waiter. "What will you have?"

"A latte, please," Sabine said.

"I'll have a French press..."

"So?" he asked after the waiter had gone. "Do you think I should call her? Write to her?"

"After you go back to Mumbai, I would get back in touch with her," Sabine suggested.

"What if she doesn't take my call? Not reply to my emails?"

"Be persistent."

"I've tried."

"Not hard enough, Hari."

"Are you sure the two of you are not mixed up in the theft of the necklace?" Hari asked.

"I swear we don't have it, Hari."

"But do you know where it is?"

"I'm working on it."

"Look, Sabine, I just want the necklace...I don't care at this point who stole it."

"I promise I'll let you know when I find out..." she pulled out her cellphone. "Heavens! Is that the time? I'm sorry, Hari, but I must fly," Sabine said. "Don't forget to get in touch with Indi..."

Back at Gema's atelier,

"Wait a minute..." Indi frowned as she looked at her computer screen. "Holy Ganesh!"

"What's going on?" Sabine came in.

"Where did you go?"

"Never you mind," Sabine replied. "Now what have you found?"

"Look at this..." Indi lined up footage from the night of the party and froze it. She minimized the screen and pulled up the cover of the most recent Hello Magazine with Arun and Bunny.

"That's the Hello Magazine cover I was telling you about," Priya looked confused.

"And here is another shot of the two of them in Gossip India," Indi said, "And the caption says 'Black widow, Bunny Mehra has set her eyes on her next victim, Arun Singh."

"I still don't understand.

"Look at these two pix," Indi put them all up side by side, "and...this one," she zoomed in on the still shot from the party.

"So? We know it's Bunny," Sabine shrugged.

"Right, but here's the ace," Indi pulled up the photo she had taken of Pooja Khanna. "Pooja Khanna and Bunny Mehra are one and the same," she said triumphantly.

"Holy shit!" Sabine's eyes began glittering. "And there was that story the other day saying Arun's deals were back on track..."

"So Bunny Mehra stole the necklace?" Indi said. "But how?

"She was never near Priya, nor was Arun."

Sabine put her hand up to silence everyone. "Let me just think this through..." She grabbed a clean sheet of paper and began drawing round circles, which she numbered.

"What are you doing?" Priya asked.

Indi nudged her, shaking her head, putting a finger on her lips, indicating she keep quiet.

"So..." Sabine began murmuring. "The trays were here...so if that tray had served the people at Priya's table...then...this tray would have served the people at JJ's table...and...I've got it!" she cried, drawing an arrow from a tray to a seat. "If I am calculating it correctly, the plate with the necklace was placed here..." she pointed at her hand-drawn map of the tables on the night of the party. "Who was sitting there?"

Indi scanned her notes.

"It was Kareena Kapoor, but let's check the footage," Indi said pulling up the footage.

"Oh my God! You think Kareena Kapoor has the necklace?" Priya said.

"Wait..." Indi said. "Here's the food being served...Kareena is on Rambo's right...so she must have switched with her husband...so that was Arvind Kapoor's seat...but the seat is empty...and here we go...look who sits down...Arun Singh...and then here's Arvind coming back and Arun stumbles...and gets up...here he is...and leaves."

Indi and Sabine looked at each other.

"Can you zoom in on that fall?" Sabine asked. "I want to see where his hand is."

"In slow motion, Indi," she stared intensely at the screen. "Frame by frame."

"There it is!" Sabine pointed. "Freeze, Indi.

"See that hand on the table...that's it!"

"What are we going to do now?" Priya asked.

"We have to get the necklace back?"

"But how?" she asked. "We don't even know where it is, or how many pieces it's in."

"It's got to be in the house."

"Whose house?" Priya asked.

"Bunny Mehra's, of course," Sabine smiled.

"But how are we going to get in?"

"We are going to talk to her ex-best friend."

*

"She what?" Nina exploded when Sabine explained what had happened. "You can't be serious?"

"I'm afraid I am," Sabine replied.

"That bitch! I cannot believe she stole the necklace! By right, that is *my* necklace!"

"I don't know that she stole it."

"Then who?"

"It was Arun."

"Arun?" Nina cried. "How?"

"I think he came upon it and couldn't believe his luck," Sabine said. "He was literally served it on a plate."

"That is lucky," Nina agreed.

"Right place, right time."

"What do you suggest we do?" Nina asked. "We can't leave it with Bunny...

"We need that necklace...Rupa needs the money...I do," she added.

"We all do," Sabine agreed.

"Now that I think about it," Nina recalled. "I saw the two of them leaving shortly after dinner.

"I remember thinking it was strange because Arun never left

a party before 3am," she added. "Especially not a party that was full of rich and famous people...he was always trying to get money out of them."

"Where does Bunny keep her jewelry?"

"Most of it at home."

"Does Bunny have a safe in the house?"

"I don't think so...she could have had one installed though..."

"Where?" Sabine asked.

"She has a jewelry box..." Nina said. "In her chest of drawers...top drawer that is always locked."

"Would she keep the Barodan in there?"

"Honestly...I don't know," Nina sighed. "But she may keep it there for easy access.

"In any case, how are we going to get it from there?"

"The usual way," Sabine said. "We're going to steal it."

Chapter 16

"Hari…" Imran sat back in his chair.

"What's up?"

"I just got a weird tip."

"Another weird tip?

"About where to find a piece of the Barodan."

"Is it real?"

"I don't know…the informant said Arun Singh has it."

"Arun Singh?"

"Apparently."

"How did he get the necklace?" Hari asked.

"No idea, man."

"What are you going to do?"

"I have to follow up on it…" Imran said. "It's not as outlandish as it seems, bro," he added. "The papers here are all talking about how Singh's real estate projects have gotten a healthy injection of cash."

"Interesting…

"I have to get a search warrant."

"Keep me posted and I'll fly back up."

*

"Are you sure having a dinner party is a good idea?" Arun asked Bunny who was sitting at the dining table, buttering a piece of toast.

"Of course! Why shouldn't we?" Bunny replied.

"I feel a little awkward…" Arun visibly squirmed. "It's just that we haven't been divorced for long and Nina has only just signed the papers...

"And here we, as a couple, would be inviting people."

"Not my problem!" Bunny snapped, interrupting him. "You've signed the papers and that's all I care about."

"Oh alright," Arun said meekly. "Who are you going to invite?"

"I thought I would invite Sonia Jaffrey, Rupa Patel and a few others...."

"But...but..." Arun stammered. "Those are Nina's best friends."

"Precisely the point, Arun darling," Bunny said, "I want her to know how well we're doing, you and I...together," she put her hand over his, and, lowering her lashes, she coyly ran the tip of her tongue over her lips.

"Oh very well," Arun relented, smiling as he thought of the untold joys in the bedroom later that evening.

"And of course now that our circumstances have changed..."

"That was luck, Bunny," Arun took a bite of a piece of toast.

"Yes, it was," Bunny agreed. "And we should celebrate it."

"I just don't want us to flaunt it too much..."

"Oh why not? We have it, don't we?"

"Bunny...you're testing karma..."

"Enough! Stop being such a ninny, Arun!" Bunny shouted at him. "You happened to be sitting in the right place at the right time and luck came to you on a silver platter...literally.

"You can't possibly be ashamed of that?"

"No...but what if someone finds out?"

"Who is possibly going to find out?" Bunny returned. "There

were 200 people there."

"But JJ..."

"JJ will file an insurance claim and get his money back...don't worry about him."

"What if someone traces the stones back to us?"

"No one will...no one has recognized me...

"Besides there are hundreds of Pooja Khannas in India."

"What about the jeweler who cut the necklace?"

"He had no idea what he was looking at?"

"What about the woman you took the stones to?"

"I don't think so...besides, she's already introduced me to a buyer."

"Really?"

"Yes! The broker for Cartier."

"Well..." Arun sighed. "I do feel a bit badly about cutting the necklace...my grandfather is probably turning in his grave."

"Stop with the sentimental remorse, Arun," Bunny chided. "It's so middle class.

"Besides, they all cut their jewelry and sold stones as they needed...it's the stones that have all the value, not the settings."

Arun pursed his lips and remained silent.

"This bit of luck has given you and me a new lease on life," Bunny said. "Now at least we can live like the Maharajah and Maharani of Barodan, even if you don't have the title."

*

"Ooohhhh!" Sonia gasped. She was seated at her desk and had just opened a thick cream envelope and looked at the card within.

She put it down and reached for her phone.

"Mrs. Rupa...I have just received an invitation..."

"Oh Mrs. Sonia," Rupa said tearfully. "I was just going to call you."

"This is simply outrageous!" Sonia said. "How can she do this? Doesn't she know our loyalty lies with Nina?"

"What are we going to do?"

"We are going to turn it down of course!" Sonia said. "And we will tell everyone else to boycott her and that treacherous man!"

"Are you going to tell Nina?"

"Naturally! She's our friend."

"Ooooohhhh, Mrs. Sonia," Rupa wailed. "This is so unfortunate."

"Right," Mrs. Sonia said quickly. She had no intention of listening to Rupa continue to wail. "I'll talk to you later."

She hung up and dialed Nina.

"Are you sitting down?" she said when Nina answered.

"Yes, why?"

"Your ex-friend Bunny is throwing a dinner party..." Sonia said and stopped.

"Nina...hello? Are you still there?"

"Yes," Nina replied. "I am."

"Well, what do you have to say to this?"

"I don't know..."

"Well you must feel something!" Sonia exclaimed. "Or is it possible that I am more outraged than you are?"

"I'm not saying anything because I don't know what to say."

"How can you not?" Sonia said. "Why aren't you angry?"

"Because I suppose I've been expecting this," Nina said. "And when I thought about how I would react, I worked myself into quite a tizzy, but now that it's really happened, I just feel numb."

"I don't understand you," Sonia said.

"Has Rupa been invited as well?"

"Yes."

"Are you thinking of going?" Nina asked.

"What a question!" Sonia replied. "Of course not!

"And in fact, I'm going to find out who else has been invited and tell them not to accept...better still...I will throw a dinner party the same night and invite all the usual suspects," Sonia added. "Then let's see whose dinner party is the more successful one."

"Don't..."

"Why?"

"Because the Barodan is in Bunny's house."

"What?" Sonia was incredulous. "Did I just hear you say that Bunny has the Barodan?"

"She has it by default."

"What the hell does that mean?"

"Remember when Arun came and sat at JJ's table at the party?"

"Yes..." Sonia sounded cautious.

"And remember how they came around with dinner, but kept the plates covered?"

"Not really, but...what? What are you saying?"

"They kept the plates covered because Priya had to go and fix her blouse and JJ didn't want to start dinner without her."

"I don't know where this is going..." Sonia said.

"Because the necklace had been hidden under a plate that was supposed to go back to the kitchen," Nina began, "but the server got mixed up and served the food...and the plate with the necklace ended up at a spot on JJ's table where Kareena Kapoor's husband was sitting, but he was off talking to someone when dinner was served and Arun sat there, remember?"

"Yes, I do."

'Yes, I remember that funny tumble he took."

"Precisely," Nina said. "He must've seen the necklace under the plate and pretended to fall pocketing the necklace when everyone was distracted," she finished.

"What in the name of God does this have to do with this dinner party?"

"Can you hold on a minute?" Nina said.

"This is exasperating," Sonia shouted. "What are you doing?"

"I'm going to make a quick call on the other line."

"Sabine?" Nina said.

"Why are you calling Sabine?" Sonia said.

"Bunny is throwing a dinner party..." Sonia heard Nina say. Sonia tapped her fingers impatiently.

"Alright, I'm back," Nina said.

"Sabine is going to get the necklace back," she told Sonia.

"This is madness!" Sonia said. "How?"

"I don't know, but let's leave that up to her, she has a plan."

"Shall I wear a piece of the Barodan tonight?" Bunny said, staring at herself in the mirror of her dressing table.

"Have you gone mad?" Arun was buttoning the cuffs of his shirt and whipped around to face her.

Bunny ignored him, sashaying across the room to a chest of

drawers. She opened the top drawer and took out a black lacquered jewelry box. "Look at this!" she sat down at her dressing table. "Aren't these pieces beautiful?

"Should I wear the earrings?" she put one up to her ear.

"Bunny, please!" Arun put on his jacket. "It would make me very uncomfortable. Please put it all away."

"Oh don't be such a spoilsport, my love," she drawled. "Just this once...before they're all gone...sold to the highest bidder.

"Besides no one is going to recognize the pieces, I promise you," she walked over to him and kissed his ear. "My man in Bombay did a fabulous job making all these pieces."

"Why don't you wear something else?" Arun said. "What about the blue sapphires I bought you?"

"Because these are much more beautiful and besides, I feel like being the Maharani of Barodan tonight," she replied.

*

Shaking his head, Arun went downstairs, headed straight for the drinks trolley in the corner of the living room. He was pouring himself a whiskey when,

"May I pour that drink for you, sir?" he heard a voice behind him. He turned around and saw a young man in black pants and a black jacket with a Nehru collar.

"Who are you?"

"Me, sir?" the man looked surprised.

"Of course, you!" Arun snapped. "Who are you and what are you doing here?"

"My name is Krishna and I am one of your waiters for this evening's dinner party."

"What do you mean?"

"We were hired to work the party this evening."

"We? Who's we? And what do you mean work the party..."

"Sir?"

"Who is in charge of this?"

Before he could answer,

"This is ridiculous!" Arun drained his whiskey in one gulp, put the glass down on the table and walked over to the staircase. "Bunny!" he called out. "Bunny!" he said again when she didn't answer, he began climbing the stairs, but halfway up, the doorbell rang.

"For goodness sake!" he fumed as he watched another young man dressed the way Krishna was open the front door.

"Bunny!" he called again. "What the hell is going on here? Caterers, waiters...how much is this costing us...?"

"There you are Arun!" he heard a male voice.

Arun looked down and saw Samir and Sonia Jaffrey looking up at him from the entrance hall. He closed his eyes for a moment and took a deep breath to compose himself.

"Yes, come down Arun!" he heard another voice.

He looked back down and saw Ramesh and Rupa Patel also looking up at him.

"Come on, *yaar!*" Ramesh said. "Let's celebrate! Your deals are all back on track...you have to tell us how you managed to get that much capital..."

Arun stood still for a moment, debating whether he should go up or down.

Finally, adjusting his shirt cuffs, he sauntered down the stairs.

"*Hai Hai*, Ramesh!" he said warmly shaking Ramesh's hand

followed by Samir's. "Thanks so much for coming...*Begum Sa-hibas...*" he acknowledged the two wives.

The doorbell rang again and two more couples came in.

"Where's Bunny?" Sonia asked.

"She'll be right down," he said and went through to the living room followed by the two men.

*

"Look at this..." Rupa exclaimed when waiters appeared with silver trays and glasses of champagne, sparkling water and orange juice.

"This is quite the party..." Rupa helped herself to a glass of champagne.

"It's alright," Sonia replied.

"Alright?" Rupa scoffed. "Mrs. Sonia, she got Indian Accent to cater it.

"And that's not cheap."

The door opened and a few more people came in.

"Oh! It's Gita..." Rupa said. "I haven't seen her in a bit."

"Gita!" She walked towards the couple that just came in, leaving Sonia alone.

"May I get you anything, *Sahiba*?" Sonia heard a familiar voice. She turned around and saw a woman in a pair of black pants, a white shirt and a black blazer. Her hair was dark and pulled back in a bun and she wore a pair of round tortoiseshell glasses. "Another glass of champagne?"

"No..." Sonia said, recognizing Sabine. "But thank you."

Sabine turned and went back to the entrance.

Sonia followed her.

"What are you going to do?" she whispered as she pretended to inspect the framed photographs.

"Nothing for the moment."

"Do you have a plan?"

Sabine stared at her in silence.

"I suppose you do...

"Do you know where it is?"

"No."

"Are you sure you're not going to get caught?"

"I'm sure."

Sonia was about to open her mouth when Bunny appeared at the top of the stairs dressed in a green floral silk sari.

"Sonia!" she said. "How lovely to see you here..." she came down the stairs with one hand on the bannister.

At the same time, the front door opened.

"Hanuuuuut!" Bunny squealed. "I'm so glad you could make it," she rushed towards him.

"And look who my date is..." Hanut waved his hands flamboyantly.

"Priya!" Bunny gushed. "What an absolutely lovely surprise!"

"When Hanut asked me if he could bring a friend, I had no idea he meant you...come in, come in..."

"Everyone!" she said loudly. "Look who's here! None other than the one and only Priya Chopra!" she announced.

"I suppose this is all part of the plan?" Sonia said without looking at Sabine.

Sabine walked away without answering.

Sonia nodded smiling inwardly. Nina was right. The girl knows what she's doing.

Chapter 17

Sabine went back into the kitchen.

"Let's get some more appetizers out," she said. "Chef...let's send out the shrimp," she instructed, "and the mini samosas and pakoras..."

She stood off to the side and pretended to read a clipboard. "Indi?" she whispered.

"Indi..." she said a bit more forcefully, adjusting the piece she had in her ear.

Suddenly she winced, pulling it out when a piercing sound filled her ear.

"Are you alright Miss Kumar?" one of the young men in the kitchen asked her.

"What?" she whipped around.

"Is everything ok?"

"Yes, of course everything is ok," Sabine said.

The man wobbled his head and smiled.

"Why are you grinning like a clown?" she said. "Get out there! The pakoras are getting cold."

"Yes, Miss Kumar," he replied and scampered towards the living room.

Sabine looked around to make sure no one else was looking and put the ear piece back. "Indi?" she said again.

"Here," she heard Indi's voice.

"Priya?" Sabine whispered.

"Here."

"Nina?"

"Yes, I am here."

"Good, we're all on,' Sabine said. "Now...we all know what we're doing," she continued.

"Yes," came the reply.

"Alright, ladies," Sabine said. "It's go time."

*

Dinner was in full swing.

Sabine watched as all 18 guests came into the dining room and sat down. The appetizers had been served and wine was being topped up when she slipped away.

"Alright, Nina," Sabine whispered. "Where am I going?"

"Where are you now?"

"At the entrance to the kitchen."

"Good...go back into the entrance hall and up the stairs to the first floor."

Sabine looked around the corner. The entrance hall was empty and raucous laughter and the clinking of cutlery against the plates could be heard.

She had just taken a couple of steps up the stairs when,

"Excuse me..."

"Yes!" she whipped around.

It was one of the guests.

Sabine sighed inwardly with relief.

"Where's the bathroom?" he asked.

"Through here," she came back down and showed the man through a small archway into a nook. "Just behind that door."

"Thank you so much."

She went back and this time took the stairs two at a time before she was stopped again.

"Nina, I'm on the first floor landing," she whispered.

"Turn right," Nina said. "Walk to the end of the hall, to the door that's at the end.

"That's the master bedroom."

Sabine padded down the hall and stopped at the door. She went to the balustrade and leaned over. Someone told a crude joke and everyone laughed. "Priya, I'm going in," she whispered.

"They are both here," Priya replied.

Sabine went back and opened the door. It creaked and she winced, before slipping in quickly. "I'm in," she said.

"You'll see the bedroom first," Nina said.

Sabine walked into a large bedroom, lit by a crystal chandelier. There was a king-size bed with a cream brocade headboard in the middle, white bedside tables with drawers and a small sofa upholstered in the same fabric as the headboard at the bottom of the bed. The sofa was strewn with shirts and pants and a couple of saris, but the rest of the room was tidy.

"The dressing rooms are on the left," Nina said.

Sabine went through a door that opened into a room in shades of taupe and cream that was almost as big as the master. Ringed by closets, it was a boudoir with a fainting couch, an armchair near a window and a large dressing table with three mirrors. In the middle, under another chandelier, similar to the one in the master bedroom, only smaller, was a round table with a large bouquet of fresh flowers, as well as white roses on the dressing table.

"The dressing room is quite something isn't it?" Nina said.

"What am I looking for?" Sabine ignored the comment.

"Do you see the chest of drawers?"

"Yes."

"Top drawer," Nina said. "There's a Chinese black lacquer box," she added. "Both will be locked."

"Is there a key or do I need to pick them?"

"The key to the chest of drawers is in her dressing table," Nina said. "Open the drawer on the right, there should be a tray of lipsticks. One of them is hollow and has a key in it."

"What about the black box?" Sabine busied herself opening lipstick tubes.

"That's a bit tricky," Nina said. "She moves that around, so the servants won't know."

"I have the chest of drawers key," Sabine said. "Where's the other one?"

"Try under the fainting couch, taped onto the rim," Nina said.

Sabine got to her hands and knees. "I don't see it."

"Gosh..." Nina said.

"Where else, Nina?"

"I'm thinking...I'm thinking..."

"What?" Sabine cried. "I thought you knew...?"

"Sometimes, she wears it around her neck," Nina's tone was apologetic.

"Bloody hell!" Sabine swore. "Priya?"

"Yes?"

"Is Bunny wearing something around her neck?"

"No, but she's wearing a pair of earrings...emeralds to die for."

"Nothing on the neck?"

"Not that I can see."

"Nina? Where's the damned key?"

"I...I..." Nina stammered.

"I'm going to pick the lock," Sabine took a small tool out of the breast pocket of her jacket.

Just as she had inserted it into the keyhole,

"Sabine," Priya's voice sounded nervous.

"What?"

"Sabine...she might be coming upstairs."

"Why?"

"She's saying something about a sari and wants to show it..."

"To whom?"

"I don't know...one of the women here."

"Stall her."

"How?"

"I don't care...think of something! Faint...just do something...you're the actress!"

*

Downstairs,

"Oooooh!" Priya moaned.

"Priya!" Hanut immediately put his arm around her. "What's the matter?"

"I don't feel so well," Priya said.

"Bunny!" Hanut said. "Where's Bunny?"

"She just went upstairs to show Gita something," someone said.

"Bunny!" Hanut cried out.

"What's going on?" a couple of other people asked.

"Priya's not feeling well," he said. "Please go get Bunny."

One of the waiters went into the entrance.

"Mrs. Mehra!" he was heard calling out. "Could you come back to the dining room please?"

Moments later Bunny walked back in. "What's the matter?" she looked around. "Goodness!" she exclaimed when she saw Priya slumped against Hanut. "What's the matter?"

"I don't know," Hanut said. "But all of a sudden, she just collapsed."

"Quickly, let's take her upstairs to my room," Bunny said.

"Ohhhhhhh," Priya moaned again.

"Shall I call a doctor?" Bunny said. "Priya...tell me what you're feeling..."

"My head...spinning...." Priya opened her eyes briefly.

"Let's get her to a sofa," Bunny said.

Hanut held Priya up by the waist and helped her towards the drawing room where Bunny plumped up a couple of cushions and helped her to lie down. "Now you just rest up," Bunny said after Priya was cozily ensconced amidst the pillows. "I'll leave you both here and get back to the party."

"No!" Priya opened her eyes and held a hand out to Bunny. "Please don't leave me," she pleaded, her eyes watering.

"But my dear Priya," Bunny said. "I must get back to my guests."

"Bunny!" Hanut whispered in her ear. "This is Priya Chopra! Who can be more important than the biggest celebrity in Bollywood?"

"Oh alright..." Bunny conceded. "Let's at least get some water or some lemonade," she gestured the server who was discreetly standing near the entrance.

"Do you think she drank too much?" she whispered to Hanut.

"Hush, Bunny!" Hanut said.

"I'm going to throw up," Priya said, her eyes still closed.

"Could she be pregnant?" Bunny whispered.

It took everything in Priya to not burst out laughing.

*

Sabine jiggled her small tool in the keyhole of the black lacquer box, but the lock was proving stubborn. "Damnit!"

"What's going on?" she heard Indi's voice.

"It's stuck."

"Yes, Bunny has trouble with it even with the key," Nina said.

"Use a hairpin," Indi suggested.

"Of course," Sabine muttered and went to Bunny's dressing table.

She bent one and inserted it into the lock and seconds later, heard a click. She opened the box, blinking as diamonds and emeralds glittered up at her. She picked out several pieces of jewelry, a couple of bracelets, three pairs of earrings and a pendant and put them in her pocket.

"Is it there?" she heard Indi's voice.

"Looks like it," Sabine replied. "Minus the earrings Bunny is wearing.

"Indi, where are you?"

"Outside the gate, next to the catering van."

Sabine put the box back, came out of the bedroom and went back into the hallway, looking cautiously over the balustrade. She came downstairs quickly and slipped back into the kitchen.

"We're in the clear," she whispered. "What are these plates

doing here?" she said out loud.

"Those are the plates from all the appetizers," someone replied.

"Are they clean?"

"Yes, Miss Kumar."

"Put them all in this box and take them out to the van."

"Now?"

"Yes! Now!" she glared at the young man. She watched as he loaded the box onto a hand truck and wheeled it out the back.

*

Outside, Indi was waiting when he arrived.

"What are these?" she peeked in the box.

"Plates to go back to the restaurant."

"I'll take care of this," she instructed him. "You go back inside."

"Who are you?" he looked at her curiously.

"I'm Miss Kumar's assistant," she replied, hands on her hips. "Go back in and tell her you handed me the box."

"Yes, madam," the boy replied.

As soon as he was out of sight, Indi reached in and pulled out a velvet pouch. She undid the zip and peeked in.

"I have the pouch," she whispered. She put the pouch in the pocket of her jacket and walked back to her car.

*

A soft knock sounded on the door. Arun turned over and buried his head in the pillow. A knock sounded again, this time a little louder. Arun opened his eyes but heard nothing more. Good! He had been dreaming. He rolled over and threw his arm over Bunny who was peacefully snoring next to him. Suddenly, he heard loud voices downstairs. Frowning, he swung his legs over the side of the bed and sat up. He sighed. His head was pounding. "I'm never drinking again," he mumbled, holding his head in his hands.

Another knock sounded at the door, this one louder.

"*Sahib?*" he heard a muffled voice. "*Sahib?*"

"Yes, yes...coming," he said and reached for his dressing gown at the edge of the bed.

"What is it?" Bunny rolled over murmuring.

"I don't know," he replied. "Go back to sleep."

Arun opened the door.

"What is it, Karam?"

"Sir...the police are downstairs..." Karam looked worried.

Arun's heart dropped into his stomach and began to pound.

"Why?" his already dry mouth felt like the Sahara.

"I don't know, *Sahib*," he replied. "They won't tell me."

"I'll just change quickly," Arun closed the door and leaned against it.

"Bunny!" he went and sat next to her. "Bunny, wake up!"

"Arun...I'm half asleep...not now...later," she mumbled. "I promise."

"It's not that, Bunny," he shook her. "The police are here."

Suddenly her eyes shot open and she stared at him wide-eyed. "What?"

"The police..."

"Yes, yes, but what do they want?" she said, irritably.

"I don't know...I'm going to change," Arun said. "Make sure you hide you know what..."

Bunny nodded and quickly got up and went to the dressing room. She pulled a small key off her neck, opened the chest of drawers and pulled out the black lacquer box. She opened it with the small key. Her eyes grew wide with shock. It was empty.

She sat down on the fainting couch with the box next to her, frowning as she thought back to the night before. She'd definitely taken the earrings out of the box...had she moved everything else? But where?

Just then,

"Bunny!" she heard Arun's voice in the bedroom seconds before he came into the dressing room followed by a couple of policemen.

"What are you doing in here?" Bunny said, pulling her dressing gown around her. "Please allow me to get dressed."

"Bunny, this is Detective Imran Khan..." Arun began.

"...Delhi Police," Imran flashed his badge. "Please don't touch anything," he said. "We have to search these premises."

"Oh no you won't," Bunny said. "Not without a..."

"...a search warrant?" Imran pulled a sheet of paper from his jacket. "Please put that box down.

"Now, if you two would please wait downstairs..." he nodded to one of his officers who was to escort them. "Let's go, ladies and gentlemen," he said to his team. "I want every nook and cranny looked into."

*

"Where is it?" Arun asked as he and Bunny had tea at the dining table.

"I don't know," Bunny replied, her hand shaking as she lifted the cup to her lips.

"What?" Arun spluttered.

"It's not there, Arun," Bunny looked worried. "I don't know what happened, but the pieces are all gone."

"What do you mean 'all gone?'"

"I mean there's nothing there," she said. "The box is empty."

"Could you have put them somewhere else?"

"No...at least I don't think so..."

"Bunny! How could you do this?"

"Do what?" Bunny shouted.

"I need the money from those stones...!" Arun said angrily.

"And you think I don't?" Bunny retorted. "I've already spent a lot..."

"What are we going to do?"

"All I have are the earrings I wore last night."

"Where are they?"

"On my...dressing table."

"Oh my God..." Arun's face sank.

"Hopefully they won't be able to tell," Bunny said, wringing her hands, "after all, there's nothing that ties them to the necklace."

"Unless they examine the stones..."

"Ah! There you are Mrs. Mehra!" Imran came in holding small tray. "I wondered if you could tell me about these earrings."

"What about them?"

"Where did you get them?"

"I...uh...I think I got those in one of my divorce settlements," Bunny stammered.

"You did?" Imran stared at her.

"I did quite well from a couple of divorces."

"I think I'll need you both to answer some questions," he

said.

"Shall I call my solicitor?" Arun said.

"I don't know Mr. Kumar," Imran said. "Do you think you need one?"

*

"And next and last on the docket," said the auctioneer, "we have a pair of emerald earrings...perfectly cut stones, Colombian in origin, originally part of a necklace made by the House of Richemont circa 1928, part of a collection of one of the royal families in India.

"Shall we begin the bidding at $500,000 U.S dollars?"

Sabine stood in the back of the room looking stoic as she watched people raising their hands, driving the price higher. She looked into the audience and saw Rupa wiping the corners of her eyes, and Sonia using the calculator on her iphone. Just then Nina turned around and caught her eye.

The two women nodded.

Chapter 18

The Emirates plane from Dubai touched down at Delhi Airport and Sabine walked off and through the airport to the entrance. She was about to hail a cab when she saw Indi leaning up against one of the columns. She grinned and walked towards her.

"What are you doing here?" she said.

"I came to pick you up."

"Why?" Sabine threw her small bag in the back of the car and jumped into the passenger seat.

"What do you mean 'why?'" Indi replied. "You're my friend and I thought I'd give you a ride.

"Isn't that what friends do?"

"What? Pick them up at airports?"

"Don't be such a smartass," Indi shook her head.

"Alright, alright, I'm sorry," Sabine grinned.

"How was Dubai?"

"Great! Rupa, Sonia and Nina all played their roles of penniless widows and divorcees selling their jewels.

"No questions asked...the pieces went straight into auction."

"We did well?"

"Pretty well..."

"How much?"

"We should end up with about 7 million a piece."

Indi nodded approvingly.

"Where is everyone?"

"At my house," she said. "The aunties got back last night."

Loud cheers and clapping greeted Sabine and Indi when they walked through the front door.

"Drinks all around!" Indi said and opened a bottle of champagne. "Will you all have champagne or does anyone want something else?"

"I'll take a martini," Nina said.

"So will I," Sonia added. "What about you, Mrs. Rupa?"

"Oh I might as well have one too," Rupa smiled.

"Everyone else?" Indi asked. "Champagne?"

She walked around filling glasses.

"And here are the martinis," she said when Laxmi came into the room with a tray.

"Alright ladies!" Sabine raised a glass. "Here's to us!"

"Cheers!" everyone clinked glasses.

"So what happens to Arun and Bunny?" Priya asked. "Are they going to jail?"

"There'll be a court case, but I don't know if they'll go to jail," Sabine said. "After all, they only found the one pair of emerald earrings."

"He should go to jail," Sonia said.

"Bunny is the one who ought to be locked up," Nina said. "She's a menace to good wives."

"And what about JJ?"

"JJ will get the insurance money," Sabine shrugged.

"What are we all doing with our shares?" Indi asked.

"I'm going to buy a couple of properties in Goa and rent them out," Sonia said. "Give myself a little income."

"I'm going to pay off my debts," Rupa said.

"And swear off gambling...?" Nina asked and Rupa nodded.

"What about you, Nina?"

"I'll turn two floors of the house into apartments and rent them out."

"Sabine?" Indi prompted.

"I don't know yet," Sabine said. "You?"

Indi shrugged. "Priya?"

"I'm going to pay off my brother's debt to Rambo Singh and start a fund for women's education in villages...do something good."

"That's very commendable, Priya," Nina said and they all nodded agreement.

"I'll probably contribute to that,' Sabine said.

"As will I."

"And me!" said another voice. They all turned around to see Gema.

"Sorry, I'm late," she walked into the living room.

"Cheers!" all the women raised their glasses.

"Well," Rupa said. "All's well that ends well," she took a sip of her martini.

"Indeed it is, Mrs. Rupa," Sonia added.

"That's a very good martini," Rupa added. "And a job well done."

Sonia rolled her eyes.

"The best laid plans of mice and men may go awry," Nina said. "But women...now that's a whole different story."

Just then, the doorbell rang.

"You expecting someone?" Gema asked.

"No," Indi frowned. "I'll just go see who it is."

*

She looked at herself in the large mirror in the hallway, pushing her hair behind her ears and smoothed down her shirt.

She opened the door.

"Hello Indi," Hari said.

Indi looked over her shoulder and saw a shadow dash back into the living room.

She rolled her eyes and made a sudden movement to close the door, but Hari put his hand on it.

"Don't shut the door, Indi," he said. "Please."

"Did Sabine do this?"

Hari didn't reply.

"Your silence answers the question," she said wryly. "What do you want?"

"I came back just to have dinner with you tonight," he said, "...if you're free, that is."

Indi stood staring at him. "You're asking a lot."

Hari looked crestfallen, leaning on the arm that was holding the door open.

"I think we can start with a drink," she said.

*

Hiding behind the wall, Sabine smiled happily. At least this had gone according to plan.

*

A couple of weeks later,

"I can't believe you're leaving," Indi said sadly.

The two women were sitting in Indi's living room.

"I have to, Indi," Sabine replied.

"But why?"

"I've always wanted to have a quiet little place in Provence and now I can buy it."

"But life here is so much easier," she gestured around the room, "especially with staff."

"For you," Sabine said. "But not for me."

"But what on earth are you going to do out in the middle of the country?" Indi asked. "You're a city girl. You're just going to get bored."

"I don't think so," Sabine said.

"At least you speak French," Indi shrugged. "I suppose there is that."

"Perhaps I'll open a little wine bar in the village."

"I still think you won't have enough to do."

"If I get bored, I can take the TGV to Paris, or fly to Rome or London or Madrid."

"I'm going to miss you," Indi said. "It was fun having you back."

"Don't get all sentimental, Indi," Sabine said. "I can't stand that."

"I know, I know," Indi nodded.

"Come on, Indi!" Sabine got up. "This means that you'll have a place to stay when you feel like a bucolic few weeks in the French countryside."

"Alright, alright," Indi walked her to the front door.

"I'm glad you came back," she said. "At least for a few weeks."

"And it was worth it."

"Yeah," Indi smiled. "That it was."

"What are you going to do with the money?"

"I may open a small modeling agency," Indi said.

"You can definitely do that," Sabine looked at her watch. "Now, give me a hug, I've got to go."

The two women hugged warmly.

"See you around, friend," Sabine extricated herself and walked towards the car where the driver held the door open for her.

She got in and rolled down the window.

"Bye!" Indi waved. "Have a safe flight."

Sabine nodded and waved. "Let's go," she told the driver.

And as they drove away, she looked back at Indi and found herself choking up. Indi was a real partner in crime and everyone needs one of those.

*

Sabine walked into the first class lounge at the airport and looked around. It wasn't very crowded and she spotted him easily, as she walked towards the cane with the silver swan head in the corner, silently sitting down in an armchair across from him.

"You're late," he looked at his watch.

"Only by thirty seconds," she said.

He smiled.

"Drink?" he asked as a waiter approached discreetly.

"A glass of champagne," she told him.

"I'll have a Macallan 25 neat."

"Thank you, Rambo," she said.

"For you," he said, "anything."

Sabine grinned.

"How could I not look after my old friend and partner's only child?" he said as the waiter placed their drinks on the table. "Besides being a brilliant idea, the timing was incredible...the perfect storm for everyone involved."

"He would never have brought out the Barodan if you hadn't threatened him," Sabine said. "And you had Priya in your hand too."

"You held out for the long game, Sabine, but it worked."

"How about a toast?" she raised her glass.

"To you," he said.

"How about to honour among thieves?" she suggested.

"No," he said, "to you...your father would have been proud, and so am I."

"You are?"

"You know your father didn't want you to have this kind of life."

"What kind of life?"

"The one you lead."

Sabine shrugged.

"Abi often said he wanted you to think of him as more normal, a father who went to work, came home in the evenings..."

"That wasn't my dad," Sabine laughed. "He would've been bored to death with that kind of life."

Rambo chuckled. "I've said before and I say again that sometimes, just knowing that a plan will work is enough."

"Not for me, Rambo."

"I know...nor for him."

"Did he always follow through? Every con? Every heist?"

"Always," Rambo nodded.

They both sat in silence for a moment.

"The plan was brilliant, Sabine."

"Thanks...brilliant, but not perfect."

"Sometimes, brilliance is in the imperfection."

"Coming from you, that's a compliment."

"What was so special about the Barodan?" he asked.

Sabine stared into her drink.

"I did this for Dad."

"And for yourself..." Rambo added.

"This was more about JJ than the necklace, wasn't it?"

"Dad always said it was the most beautiful necklace in the world," Sabine changed the subject.

"Your father was fascinated with the necklace, yes..."

"Do you know why?" Sabine asked.

"For starters, it was a beautiful necklace," Rambo said. "But beyond that, I don't know."

"Was there any link between the House of Barodan and Nawanagar?"

"Maybe..." he shrugged. "But there are other necklaces, Sabine and we know you're very good at what you do."

Sabine was silent as she stared at the bubbles in her glass, twirling it in her fingers.

"Anyhow, both of you got what you wanted."

*

Finally,

"I lost five years of my life, Rambo...

"Five years of staying off the grid, I gave up my life, my friends...disappeared."

"I see."

"I wanted him to feel what I felt...the anger, the sadness...at losing something that mattered.

"That necklace is really special to him," she added. "His mother gave it to him on her deathbed...it was all he had of her."

"How the hell did his mother get it?"

"She never told him, but..." Sabine said, "the mother was a teacher and it is possible that she taught in the Barodan Palace around partition."

They two finished their drinks and Rambo ordered another round.

"Did you get the money from JJ?"

Rambo reached into his breast pocket and took out a check.

"All's well that ends well," Sabine said.

"I have to admit, I was a bit worried you would get caught."

"Is that why you stayed?"

"Maybe...couldn't let you get thrown in jail...not here."

"Sir, the flight for London is boarding," the waiter came over and said to Rambo.

"Thank you," he replied, getting to his feet with the help of the cane. "Where are you headed?"

"Paris."

"Well, my dear, I shall see you along the trail," Rambo said and began to walk away.

"Rambo?" she said.

"Do you really think my father would have liked the Barodan job?"

"He would have loved it."

Sabine smiled. "Thanks, Rambo.

"That makes it all worth it."

ABOUT THE AUTHOR

Kim Akhtar is a writer and a wine sommelier.

To date, she has written and published five books, Roca Editorial (Barcelona).

Dividing her time equally between writing and her wine studies, she is currently studying for her WSET diploma and is a wine director with the Stephen Starr group.

As such, Kim Akhtar has woven a rather unique, multifaceted career path that has taken her into diverse worlds, allowing her to build a wealth of experience that has at its core her determination to always follow her passions.

Shortly after graduating from college, Kim established herself in the world of rock and roll as the assistant manager to The Cure. She went on to work for Tim and Nina Zagat when they launched their now famous restaurant guides and whom she credits with introducing her to the top chefs in New York City in the 90s and to the New York City dining scene. Following her time with the Zagats, she dove into television news, working closely with Dan Rather starting as the PR person for the CBS Evening News with Dan Rather and Connie Chung, and moving into his office as his chief of staff.

After fifteen years at CBS News, she switched gears and decided to go back to Europe, to Spain where she embarked on a full-time career as a flamenco dancer and began seriously studying wine, spending a chunk of time in Beaune, Burgundy.

Back in New York, Ms. Akhtar worked with various public figures, handling media appearances, public events, whilst keeping her hand in the wine world, building and curating important wine collections for prominent individuals in New York and Paris.

Ms. Akhtar is multilingual, fluent in English, French, Spanish, Italian, with a working knowledge of Arabic and Urdu.